George Prime, Alicia Prime Bayne

## Autobiographic Recollections of George Pryme, Esq. M.A.

Sometime Fellow of Trinity College, Professor of Political Economy

George Prime, Alicia Prime Bayne

**Autobiographic Recollections of George Pryme, Esq. M.A.**
*Sometime Fellow of Trinity College, Professor of Political Economy*

ISBN/EAN: 9783337133832

Printed in Europe, USA, Canada, Australia, Japan

Cover: Foto ©Raphael Reischuk / pixelio.de

More available books at **www.hansebooks.com**

# AUTOBIOGRAPHIC

# RECOLLECTIONS

OF

# GEORGE PRYME, ESQ. M.A.

SOMETIME FELLOW OF TRINITY COLLEGE,

PROFESSOR OF POLITICAL ECONOMY IN THE

UNIVERSITY OF CAMBRIDGE,

AND M.P. FOR THE BOROUGH.

*EDITED BY HIS DAUGHTER.*

CAMBRIDGE:

DEIGHTON, BELL, AND CO.

LONDON : BELL AND DALDY.

1870.

# DEDICATION.

MY DEAR PROFESSOR SEDGWICK,

I REJOICE that you permit me to dedicate to you these Recollections (many of them interwoven with your own) of my Father, nearly seventy years of whose life was gladdened by your friendship.

Believe me to remain, with every sentiment of respect and regard,

Yours very affectionately,

ALICIA BAYNE.

40, YORK TERRACE, REGENT'S PARK,
*Feb. 8th*, 1870.

# INTRODUCTORY CHAPTER.

"We die, my friend;
Nor we alone, but that which each man loved
And prized in his peculiar nook of earth
Dies with him, or is changed; and very soon
Even of the good is no memorial left."

WORDSWORTH.

" IT may at first sight appear that a man is not the best delineator of his own character. Yet in a circumstantial narrative of his life he must inevitably expose a variety of traits and sentiments, from which others may form an accurate estimate." Nor is the value of an Autobiography confined to its own subject. So much which is traditional dies with every one that it is sure to become valuable, if its writer has lived and taken part in an eventful period, as a contribution to the social history of his time.

There are few now left who have crossed the chasm which separates our century from the last, who can tell us from their own personal observation what people ordinarily thought and did before the year 1800. My Father was one of the few who could give a picture of an age which is in character, though not in time, so far removed from our own[1]. In the year in which he was born (1781), Frederick the Great being still king of Prussia, the Dauphin of France (son of Louis XVI.) was baptized, and the Prince of Wales (George IV.) declared of age. Walpole, who had seen Marlborough's funeral, was writing to Sir Horace Mann, Mr Pitt and Mr Wilberforce making their first speeches in Parliament, Dr Johnson finishing his *Lives of the Poets*, while America being still our own and communication with it all-important, it took six weeks to transmit news which is now sent in a few hours.

The vast discoveries in Science, the revolution in our means of locomotion, the luxury and the ease which have followed in consequence, have altered many of our customs, and effaced much that was peculiar in our modes of life. Such a complete transition from old to new cannot easily occur again. We have ceased to be surprised at our own experience, and shall soon cease to believe that things were not always as they are now.

It was with these impressions that I suggested to my

[1] " The changes (says De Tocqueville) which have taken place in the habits of society, as I faintly recollect my boyhood, seem to have required centuries."

Father, in August 1861, to let me write from his dictation as much as he could recall of the different scenes in his varied life. He was pleased with the proposal, and we commenced at once. Our progress was slow, as I could only write a few weeks in each summer, and except in the description of his childhood and early youth, he followed no plan, but dictated as memory or fancy suggested. I was occupied in the intervals in arranging and bringing into order the various parts, which consisted of innumerable detached particulars. The Book, so far as my Father was concerned in it, was completed in the autumn of 1868. There still remained for me more than a year's work in linking the narrative together where it seemed necessary (which I have done in smaller type in order distinctly to mark the difference), and in adding such notes as I thought might serve to illustrate the singular changes in laws, manners, and customs, which were comprised within the compass of my Father's life. The letters which I have printed (by permission of the writers, if surviving, or their representatives, if I had any doubt of the propriety of using them), are inserted on my own responsibility. My Father never suggested my doing so, or even mentioned that he possessed them, but I have used my privilege as an Editor and Executrix to supplement his "Recollections."

Although a work of some labour, this has been one of pleasure to me, and I think it was also to my Father. One would not altogether die ; and although he was really too little occupied with himself to have initiated such a

Memorial, I think that he was pleased to have it done for him.    He could not but be conscious that he had not lived in vain, though he never asserted it himself.    He could not forget that he alone laid in the University of Cambridge the foundation of Economic Science, which although it has been pleasantly called by Mr Carlyle "the dismal Science," yet has, I suppose, really assisted our Statesmen

> "To scatter plenty o'er a smiling land."

This was far from his only contribution to the benefit of mankind ; but as this fact will appear in the course of his Recollections, I need not dwell upon it here.

I hope that nothing will be found in these pages to wound the feelings of the persons spoken of if living, or their surviving relatives if deceased.   My Father was most anxious about this point, and always suppressed an anecdote or a name where he thought that there was a possibility of giving pain.   A few remarks about public men may be looked upon as constituting exceptions to this his guiding rule, but it is only *as* public men that they are spoken of, and such are accustomed to have their actions freely canvassed.

On the other hand, I trust that some will be pleased with the sketches of persons who have played important parts in their day, whose actions still "smell sweet and blossom in their dust[1]," but of whom no lengthened Memoir has been or could be written, since a part of the beauty of their particular life lay in its partial concealment.

[1] James Shirley, ed. Dyce, Vol. vi.

I must add one word more to express my thanks to my friend Canon Blakesley, to whose kindness in reading my proof-sheets I owe the correction of some misprints, and other inadvertencies which had escaped my own eye.

A. B.

# AUTOBIOGRAPHIC RECOLLECTIONS

OF

# PROFESSOR PRYME.

## CHAPTER I.

### 1781—1796.

*Huguenot descent—Abraham de la Pryme the antiquary—Kingston-upon-Hull—Birth—Wensleydale—Nottingham—First School—Great Frost—Severe illness—Clergy of those days—Card-playing—Old Lady of Queen Anne's time—Nottingham Election Riot—John Wesley—Bunny—Sir T. Parkyns—Sherwood Forest—Mr Beetham—Schoolfellows—News from France—Lord Howe's Victory—Sports and old customs—Dinner parties—Mr Wilberforce—Nottingham Assizes—Two curious trials—Adam Smith.*

I AM descended from one of about eighty Huguenot families who migrated from French Flanders during the siege of Rochelle, and settled at Hatfield near Doncaster in Yorkshire[1]. They obtained a licence from King Charles I. for a religious service to be used in their own languages

---

[1] " Hatfield was formerly a Royal village, in which the King had a palace ; so there is part of the palace standing (circa 1694), being an indifferent large hall, with great courts and gardens about the same."—A. de la Pryme's *History of Hatfield.*

I

(French and Dutch). This was at first celebrated in my ancestor's house in the Levels of Hatfield Chase, till the Chapel of Santoft was erected for that purpose. Charles de la Pryme was the first of the family who came to England. He was descended from Alexander Priem who followed Philip of Alsace to the second Crusade in the 12th century, and received a patent of gentility and a grant of arms, being a Cross and poniard quarterly; the Crest a Cross upon a wreath (the heraldic representation of a turban). The motto *Animose certavit.* *Priem* is the Flemish word for a large dagger or poniard.

Charles de la Pryme was a Huguenot, and the desperate resistance of Rochelle, which was besieged in 1627, rendered a residence in French Flanders so insecure and uncomfortable that his zeal induced him to take the sad alternative of sacrificing, at least for a time, his country to his religion. He and his family therefore came over, with others induced by the same motive, to England, about 1628-30, and joined with Sir Cornelius Vermuiden and others of their countrymen in the draining of the great Fens in the Levels of Hatfield Chase[1]. The knowledge they must have derived from the similar situation of their native country rendered them peculiarly fitted for such an undertaking; but either through the disadvantageous terms of the contract, or unexpected obstacles in executing it, although "for a time

[1] Mr Smiles, speaking of the Huguenots who came to England at this time, says, "their distinctive existence as a Dutch-speaking or French-speaking part of the community gradually ceased. Their blood eventually mingled with the best in England. Lord Palmerston was lineally descended from the daughter of one of the Houblons, who furnished the Bank of England with its first Governor......Among other well-known names are the De la Prymes, the Tyssens (of Foulden), the Crusos, and the Corsellis. But many of the immigrants changed their foreign-sounding names in the second generation, and are no longer traceable."

they lived like Princes, most of them were undone, and Charles de la Pryme lost many hundreds of pounds by it[1]." On his settling in England he, probably from an anti-Popish feeling, changed his arms. The last Herald's Visitation was made by Warburton. He published a quaint map of Yorkshire, putting the arms of the nobility and gentry round the margin. Amongst them are those of the de la Prymes —*Az. a sun in his splendour or.* These I find on the old plate, seals, &c., that I possess. Many years ago, finding what were the real arms, I adopted them and placed them over my house at Cambridge. They are still used by the last descendant of those of the family who remained at Ypres. The French and Dutch languages were preserved among these emigrants for at least two generations, and the de la Prymes retained an estate in Flanders, which after the revocation of the Edict of Nantes one of the family endeavoured unsuccessfully to recover.

When Charles de la Pryme died is uncertain. He left two sons, Mathias or Matthew, and Abraham, of which latter nothing is known but that he died in 1687, and was, according to the account given by his nephew, "an honest, learned, pious, wise, and understanding man." Mathias, born in 1645, married Sarah daughter of Peter Smaqué, "a rich Frenchman that with his whole family was forced from Paris by persecution for his faith, and was come to live also in these Levels." They were married April 3rd, 1670, in the Dutch

---

[1] Abraham de la Pryme in his *History of Hatfield* says, "Sir C. V. at the incredible labour and charges of £400,000 did discharge and drain Hatfield Chase, whose name deserves a thousand times more to be honourably mentioned and revered in all our histories than Scaurus's was in those of Rome, for draining a great lake in Italy not a quarter so big as this." Sir C. V. after spending an additional sum in litigation died in indigent circumstances.

Congregation assembling in the great Hall called Myn Heer Van Halkenburg's that stands in the Levels. His eldest son Abraham, was born 15 Jan. 1671, not at Hull, as Tickell in his history of that place says, but at Hatfield[1]. His literary distinction may render a detailed account of his life not uninteresting. Ample and authentic materials for it are extant in two folio MS. volumes written by himself.

He says, "I was the firstborn, and was born the 15th of Jan. 1671 (to all the miseries of life). My father can speak Dutch and nothing French, but I nothing yet but English. In 1680 my father shifted dwellings and went and lived at an old great large Hall in the Levels, which was built by Myn Heer Van Halkenburg, one of the great drainers of this country, and 200 acres of land belonging thereto, and we live now of that Hall yet." (The same wherein his parents were married.)

Of his early education nothing appears but that insatiable eagerness after knowledge which he always retained. When only ten or twelve years old he began to write what he calls "Ephemeris vitæ, or a Diary of my own life, containing an account likewise of the most observable and remarkable things that I have taken notice of from my youth up hitherto." His father, who still leaned to the Presbyterianism of the Huguenots, wished to send him to the University of Glasgow, but Abraham, who was inclined to High Church principles, with difficulty gained a victory in favour of Cambridge, where he was admitted at St John's College in April 1690. In addition to the usual studies he applied

[1] I give the entries from the Register of Sandtoft. "Le 4 d'Avril, 1670, sont mariés Matthew Pryme et Sara Smaqué." "Le 15 Janvier, 1671, naquit Abrah. fils de Math. Pryme et de Sarah Smaqué, et a été baptisé le 22 du dit mois à Santoft, son Parein est Abr. de Prim et sa Marcine Françoise Sterpin femme de Abr. Beharal."

himself with great diligence to Natural History, Chemistry, and what in the present age will be read with a smile, Magic. The ardent curiosity and inexperience of young minds made them yield easily to the superstition of the times, and this study seems then to have been common among the more courageous students at that time ; nor were the fellows of his College exempt from such errors. He with some of his friends attempted to hold intercourse with the world unknown, and he expresses his mortification that "nothing appeared, *quamvis omnia ritè peracta.*" His mind however soon became emancipated from every species of superstition ; and on a future occasion he took pains to expose the improbability of præter-natural appearances. He took his degree of B.A. in January 1693. Soon afterwards he had the curacy of Broughton, near Brigg, in Lincolnshire, where he devoted himself chiefly to researches into the topographical antiquities with which the adjacent country abounded. The most important of these are published in the *Philosophical Transactions.* In 1696, having exhausted all that his neighbourhood afforded of this kind, he went to live at Hatfield, the better to carry on his history of that place[1], where he describes himself as "so exceedingly busy in old deeds and charters which they send me in on every side that I cannot take time to think or write of anything else." He entered into correspondence with the Dean of York, Dr Gale, the celebrated antiquary, and with Sir Hans Sloane : with this latter on subjects of natural history and marine petrifactions. He was led to attempt a solution of the bearing of these phenomena upon the Noachian deluge, which was also published in the *Philosophical*

---

[1] This is now in the British Museum with his other works, but all are mutilated and imperfect.

*Transactions.* Natural history and chemistry were then completely in their infancy, and the essays of these times, and
among them his papers in the *Philosophical Transactions*,
have been superseded by recent discoveries and more improved systems. Yet justice requires us, while we admire
the modern superstructure, not to forget the merits of those
who laid the early foundations, or by unsuccessful attempts
shewed what parts of them were unsound. They laid the
groundwork of what has been since done more accurately
and completely; and by narrowing the limits of conjecture,
contributed to the discoveries of those who might otherwise have been occupied, like them, in ill-directed researches
and in deducing erroneous theories. He next applied himself to "methodising, &c." the old records and antiquities of
Kingston-upon-Hull, and to this task he devoted himself
with more than his usual industry and extensive research[1].
But having gathered and gotten all the antiquities relating
to that town and neighbourhood, he "began to grow somewhat weary thereof," and anxious to obtain some preferment, that he might retire from the hurry and laborious
duty of the Divinity Readership of the High Church there.
The state of his finances was a still more cogent reason.
His father had left him an estate at Hatfield and another
in Lincolnshire, which with the emoluments of his cure
produced a handsome income. But his tours in every direction and his studies led him into great expenses. "My zeal,"
says he, "for old MSS., antiquities, coins, and monuments,
almost eats me up, so that I cannot prosecute the search
of them so much as I would. I am at very great charges

---

[1] Two folio vols. are now or were in Lord Shelburne's library, containing extracts from the ancient Records of Hull. As also the following
MSS. *History of Ripon, Selby, Doncaster, and the West Riding*, in
one vol.

in carrying on my study of antiquities, in employing persons at London, Oxford, &c., to search records, &c., even to the danger and hazard of my own ruin, and the casting of myself into great debts and melancholy."

In 1701 the living of Thorne was given him by the Duke of Devonshire. About the same time he was elected Fellow of the Royal Society, an honour then bestowed more sparingly and discreetly than at present. He did not long enjoy these acquisitions, but died soon after in his 34th year[1]. He was a man of genuine and fervent piety; great purity and simplicity of heart; warmth and sincerity in friendship; unassuming manners and singular modesty. He was never married; nor does it appear that his studies ever allowed him leisure to fall in love.

His monument, with those of several others of his family, is in Hatfield Church, and the inscription on it runs in this quaint strain:

"Here lies all that was mortal of Abraham de la Pryme, F.R.S., Minister of Thorne, in the County of York; son of Matthew de la Pryme and Sarah his mournful relict. He died June 13th, 1704, aged 34.

Tho' snatched away in youth's fresh bloom,
Say not that he untimely fell,
He nothing ow'd the years to come,
And all that past was fair and well:

---

[1] "1704. June 20. Was much concerned to hear of the death of my kind friend, Mr Ab. de la Pryme, Minister of Thorne, who, visiting the sick, caught the new distemper or fever, which seized him on Wednesday, and he died the Monday after, the 12th inst., in the prime of his age."— Thoresby's *Diary*, 8vo. p. 455.

Joseph Hunter, F.S.A. says of him, "He died before he had the opportunity of pouring upon the world the results of a meditative life, of which it may be truly said that in a short time he had fulfilled a long one."

> "A painful priest—a faithful friend—
> A virtuous soul—a candid breast;
> Useful his life, and calm his end—
> He now enjoys eternal rest."

Abraham's property devolved on his death to his only brother, Peter, who married in 1695 Frances, daughter of Francis Wood, of the Levels, and died in 1724, leaving Abraham and Francis, born respectively in 1697 and 1702. The eldest succeeded to and resided on the estate.

Francis, who was thus descended in the fourth degree from Charles and was nephew to Abraham, was my grandfather, my father being his only surviving son. He endeavoured, and successfully, to increase the portion of a younger brother, and settled as a merchant at Kingston-upon-Hull[1]. He was a magistrate, and took a very active part in the affairs of the town. During the seven years' war, 1756 to 1763, the national feeling was so strong against anything French, that my grandfather dropped the prefix of de la, and henceforth called himself Pryme only. I have seen his signature written both ways. In Nichols's *History of Kingston-upon-Hull* he is mentioned among the list of mayors also differently:

> 1749.    Francis de la Pryme.
> 1766.    Francis Pryme.

My father continued to do so, but the original name has been revived in the person of my son, who was so registered at his baptism.

---

[1] "It was a favourite resort of the great wool-merchants, about one-third of them being foreigners, especially Flemings and Florentines...... Edward I. bought it of the Monks of Meaux in 1293, and ordered that it should be henceforth known as the King's Town—whence Kingston-upon-Hull, or, as it appears for the first time in an old writ, 'Kyngeston super Hull.'"—*English Merchants*, by H. R. Fox Bourne, Vol. i. 53, 54.

The De la Poles did the same. I remember the last of that famous family, a brother and sister, who lived in their own house at the corner of Bowl-Alley Lane. There is an institution in Hull called the Charter House, for decayed merchants, founded by their ancestor Michael de la Pole, son of the first mayor of Hull, Earl of Suffolk, and Lord Chancellor in the reign of Richard II., similar to the one in London, but without a school. It has a chapel, and on the walls of it are some inscriptions relating to the De la Poles.

Hull was formerly enclosed, partly by water and partly by walls, which latter stood where the docks now are. In my grandfather's time the gates were closed at ten o'clock at night, and could not be passed without an order, which rule was so rigidly enforced that my great aunt (his sister), who resided a little way out of the town, used on the evenings of the assemblies to sleep at her brother's house[1].

"The mighty Humber," as it has been called, on which the town is situated, is formed by the union of the Ouse and the Trent. It is between two and three miles broad opposite to Hull, but we had to cross, before steamers were used, in sailing vessels, from Barton in Lincolnshire by a circuitous passage of five miles. These sailing vessels had large oars to assist them, each requiring two men to row. I remember crossing in the first steamer about the year 1812[2].

[1] "Hull was *then*, previous to 1780, one of the gayest places out of London. The theatre, balls, large supper- and card-parties, were the delight of the principal merchants and their families. They dined at two, and met at each other's houses for sumptuous suppers at six o'clock. Cards followed."—*Recollections of William Wilberforce, Esq.*, by J. S. Harford.

[2] The first passenger steamboat in England, *Bell's Comet*, was started in 1812. One had in 1811 plyed on the Clyde. The first steam-packet that made the passage from London to Margate was named the *Thames*.

I was born at Cottingham, at a small country house, which my father had there, on August 4th, 1781. My elder brother died in infancy. My mother was Alice, daughter of George Dinsdale, who lived at Nappa Hall, in Wensleydale, Yorkshire, then the property of Lord Bolton. It had belonged to my collateral ancestors, named Metcalfe, one of whom had been High Sheriff, and there was a tradition in our family that on that occasion he took only Metcalfes, like the clans in Scotland, as his attendants when he met the judges at the assize towns[1]. Another of them speculated in the South Sea scheme, and his estate was confiscated to the sovereign, who afterwards granted it to Lord Bolton. One of this family of Metcalfes left me a legacy as a relation. Mary Queen of Scots, during her imprisonment at Bolton castle, passed two nights at Nappa Hall. I have slept in the very room which she occupied in the former; a long low room, and to gratify my wish some servants had to give it up. While there she attempted to escape by a Pass, since called *The Queen's Gap*, and had nearly succeeded. There is an inscription on a board near the Pass relating the circumstance.

I never saw my grandfather Dinsdale, but have heard that he was a man of urbane manners, and of such influence in his neighbourhood that he refused to qualify as a magis-

Sir M. I. Brunel wrote: "In 1814 I was refused a bed (at the York Hotel, Margate) because I came by a steamer, and every one of the comers met with an unfriendly reception."

[1] "Nappa Warren and Hall, the seat of the ancient Metcalfes. In 1556, Sir Christopher Metcalfe, being High Sheriff of Yorkshire, met the judges of assize attended by 300 horsemen, all of his own family and name, mounted on white horses" (for which Jervaulx is famous), "and clad in uniform habits......King James was entertained there by Sir Thomas Metcalfe, called the Black Knight of Nappa."—*Three Days of Wensleydale.*

trate when often pressed to do so, on the ground that he could do more good in giving his judgment on the disputes referred to him, by which the parties always abided. My father died in my childhood in consequence of a fall from his horse. He was buried at Ferriby, a pleasant village on the banks of the Humber, in a family vault which my grandfather, who had a country house there, had made. I have a vivid remembrance of the terror I experienced when I was taken from the mourning coach to see his burial. He left considerable property in the outskirts of Hull to me and to my mother: she however removed to Nottingham to be near her brother, the Rev. Owen Dinsdale, rector of Wilford, a village about two miles from that town, from which it is separated by the Trent.

Nottingham was celebrated for its spacious market-place, and its excellent ale. At that time no public brewery existed, every one brewing for themselves; one was attempted to be established but did not succeed, and the first that did answer was undertaken by two attorneys of large property. The manufacture of English lace by machinery had not then begun. The first machine was invented about 1801 or 1802, by a clever operative named Heathcoat. It excited great opposition among those who had made lace in their own way, and they frequently burst into the factories by night and broke the frames, doing, however, no other damage. This drove Mr Heathcoat to establish his machinery at Tiverton in Devonshire, which borough he represented after the Reform Bill passed.

In April 1787, being five years and eight months old, I became a day pupil at the academy of the Rev. John Blanchard[1], at Nottingham, who was a good classical scholar.

---

[1] Mr Blanchard afterwards became rector of Middleton near Beverley, Yorkshire, and died there in 1827.

When I was ten years old, having made some progress in the Latin language, and observing that some of the boys were reading Greek, I prevailed on my mother to buy me a Greek grammar, and made myself acquainted with its contents without the knowledge of my master or of his classical assistant, the Rev. L. Chapman; and was able to read the Greek Testament, and explain the inflections, before I was eleven years old. Kirke White and his brother Neville were among my schoolfellows. Kirke White, like many other persons of literary eminence, showed no peculiar ability while at that school.

[He lies buried in Wilford church.]

In the winter of 1788—9, at the time of King George the Third's long and dangerous illness, and of a prolonged and intense frost, when the rivers Trent and Thames were frozen over, so that persons walked across them for ten days or more[1], I was attacked by a severe fever, and was attended by Dr Storer of Nottingham, the most eminent physician in that part of the country. After prescribing every medicine that he could think of as suitable to the case, he called one evening on my mother but declined seeing me, as he said everything had been tried, and that giving more medicine was only harassing me in vain. He, however, asked a few questions about me, and was told that I had repeatedly begged for brandy. He mixed some in a wine-glass with water, which I eagerly drank, and asked for more; he then mixed a second glass. The next forenoon he called to enquire if I was still alive, and was told that I had had a good night and was much better. He saw me, and from that time I steadily recovered. Many years after I sat next him

[1] "The frost commenced on the 24th Nov. 1788, and continued with increasing severity for 51 days."

at a dinner-party in Nottingham, and asked him if he remembered the incident. He said that he recollected it perfectly, that at the time he gave me the brandy he thought it the most improper thing that I could have taken, but that as he believed I had but a few hours to live he wished to make them more comfortable, and that he attributed my recovery entirely to the brandy affording a stimulus which his medicines had failed to do.

During that illness my uncle, who always considered me as almost his own child, came every day from Wilford to see me, and instead of crossing the Trent by the Ferry he walked over it. When the ice and snow melted the river rose to a great height, and so suddenly, that the poor people were imprisoned in their houses. The rectory at Wilford stood on higher ground than the village, so that the water only reached the doorstep. My uncle got the people out of their houses from the upper windows by means of a boat, and took about six and thirty into his own house, lodging them in some spare attics that he had. Luckily there were one or two flitches of bacon hanging in the kitchen chimney, so they were fed as well as sheltered for some days.

My uncle was a good and conscientious parish priest, but he was a sportsman, as clergymen were in those days. He used to shoot quails in the high-lands, Clifton, &c., not far from Gotham, which is a village six miles from Nottingham. The three wise men are said to have lived there, and there was some little evidence existing in my time of their having acted as the legend runs, in so far as regards their surrounding with a hedge the tree in which they found a cuckoo. There is actually at Gotham a tree so surrounded. Barnaby in his diary of 200 years ago speaks of the wise men of Gotham.

Among other recreations my uncle belonged to a bowling

club, which met once a week to play at bowls at a village
called Basford, three or four miles N.W. of Nottingham.
They played both before and after dinner, and dined at
3 o'clock. He dined on week-days at 2 o'clock, and on
Sundays at 1 o'clock. He always had his churchwardens
to dine with him on Sacrament Sundays. After dinner
and previous to the second service they discussed how to
apportion the money collected in alms. The custom of
saying the Lord's Prayer in the pulpit is now being given
up by some. I remember its being commenced, and that
when I asked my uncle his reason for using it, he answered
that its adoption was becoming general in the villages around.

It was an age of cards, and clergymen were not ashamed
to play. My mother went annually on a visit to a lady near
Nottingham. On two or three occasions there were six
ladies of the party, and for three days they played at quadrille, commencing directly after breakfast, without ceasing.
Four were occupied at the card-table, and two were at
liberty, but they took their turns to go in as the others went
out. "The partners changing, but the sport the same." Such
was the love of card-playing in those days[1]!

I am reminded of one very great contrast between this and
the age I speak of. China roses, which now grow on every
cottage-wall, were, when first introduced into England, kept
during winter under glass. I remember some pots of them
being sent as a present to my uncle in the Spring, with a
request that they should be returned in the Autumn in order
that they might be put into the greenhouse[2].

---

[1] My mother has seen the blinds down in a room lighted up in the
middle of Sunday at the Green Dragon, Harrogate, while a lady of title
from Ireland and her friends were playing.

[2] "China Rose, Rosa Indica, brought from China about 1789."—
Haydn's *Dictionary of Dates.*

1789. The King's recovery was in the spring of this year. I was taken to see the illuminations in honour of it in Hull, when on a visit there after my illness. It was probably during this stay that I went to drink tea at a friend's house in order to meet a lady above ninety years old, who retained all her faculties, and perfectly remembered Queen Anne; and told us of seeing her, when a child, driving in her carriage through the streets of London. Drinking tea was a more expensive refreshment then than now. I have seen an advertisement offering tea at a very high price, and particularly describing the private house where it could be obtained; for at that time there was no numbering as now[1].

In the year 1790 a fiercely contested election took place for Nottingham. The candidates were Robert Smith of the bank of Smith, Payne, and Smith, in London and Nottingham, who afterwards became the first Lord Carington; Daniel Parker Coke, a barrister on the Midland Circuit; and Captain Johnson, a military officer then stationed at Nottingham (their unsuccessful opponent); he was of Whig politics; the two first were supporters of Pitt's government. Mr Smith was unpopular with the mob on account, as was supposed, of his haughty manner. On one of the polling days I, being at a window in the market-place, saw the people set ladders against the Exchange Hall, burst through the windows, and

---

[1] Numbering houses in London was not enforced till 1805. The following is such an advertisement as that alluded to. "These are to give notice to persons of quality, that a small parcel of most excellent tea is by accident fallen into the hands of a private person to be sold; but that none may be disappointed, the lowest price is 30s. a pound, and not any to be sold under a pound weight, for which they are desired to bring a convenient box. Enquire at Mr Thomas Eagles, at the King's Head, in St James's Market."—*London Gazette*, Dec. 16, 1680.

seize a depôt of constables' staves, which they cut into blud-
geons and threw out to the people below. One of them was
aimed at the head of Mr Smith as he was leaving the hustings in the market place, but he was saved by having on an
exceedingly high-crowned hat such as was then fashionable[1].

1791. John Wesley died March 2nd. I remember going
to hear a funeral sermon upon him, and that my mother, who
was a distant relation of his, put on mourning for a week.
John Wesley differed but little from the Church of England.
He did great good in stimulating the clergy to a different
style of duty. If a rector performed the service on a Sunday,
and visited the sick *when sent for* it was thought quite
sufficient.

I saw the lying-in-state of a Duke of Newcastle at the
Blackamoor's Head in Nottingham. The minute-bell tolled for
a long time. Indeed it tolled for every gentleman who died
in those days.

[It tolled for one day and night for the great Marquis of
Rockingham, who lay " in great and solemn state at York and
was buried in the Minster." Funerals must have been very different
in those days. Mr Dinsdale of Wilford, writing to my father,
describes that of a friend, a lady: " I was one of twelve pall-bearers.
The entrance into the hall was very solemn indeed. It was all
hung with black, and lighted with lamps. The Church was also
hung with black cloth, even the pillars, from top to bottom. The
coffin was highly ornamented with large plumes of feathers from
London."]

In the summer of 1792 I was placed with the Rev.
William Beetham, Vicar of Bunny in South Notts. He

---

[1] "On July 12, 1865, about 10 A.M., an attack was made by *the Lambs*
on a Committee room of Morley and Paget (Nottingham) and it was
completely gutted." One cannot here say, *Tempora mutantur et nos
mutamur in illis.*

proposed to take six pupils. I was the first, and was for a year and a half without any companion. The solitude of this interval, during which I rambled alone amid the woods and fields of that, as yet unenclosed, country gave a meditative bias to my mind, insomuch that when other boys gradually filled up the number I still preferred my solitary walks, which prevented my being popular with them. I used to read a great deal in my leisure hours,—the Arabian Nights among other books, and believed in them implicitly; the first thing which shook my faith was the account of the boatman of a ferry who had the head of an elephant. Boswell's life of Johnson, which had only lately appeared, and Cowper's Task, also delighted me at this time. One of these early companions of my youth was George Davys, since Bishop of Peterborough, who always behaved with great kindness to me. There was some family connection between us, as my uncle at Wilford had married his aunt, the widow of the Rev. J. Cockshutt Twisleton. Another was Benjamin Clarke Raworth, son of a country gentleman in Leicestershire, and almost the originator of the Cambridge Calendar, which he edited for some years, and of which Mandell of Queens' had a complete collection from the first; these were purchased at the sale of his books by Dr Edleston of Trin. Coll.[1]

A third was Francis Hurt, whom I afterwards met in the House of Commons, where he sat for Derbyshire. Among several others who came after a time I specially remember Verelst, because he was the son of a retired Indian Officer who lived in Mason the Poet's parish, and he used to tell me anecdotes of him. Mason was called the "Swan of the Humber," having property near Hull, and in Holderness.

In the same village lived Sir Thomas and Lady Parkyns

---

[1] Cambridge Calendar, first published in 1796. Oxford Calendar, circa 1809.

of Bunny Hall, with whom we often dined before our numbers increased, and always took tea once a week. They dined at 2 o'clock, drank tea at 6 o'clock, and had a hot supper at 9 o'clock. These were the customary hours of that and the preceding generation. Sir Thomas's first wife was his great niece, which was a lawful marriage then, being legally considered in the same degree as a first cousin. His eldest son was afterwards created an Irish Peer by the title of Lord Rancliffe.

Sir Thomas always drove with four horses to his coach. He had a walled deer-park, said to be three miles in circumference, containing two deer-leaps ; Sherwood Forest was about eight miles distant, and the country between it and the park was unenclosed. When formerly the hunters of the wild deer had chased them up to one of these deer-leaps, where the ground was elevated on the outside and hollowed within, the animal taking this leap found safety in the park, and became the property of the owner.

I can remember Sherwood Forest, or Shire wood, which is traditionally associated with "Robin Hood and his merrie men," the boundary between Nottinghamshire and Lincolnshire being formed by it; when, as a child, I posted over it from Nottingham to Mansfield there was no road, only a track which was pointed out by some groups of trees called the Shire oaks, left standing for that purpose after the forest was cut down. And they were still standing of late years. After that time a road was made, and a mail coach ran along it.

[It is now traversed in forty minutes by rail.]

There was a monument in the church to Sir Thomas Parkyns' father. It was sculptured in his lifetime by his own order. He was represented in the attitude of a wrestler, just preparing to attack his opponent.

[The present Vicar, the Rev. A. C. Kingdon, has obligingly copied for me the Inscriptions.]

Round the shoulder of the figure,

"Artificis status ipse fuit."

That on the monument runs thus:

"Quem modo stravisti longo in certamine tempus
Hic recubat britonum clarus in orbe pugil
Jam primum stratus; præter te vicerat omnes;
De te etiam victor quando resurget erit."

"Tempus edax rerum."

He left a yearly charge upon his estate of a small sum of money to be given as prizes to the best and second best wrestler. These wrestling matches were well attended, but his son, who was a quiet sedate man, never went to them[1].

Mr Beetham was a good classical scholar, but did not confine his instructions to Greek and Latin. Amongst other things he explained to us the progress of the French revolution, and pointed out on a map the course of the Austrian and Prussian allied armies, when they advanced into France in support of Louis XVI. It was while at Bunny that I heard of Louis's execution.

[Jan. 21st, 1793. How long this sad news would be in coming to this remote village we may judge from the fact that the murder of Marat by Charlotte Corday did not appear in the London Papers till nine days after it occurred.]

One day we heard the village bells ringing a merry peal. Mr Beetham sent me to the church to enquire the

---

[1] "Sir Thomas Parkyns' *Inn-Play, or Cornish-hug Wrestler*, 4to. printed by William Ayscough, 1714, is the earliest Nottingham book which I have met with (Bodl.)."—Cotton's *Typographical Gazetteer.*

reason, and I was told that Lord Howe, the admiral of the fleet, had on the first of June (1794) defeated the French, and captured seven sail of the line[1]. This was the first of several naval victories during the war with France.

In addition to wrestling, badger-baiting was a sport still existing. I have seen wild badgers in Rancliffe wood.

Many old customs still lingered in this part of Nottinghamshire. The curfew tolled at Bunny, and the first time I heard of Gray's Elegy was when Mr Beetham quoted to us the first stanza in reference to it.

[His lessons seem to have abounded with illustration. I have heard my Father say that in construing the line of Horace, *In silvas ne ligna feras*, he said, "no need to carry coals to Newcastle."]

I have seen the maypole at Bradmore, a village one mile north of ours, and the people dancing round it. It was made so that it could be lowered to the ground, in order to be dressed with flowers, and raised again[2].

There was a belief in parts of Yorkshire that a person watching in the church-porch on a particular eve, St Mark's, would see pass by it the forms of those in the parish who were to die within the year. It extended so far south as Notts, for I and two or three others of Mr Beetham's pupils obtained his leave to watch one year, but, as may be supposed, we saw nothing.

In every village there was a weaver, and he was never called by his own name, but *the Weaver;* which illustrates the origin of some of our surnames. At Bunny the weaver was the parish-clerk. He had his little workshop open to

[1] This day was for a long while designated as "the glorious 1st of June." The last survivor of this battle died Feb. 1869.

[2] The two parishes are now united, and neither Curfew nor Maypole distinguish them from others.

the street, and we boys often stopped to see him at work. Nearly every cottage and farm-house had a spinning wheel, and the people bought the flax and spun it, and then gave it to the weaver after bleaching it themselves.

I spent many of my vacations with my uncle at Wilford, and after I was ten years old was often invited with him out to dinner, and usually found myself the only youth of the party. In this way I met again Mr Wilberforce at Mr Samuel Smith's, brother to Mr Robert Smith, M.P. for Nottingham, afterwards Lord Carrington.

The first time I ever saw Mr W. he talked to me as I stood between his knees about my father and grandfather, whom he remembered. I regret very much that I lost in after years, through a mistaken delicacy of political feeling, the opportunity of knowing more of him.

At that period it was usual for gentlemen's sons to wear scarlet coats occasionally. I recollect having two or three as a boy, and wearing them with ruffles, shorts and silken stockings. They were made as swallowtails. In my shoes I wore silver buckles.

The usual dinner-hour of good families, when alone, was two o'clock. Dinner parties were from three to four o'clock. Only thirty years ago a country-woman calling upon a conveyancer at Hull at two o'clock, was told that he was at dinner. "What," said she, "has he turned fine gentleman?" I remember it being mentioned as a strange thing, "They are going to dine by candlelight." There was but little conversation at dinners except about helping and eating. The wine was not *on* the table, and if you wished to take wine with a lady you asked her what she would take, and then called to the servant to bring two glasses of it from the sideboard. Next came the decanters *on* the table, when people, on taking wine with each other, helped themselves :

and lastly the present fashion of handing it, which is near akin to the first one. The first time I saw this better and quieter way was at Lord Althorp's.

When I was at Bunny I was invited by some kind friends at Nottingham, named Storer, to stay two or three days with them during the assizes. One evening there was a small party, including two or three barristers, one of whom I remember as Mr Manners, afterwards Lord Chancellor of Ireland. These were discussing and disputing about some point of law which had been argued that day in the court; I, who had been present, ventured to state it differently, on which Mr M. said, "he is quite right." Henceforth I was always invited to stay at that house during the assize time, and from this period I date my bias to the legal profession.

I remember a trial occurring which exemplified the severity of the law at that time. The penalty was death for stealing 40s. from a dwelling-house and 5s. out of a shop, there being a peculiar protection for the latter, on account of the ease with which the theft could be committed. The trial in question was before Baron Thompson; a man had gone into a better kind of public-house, and called for a pint of beer; it was given him, as was not uncommon then, in a silver cup, valued at 40s. He drank it, and paid for it, and put the cup into his pocket. His guilt was clearly proved, but Baron T., unwilling to pass sentence of death for so slight an offence, in charging the jury asked to look at the cup. After examining it and tapping the bottom he said, addressing the jury, "It will be for you to consider whether the bottom of this cup may not be of copper." The humane hint was taken, and the jury gave the verdict "Guilty of stealing a silver cup of the value of 38s."

My first introduction to Political Economy may be said to

have taken place while at Bunny. Raworth and Verelst were elder pupils, come to finish their education before going to college. V. went one day to Nottingham and bought Adam Smith's *Wealth of Nations.* These two and Mr Beetham read it, and I, being curious, also read three or four chapters, but found it too deep, as may be supposed, for one of fourteen years old. We were all interested in the division of labour, and in the fact that with it ten men could make, amongst them, upwards of forty-eight thousand pins in a day, whilst separately they could not have made more than two hundred.

I remained at Bunny during three years and a half, and was then removed to the Grammar School at Kingston upon Hull, in January, 1796. It was the great seminary for boys in the East Riding of Yorkshire.

# CHAPTER II.

## 1796—1799.

WHEN my uncle took me to call upon Dr Joseph Milner, I well remember that he expressed his satisfaction at receiving me, as he attributed his appointment to the mastership chiefly to the influence of my grandfather, Francis Pryme, who had disapproved of a very ordinary man whom the Corporation were about to appoint, the nephew of one of them, and had written to his friends in the West Riding to enquire if they knew of a proper man. In this way he heard of Joseph Milner, who had been of St Catherine's College, Cambridge, a Senior Optime and second Chancellor's Medallist, B.A. 1766. My grandfather was supported in his resistance to the inferior candidate by Alderman Wilberforce, father of the celebrated philanthropist, who was himself in his early youth educated at this school.

I became Joseph Milner's scholar at the age of fourteen.

The school numbered about forty-five boys, for whom there were also provided two assistant masters. I was examined on entering, and passed well as to construing Greek and Latin, but was found deficient in composition, to remedy which I was restricted for three or four weeks to translating from English into Latin prose. I was then placed in the highest class, in which was also my friend the present General Perronet Thompson, just then beginning to construe the Iliad of Homer, which we went through, omitting the description of all battles and combats after the first.

Joseph Milner seemed to me a man of *strong* mind, of independent habit of thought, and of enlarged views. Having previously been under masters of considerable ability and knowledge, I was not likely, in forming an opinion of him, to be biassed by the prejudices of childhood. Perhaps he had not what is called a knowledge of the world; his confined situation and studious life allowed little opportunity of acquiring it.

As a schoolmaster he discarded many old prejudices. He rarely latterly inflicted corporal punishment, preferring impositions or restraints. I well remember the caustic yet temperate ridicule with which he remarked on the custom of getting by heart the Latin Syntax before some progress was made in the language; or the "Propria quæ maribus," "As in præsenti," &c. &c. at any time, which he said damaged the taste for harmonious versification. When some proficiency in the Latin language was obtained, he directed us simply to read a book, so as to be able to answer questions on the substance of it. At the close of the lessons he poured forth remarks on the subject, and illustrated it from his rich fund of collateral knowledge. In like manner he abstained from making the Greek Testament the first book from which to construe, as being of inferior elegance to other Greek works. He was attentive to the correct use of the English language in construing, &c., and gave a course of Lectures to the elder boys on Lowth's English Grammar.

These things may seem little at the present time, but seventy years ago they were bold innovations.

I have said that Joseph Milner would not permit the Greek Testament to be used as a lesson-book. At a later period, however, we had a chapter a week, after which he expounded his religious views, which were Evangelical, but avoided the vexed question of Predestination, and required no answer as to doctrinal points.

On these occasions, while he enforced his own opinions, he spoke often with kindness, always with forbearance and charity, of those who differed from him. I was convinced of the truth of his views, and have ever since adhered to them. He was in fact the Simeonite of that part of the country, but yet a most unaffected man. He was eight or ten years older than his brother, the Dean of Carlisle, whom he had himself sent to College, and who afterwards assisted him in the School. He, the Dean, was Senior Wrangler in 1774, and President of Queens' College, Cambridge.

1797. Admiral Duncan's victory over the Dutch occurred this year [battle of Camperdown]. His fleet was dispersed the next day by a violent storm; one of his prizes, Admiral Wynter's ship, took refuge in the Port of Hull, and I saw some of the wounded sailors brought ashore on mattresses to a temporary hospital provided for them.

During my abode at Hull and while we were at war with France, an invasion was much apprehended, and an encampment was formed on the sea-coast about eighteen miles distant from it. A ship of the line was stationed in the Humber, and the ancient garrison maintained in military efficiency.

[I have heard my grandmother speak of this fear of invasion, and the preparations for it. She told me that the nuns (probably those of York) were engaged in making lint for the wounded.]

Nearly every merchant's ship was boarded on its return by a press-gang. I have witnessed the weeping and wailing of the wives and mothers of the sailors who had gone to Southend, at the entrance of the harbour, to meet them, and who saw them carried off to join the Royal Navy without the opportunity even of exchanging a word. I was present during one instance of determined and effectual resistance by the mercantile crew of the "Blenheim," a Greenlander. That fishery required a number of hands on each ship; the sailors, armed with their harpoons, knives and lances, resisted the attempt of the press-gang to board them, and one of the latter was so severely wounded that he died soon afterwards. The master of the "Blenheim" was tried for murder at the next York Assizes, but acquitted on the proof that his sailors had confined him (perhaps no unwilling prisoner) to his cabin during the conflict.

[The same features of misery appear in some Chinese verses of the 8th century which I am kindly permitted to insert by their accomplished translator.]

## THE PRESS-GANG.

*From the Chinese of Thou Fou, a popular poet of the eighth century.*

The summer sun was sinking low
   As I went up and down,
To find a place where I might rest,
   Within Chekao's town.

The Imperial press-gang at that hour,
   Came up the self-same way,

Who in the time of darkness make
    The sons of men their prey.

\*     \*     \*     \*     \*

On rolled the night—both shouts and screams
    Died off to silence deep ;
Still, ever and anon, I heard
    Choked sobbings round me creep[1].

\*     \*     \*     \*     \*

I witnessed the last assizes that were holden at Hull, which, with a few adjoining villages to the west, formed a county of itself; the Judges of the Northern Circuit came there once in three years, or oftener, if urgent criminal business required it.

I remained at Joseph Milner's school till his death in Nov. 1797, shortly after he had been appointed Vicar of the Holy Trinity Church, chiefly through Mr Wilberforce's influence. I was then within two years of the usual period of entering at a University. During those two years I resided at home reading alone, and was occasionally helped over difficulties by the Rev. Richard Patrick, Vicar of Sculcoates, a suburban parish of Hull, in which my mother and I, having property there, then resided. He was an excellent classical scholar, and kindly volunteered his assistance to me. His knowledge was varied, and he wrote a book entitled "Geographical and Commercial Essays, edited by E. H. Barker," for he was unwilling to give his own name.

[Mr Patrick was a friend and correspondent upon Oriental Literature of Archdeacon Wrangham. In one of his letters to the latter he says, "I was surprised and sorry when I read your

---

[1] Translated by Sir F. H. Doyle, *Poems*, 1866.

past favour to me. To despond is not the high road to conquest. * * * Mr Pryme, who would have entered the lists with you,
an equal prizeman as yourself, is laid up in a serious sickness and
writes me word that he declines *this* literary conflict. But between
ourselves, why should you limit your views to a Cambridge βραβεῖον
καὶ μοῦσα? write for the world, and publish your remarks on this
sublime and solemn subject (i.e. the conversion of the Hindoos)."]

Previously to my going up to Cambridge I passed the
summer of 1799 at Sedbergh, a small town in the N.W. of
Yorkshire, with the celebrated John Dawson, with whom
several University students were wont to read during their
long vacation. He was the son of a yeoman in Garsdale.
He had availed himself of some books belonging to his
brother, an excise officer, to gain a knowledge of arithmetic,
and of the rudiments of mathematics, and then became an
*itinerant* schoolmaster; for many parts of that mountainous
district were not sufficiently peopled to maintain one capable of teaching anything beyond mere reading and writing.
He stayed two or three months at a time in one house, by
arrangement, teaching the children of the family and neighbourhood, and then removing to another. In the meantime
he was pursuing his own mathematical studies. It was at
length settled, by the assistance of some friends, that he
should become an apprentice to Mr Bracken, an eminent
surgeon at Lancaster. After this he commenced a medical
practice at Sedbergh, which soon became considerable, and
enabled him to retire, and devote his attention exclusively
to mathematical training. His plan was to let his pupils
read by themselves in a room at his house, where he attended six hours in the day, and assisted them by explaining
such difficulties as arose. The lodging for the men at
Dawson's was 3s. 6d. a week, and we dined together daily
at one or other of two small inns, our dinner costing one

shilling a day. Mr Dawson died in 1820. There is a bust of him in the chancel of Sedbergh Church.

Many of his pupils attained high honours at Cambridge, some of them being senior wranglers. Among those in my time were March Phillips and Adam Sedgwick. The former was a fellow-commoner of Sidney Sussex College. He was eighth wrangler and first classical medallist. He took a fellowship, but afterwards resigned it, and moved to Trinity. He became Under Secretary of State—the permanent one—kept it for some years, and then went to live on his estate, Garendon Park in Leicestershire. The other, the now celebrated Adam Sedgwick, was, when I first went to Sedbergh, a boy at the Free Grammar School, the older boys of which and Mr Dawson's pupils used to play together at cricket on Saturday afternoons. In this way commenced the life-long friendship which I have had the gratification of enjoying with him. His father was the vicar of Dent, a parish which comprised the whole of a small neighbouring valley. I met him at the annual dinner of the Book Club, to which Dawson's pupils were admitted as members. He told me that he had known my Uncle Dinsdale at College, and that after one long vacation it was arranged, on account of the difficulty of travelling, that they should ride together up to Cambridge (each on a horse of their respective fathers, which they sold when they arrived there), sending their trunks by the stage waggon.

Mr Sedgwick was a most amiable man, and highly esteemed in his parish, of which his father also had been the vicar. On his decease, some years afterwards, the living was offered by the trustees (some of the principal inhabitants of the parish) to his son Adam, who, being Professor of Geology at Cambridge, declined the appointment. It was then given to his younger brother.

I had my pony with me while at Sedbergh, and in one

of my earliest rides I observed along the horizon a high
range of clouds resembling hills. It was towards sunset, and
I was lost in a reverie of admiration, saying to myself, "if
I did not know that these were clouds I should take them
for hills;" but to my surprise, as I rode further onwards,
I perceived that they did not disperse, as I had expected,
but settled into solid substance. In fact they were the hills
of Wensleydale. During my residence at Sedbergh I went
to visit a relative who lived among them, so that I am able
to describe from memory this beautiful valley. It is above
twenty miles in length, and is bounded on each side by
mountains, which at that time prevented much intercourse
with the rest of the country. My maternal great grandfather
was summoned as a witness to York assizes. He travelled,
as was the usage at that time, on horseback, followed by his
servant on another horse, carrying his portmanteau. The
distance he had to traverse was about eighty miles, and when
they got near to York the servant exclaimed to his master,
"I didn't think the world had reached so far." I remember
another instance of the simplicity of the poor inhabitants of
the Dale. A female servant, who came from one of the
remote glens, on seeing, for the first time, the coach of a
neighbouring family, who had come to call at my grandfather's, said that "the mountebanks were come." Itinerant
quack doctors who erected a stage, sold their nostrums, and
held a jocose dialogue were so called. I have frequently
seen them in my boyhood. The lower orders in the Yorkshire dales believed in fairies and brownies; and my nurse
used to tell me stories of them, and how people in crossing
the moors had met them. She described them to me as
very little well-formed people, with a great deal of super-
natural power. She was an intelligent woman, and in her
Bible were written these lines, which I never saw elsewhere:

" Nanny Casson, her Book;
God give her grace in it to look:
Not only to look but understand,
For learning is better than house or land.
When house and land are gone and spent
Then learning is most excellent."

[The last two lines are well known, but of them it is said in
*Notes and Queries*, " We are unable to trace the origin of this
familiar couplet." Old Cocker has the following readings:—

When Honour's sun declines and Wealth takes wings,
Then learning shines, the best of precious things.
*Urania*, Lond. 1670.

When lands and friends are gone and Wealth takes wing,
Then learning's priz'd, then learning's a brave thing.
*Morals*, p. 62, 1675.]

I have been told of a man who had not led a very good
life, returning to Askrigg one evening almost drunk, and
affirming that the devil with hoofs and horns got on his
back, and clung to him all the way till he reached home,
when he left him. The poor people all around believed in
the *reality* of the story, but it was truly nothing more than a
trick to frighten and reform the drunkard.

The death-watch was also believed in, and I have heard
an educated woman relate particulars of her hearing it. The
Dales-people called the re-appearances of the dead *flayings*,
from *flay*, a North country word, to be *frighted*. Such were
seen and described to my mother when she was a girl.

[I asked Professor Sedgwick for *his* definition of this word, which
is, I imagine, unknown in the south, and I give his expressive
answer:

" Flayings are things to cause terror. Hence in a more special
sense they are *ghosts* or goblins. A haunted house is a house

infested by flayings. I have heard the word myself a hundred times."

Wensleydale was once pre-eminently Catholic, as its ruined Abbeys and Churches and lingering customs bear witness to. One of my father's relations, writing to him about the year 1825, says of a friend, " she died on the eve of St Simon and St Jude." On the other hand much had been lost, as this story related by him will shew. "An aunt of mine was once staying in a little village in the West of Yorkshire, and saw a woman spinning in her cottage on a Good Friday. She entered into conversation with her, and told her about our Lord's good works, and His crucifixion, to all which the good dame listened with attention, and then said, ' Pray, Ma'am, did you know him ?'"]

An extensive forest formerly existed in the upper part of the valley. At the village of Bainbridge, near the centre of it, there was an hostel or small inn, and a horn was sounded every evening at sunset ("from the feast of Holy Rood, Sept. 27th, to Shrovetide"), to apprise bewildered travellers where they might come to for shelter. A small endowment had been left for that purpose, and though the forest had disappeared, the horn continued to be sounded within my own recollection. A soft air was played upon it, which, from the reverberation of the rocks, could be heard afar off. I remember one evening at Hawes, a distance of three or four miles, walking with a companion, who suddenly arrested my attention, saying, "Hark ! there's the forest horn," and we were silent till it ceased.

There are traditions in the Dales of its men having joined in the wars with Scotland ; and I have had repeated to me parts of old ballads shewing this, but I only remember a line here and there, speaking of the gathering of men that went from Wensleydale to Flodden,

" And lusty lads from Semer-water's side."

Semer-water is the only lake in Yorkshire. It covers a space of more than a hundred acres. It is high up on the hills, so high that at its outlet by a little brook, it falls by a gradual descent of 2 or 300 ft. into the Yore[1]. Another ballad was supposed to have been sung by the milkmaids on the same occasion :

> " There's nae more lilting
> At our kye's milking,
> Sin our braw lads are awa[2]."

[There are many lovely spots in Wensleydale which I have heard my father dwell upon with delight. Such is "the waterfall of Hardraw Scar," (I quote from an old letter) "which dashes down 120 feet in front of Stag's Fell, a hill which rises immediately behind the fall to a height of 1,200 feet above the bed of the river Ure. The little valley above this fall is called Forsdale, and here were the monks first established who afterwards settled in the more fertile fields of Jerveaulx. Also, not far from Bolton Castle, the Church of Aysgarth" (his uncle's first living) "which stands alone in a romantic situation overhanging the river, which dashes from rock to rock and forms a number of small falls, beneath the overhanging woods: but all this is much *changed* now by the erection of a cotton mill." The alteration in the manners and customs of the inhabitants of these sweet Yorkshire valleys, following upon

---

[1] For account of Semer-water and buried city, see *Three Days of Wensleydale.*

[2] THE FLOWERS OF THE FOREST, WRITTEN ON FLODDEN.

> " I have heard of a lilting, at our ewes milking,
> Lasses a lilting, before the break of day ;
> But now there's a moaning on ilka green loaning,
> That our braw foresters are a' wede away."

To lilt (lulla Lu. Goth., to sing), thus to sing by not using words of meaning, but tuneful syllables only. Brockett's *N. C. Words.*

To jerk, or rise in the gait or song.—*Craven Dialect.*

mechanical changes, was long in coming, but it has come at last; and to judge from the account, in his charming *Memorial*, of his own Dent by Prof. Sedgwick, it is one in many points not for the better.]

My grandmother Dinsdale told me of her being at Hawes Church one Sunday in the year 1745, and hearing the guns of the Scottish army, engaged, while on its march, in some slight skirmish[1]. One of my aunts also related an anecdote bearing in reality on this march, but which she meant as an illustration of the necessity of caution in entrusting children with a secret. The officers of the Pretender's army were billeted on private houses, and some were sent to one whose inmates, fearing for their plate and valuables, had hastily put them into a cupboard by the fireside. The soldiers observing a little child looking constantly towards the cupboard demanded to have it opened. The master of the house made an excuse, saying he had lost the key, but the soldiers declared that if he did not find it they should break it open. When they saw its contents they exclaimed, "Is that all? we thought there might be fire-arms concealed." And they touched nothing.

There is a traditional story here of Charles Edward's escape. He was in Scotland after the retreat from Derby for some time before he could make his escape. An officer was sent with a company to search for him, and came to a farmhouse where he was concealed. The farmer, under the pretence of his being a beast-jobber, sent the prince into the field. The officer followed him alone, and told him that he knew him, that he had fought against him, and would fight

---

[1] "Few events of historic note occurred in the valley of the Yore, except in 1745, when a detachment of the Highland army marched through on their celebrated advance to Derby."—*Three Days of Wensleydale.*

3—2

again, but that he would not avail himself of a discovery like this, and then gave him some valuable advice as to how he might best escape.

Whilst I was at Hawes we called on the Mr Parkes, two bachelor brothers, who lived together in Swaledale. A third brother was a merchant in Liverpool, and made a large fortune. This was the father of James Parke, now Lord Wensleydale, and to him these uncles left their estates. When I wrote to congratulate him on his peerage, more than fifty years later, I said how gratified I was that, although the greater part of his property was in Swaledale, he had chosen Wensleydale for his title.

[The time had now come when my father was to exchange his quiet life in these primitive northern vales for the unknown world of men and things in the South.]

# CHAPTER III.

## 1799—1804.

IN October, 1799, my uncle Dinsdale went with me to
Cambridge, where I had been previously admitted of
Trinity College. As we entered the town and looked out of
the post chaise, my uncle, who had not been there since 1782,
was scandalised at seeing the M.A.s wearing round hats.
Cocked hats had formerly been universal among those of
them who did not wear a cap. He remarked too, that in his
time the streets were not paved, and that the run of water
had been in the *middle* of them. We staid two nights at the
Rose, which occupied with its stables and chaise-houses the
whole of what is now the Rose Crescent.

I was shortly introduced to Mr Lambert, the senior resident
Fellow and Bursar of Trin. Coll. We supped with him the
next evening and met the Vice-Master, Mr Davies, and the
Senior Dean, Mr Renouard. My natural awe of these dig-

nitaries was much increased by their addressing each other, not by their names but by their titles of office. Mr Lambert was a college contemporary and intimate friend of my uncle, who had graduated in 1762 as twelfth wrangler, and to whom, as wishing to marry instead of sitting for a fellowship, the college had presented the small vicarage of Aysgarth, in his native valley of Wensleydale, which he afterwards resigned for the rectory of Wilford.

Mr Jones, the Tutor, on whose side I was admitted, was remarkable for the attention he gave to the progress of his pupils, and for his kind and guardianlike interest in their general conduct and welfare. His lectures on Moral Philosophy and Metaphysics, given to the Junior Sophs, were most able and comprehensive, and so much valued, that some of the students sought permission to attend them a second time. A few years after his death I offered one of his executors to edit them. He made enquiries about them, but they were not to be found, having been destroyed, probably by those who did not know their value. His only publication was an excellent Sermon on Duelling, preached after a fatal encounter between two students of the University.

Mr Sheepshanks was assistant Tutor. He was an admirable instructor, taking pains to make us thoroughly understand what we read. None of us durst have said what Hunt, the translator of Tasso, said in answer to his question, "What is the centre of percussion?" "I don't know, Sir, what the centre of percussion is, but I can do the proposition about it." He was most kind and attentive, and I have known men stay a quarter of an hour after the lectures to have something explained to them by him. At a party where he was praised in his capacity of Tutor, I remember it was objected by one of his pupils, that he dilated too much upon self-evident truths, and instanced that he would

give three or four definitions of a straight line. "On the
contrary," said Macfarlane, "he distinctly shewed that a
straight line was an idea so simple that it could not be
really defined."

Mr Sheepshanks took a living in Cornwall and became
an Archdeacon. He wrote to me when I was in Parliament
to enquire something about an act, and asked if I remembered him? In answer I said, not only that I remembered
him, but that I availed myself of that opportunity of expressing to him my gratitude for all the pains he had taken
with me, and for which I feared I had not been sufficiently
thankful at the time. He was much gratified with this, and
called upon me when next he was in London. When he
died I wrote a notice of him for the Cambridge papers,
and also sent it to a Cornish one, being unwilling that he
should pass to the grave without some mention of his excellence. I received in consequence letters of thanks from
two or three of his relatives. Such men as Jones and Sheepshanks have passed away, the numbers in the lecture rooms
have increased, and the necessity for private tuition has in
consequence arisen.

[It may be interesting to compare the account given by my
father's relative, of whom he spoke in the first chapter, of *his* arrival
and introduction to University life, with his own of more than a
hundred years later. He says, "in this year, 1690, about the end
of April, I set forward for Cambridge to be admitted there an
Academician. We travelled forty-six miles from the Levels to
Sleaford beyond Lincoln Heath, and so came through the fens of
Ely to Cambridge. We arrived at Cambridge May 1st (which I
took to have been a much fairer town than I then found it to be):
and I was admitted of St John's College. I was examined by my
Tutor, then by the Senior Dean, then by the Junior Dean, and then
by the Master (Dr Gower); who all made me construe but a verse
or two apiece in the Greek Testament, except the Master, who

asked me both in that and in Plautus and Horace. Then I went
to the Registrar to be registered member of the College. We go to
Lectures every other day in Logic, and what we hear one day we
give an account of the next. Besides, we go to his (the Tutor's)
chamber every night to hear the Sophs and Junior Sophs dispute,
and then some one is called out to construe a chapter in the New
Testament, after which we go to prayers, and then to our respective
chambers[1]."]

Hunt, of whom I spoke just now, was a relation of Monk[2].
He was a good classical scholar, having already gained the
Latin Ode. When he made that speech in the lecture room
he was only cramming in Mathematics in order to obtain a
Senior Optime's degree, which was requisite to enable him to
be a candidate for the Chancellor's Medal. He suffered a
grievous disappointment in losing this, which it was supposed was owing to the two Grants degrading. They were
brothers, and both of Magdalene College, and such friends
that they read together and helped each other. They were
respectively third and fourth Wranglers, and first and second
Medallists, only changing places. It was not necessary in
those days to plead sickness for degrading; a man had
nothing to do but to remain up at the University and not
send in his name for examinations. This case was so forcible an instance of the evils of degrading, that a Grace
passed the Senate to forbid a man who had degraded, except
by permission, going out in honours.

[Mr Hunt translated Tasso's *Gerusalemme liberata*. My father
told me that he had compared one Canto of the original with the
four chief translations, and that he considered that Mr Hunt's was
the best.]

_____

[1] MS. of Abraham de la Pryme.
[2] Afterwards Dean of Peterborough and Bishop of Gloucester and
Bristol.

Trinity College consisted anciently of three halls ; King's Hall, near the clock tower, in which is placed the statue of King Edward III., with the inscription under it, " Fama super æthera notus ;" Merton Hall (corrupted to " Mutton Hole") in the S.E. corner of the great quadrangle ; St Michael's House was the third. This last was near the present kitchen, which has a vaulted and timbered roof, and the tradition is that it was the ancient chapel. Henry VIII. put them all together, and added some revenues from dissolved monasteries. The college presents to the vicarages of these. Hitchin and Ware, I think, are two of them[1]. Profligate as he was, he was a good theologian, and gave appropriately the name of Trinity to the three that he had merged into one. His statue is over the great gateway, although the inscription beneath it refers to King Edward :

"TERTIUS EDVARDUS AULÆ FUNDATOR REGIS."

[Cooper, in his *Annals of Cambridge*, makes no mention of Merton Hall as a part of Trinity College, but describes the union (1546) of King's Hall and Michael-house, of certain houses called Fyswycke Hostell, and Hovinge Inne, and of an adjacent lane into a "college of literature, the sciences, philosophy, good arts, and sacred theology to be called *Trynitie College*." How then is the common name for that corner of the Great Court to be accounted for? Perhaps in this way. There was "a certain stone house situate in the Town of Cambridge called ' *Mertone Halle*' belonging to Merton College, Oxford, which was exchanged with King Henry VI. for the Manor of Margaret Stratton, in Wiltshire, and given to King's College. It was afterwards resumed, and King's College released all claim. It was much nearer to Trinity than to King's, and may have been where the S. E. corner of Trinity quadrangle now is. It is a pity when old names are changed, e. g. there is a small street (Park-street) near to Jesus College. I remember when it was called "Garlic Fair Lane," and that name,

[1] See Chauncy's *History of Herts.*

now lost, helped to preserve the fact that there was a fair called Garlic fair granted to the Nuns of St Rhadegunda by King Stephen, on whose convent Jesus College stands, the cloisters being, it is supposed, the original.]

The first day that I dined in hall as an undergraduate was a feast day, the anniversary of the accession of George III. In my uncle's time the dinner hour was at noon, but now it was at a quarter-past two o'clock in term time, on account of the disputations in the Mathematical Schools commencing at three o'clock. Some years after it was altered, the hour of the schools was changed to twelve, and that of the dinner to four o'clock, as at present. Our habits were to take some relaxation after dinner, to go to chapel at half-past five, then retire to our rooms, shut the outer door, take tea and read till ten or eleven o'clock. There was supper in the hall at a quarter before nine, but very few partook of it. On Sundays we dined at a quarter-past one, and the afternoon University sermon at St Mary's, which was well attended by the students, was at three o'clock. The Vice-Chancellor's weekly dinner-parties were at half-past one, and all his company attended him to St Mary's.

[In Dewes' time (the 17th century), the dinner hour at St John's was at 12, and the bell rang for morning chapel at 5 o'clock. I add Bp. Watson's prophecy of the degradation of Cambridge. "An evil custom has of late years been introduced into the University which will in its consequences destroy our superiority over Oxford, and leave our scholastic exercises in as miserable a condition as theirs have long been. It is the custom of dining late. When I was admitted, and for many years after, every college dined at twelve o'clock, and the students, after dinner, flocked to the philosophical disputations which began at two. If the schools either of philosophy or divinity shall ever be generally destitute of an audience there will be an end of all scholastic exertion." While writing this Bishop Watson mentions the dinner hour as three.]

There were two coffee-houses in the town, where men used to take their tea or coffee on summer evenings, when there was no fire in their rooms. Frank Smith kept one in Bridge Street, opposite the Round Church. The other was at a room in the Rose Inn, set apart for that purpose, facing the Market Place. The same system existed then as now of supplying bread and beer from the butteries. In my first year nothing but brown bread was served from them. There was a great scarcity in this year, as there had been also in '96. The excitement *then* was very great, the poor people entertaining an idea that the millers and bakers combined to keep up the prices. Wheat now rose to more than 120s. a quarter, and the brown bread act passed into law. The season had been so backward that I saw cattle penned into fields of green oats which were past all hope of ripening.

[The highest price which the quartern loaf ever attained to was on March 3, 1801, 22½d.]

I previously knew no undergraduates of Trinity, as those of my schoolfellows who had come to the University were of other colleges : but the freshmen soon formed acquaintances by sitting near each other, and in this way I became intimate with four or five men, who with myself were just at first very studious. Shortly after however we fell into idle habits. Rowing on the river was not then the custom, but we took a boat one day, rowed down to Clayhithe, hired a net to fish with, and rowed back in the evening. This was my only excursion during my first term.

The Vice-Chancellor, Mansel, in his inaugural speech in the Senate-House, inveighed against the "togatum ocreatum-que genus"; the dress of the time was so different from that of the present day. Shorts of any colour, and white stockings, were the only regular academical dress, gaiters were for-

bidden. It was usual for the undergraduates, or at least
the more particular ones, to dress daily for the dinner in
hall in white waistcoats and white silk stockings, and there
were persons who washed them for us, as things too special
for a common laundress. There were two or three undergraduates who wore powder. My namesake, Richard Prime
of Trinity, was one of them[1]. The rest of us wore our hair
curled. It was thought very rustic and unfashionable not to
have it so. Wigs were still worn by the Dons and Heads,
with two or three exceptions. Cory, the Master of Emmanuel,
was, I have heard, the first to leave his off, complaining of
headache. Dr Barnes of Peterhouse preserved his to the last.
In Mr Daniel Sykes's time, which was twenty years before
mine, the Senior Fellows of Trinity wore wigs, and he was, as
he told me long afterwards, concerned in a practical joke
respecting them. There was a barber's shop just within
the gate of Trinity, near Bishop's Hostel, where the Fellows were powdered and the wigs dressed. It existed
even in my time. Sykes and some others bribed the
barber one Saturday night, when he had the Sunday wigs
to dress, to give them up; and getting out upon the library
parapet, placed them on the heads of the four statues
which face the hall. The next day the Seniors missing their best wigs were in a state of great excitement,
and obliged to go to dinner in their old ones. Coming
out of hall into Neville's Court, and looking up, they saw
them on the statues. The perpetrators were never found
out.

I have heard my uncle say that as a boy he wore a wig,
and that it was common for boys to do so. Footmen wore
their hair tied up behind in a thick loop called *a club*. Gen-

---

[1] Afterwards M.P. for West Sussex.

tlemen had theirs in a thin one and it was named a pigtail. Dr Hubbersty, of Queens' College, was the last person I saw in one. In every well-ordered house there was a powdering room. Pitt's tax sent powder out of fashion. People paid it for a year or two, and then gave up wearing it. Pitt is not so much to be blamed for imposing this tax, for he was at his wits' end to supply means for the French war. Every common soldier was obliged to wear it, and I believe, one cause of its disuse was the scarcity of '96 or '99, when the government forbad it, as flour was greatly employed for that purpose, and was then too dear to be so wasted.

In my uncle's time, the great feast-day, or Commemoration, was on Trinity Sunday. This was now changed to the 16th of December, and continued so for many years. The feast began with service in the chapel, and after that was over, the names of the Benefactors of the college were read aloud, and this was followed by an English declamation. In this year (1799) it was gained by Lord H. Petty (afterwards Lord Lansdowne). Being near its close he chose for his subject, *The improvements of the Eighteenth Century.*

The Christmas vacation came, my acquaintances dispersed to their homes, and I remained behind. When left to reflection, I saw the importance of earnestly pursuing my studies, and avoiding those idle but agreeable companions when they should return. I was fond both of fishing and shooting, but I made a vow never to take a gun, or fishing-rod, or cricket-bat, in hand *at Cambridge* till I had taken my degree; for I felt that total abstinence was the only safe-guard against excessive indulgence in these amusements.

I then sought the acquaintance of a more studious set, and gradually acquired one of the great advantages of college life, the intercourse and collision with men from different parts of the country, and of originally different tastes and habits, thus, to use the expression of a friend, "rounding off the acute angles of the mind."

1800. In this year Dr Glynn died. He was Fellow of King's College and an eminent physician at Cambridge. He was buried in the chapel by torchlight, as also was Dr Farmer of Emmanuel College in '97 (these were the last). A funeral sermon was preached on him the Sunday following, by Mr Michell of King's. He was also celebrated for having gained the Seatonian Prize, by a very good poem, called *The Day of Judgment*. I remember waiting with some others outside St Mary's Church, in my freshman's year, to see him. He usually wore a scarlet cloak and three-cornered hat; and carried a gold-headed cane. He also used pattens in rainy weather[1]. Our ancestors must have been badly off before umbrellas were introduced. Even so late as the latter end of the century, there was only one in Cambridge, and that was kept at a shop in Bene't Street, and let out by the hour! The early umbrellas were very clumsy. They were made of oiled cloth and were very flat, people not being then aware of the philosophy that fluid will not penetrate if it falls slantingly, and were carried by a ring fastened to the top, so that the handle often got dirty[2].

In the Easter vacation the examination for Trinity Scholarships took place. Freshmen were *then* allowed to be candidates, and I with four or five others of my year were elected. Among them were James Parke, now Lord Wensleydale,

---

[1] Hogarth wore a scarlet roquelaure and cocked hat, and "Newton, Cowper's friend, trudged through the mud in the rainy season from the parsonage to the church at Olney in pattens."—Bruce's *Life of Cowper*.

[2] Paris in 1773. "Those who walk always carry an umbrella, which is so exceedingly convenient that I wonder the people in London do not adopt it." *France on the eve of the great revolution.*—Admiral Collier.

and Thomas Coltman, afterwards one of the justices of the Court of Common Pleas. My uncle told me that in his time the examinations for Scholarships were not conducted as now, in a regular order in the hall, but that the Seniors sent for one, and sometimes two or three students together, and examined them in some Greek or Latin book in their own rooms, and afterwards they would say to each other, "So and so has done well, I think he will do for scholar," or the contrary, as it might be. Undergraduates were so young in his time that they were often spoken of as "lads." My relative, A. de la Pryme, in his MS. says, in 1693, "This year there was admitted of our college one Needham, a freshman of about twelve years old, a meer child : but he understood very perfectly $y^e$ Latin, Greek, and Hebrew tongues. But this is nothing in comparison to one of our present Fellows, Mr Wotton, who when he came up to be admitted was but eleven years old, and understood (as I have heard from all the college and multitudes of hands besides) not only the aforesaid languages, but also the French, Spanish, Italian, Assyrian, Chaldean, and Arabian tongues. When the Master admitted him he strove to pose him in many books, but could not."

I wished to have sat in the previous December for the Craven Scholarship, but my tutor advised me not, fearing, as I had received my education at a private school, that I should not be sufficiently prepared, and saying that I could try for the next. Parke obtained it, and there was no other vacant while I was eligible.

At the annual college examination, in June, in the lecture books of the year, I thought I had passed very well. When the list appeared, to my bitter mortification, I found my name placed in the second class. The next morning, Mr Sheepshanks, the assistant Mathematical Tutor and one of

the examiners, called at my rooms to inform me that there
had been a mistake in casting up the number of marks by
which the places were regulated, and that I *was* in the
first class.

After this agreeable surprise I was soon destined to a
disappointment. I had sent in a pair of Epigrams for the
Browne's Medal. One evening in June I received a message
from Dr Mansel, Master of my college, and Vice-Chancellor
of the year, requiring me to call on him. He told me that
the Prize was adjudged to me, but that he would suggest an
alteration in one of the lines. For this purpose he shewed
me the MS., and to my dismay I perceived it was not mine.
I had chosen the same motto, " Scribimus indocti doctique,"
as G. J. Durham of Bene't College, and the judges had opened
my sealed paper instead of his. The day after Dr Mansel
sent for me again to say that he had examined more particularly my epigram, and to encourage me by his com-
mendations.

[The name of Bene't remained until after 1820, when its ancient
one, Corpus Christi, was resumed.]

The three Browne's Medals were the only classical prizes,
except the University Scholarships, for which undergraduates
could compete. The Prose Essays were the only prizes for
which B.A.s could compete. Prizes have since that time
multiplied exceedingly, and, as I think, to an extent which
much diminishes the credit of obtaining them. It may,
however, be urged that the number of students is also much
increased.

The system of private tuition had not then become common, and the lectures of the tutors during term-time were by
many of the students (myself included) deemed sufficient.
A grace of the Senate was then in force prohibiting any

student from taking an honour who had read with a private tutor within two years of his degree. It was repealed after I ceased to be Fellow.

I passed my first long vacation with my former tutor, John Dawson. When I returned to Cambridge in October it was to rooms in Bishop's Hostel, to which I had become entitled as soon as I was elected scholar.

I now cultivated the acquaintance not merely of studious men, but of several who were good companions, and whose pleasant conversation afforded more relaxation than that of hard reading men only. Among them were Sir George Rose, the late Master in Chancery, whose wit and humour still delight London society; Courtenay, celebrated judge of good cookery, late M.P. for Barnstaple; Kenyon of Peterhouse, afterwards a poet and the friend of poets; and Sir Molyneux Nepean, eldest son of the Secretary to the Admiralty. With all of these I had the gratification of renewing my acquaintance in after life.

When I first went to Cambridge the habit of hard drinking was almost as prevalent there as it was in country society. It was usual to invite a large party to partake of wine and a moderate dessert after hall. The host named a Vice-President, and toasts were given. First a lady by each of the party, then a gentleman, and then a sentiment. I remember one of these latter: "the single married and the married happy." Some of them were puns, and some not very decorous. Every one was required to fill a bumper to the toasts of the President, the Vice-President, and his own.

While on the subject of toasts I may just advert to those which the Jacobites had used and which went out with the century. The song of "God save the King" is supposed to have been one of them. It was introduced no one knew

4

how, and written by no one knew whom[1]. The line "on thee our hopes we fix," seems to apply rather to one hoped for, than to one already *on* the throne. It was usual for the Jacobites to give as a toast, "God bless the King and confound the Pretender." It was not unusual to have a bowl of water in the centre of the table, and when drinking the King's health, to hold the wine-glass across it, thus intimating "The King over the water." The following lines were intended by their ambiguity to soothe both parties :

> "God bless the King, I mean the Faith's defender,
> God bless—no harm in blessing—the Pretender ;
> But who Pretender is, or who is King,
> God bless us all—that's quite another thing[2]."

I had a little book called *The Cries of London*, of which the only one I remember was supposed to allude to Jacobites in disguise, thus :

> "To live by Hurdy Gurdy I pretend,
> But for to spy your ways is all my end."

[This book has been looked for in vain in the British Museum and Cambridge University Library.]

"Buzzing," unknown in the present day, was then universal. When the decanter came round to any one, if it was nearly emptied, the next in succession could require him to finish it ; but if the quantity left exceeded the bumper, the challenger was obliged to drink the remainder and

---

[1] "God save the King" was composed by Dr Henry Carey, so it is said in *Notes and Queries*, in honour of the then reigning monarch George II. It was produced by the author for the first time at a dinner given by the Mercers' Company.—See *Notes and Queries*, 2nd Series, Vol. x. p. 301.

[2] The above lines were composed by John Byrom, who wrote the pastoral of *Colin and Phœbe* in the Spectator.

also a bumper out of the next fresh bottle. There was throughout these parties an endeavour to make each other drunk, and a pride in being able to resist the effects of the wine. If any one wished to go to chapel he was pressed to return afterwards.

In my second year, I and several of my acquaintances, among whom were my friends Monk and Pepys (late Bishops of Gloucester and of Worcester), agreed to press no one to drink at our own wine parties, ourselves decisively to resist doing so elsewhere, and to separate at chapel-time. When invited by any one who had not joined this temperance compact, we stated the conditions on which we would accept the invitation. Our attempt succeeded, and by degrees prevailed almost generally. Supper-parties about nine o'clock were frequent, at which we met an hour or two before to play whist.

Smoking was allowed in the Trinity combination room after supper in the twelve days of Christmas, when a few old men availed themselves of it. Among *us* undergraduates it had no favour, and an attempt of Mr Ginkell, son of Lord Athlone (a Dutch family mentioned in Macaulay's *History of England*), to introduce smoking at his own wine-parties, failed, although he had the prestige of being a hat-fellow-commoner.

1801. In April of this year was fought the great battle of Copenhagen. We were not at war then, but it was supposed that there was an understanding between Buonaparte and the Danes, and therefore the government instructed Nelson to demand the surrender of the Danish Fleet. This was refused, and the battle fought. A motion was made in the House of Commons blaming the ministry. There was a small Foxite minority. One Whig, and only one, Mr Morris, a barrister, who had married a daughter of Lord

Erskine, voted in the majority, saying that he thought the ministry had made out their case. Only a few years ago one of the leading Tory members of the House of Commons asked the Foreign Secretary if he had not found in the secret papers evidence sufficient to warrant the battle of Copenhagen? and he replied that he had. Mr Morris was not alive to hear it. It was supposed at the time that he had had some hint given him, which he was too honourable to reveal, but which had shown him that more was known than was supposed, and that ministers had very good reason for their policy.

At the annual college examinations, which for the second year were chiefly mathematical, I was again in the first class. I sent in two sets of Epigrams in competition for the Browne's Medal, and obtained it by that set which, in my own erroneous estimate, I had thought inferior to the other. A candidate in the year before had consulted a mathematical friend, who advised sending in what he himself (Newton of Pembroke) thought an inferior set, which was pronounced the best, though it did not gain the prize. Though I had written very few Latin verses, and no Greek ones, previous to my coming up to college, I resolved to write for the Greek Ode. I heard afterwards that there were doubts about three, that Professor Porson had been consulted, and had carried them about with him for a few days that he might consider them, and I had reason given me to suppose that mine, which was unsuccessful, was one of these three. The utmost secrecy is always observed among the examiners, but on this occasion the letter enclosing my name was written on such thin paper that it was quite discernible. A friendly intimation of this was given me by a gentleman to whom the Vice-Chancellor mentioned it. My Ode had some errors in it, which I easily discovered and avoided in the next trial.

In October of this year was concluded the Peace of Amiens. I remember seeing the mail-coach which brought the news decorated with blue ribbons.

In 1802, my third year, I determined to make a great effort to obtain the Greek Ode: there were at this time no college examinations for the third year; I therefore gave up two or three weeks exclusively to the perusal of Pindar and the choruses of the Greek tragedians. I then composed my Ode (the subject was *Pompeii Columna*), and it obtained the prize, Porson being again the judge. Dr Proctor was Vice-Chancellor, and sent for me to tell me of my success. He kindly complimented me on it, and said that Porson was consulted and had no doubt about it. He then enquired whether I had been educated at any of the great schools? I answered no, but at a foundation school of which the head master was the Rev. Joseph Milner, of his own college (St Catherine's). He seemed unaware of his existence, but said that there was the more credit due to me. I had the gratification of reciting my Ode in the Senate House at the Commencement, and also of presenting a printed copy of it to Mr Pitt, who received it from me very courteously. It happened to be one of the public Commencements, which then took place at intervals of three or four years. This was not the only occasion on which I saw Mr Pitt, for being Member for the University, he usually came there twice a year to visit his constituents. His stately form and cocked hat, then not quite obsolete, attracted the attention of every one. He is admirably represented by the statue in the Senate House, from the pedestal of which I can almost fancy him walking forth[1].

[1] " He had an almost military manner of walking as he put one foot before another."—Extract from the *Cambridge University Calendar* for 1807.

At that time the scholars of the third year were required to reside half the long vacation, for the purpose of reading the lessons in chapel and the Latin grace after dinner in hall. I chose the latter half, and remained till I took my degree. One of the books then read for a degree was that of Roger Cotes, a great mathematician, who died at the early age of 33, of whom Sir Isaac Newton said, "had Cotes lived longer we should have known something."

A few months before I took my degree, Dr Mansel met me accidentally in the walks, asked me about my preparation for the Senate House, and advised me not to shut myself up with my books, but to mix in society, and so relax the strain upon my mind. I therefore persevered in joining in miscellaneous company as well as that of the more studious men.

To these latter were now added Frederick Pollock. He came up in my third year, and I met him at Wilde's rooms, who had been educated at St Paul's school, like himself. When he was introduced to me as a freshman, I felt sure he would prove a very superior man, and, contrary to the then usual custom of not visiting our juniors, I called upon him. He was Senior Wrangler, and resided in College until he was elected Fellow. We became excellent friends, and afterwards on my visits to town, while both of us were still unmarried, I used to breakfast with him in Serjeant's Inn, and enjoy his conversation. He ever retained a fondness for any ingenious mathematical point or problem. I remember that on one such occasion we talked of Optics, and of that *crux* in Optics, single vision, and that I said to him, "the assumption of our seeing an object with both eyes apparently in the same place is erroneous, for it is *not* so (in point of fact), as stated in Wood's *Optics*. Set up a gnomon between the eyes, and shut one and then the other, and you will see the object you are looking at first to the right and then to the left, or *vice versâ.*" Pollock agreed that it was as I pointed out. He is now Chief Baron of the Exchequer; where he shows the same exceeding clearness of judgment that he had previously done in matters of science.

There was a severe frost and deep snow during the examination for the degree (January, 1803). We were bitterly cold, for the Senate House was not then artificially warmed. The examination lasted four days.

[It may be interesting to some to know how differently things were managed little more than a century before. "January, 1694. This month we sat for our degrees of B.A., we sat three days in the College and were examined by 2 fellows thereof in Rhetoric, Logic, Ethics, Physics and Astronomy; then we were sent to the public schools, there to be examined again 3 more days by any one that would." After the degree had been conferred by the Vice-Chancellor (much as is done in our day), each one knelt down and prayed by himself at the tables in the Senate-House[1].]

As I had divided my time almost equally between my classical and mathematical studies, I had not expected to do more than just obtain a place at the bottom of the Wranglers' list. When the brackets came out on the morning of the last day of examination, I began to look at the place whereabouts I hoped to be, and not finding my name as I read downwards, felt dismayed, till, casting my eye upwards, I saw my name in the second bracket, as sixth wrangler[2].

[1] MS. of Abraham de la Pryme.
[2] The names of the Wranglers of 1803 were:

| | | | | | | |
|---|---|---|---|---|---|---|
| Starkie | Joh. | Parke | Trin. | Thomson | Jes. |
| Hoare | Joh. | Pryme | Trin. | Davys | Chr. |
| Mandell | Qu. | Rose | Trin. | Ewbank | Qu. |
| Wiles | Trin. | Wood | Pemb. | Carrighan | Joh. |
| | | | | Coltman | Trin. |

I had an opportunity soon after of asking one of the moderators, Mr Dealtry, who had also been educated under Joseph Milner, how I had obtained a degree so much beyond my expectations. He told me that it was not the extent of my knowledge which had placed me so high, but that, within a certain limit, I had done almost everything clearly and well. I had aimed in my reading thoroughly to understand every proposition, and thus found the benefit of it, being placed above those who adopted what is called the system of cramming. Two of my acquaintance, who had recommended to me that course, and themselves read much deeper than I had, and whose prospects I had envied, were far below me on the list.

There are many evidences at Cambridge of the mistakes of hard readers. I knew a Mr Bolland of Trinity. He had the character of being a hard reader; he shut himself up and avoided society, and was after all but in the third class at the college examinations. His chance of a Fellowship seemed hopeless, for it is very rare for a second classman to gain one. I spoke to him, and told him that I thought he would do better if he read less, and gave his mind time to digest. He said he would take my advice, and he became seventh wrangler, and afterwards was elected Fellow. It was Wrangham, I think, who got the Browne's Medal for an Epigram, with the motto, "Ne quid nimis." He took for his illustration a reading man. I remember the first, and part of the last line:

> "Perlegit Eutrapelos libros malè sedulus omnes,
> \*          \*          \*          \*          \*
> \*          \*          \*          \*          \*
> \*          \* ut discas plurima, pauca legas."

[My father, while College Examiner, did many kind things of this sort. To one young man he advised a private tutor, and on his saying that he could not afford it, offered to let him come to his rooms once or twice a week that he might help him. This gentleman became a Fellow, and long afterwards, on receiving a dignified appointment in the Church, wrote to his old friend reminding him of that early kindness and assistance, and saying that he considered his success in life was partly owing to it.]

In August I accompanied an Address from the University to the King.

I saw Lord Nelson on this occasion coming away from the Levee, which had been previously holden at St James's, in a sedan chair. The chairmen happened to set him down as I passed, and I saw him distinctly through the glass windows. It is usual for the Sovereign to receive addresses from the Universities on the throne. The King walked to it from an adjoining room after the Levee. Immediately after he had passed through the antechamber, Dr Hurd, Bp. of Worcester, was following him, when Lord Alvanley, Chief Justice of the Common Pleas, reminded him that the Vice-Chancellor, Dr Sumner, Provost of King's College, had on *that* occasion precedence of every one, and that he ought to stand aside till he had passed. Dr Hurd seemed much displeased, and exclaimed, "A Bishop called to order!" He was the translator of Horace's *Art of Poetry*, and the friend of Bp. Warburton.

The King's bearing, though he was an elderly man, and stooping, struck me as dignified, and he was both unaffected and courteous in his manner of receiving us.

It was in the long vacation of this year that the idea was suggested of forming a corps of University Volunteers. The fear of invasion was universal, and the volunteer movement had begun elsewhere. The heads were greatly opposed to it as an unacademical thing. We formed ourselves into a committee, consisting of several M.A.'s, and two delegates from the large and one from each of the small colleges, and met at the rooms of Mr Johnson, Fellow of King's College. I was one of those from Trinity. We then put ourselves in communication with the government, and when we found that it approved of our plan we went to the Vice-Chancellor, who with the Heads withdrew his opposition. In order to give as little offence as possible we adopted a grave uniform. It consisted, as far as my memory serves me, of a dark blue jacket, black stock, grey trowsers, and short black gaiters. The corps, consisting of 180 men (44 from Trinity), included Lord Palmerston. We practised on Sidney Piece, now enclosed in the master's garden, and sometimes on Parker's (or *Parkhurst* according to Dr E. D. Clarke) Piece. On a grand field day we went to Cherry Hinton Chalk Pits. On going afterwards to Lincoln's Inn I found a company formed of the four Inns. Some wit had named them "the devil's own." This name, by which some of the legal volunteers are called at this day, is only a revival of the saying[1].

I continued to reside in college, reading chiefly for a Fellowship. In the autumn of this year (1803) I gained the prize given by Trin. Coll. for an English Essay by a B.A., on the character of King William the Third, to be recited in the Chapel on the fourth of November in each year. I had been educated in the extreme Tory (then called Anti-Jacobin)

---

[1] "The apprehension of a French invasion excited such a general enthusiasm in all parts of the country that before the end of August (1803) Mr Addington estimated the number of volunteers at upwards of 300,000."—*Lord Sidmouth's Life,* Vol. II. p. 226.

The University of Cambridge gave £2,000 out of its Chest to the general subscription.

opinions. The state of society was at that time so politically exclusive, that I never met any one who expressed a different sentiment, till a solitary instance occurred in my second collegiate year. My reading for the above-mentioned essay had suggested some doubts to my mind as to the correctness of my political creed, and subsequent study of English History and Law gradually changed it to those moderate Whig opinions which I have ever since entertained. My first public opportunity of acting on these convictions was at the general election in May, 1807.

1804. Early in this year Dr Claudius Buchanan, Principal of the College at Calcutta, offered to the University four prizes. First, for the best Greek Ode on the subject " Γενέσθω φῶς," (the words of the Septuagint translation of Genesis) " Let there be light," which I took in its literal sense as meaning its creation, and obtained the prize. It was published as required. Dr Buchanan, with whom I afterwards became acquainted, told me that he had meant it in the metaphorical sense of spreading the light of the gospel in India. The other prizes were, Second, a Latin Poem on "Collegium Bengalense," which was not awarded. Third, an English Poem on India, obtained by Charles Grant, afterwards Lord Glenelg. Fourth, an English Essay, which was adjudged to Mr Cockburn, Fellow of St John's Coll., afterwards dean of York. I mention them here as they have long been omitted from the *Cambridge Calendar*.

I also obtained in this year the first University prize for a Latin Essay (Members' Prizes). The subject was "On the Causes of the Decline and Fall of States[1]." I confined my view to the States of Antiquity, omitting that of

---

[1] The Second Prize was adjudged to James Parke, afterwards Lord Wensleydale.

the Jews, and mentioning that I did so as it was influenced by the direct dispensation of the Almighty. I then
knew little of Modern History and nothing of Political
Economy.

# CHAPTER IV.

## 1804—1808.

IN October, 1804, I migrated to Lincoln's Inn, took chambers in Stone Buildings, and began to study Law. The
state of travelling was *then* such that we reached London in
the course of one day, *i.e.* in about eight hours, the coach
stopping when half way that we might take luncheon. In
my uncle's time it stopped all night. Some years before that
again it took two whole days to perform the journey with the

same horses, staying all night at Epping. When they went through in one day there was one change. I have heard a person, much older than myself, say that she used to start at six A.M. and get into town between nine and ten P.M. ·When the *Telegraph* was announced to do it in seven hours, people anticipated that it would never last, and that the horses would shortly break down from fatigue. The coaches went very slowly: a man walking between Bury St Edmund's and Newmarket was offered a lift on one as it passed him. He had been in the habit of accepting it, but on this occasion said, "No, thank you, I'm in a hurry to-day." I myself have travelled with my uncle from Nottingham to Hull by coach, when it took two days to perform the journey (72 miles), and have witnessed two men, who spoke to the coachman as he left Newark, arrive on foot at the half-way house between that and Lincoln, a distance of 16 miles, just as we drove out of it after baiting the horses. Some years ago there was found at the back of a drawer in an inn at York an old hand-bill, stating that a stage coach would run between York and London, doing the distance, 200 miles, in four days. It mentioned the places where it would stop for the night, and added the positive assurance that the journey should be accomplished in *that* time. The landlord who discovered this relic very sensibly framed it, and hung it up in his commercial room.

The originator of mail-coaches was one Palmer of Bath, and they were started in 1784[1]. It is within my memory that one was commenced from Hull to York. Before that time letters were conveyed on horseback, and I have

---

[1] The first was at Bristol. Gen. Palmer is said to have received £100,000 for his father's introduction of the Mail-Coach system. The late Lord Campbell mentions going by one from St Andrew's, Scotland, to London, and being three nights and two days on the road.

seen the post-lad with a portmanteau strapped behind him on his horse, of which he could so easily have been robbed, riding between Newark and Nottingham.

Pack-horses were used for conveying goods, and I have seen long strings of them with their panniers in the North of Yorkshire and in Devonshire.

A gentleman of olden time travelled, when alone, by "riding post," that is, hiring for eightpence a mile at each stage two horses, with a post-boy, who carried the portmanteau behind him, and took the tired horses back when fresh ones were had. Every gentleman visited London at least once in his lifetime[1]. Pillion was the usual mode of conveyance for women among farmers, and even the gentry. I have seen hundreds riding so.

When I first saw Lincoln's Inn Fields, the centre, which is now enclosed by palisades, was a mere grass field surrounded by posts and rails, and sheep were feeding on it[2]. Many of the great lawyers of the time had houses there, among them Lords Kenyon and Erskine, and Sir Frederick Morton Eden. This last proposed making it into an ornamental garden, and Erskine said, "If so, it must be called *the Garden of Eden.*"

London was in fact very different from what it is now, even in the parts that seem to us at this time quite old. The Foundling Hospital stood nearly alone, Hunter Street

[1] Lord Clarendon says in his *Life* " that few gentlemen made journeys to London, or any other expensive journey, but upon important business, and their wives never ; by which providence they enjoyed and improved their estates in the country, and kept good hospitality in their house, brought up their children well, and were beloved by their neighbours."

[2] Pennant says that "In the centre of this square Lord Russell was beheaded (1683), being the nearest open space to Newgate, where he was imprisoned."

and those other streets now around it being unbuilt. At its back were green fields and crooked lanes. I kept my horse in Gray's Inn Lane; within half-a-mile of it, on the north side, were fields and rural rides. Islington was a village. In the Strand, near to Catherine Street, was a block of buildings, similar to Middle-Row, Holborn; this was the once famous Exeter Change. The wild beasts were in rooms upstairs, the shops below had casement windows. By Northumberland House the way was so narrow that I witnessed an accident to a small cart, which was overturned there from that cause.

Portland Place was bounded on the North by a wooden railing with a stile in the middle, beyond it were fields. At the other end (the south) was the Duke of Gloucester's house in a garden. Portland Place was therefore at that time scarcely a thoroughfare. Two small streets led into it at either side of the duke's house. In the centre of Portland Place, on the left-hand side, was Lord Mansfield's residence, which was larger than the others, and still preserves something of its ancient aspect. The present Regent Street was composed of several small streets, the pulling down of which I saw. It was then re-named, in compliment to the Prince of Wales, whose regency lasted a decade, as did also his reign. I have a map of the year 1770, bought by my father when he visited London, in which Portman Square is represented as complete only on the south side, the other three are blank; Baker Street did not exist, and between the Square and the New Road were fields. My mother went once or twice before she was married to visit a cousin who had been domestic chaplain to George II., and had apartments in Kensington Palace, and she has told me that the road between Kensington and London was so dangerous at night that there was a horse patrol.

Modern Belgravia I remember as a set of swampy meadows, called St George's Fields.

The streets were lighted by lamps fed with whale oil. A scheme was just at that time started, and I among others received a circular, by a man named Winsor, proposing that London should be lighted with gas. It met with no approval, and fell to the ground. But at a later time it was tried on one side of Pall Mall, and the contrast between the two modes of lighting was then so forcibly illustrated, that its success was established.

Soon after my arrival in town I became a member of a debating society, called "the Academical," from the rules requiring a candidate to be a member of an University or Inn of Court. We met once a week at a room in Bell Yard, between Lincoln's Inn and the Temple, for debate. Recent politics, or allusions to living statesmen, were excluded. Modern History and Political Economy were occasionally touched on, and were subjects wherein I felt my deficiency. Brougham, Copley (Lord Lyndhurst), Charles Grant, afterwards Lord Glenelg, and his brother Robert, Francis Horner, Bowdler and Clason (both of these latter died young), were distinguished speakers. Campbell, afterwards Lord Chief Justice, was also a member. Bowdler was a very eloquent and a very religious man. Dr Bateman was our President. He was a rising physician, and we chose him for the speaker, as it were, of our little parliament, because we had so many lawyers among us. The first night on which I joined I remember Copley opening the debate by a motion to this effect : "That the reign of Charles the Second was favourable to civil liberty." "This," said he, "may seem a paradox, but I care not for the character of the Sovereign, and shall dwell only upon the measures and political acts of the time."

Francis Horner was four or five years senior to me. When I first saw him at the "Academical," he spoke directly after my maiden speech there. I forget the subject of the evening, but remember that I was very timid and nervous. In his speech Horner very kindly alluded to "the gentleman whom they had just heard with pleasure for the first time, and whom he, and he doubted not the rest of the company, would have much pleasure in hearing again." Doubtless he saw my nervousness and wished to reassure a timid young man. His character for statesmanlike views stood so high, that Lord Carrington, who owned two close boroughs, placed him, without expense of any kind, in one of them. When in Parliament he took a very active and effective part respecting the orders in Council which imposed considerable restrictions on foreign trade[1].

I must here mention my first acquaintance with Political Economy. I had heard, even when a boy, of Adam Smith's *Wealth of Nations*, a book much seen on University shelves, but seldom read. I now bought it, and devoted every Thursday to its perusal, always going over a second time what I had read on the preceding week. In this year, 1805, when on a visit to Mr Lomax of Netley Place, Surrey, I met Mr Malthus, author of the celebrated work on *Population*. He said that his theory was first suggested to his mind in an argumentative conversation which he had with his father on the state of some other countries.

I dined daily in hall during term-time. It was not usual for the fellow-students to converse without previous introduction. We therefore arranged our parties before

[1] Mr Horner died early. "A life too short for friendship, not for fame," for his death was admitted to be a public loss. Sidney Smith said of him, "There was in his look a calm, settled love of all that was honourable and good, an air of settled wisdom and sweetness."

taking our seats at table. Among my acquaintances was
Mr Sugden, now Lord St Leonards, who was practising as
a conveyancer under the Bar, and therefore ranked only as
a student. He had published an able and acute pamphlet,
showing that the usury laws had only increased instead of
limiting the rate of interest, by means of evasions which
legislation could not prevent. I soon discerned his acute and
vigorous mind. At that time conveyancers scarcely ever
went into court, and never attained to the honours of the
profession. One day I suggested to him whether, with his
abilities, he had taken a right course, and whether he should
not practise in the Court of Chancery? He answered me
that he was not anxious for the honours of the profession, and
sought only an income, which he was taking the surest course
to obtain. Since then conveyancers have sometimes appeared as counsel in cases touching wills or conveyances
which they themselves had drawn; and on such occasions
as these Mr S.'s superior powers of arguing were manifested,
and led to his becoming in succession Solicitor and Attorney
General, and Lord Chancellor both of Ireland and England[1].

I saw Pitt, Fox, Sheridan, and Windham in the House of
Commons: but I never heard a debate of any consequence
at that time. I heard Pitt speak, but shortly, and Fox more
at length both in the House, and on the hustings at Covent
Garden, in a general election. Windham was not splendidly
but soundly eloquent, clear, sensible, fluent, and to the
point. He was the introducer of that most valuable measure
"the Limited Enlistment Bill." Canning was pointed out to
me, but I do not remember hearing him speak. He was
good-looking, though not handsome, with a great appearance

---

[1] Edward Burtenshaw Sugden was born in 1781, called to the bar
in 1807, went into the Court of Chancery in 1817.

of intelligence in his face. The *Anti-Jacobin* had not long come out. Davys and I read it together with exceeding interest.

I was present one day in Westminster Hall at the impeachment of Lord Melville. Erskine was Chancellor and presided.

Suddenly (May 3, 1805) the news came that the French Fleet had escaped our blockade, and that Nelson had followed them to the West Indies. A cousin of mine, who commanded a small vessel, was under orders to sail somewhere, but hearing of this event came instantly to England with the news. Instead of being blamed he was given another step in the navy. People were great martinets in those days. On his way Nelson stopped at a principal island, and asked for troops. The governor promised them, and said they could be ready in a week or ten days. "I must be under weigh at sunset," replied Nelson, and he took the men as they were.

Having again obtained the first prize for the Latin Prose Essay, the subject being "On the Researches and Discoveries made by the French in Egypt, during the expedition of Napoleon there," I returned to Cambridge in June, 1805, to read it in the Senate House, and remained there till the examination for Fellowships, when I was elected on the first of October, along with my friends, Monk and Coltman.

I now gave up my rooms in college and went back to Lincoln's Inn, and there applied myself more exclusively to my legal studies, and became one of five pupils in the office of Mr John Atkinson, an eminent Special Pleader, where we drew declarations, pleas, &c., which were filed among the records of the court previous to trial, and also gave opinions. These were matters of much more technicality and nicety than at present. Improvements had indeed begun, as parties were often allowed by the Courts a judge's order to amend an error on paying the extra cost occasioned by such amendment. Subsequent acts of parliament have done much to diminish the expense of litigation, and to prevent a case being decided upon a legal quibble.

One of my fellow-pupils at Mr Atkinson's was Mr Hope Vere: with him I formed an intimate friendship, which continued through life[1]. In later years we used to breakfast at each other's rooms every Sunday morning, when I was in town, and afterwards attend divine service. Sometimes we went to hear Sidney Smith, who used pointed and forcible expressions in his sermons.

I used to frequent the students' box in the Court of King's Bench, in order to hear Lord Ellenborough's (Chief Justice) judgments. I think he succeeded Lord Kenyon, whom I remember, when a little boy, as a judge at Nottingham. K. was not a very educated man, and made many mistakes in a habit he had of quoting Latin upon every occasion. He was once happier in a translation. Some one was applying "abiit, evasit, erupit." "Yes," said Kenyon, "that means over the hills and far away."

An unusual thing occurred in the fact of Lord Ellenborough's joining, as a cabinet minister, Addington's short administration, which concluded peace with France in the autumn of 1801. Such a thing had not occurred for two or three hundred years, nor has happened since; it being thought undesirable to join the high judicial functions with

---

[1] James Joseph Hope Vere, M.P. for Newport, Hants., of Craigie Hall, co. Linlithgow, and Blackwood, co. Lanark, Scotland. He died May 19, 1843. I regret that my father has not given any sketch of Mr Hope Vere, whose elegant manners, refined yet vigorous mind, and delightful conversation, charmed all who knew him well.

those of the administration[1]. Addington was a feeble well-meaning man, and had never committed himself against the peace with France as Pitt had, who, it was said, stood aside for this purpose.

[My father's change from College to legal life elicited the following letter, which I showed to an old pupil of the writer, who honours his memory and on whose judgment I can rely, and he approved of my publishing it, adding, in reference, I suppose, to its quaint pedantry, "he wrote better Greek than English."

Mr Tate was a great scholar, and a most simple and kindhearted man. He was master of the school at Richmond, Yorkshire, and had many pupils who distinguished themselves at Trinity, among them Dean Peacock. He was afterwards Vicar of Edmonton, and Canon of St Paul's. Sidney Smith described him as "one of the kindest and best men that ever lived."]

" RICHMOND,

*Saturday,* 11 *Jan.* 1806.

" DEAR SIR,

"Your very valuable and magnificent, as well as most gratifying, present of the three volumes of Suidas, bound, I dare say, exactly to your wish, came safe to hand on Thursday, but too late for acknowledgment by the post of that day.

"I take the earliest opportunity therefore of assuring you, that you could not have devised a more delightful method of obliging me. Indeed, so handsome a gift could not fail to demonstrate the respect and good-will of the munificent giver: and I am only desirous that you should believe your

---

[1] See some very judicious remarks of Mr Wilberforce in his *Life,* Vol. III. p. 258.

purpose has been most completely answered, if you wished
to convince me, that any little service I may have been
fortunate enough to render, was not ungraciously received.
May your relinquishment of classical amenity for legal toil,
as you share it with Blackstone and Jones, so turn ultimately
(as it did with them) to your own honor and the good of your
country. You have met with the former's most beautiful
*Lawyer's Farewell to his Muse;* and of the latter you need
not be told how much he realised the Attic image of that
most beautiful strophe which ends

Τᾷ Σοφίᾳ παρέδρους
Πέμπειν Ἔρωτας—the amenities and graces of literature,
Παντοίας ἀρετᾶς συνεργούς.

And believe me, dear Sir, you carry with you into the arduous profession of jurisprudence, my most cordial good
wishes, that you may in like manner embellish forensic rudeness with literary elegance, and give the fascinations of grace
to the solid and the severe.

"Whenever your nearness to this place may conveniently
allow, I hope you will not scruple to try at Richmond the
hearty welcome

"of, Dear Sir,

"Yours faithfully and affectionately,

"JAMES TATE."

"*G. Pryme, Esq.,*
*No.* 3, *Stone Buildings,*
*Lincoln's Inn, London.*"


Oct. 21, 1805. The battle of Trafalgar was fought and
the death of Nelson took place. Monk's remark was, "Shall
we be able to say any more of it than 'Diem proferet Ilio'?"

His body was brought to England, laid in state at the Admiralty, and was buried in St Paul's. I witnessed the procession, Jan. 9th, 1806.

[A friend who saw it also, told me that the car was so badly arranged that the coffin nearly fell out of it as they were passing Northumberland House.]

A fortnight later Mr Pitt died. The King sent for Lord Grenville. He declared that he was engaged to Mr Fox, and so the King was obliged to permit the latter to be in the cabinet. It did not last long, breaking up on their wishing to give the Roman Catholics in England and Scotland three more steps in the army, and thus make them on an equality with those in Ireland. The King, who had been displeased with Mr Pitt's advocacy of Roman Catholic Emancipation—not the full emancipation of late years, but a relaxation of existing restraints—disliked this, dismissed them in March, 1807, and sent for Lord Liverpool. It was said of this short administration, which obtained the sobriquet of "All the Talents," that it lasted a year, a month, a week, and a day. Canning wrote thus of it :

"So round some cliff when now the tempest roars,
And the weak linnet downwards turns her oars,
The royal Eagle from his craggy throne
Mounts the loud storm majestic and alone,
And steers his plumes athwart the dark profound,
While roaring thunders replicate around.
But now roused slowly from her opiate bed
Lethargic Europe lifts the heavy head,
Feels round her heart the creeping torpor close,
And starts with horror from her dim repose."

*All the Talents*, 1807, Dial. 1. p. 47.

An election took place at Cambridge, and Lord Henry Petty[1] was returned in Mr Pitt's room. Not being yet an M.A. I could take no part in it. The question of a statue to Mr Pitt was now mooted at Cambridge. A grace for this purpose was rejected in the caput by one dissentient voice ; but at a private meeting at Trinity Lodge a subscription was commenced, and in a short time more than £7,000 was given by 616 members of the University, past or present.

[Nollekens, who had never seen Mr Pitt, was appointed the sculptor. He drew inspiration from West's drawing and description of him when, "in an attitude of triumph," he left Windsor Castle after an interview with the king, in spite of all opposition. "He received 3,000 guineas for the statue, and for the pedestal 1,000 guineas. He also executed at least 74 busts in marble ; and there were upwards of 600 casts taken at 6 guineas each."]

I will now speak a little of the amusements of the town, which in my time were not very varied. The stage was, however, in its zenith, although Garrick's sun had set. I saw Mrs Siddons in all her great characters. In the pure pathetic I preferred Miss O'Neill. In one or two plays her representation gave me positive pain, it was so natural, and I resolved never to see her in those again. I went once with two or three other men to a masquerade at Ranelagh. We went in domino (a long cloak) and mask. It must have been already losing its favour, for from the dresses we took the company to have been third-rate. Among it were some who played the part of housemaids, and occasionally brushed both floors and guests with their long-handled brooms.

[This party to Ranelagh, to which my father affixed no date, must have been in a former visit to London. "The Peace Fête

---

[1] Afterwards Marquis of Lansdowne.

was held there in 1803, and in 1804 it was pulled down, and part of the grounds thrown into the Old Men's garden at Chelsea Hospital."]

I once accompanied Dobree and a party to Vauxhall. Avenues of trees, lighted by coloured lamps, a rotunda for music in the centre, and arbours all around for private suppers, made its charm. There was also a public supper-table. For ladies the proper thing was to go about seven, and leave between nine and ten o'clock, before the revelry began.

There was an exhibition called "The Invisible Girl," which excited great attention and much curiosity to know how the effect could be produced. It consisted of a globe, about a foot, or rather more, in diameter, having four trumpet-like orifices, by speaking into which an answer was returned as if the girl had been within. It was suspended by a small chain from the ceiling and was surrounded by a square railing. This was described to the Rev. Dr Milner, President of Queens' College, Cambridge, and he conjectured that there must be, opposite to these trumpets, little holes in the railing conveying the sound by tubes to some one in a room below. I went to see it, and clearly found the fact to be so, though it was not very apparent, from the closeness of the rails to the mouth of the trumpet. While I was there the invisible girl said, "What is that gentleman peering so curiously about for?" Dean Milner was a very acute and sagacious man, and the conjecture I have mentioned proved it.

With regard to dress, I remember shortly after my going to reside in London the introduction of tight pantaloons, over which were worn a pair of black boots called Hessians. They came up in a point to within a few inches of the knee, and from this depended a tassel. But the most fashionable morning dress was pale yellow leather breeches with top-boots, in which the men of distinction promenaded in Bond Street from two till four o'clock. It was to be supposed that they had been riding, or were going to ride[1]. Charles James Fox was frequently there, but dressed in the old-fashioned costume, which we see in his portraits. His waistcoat had immense pockets with a flap over them. I saw him at an election in Covent Garden, when one of the crowd called out, " Holloa ! you with the salt-box pockets," in allusion to Fox's large waistcoat. Such pockets and flaps were called by this name. Coltman, who stood next me, and I, thought this a clever hit.

Beau Brummell was pointed out to me. He was then the reigning dandy. I remember my tailor saying, " Mr Brummell wears it so."

1806. Charles James Fox died in September. He was Foreign Secretary, and Lord Grenville Premier. Lord Grenville was one of the ablest statesmen of his day. I have seen him. He was third son of the famous George Grenville, whose name will be for ever connected with the letters of Junius.

I was called to the Bar in Michaelmas Term of 1806 (Nov. 15), on the same day with the late Lord Campbell. In this way commenced an acquaintance, perhaps I might say a friendship, which lasted through life. I may here mention an anecdote respecting him, which shows how remarkably his energy and ability of character had thus early manifested itself. His connection with the *Morning*

---

[1] March 18, 1796. " No business in the House of Commons ; but Popham, an old M.P. represented to me that I was disorderly in wearing my spurs in the House, as none but County Members were entitled to that privilege." *Lord Colchester's Diary*, Vol. I. p. 45.

*Chronicle* at that time is well known. Mr Spankie, afterwards serjeant-at-law and M.P. for Finsbury, was the editor of that paper. He was walking one day with a friend in Bloomsbury Square, when Campbell passed them, on which S. remarked that he, Mr C., had relinquished his engagement with the newspaper in order to practise at the Bar. " Has he done wisely," said the other, " to give up such a certainty for so precarious a profession ? " to which S. replied, " You might have remarked his stiff gait and figure; were he to set up for a dancing master he would probably not be able to dance like Sir John Galini[1], but I am quite sure he would make a fortune by it." Campbell had a quiet humour. Some one repeated to us at dinner in hall an epigram of four lines. The next day another enquired of Campbell if he had heard it ? " Yes," said he, and repeated them, adding two more lines of his own without the least alteration of countenance.

[My father would not put them down though he remembered them, lest they might hurt the feelings of any survivors of the name which occurred in them.]

During this winter symptoms of a pulmonary affection appeared, and I was advised by Dr Willan[2] to pass several weeks at Ventnor, in the Isle of Wight, and from this change I derived some benefit. As I went down I saw, not far from Guildford, a man who had been found guilty of robbing a mail-coach, hanging on a gibbet, dressed in a red coat. The gibbet was an iron frame-work, a few feet from the ground, where no hand could reach, which encompassed the man and

---

[1] Sir J. Galini was the most celebrated dancing master of the time, and knighted for his eminence in that line.

[2] Robert Willan, M.D. and F.R.S., an eminent physician in his day, born at Sedbergh, 1757, died at Madeira, 1812.

prevented his bones from dropping through. A fragment of one was remaining within my memory on Caxton heath in Cambridgeshire.

Feb. 23, 1807, was memorable for the final carrying of the slave-trade question in the House of Commons, 283 to 16. This was the last act of the Grenville administration.

[I place here extracts from two letters which my father received from his uncle about this time, as it will show how liberal the old tory rector was, and how he sympathised with his nephew, although the political opinions of the latter *had* changed, and how he directed his attention to the best models.]

"WILFORD,
*April* 30, 1807.

"DEAR GEORGE,

"I was duly favor'd with your Letter, and must now certainly acknowledge myself your Debtor. How our Epistolary Account stood before I cannot take upon me to say, but upon y$^e$ Receipt of this, we must strike a Balance, and open a fresh Account. Spring, or rather Summer, has burst upon us all at once; so sudden, and so pleasing a change in the appearance of the Country in three or four days I never remember; and I shall hope to hear that this genial Warmth has produced as great and sudden an Alteration in your state of Health.

"I suppose that you will go down to the Election at Cambridge. I have long been sick of Politics; however I certainly condemn the late Ministers for that Conduct which was y$^e$ Occasion of the Change; and I only wish there were more Characters both in and out of the Cabinet, similar to that I lately read of Lord Somers: 'Lord Somers,' re-marks Mr Walpole, 'was one of those divine Men, who like a

Chapel in a Palace, remain unprofaned, while all the rest
is Tyranny, Corruption, and Folly.  All the traditional Accounts of him, the Historians of the last age, and its best
Authors, represent him as the most incorrupt Lawyer, and
the honestest Statesman, as a Master Orator, a Genius of the
finest Taste, and as a Patriot of the noblest and most extensive views; as a Man who dispensed Blessings by his Life,
and planned them for Posterity[1].'

*       *       *       *       *       *

"The Pipe of Port arrived about a fortnight ago, and
I hope, without any depredation being committed.  I am not
likely to read those Articles in y^e *Edinb. Review* which you
pointed out, as from a dislike of their Principles, I made a
Motion at our last meeting to have it discontinued, and which
was adopted Nem. Con.: so that I am not singular in my
opinion of that Publication.

"If you can (as I know you do) admire fine writing,
though against your Politics, pray look at an address to
Lascelles, signed by hundreds of names in the '*York Herald*,
July 11, 1807,' a newspaper so called; it is guessed it came
from Dr Colthurst.  I copied it: one proof of its being an
*elegant* extract.  As another morsel, admire this immensely
glorious *visio* in Milton's lesser works: 'O, quæ in immenso
procul antro recumbis, *otiosa* Æternitas, monumenta servans
et ratas leges *Jovis!*'  It should be, Fati! though in Classical Metaphysics it is the same.  In his Poem to his Father
is *this* line: '*Æternæque moræ stabunt immobilis ævi!*'
Th' eternal *pauses*, ever fixed.

"We have got over y^e Hurry of Visitation, Confirmation,

---

[1] Lord Somers' motto was, *Prodesse quam conspici.*  He was the
favourite character of Sir Jas. Mackintosh.  His portraiture is beautifully
given by Addison on the day of his funeral in the *Freeholder*, No. 39.

&c. &c. Our new Archbishop pleased us all much by his Affability and Condescension.

> " I remain, dear George,
>
> " Your affectionate Uncle,
>
> "OWEN DINSDALE."]

There was a general election in May, 1807. I went down to Cambridge about ten days before to take my Master's degree and enjoy a little holiday. The candidates for the University were Lords Euston and Henry Petty (the previous members, whigs), and Sir Vicary Gibbs (Attorney General) and Lord Palmerston (tories). Being now M.A. I took an active part, and was one of about forty who had promised our votes to Lord H. P. only. The polling was then limited to one day. Finding in the afternoon that he was hopelessly at the bottom, and that Lord Euston was third on the poll, we held a meeting of Lord H. P.'s committee, and with his approbation resolved to divide our votes. We returned to the Senate House to do so, and thereby placed Lord Euston unexpectedly at the head of the poll. The final numbers were Lord E. 324, Sir V. G. 312, Lord P. 310, Lord H. P. 265.

[Such was my father's retentive memory at past 80 years, that all the numbers given by him of majorities and minorities while dictating this volume, were without reference to books. I remember only one exception, when he said in mentioning this very election, in reference to Lord H. P.'s number of votes being, as he thought, 267, "I am not sure it was not 265, but I'll look to be certain, for I dislike inaccuracy." Invariably after writing numbers from his dictation, I looked in an excellent *Register of Contested Elections*, and found them correct.]

It was during this visit that I saw a little of Lord Byron, who was then a nobleman at Trin. Coll. I used to sit nearly opposite to him at the Fellows' table. We entered into con-

versation about Nottinghamshire, and on other subjects.
He was unaffected and agreeable, but we Fellows did not
think him possessed of any great talent, insomuch so, that
when the *English Bards and Scotch Reviewers* appeared without his name, Monk and Rose and I would not believe that
*he* was the author.   I knew Miss Chaworth before her marriage with his rival.   She was not beautiful, but there was a
soft expression of countenance, and an innocent simplicity of
manner, which prevented my feeling any surprise at the
intensity and duration of his affection for her.   The portrait
in the *Illustrations of Byron* gives a very inferior representation of her.   Her mother was married again to a clergyman
named Clark, and they all lived at Annesley Hall, a few
miles from Wilford, and were intimate with my uncle and
his wife.   I remember once walking home with her and
another lady after meeting her at a friend's house in a
morning call.

I have seen Mr Musters, whom she preferred to Lord
Byron, in the grand stand at Nottingham races.   He was one
of several gentlemen riding their own horses.   He was a fine
handsome man, of old family, but with a dilapidated fortune.
Miss Chaworth had a female friend living with her who had
been her governess, and who was supposed to urge Mr M.'s
suit, which was considered to be more addressed to her estate
than to herself.

In the following long vacation I went, as I had done the
year before, to Scarborough, then in great repute as a sea-
bathing place.   Afterwards it declined, but the railroad has
restored it to far more than its former prosperity.   At that
time there was no bridge from one cliff to the other.   Hun-
tresses' Row, and a few other lodgings, had been built to the
westward of the old seaport town, but the north and south
cliffs had no houses upon them.

On account of my still indifferent health I passed the
winter of 1807-8 at Exmouth. The continent was then
almost inaccessible by reason of the war with Napoleon.
I rode from Wilford, and was ten days on the journey,
passing on my way the ruins of Kenilworth. I recollect
hanging the reins of my horse over a gate and gazing on
the castle, which so many years later was to give its name to
Walter Scott's delightful novel.

There were above twenty other young valetudinarians at
Exmouth besides myself, of whom few lived many years.
Two of them however, with whom I then formed a friendship, survived; Hudson Gurney, now in his ninetieth year,
and Joshua Spencer, an Irish landowner, who was afterwards
M.P. for an Irish borough. He was the elder brother of Sir
Brent Spencer, and a literary man. He introduced me to
his sister, Mrs Drewe (of the Grange, Devon), one of whose
daughters, then a little girl, afterwards became the wife of
Lord Gifford. Having thus passed the Rubicon, I was admitted to the exclusive excellent society of Exmouth. I
became a member of the Whist Club, and frequented the
card-parties and dances, at which latter I could only be a
spectator. We went to them in sedan-chairs, an admirable
invention for an invalid who was unwilling to resign society.

[I have found among my father's papers an invitation to one
of these parties couched in the quaint, courteous phrase of the
time of Mrs Delany. "If Mr Pryme is not afraid of a hot-room
and three or four card-tables, Mrs Drewe will be very happy to
see him in her drawing-room this evening." My father returned
to London in the beginning of May 1808, riding thither from
Exmouth, making his route by "Lyndhurst" (as I find in an old
pocket-book) "in the vicinity of the New Forest, enchanting beyond description, and abounding with residences between Lymington
and Romsey."

"'Tis sixty years since" my dear father took that *long* journey,

6

probably to avoid the inconveniences and delays of coaches.  He was before his age in many ways, and foresaw the necessity of some of its "coming events," as the next paragraph will show, but he never could have dreamed that any child of his might go from Exmouth to London in six hours.]

At that time the only public conveyances in London were hackney-coaches and sedan-chairs; these latter regularly plied[1].  There were stands of them, and places where people knew to send for them.  The hackney-coaches held four persons and were drawn by two horses, the charge being one shilling a mile.  They were so large that they could easily contain six persons, and if that number went in them an extra fee was given to the driver.  I suggested to Mr Newport, a coach-owner, at whose livery stables I kept my horse, the plan of carriages taking passengers at so much apiece, along the chief thoroughfares.  He inclined to approve, and said he would mention it at a meeting of proprietors shortly to take place.  He afterwards told me that he had done so, but they were of opinion that it would not answer in a pecuniary point of view.  Would that they could return to earth for an hour to see the omnibus of the present day!  The first change was to a few chariots with the same fare and horses, but pleasanter for one or two persons than the gloomy coach.  Then came a few gigs with one horse, and a little seat by the side for the driver, the precursor of the "Hansom"; and lastly the closed cab and the omnibus[2].

[1] Rich people of course had their own, which were often lined with silk or satin, and always stood in the hall ready for use.

[2] In 1802 there were 1100 hackney coaches, in 1815 no more than 1300.  In 1823 cabs were introduced, at first 12 in number.  "In 1829 the first pair of London Omnibuses were started: they were constructed to carry 22 passengers, all inside; the fare was one shilling, or sixpence for half the distance, together with the luxury of a newspaper.  A Mr J. Shillibeer was the owner of these carriages, and the first conductors were the two sons of a British naval officer."  *History of Signboards.*

I remained in London till the long vacation of 1808, but my weak state of health still continuing, I again consulted Dr Willan, who told me that he thought my life depended on my ceasing to reside there. I enquired if he considered that Cambridge had a good air, and he declared it to be an excellent one. I therefore resolved to return to Trinity College. This was a severe disappointment to me, for I had formed hopes of succeeding at the Bar, and these hopes were nourished by Mr Atkinson's having latterly entrusted to me his more difficult cases, and told me that as soon as I began to practise he knew of three or four solicitors who would become my clients, men whom he had deputed me to see for him in his occasional absences. But other considerations were paramount to these, and I retired from the arena where I had hoped to have won some distinction.

# CHAPTER V.

## 1808—1813.

I ARRIVED at Cambridge in Oct. 1808, on the morning of the day on which the body of Prof. Porson was brought from London for interment in Trinity College Chapel. We dined early, and the ceremony took place after the dinner. The coffin was deposited in the Hall as was then usual, and some of the scholars, according to ancient custom, laid upon it Greek and Latin elegiac verses. These were afterwards pinned to the pall, when the procession moved to go round the quadrangle to the chapel.

["His remains repose at the foot of the statue of Newton. His epitaph *is his name alone.*" His age was 48.]

Porson, as Greek Professor, had rooms and commons in college and £40 a year. He had ceased to be a fellow at the end of seven years from his M.A. degree, as he did not take orders. He had applied for one of the two lay-fellowships, but Ramsden told us that Postlethwaite (a former Master) refused it to him on the ground of his frequent intoxication being a bad example to the young men. A sum of money had been therefore subscribed by his friends, and appropriated to his use, and when he died, there being a surplus, it was employed in founding a " Porson Prize" for the best Greek verse translation from the English Dramatists. Porson edited four plays of Euripides, and Monk two others. Porson was a witty, playful man. The translation of the "Three Children Sliding on Dry Ground" is given in his Life, but not the anecdote of the occasion which gave rise to it. One day in hall, something leading to it, Porson said " Many of our nursery rhymes are translations from the Greek." " Indeed," said Tate, who was a clever but simple-minded man. " Yes," replied Porson, " that one of the children sliding on dry ground is from Athenæus's after-supper songs, and to-morrow I will show it you." Next day he came into hall with the verses very classically rendered into Greek. I doubt if more than one or two others besides Tate were taken in ; the rest *laughed in their sleeves.*

[The Mr Tate here alluded to was probably a William Tate of Trinity, who took his degree in the same year (1794) as James Tate of Sidney, but if it had been the latter it need have been no reflection on his Scholarship. Professor Dobree told Professor Sedgwick that " he shewed these beautiful Greek Iambics to a celebrated German Scholar, who was mightily puzzled by them."]

Smoking was the custom in our Combination Room after supper during the twelve days of Christmas, and with the wine, pipes and tobacco-box were laid on the table. Porson was asked for an inscription for the latter (a large silver one), and he said, "Τῷ Βάκχῳ." When on a visit to Dr Routh, President of Magd. Coll., Oxford, he attended a feast during which he went to sleep in the Common Room, and on his waking found the punch-bowl empty, the candles nearly burnt out, and only two persons remaining, on which he exclaimed οὔτε τόδε οὔτε τἄλλο.

When Porson was in a reading humour he would sit up all night for about ten days, coming to morning chapel, and repeating, which was not usual, the responses *aloud*, in a grave sonorous manner, and so as to be heard all over the chapel. After this he would go to bed and sleep for some hours.

I now relinquished my legal studies, supposing that I should never be able to follow the law as a profession, and I devoted my time to reading modern literature, and studying the Italian language. Much as I had liked the collegiate life during my former residence as an undergraduate, I found the life of a fellow, mixed though it was with the melancholy of disappointed views, still more agreeable. In sauntering about the secluded bowling-green, or the stately cloisters, I oft repeated to myself the lines,

> "What are the gay parterre, the chequered shade,
> The morning bower, the ev'ning colonnade,
> But soft recesses for uneasy minds
> To sigh unheard in to the passing winds[1]?"

---

[1] Pope, as quoted by Lady M. W. Montague. It was with similar feelings that "the melancholy Cowley" wrote

> "O chara ante alias, magnorum nomine regum
> Digna Domus! Trini nomine digna Dei.
> Ah mihi si vestrae reddat bona gaudia sedis,
> Detque Deus doctâ posse quiete frui."

These saddened moods were cheered however by the delightful society of such friends as Monk, Sedgwick, and C. J.
Blomfield. This last was a fine classical scholar. I heard
him recite his Greek Ode (on the Death of Nelson), in 1806,
with remarkably clear and harmonious enunciation. He
shewed me the letter in which Lord Spencer, who was
a good Greek scholar, offered him a small living, merely
from having read his edition of "Prometheus." Monk was
the only son of an officer in the army. His mother, who
was early left a widow, was of a good old Monmouthshire
family. After he was Bishop of both Gloucester and Bristol
he told me that he devoted a tenth of his Episcopal income
to the augmentation of small livings; also that when the
Duke of Wellington gave him the bishopric of Gloucester
the income was smaller than that of the deanery of Peterborough which he relinquished. The Duke said to him,
"We must not leave you worse than we found you," and
added to it a canonry of Westminster.

There were several other clever men in residence, "grave
and reverend Seniors," of whom I will give a short sketch
in this place, as it will illustrate the manners of College
life in the period preceding mine. Greenwood was a man
of great humour and good sense. His judgment was so
esteemed that the Fellows often appealed to him for his
opinion. He was the son of a statesman in the North
who possessed land which had been in his family from
the time of the Saxons. After his University education
was finished he became Tutor to the sons of Ld. Stamford,
who in recognition of his admirable conduct while under his
roof, afterwards gave him a living tenable with his Fellowship.
He said things drily himself and left others to laugh. He
once observed that he did not like pancakes for the thought
of their derivation (πᾶν κακόν). A guest having made himself

very disagreeable in Hall by his pert and forward conduct,
was silenced by Greenwood, who was at the time acting for
the Vice-Master, in the Combination-room.  The large silver
snuff-box was handed round, and came in turn to this man.
"This snuff-box," said he, "is large enough, Mr Vice-Master,
to hold the freedom of a Corporation."   "Large enough, Sir,
to hold any freedom but *yours*," was the reply.

[Another anecdote occurs to me which my father has omitted.
One of the Fellows, long since deceased, had wearied the others
out during dinner by his unseasonable attempts at facetiousness.  At
last, struck by the general silence, he remarked to the Vice-Master,
" I am sure it cannot be said that I have not done my best to
divert you all."   He was answered by Dr Ramsden, a very serious
man, whom he constantly attacked with profane, impertinent talk,
" In auntient (*sic*) times, Sir, there were persons set apart for that
purpose."  The retort was received with a laugh that rang through
the Hall, and there is one still living who heard it.]

Ramsden had a good deal of imagination, and it was said
that his Greek Ode was the best ever written.  He once
preached an Assize Sermon.  It was on a Fast Day, one of
those observed during our war with France.   " What makes,"
said he, "the heart of a nation ?  The Iliad and the Odyssey, the Cathedral choir and gloom, the trumpets of the
Judges," pronouncing the *u* in the latter word *oo*, as in
broad Yorkshire.  This was called " The Trumpet Sermon [1]."

[These are only a few of the things enumerated in the Sermon
as explaining how a heart comes to a nation ; there is much truth

---

[1] The Normans brought with them into England civility and building, which, though it was Gothic, was yet magnificent.  Upon any
occasion of bustling in those days, great Lords sounded their trumpets,
and summoned those that held under them.  Old Sir Walter Long of
Draycot kept a trumpeter, rode with 30 Servants and Retainers ; hence
the Sheriff's trumpets at this day.  *Aubrey's MS. Ashmolean Museum.*

and beauty in the whole passage, but the various constituents are oddly placed. I add a few more. "It comes by sympathy, by love, by the marriage union, by friendship, generosity, meekness, temperance, by every virtue and example of virtue. It comes by sentiments of chivalry, by romance, by music, by decorations and magnificence of buildings, by the culture of the body, by comfortable clothing, by fashions in dress, by luxury and commerce. It comes by the severity, the melancholy, and benignity of the countenance; by rules of politeness, ceremonies, formalities, solemnities." When I read this passage to my father last summer, some years after he had alluded to it as above from memory, he said, " I should be inclined to think that these may be the results not the causes of the heart of a nation."]

There is no English word to describe the then Vice-Master Renouard's ways. One must use the French one, *étourderie*, though he was an Etonian and the son of a gentleman. He had a habit of inapposite quoting, and Porson used to set traps for him, as for instance, when one day a custard-pudding was set on table, Porson said, "This pudding, Mr Vice-Master, is too slippery to be eaten." "Yes," says R., "*vultus nimium lubricus aspici.*" Porson nearly broke him of this habit.

There was an agreeable society formed by the intercourse of the most cultivated of the Fellow-commoners with the junior Fellows. Among these former were Mr Spring-Rice and the Honourable Mr Kinnaird. This latter had much to tell us, for he had managed to travel on the Continent during the war. While quite a young man he was studying at a German university, and when he left it, wishing to see France, he had his passport made out as a German. Two or three times he felt sure that he was suspected, but nothing happened till a French officer informed him that he was certain that he was an Englishman, and advised him not to go to Paris; "There," he said, "you must be discovered; but if you keep in the country

you may perhaps escape observation." Had Mr K. met
with less friendliness, he might have become like Dr Arch-
dall-Gratwicke, one of the *détenus* after the peace of Amiens.

In addition to the society of the Fellows of Trinity, I
was often a visitor at the Lodge. The Master, Bp. Mansel,
was a widower, and had three daughters nearly grown up, and
three much younger. Mrs Pearson, wife of the Master of
Sidney, acted as lady of the house when he gave parties.
We had frequently music, Blomfield played on the violin,
and if a dance was improvised, the Master would himself
turn an organ.

[In 1809 my father obtained the Seatonian Prize. The subject
was "The Conquest of Canaan."]

In October of this year, 1809, I was chosen to be one
of the five college examiners. Their province was to examine annually the undergraduates of the college in what
had been the lecture subjects of the academical year ; the
usage being to arrange four classes, which comprised about
one-half of those examined, and to publish these in the Hall,
to the exclusion of the names of those of inferior merit.
A small prize of books was given by the college to those
in the first class. I had formed a strong opinion that many
of the questions given at examinations were unimportant and
too minute ; for instance, I remember a question proposed
to myself in the year 1800, "Give the names of the four
Roman Legions that were stationed in Britain when Agri-
cola was governor ;" and again, at a later period, but ante-
cedent to the time I am now speaking of, "What was the
year, month, and day of the birth of Cicero?" Blomfield
entertained the same opinion, and we agreed to give no
question unless we thought that the knowledge which would
enable a student to answer it was of some utility. It also

seemed to me desirable that the classes should extend to *all* who were examined, for I had ascertained that many who thought they could not do well enough to be classed became indifferent, and made but little previous preparation. I argued the matter with my colleagues one by one, and induced them to agree with me, to divide the whole number into eight classes instead of four, and to add a list of those who were not thought worthy to make a ninth. In the following year I was again an examiner, and one result of the alteration was, that the lowest man gained more marks than the highest on the supplementary list of the preceding year. In June, 1812, the examiners, of whom I was no longer one, the usage being to serve but two years, resorted to the old system of four classes only, without naming the inferior men. In June, 1813, I took the examination for a sick friend (Sedgwick), and at our meeting for previous discussion we agreed, by three against two, to classify or name all the examined, and that system has been pursued ever since.

Among those whom I examined was Charles Babbage, who had the reputation, even in his first year, of being an excellent mathematician. On the occasion of his first examination in the lecture-books he gave up a small roll of MS. as if in answer to my paper. I found it to contain some clear demonstrations and able remarks on a subject connected with one of my questions on the *Binomial Theorem*, but not properly an answer to it. I told him the next day that on this account I could not give any marks for it. He answered that he did not wish to be classed, but only to show the examiners that he was not wanting in knowledge of the subject. From a similar fancy he would not compete for Mathematical Honours on taking his degree, though I believe if he would have done so he could easily have been

Senior Wrangler.   Notwithstanding this, his eminence in that line became so well known, that some years afterwards, when the Mathematical Professorship was vacant, and he was travelling abroad, he was unanimously elected to it without his knowledge.

When examiner I used to ask the first-class men to a wine-party, and get two or three junior Fellows to meet them. Monk, who was assistant Tutor, used to like to come.   I remember Romilly saying, "I am much gratified, Sir, by this honour."   Later in life we were on an equality and inti-mate friends.

It would scarcely be believed how very little knowledge was required for a *mere* degree when I first knew Cambridge. Two books of Euclid's *Geometry*, Simple and Quadratic Equations, and the early parts of Paley's *Moral Philosophy*, were deemed amply sufficient.   Yet in the year 1800 three students failed to pass even this test.   The requisite quantum of knowledge was gradually increased, and in time a Clas-sical Examination (the Littlego), at the end of the fifth term, was a bridge that had to be crossed.   Later still, 1851, those students who did not compete for mathematical honours, were required to attend the lectures of some one of thirteen Professors, and to pass an examination therein to the satis-faction of him and another examiner, specially appointed for the year.   This rule of compulsory attendance on Professorial lectures increased my class to between fifty and sixty.

In October, 1810, we kept the jubilee, or fiftieth year of the King's reign.   Some one thought it was wrong, and should be celebrated when the fifty years were completed, but Mr Simeon said "No," that "in the Jewish dispensation the cycle was forty-nine, or seven times seven years."   Trinity College being a royal foundation, all of what I may call kingly days were kept; the Restoration (May 29), King

Charles's death (Jan. 30), Gunpowder Plot (Nov. 5), the King's birthday and accession. Those days that were Fasts became almost Feasts in this way; as it was not thought right to eat till after evening chapel, the dinner-hour was altered to four o'clock, and we had prayers at half-past three. Supper was on those days discontinued, and the commons of that meal were added to the dinner; with fish, of course, in addition. During the French war we had an annual fast as directed by government. Good Friday was of course a fast. The Prince of Wales was made Regent in this year.

[I must introduce the following characteristic letter by saying that my Father took a great interest in the " new system of education by means of mutual instruction," propagated by Joseph Lancaster and Dr Bell. He was one of those who welcomed the former at Cambridge, and took an active part in the establishment of schools there on his plan. The letter is franked by " Kent and Strathearn," and has a huge seal; the portrait of the King, surrounded by a motto, "The Patron of Education."]

" *To G. Pryme, Esq.*

" Royal Free School,
Borough Road,
4th mo. 10, 1810.

" Respected Friend,

" After my arrival at Ipswich, by means of Dr Wallis, I had an audience of all the Clergy and Magistrates who could assemble at his house on so short a notice—and being Candid Liberal men—their doubts vanished like chaff before the wind, and they came forward most cordially with all their united strength to support my propositions for a School. Probably thou hast seen the Ipswich Resolutions.

I particularly call thy attention to the first *Resolution*, as breathing a spirit worthy not only the clergy of Ipswich, but that of Alma Mater itself. I beg thou will recollect the person or persons who told thee the Royal Patronage was withdrawn from the plan of education of which I am the author, and inform them from me that they have been grossly imposed upon, and that there neither is, nor was, the shadow of a foundation for such a report, and that with whom ever it originated it was a base fabrication, intended to injure my plans, and a libel on the generosity and liberality of my Royal Friends and Patrons. Inform them, if thou please, and any one else, that the Royal subscriptions are *nobly paid*, and that they are given annually on the word of a King, received by command from his own mouth, from a King too who knows how to keep his word as well as when to give it; and let them know that they are not the only persons who have been so grossly imposed upon. The Bp. of Chichester was once misinformed in a similar way, and wrote to me under the impression. I immediately sent the Bishop's letter down to Windsor to the King at once, and immediately had the Royal answer under the King's seal in writing. 'His Majesty commands me to assure you, the Bp. of Chichester is misinformed as to any intention on his Majesties part of withdrawing from you his patronage.' Let them know also, that I am assured from the highest authority, *that* of one of the King's own Sons, that he has had from their mouths assurances of their high approbation and support to my plans, on his giving an account of spending two hours in my School, and having besides a long and interesting Series of letters with me on the subject. My Friend, the Royal Family saw and heard for themselves, and are not to be so deceived and bamboozled by the intrigues of bad men as to be out of the evidence of their own senses, nor are they such weather-cocks as like children to do noble actions one minute and undo them the next.

" I beg my sincere and best respects to our Friends Tavel and Monk, and to Wm. Hollick, Dr Thackeray and Plumptre, Professor Smythe and any other enquiring Friends.

" I am going to Lecture at the Surrey Institution this evening (Leverian Museum formerly), and at the Russell Institution, Russell Square, of which my Friend the Duke of Bedford is President. You have nothing to do but to have courage, and act nobly and liberally like yourselves, and the whole nation will support you, and this was and is the King's opinion, that such is the intrinsic merit of the plan that it only wants to be known and understood by men of liberal and candid minds, for it to make its own way from one end of the nation to the other. And this opinion has been confirmed by the good sense and approbation of the British public, notwithstanding all the croaking of the miserable alarmists crying out 'The Church in Danger,' which in plain English means no more than that the parties raising the outcry are delirious, and imagine themselves starved and hungry, and in great need of a few loaves and fishes, when they are really in a prime fat condition, and need physic more than food to prevent their days being shortened by having A PLETHORA.

" I remain, with a very high sense of the kindness shewn me by the Gentlemen of the University of Cambridge,

" Thy obliged and Respectful Friend,

" JOS. LANCASTER.

" P.S. Please to excuse haste, my business has accumulated wonderfully since I have been out of Town, and my tables are covered with letters and replies, &c. &c."

In January of 1811 I visited Bath for a few weeks. The mail-coach from London to Bath started at 4 A.M. and arrived there late at night. There was also a conveyance called the "two-day coach." It was intended for invalids, and for such people as did not like to make the long journey (106 miles) in one day, and I went by it. We started at 10 A.M. and dined and slept at Reading, reaching Bath the next afternoon. In former days people often carried a diamond-pointed pencil and wrote with it on inn-windows, probably because they had nothing else to do in the days of slow travelling. I have seen such windows written all over with doggerel verses and with names.

[Swift wrote "*upon a window where there was no writing before*" these lines :

"Thanks to my Stars, I once can see
A window here from scribbling free."]

Bath was still a fashionable resort, but the race of fine people who in Walpole's and Mr Pitt's time had frequented it had passed away, and there was no one of any note there when I visited it. Beau Nash was gone, and with him the spirit of gaiety. There was a public ball at "the Upper Rooms" every Monday and Thursday, and another at "the Lower Rooms" on Fridays. The best people however would not dance there, and private balls were beginning to injure them. Minuets were out of fashion, although they were still danced at the court balls. The master of the ceremonies at Bath always opened his own ball with one. In the morning people drank the waters, and afterwards attended auctions "to cheapen silks and satins."

Sheridan frequented Bath for some years, and of course mixed in the best society; old Lady Cork, among other anecdotes which she told my wife, said that they (the Sheridans) found it difficult to get acquainted with the Duke of Devonshire and his family, but that some time after when they had become so, these latter in writing to her declared that they found the S.'s so agreeable, that they were staying at Bath longer than they intended on their account. I knew a little of Matthews, who had fought a duel with Sheridan. It took place in some meads near to Bath, the Cathedral bells of which were ringing at the time.

Sheridan has been reputed to have constantly avoided the payment of his debts. I can state on good authority one instance of his right feeling and honourable conduct. Mr Alley, a young Irish gentleman, came to London to study for the Bar. A considerable sum of money was due from Sheridan to some deceased relative of his, the payment of which had been often promised. Mr A. obtained an interview with S., and stated that without it he could not complete his legal education. S. said that he expected on a certain day to receive a large sum, and would positively pay what was owing. Believing this assurance, Mr A. told it to some of his friends, who ridiculed his reliance on any pecuniary promise of Sheridan. He therefore did not call for it on the day appointed. After two or three weeks, an acquaintance to whom he mentioned it advised him to ask for it, as the application would cost him nothing but the trouble of making it. He resolved to call again, and was received by Sheridan with a burst of indignation. "Why didn't you come at the time appointed? you know not," said he, "the temptations I have had to combat in keeping this money for you. As you told me that your prospects in life depended on it, I sealed it up and have kept it for you in my bureau;" so saying he took out the packet and put it into Alley's hands, who made such

7

a good use of it that he attained great eminence as a lawyer
in the Criminal Courts. This anecdote was told me by Mr
Benjamin Hart, afterwards Mr Thorold of Harmstone, near
Lincoln, who had it from Alley himself.

On my return to Cambridge early in this year, 1811, my
health being improved, I meditated resuming my profession
as a provincial barrister, and put on my wig and gown for the
first time at the spring assizes at Cambridge. In the course
of two or three years I gradually joined the Norfolk Circuit
at all the assize towns; and in due time I acquired a larger
professional income than is, I believe, now attainable by a
provincial counsel under the altered laws. When I got my
first wig the bill described it as a "tie-peruke." The barrister's wig is but the dress wig of a gentleman of the old
time. I remember on circuit at the Judge's dinner at Cambridge and Norwich, it was the custom for all to be in their
wigs and gowns. Serjeant Frere got up a petition to the
judges to ask them to permit their discontinuance, which
they agreed to on the condition that they themselves should
not be expected to wear them[1].

In March, the Duke of Grafton, Chancellor of the University, died. The Duke of Gloucester (Prince William),
nephew to the King, who had graduated at Trinity College
many years before, was a candidate for the vacant office.
His hostility to West Indian Slavery gave him many supporters among those who, for political reasons, would have
preferred his opponent, the Duke of Rutland, and he was
elected by a majority of 117.

The Installation which followed was extremely grand, for
there had never been one in any one's recollection[2]. The

[1] Lord Eldon, while Chancellor, wore his wig whenever he appeared in
general society.

[2] For a curious account of it see *Camb. Univ. Calend.* for 1812.

Duke of Grafton had been elected in 1768, and had therefore filled the office during forty-three years. He was one of the King's ministers at the time of his election, and one of those statesmen against whom the letters of *Junius* were directed. He never had the good taste or feeling to come down to Cambridge during the long period in which he held office there. Mansel was master at the time that the Duke of Gloucester was elected, who had been in the habit of coming occasionally to Trinity Lodge. On these visits Mansel used to ask some of the resident fellows (myself among the number) to supper. The Duke was a very simple-minded man. I remember his quoting an epigram which had been lately made, and asking who was the author of it?

ON DR DOUGLAS' MARRIAGE WITH MISS MAINWARING.

"St Paul has declared that persons though twain,
 In marriage united one flesh shall remain:
 But had he been by when, like Pharaoh's kine pairing,
 Dr Douglas of Bene't espoused Miss Mainwaring,
 The Apostle no doubt would have altered his tone,
 And said these 'two splinters shall make but one bone.'"

I must now mention that Mansel was fond of writing epigrams, and that he used to repeat them in hall, prefacing them with "that wicked man Vince has made another epigram!" Vince was a dull matter-of-fact man, I mean so far as *esprit* in conversation was concerned, though a first-rate mathematician, a Senior Wrangler, and author of the Treatises which the undergraduates read and studied. He heard

The Duke arrived on Friday, June 28th, in his coach and six, and left after witnessing a balloon ascent from the great Court of Trinity, on Wednesday, July 3rd.

of this particular epigram being attributed to him, and actually called on Dr Douglas to assure him that *he* did not write it. D. was quite a gentleman, and said that he never suspected that he did[1]. When the Duke of Gloucester enquired as to the authorship of this epigram, Greenwood, who was sitting opposite to him gravely said, "I believe Prof. Vince, it was always attributed to him." The Duke was quite satisfied with this answer. I watched Mansel, who had great command of countenance, and I thought he seemed relieved to have the matter over. I have lately read an article in the *Quarterly Review* on Epigrams, and thought it written in a high and good tone. My own feeling has ever been that epigrams are perfectly fair on deformity of conduct, but not on personal deformity.

The vacancy in the University Representation made by Lord Euston was again contested by Lord Palmerston, then still a tory, and by John Henry Smyth, of Heath in Yorkshire, a whig, who had obtained three Browne's Medals. The numbers were P. 451, J. H. S. 345.

1812. Mr Spencer Perceval was assassinated May 11. I was staying in town at the Tavistock Hotel. On that evening Perronet Thompson came to me and told me that Perceval was shot. Within the hour he had gone down with his father (M.P. for Midhurst) to attend the debate, and had heard this news. I said, "Let us go and see what is doing," so we walked about the town, and saw people standing at their doors, discussing this strange event. The excitement

---

[1] The late Sir Astley Cooper told me that he had asked Prof. Vince to call upon him, giving him his address in —— Square, and that he had promised to do so. Meeting him some time after, Sir A. C. enquired of the Professor why he had never been to see him? "I did come," said V., "but there was some mistake; you told me that you lived in a square and I found myself in a parallelogram, and so I went away again."

was intense, and it was thought that this might be the commencement of a concerted plan for revolution. Perceval was
a bad minister and very unpopular, but a man of considerable talent, and who had avowed strong religious feeling.

I think it was in this year, or thereabouts, that Mr
Pigott, Rector of Gilling, Yorkshire, and formerly Fellow
of Trinity College, communicated to Hailstone, our Bursar,
his intention to bequeath to the college, as he had no near
relations, his advowson of Gilling, and to give immediately
£12,000 for the purchase of two other livings. All matters
requiring the college seal are administered by the Master
and the sixteen resident Senior Fellows, which number just
included Professor Monk and myself. He proposed to me,
and I thoroughly agreed with him, that as the College had
many livings in its gift of too small a value to induce any
fellows to take them, it would be better instead of purchasing more livings to appropriate this sum to augmenting
five of them, thereby quickening the succession, which was
often delayed till long past the prime of life. We privately
proposed, and gradually persuaded others among the sixteen to accede to this plan, which also contemplated, with a
view to a more prolonged residence, and a better observance
of religion, to augment those livings only, the population of
which exceeded eight hundred, and to make the extra payment for each year conditional upon residence for a certain
number of months, unless leave of absence should be granted
by the bishop on account of the ill-health of the incumbent.
When the proposal came before us *officially*, the Bursar, who
was a native of Yorkshire, was commissioned to see Mr
Pigott and obtain his consent. This was readily given, and
Hitchin, Ware, and Masham were among the livings so dealt
with.

The slowness of the succession to livings may be illustrated by the following instance. The Rev. John Davies, Vice-Master, told me that he had long wished to marry a lady who was a distant relation of his, but had never ventured to declare his sentiments to her; that he lingered on in "hope deferred" till in his fifty-second year, when the offer of a living came to him. But he thought it too late in life to make the change, and resolved to die in college. This was the person to whom I have alluded in my "Ode to Trinity College."

> "He deemed too much of life gone by:
> Fate had dissolv'd each early tie,
> And left no wish, but here to die."

# CHAPTER VI.

## 1813—1815.

IN August, 1813, I was married to Miss Jane Townley Thackeray, daughter of the late Thomas Thackeray, Esq., an eminent consulting surgeon at Cambridge, and sister to Dr Frederick Thackeray, physician in the same town. We at first resided at Barnwell Abbey[1]. We had only two children, and they were baptised by the christian names of Charles and Alicia, and were entered in the parish register under the ancient surname (de la Pryme) of my forefathers.

I have hitherto only spoken of my University life; I will now attempt to trace the beginning of my social and political relations with the Town of Cambridge, which increased with advancing years, till they culminated in that point which it

---

[1] It had belonged to the Augustine Canons, and Richard II. when he held a Parliament at King's Hall (Trin. Coll.) took up his abode there.

has ever been my pride and pleasure to look back upon, my being chosen to represent the Borough of Cambridge in three parliaments. Not long after I quitted college I attended some public meeting which took place, and made a short speech, apologising for myself, as a member of the University, for taking part in the affairs of the Town, but hoping that as I had become a householder it would not be deemed improper. This remark was greeted with approbation by some of the principal inhabitants of the Town, who said they wished that such participation by University men in their affairs was of more frequent occurrence. I was soon after elected a Paving Commissioner, and took an active part in all local matters.

I now steadily pursued my profession. One of my first briefs at Cambridge was in defence of an undergraduate, charged with wilfully setting fire to his College. Sir William Garrow, Solicitor General, was specially retained ; Mr Best and I were his juniors. I had to see Garrow three or four times in London, and give him particulars of the case, as I had attended every deposition of witnesses before the committing magistrates. He was very kind to me, and gave me many valuable hints for the conduct of cases, more especially as to a cautious discretion in examination, which I afterwards found of the greatest use. My client was acquitted.

Verdicts sometimes turned upon curious technicalities. I remember being counsel for the prosecution in a murder case at Ely. Two men had been in the habit of poaching. One night one of them called the other out from his bed, and he was never seen more. The former had murdered and buried him in a little grove of trees not far from his house. Yet, though the guilt was clearly proved, there was some fear lest the murderer should escape on the technical objection that the boundary of the county ran through *that* grove, and it could not be strictly proved in which county the murdered man was found. It was however stated that it (the boundary) was on one side of a crooked ditch. Seeing Mr Page in court, who had a great knowledge of the Isle of Ely, I appealed to him, though he was not called as a witness. He agreed to be sworn, took his place in the witness-box, and gave evidence as to which side of the crooked ditch the county was. This decided the matter, and but for this the murderer would have escaped. He was hung and left on the gibbet. As the law stood, a prisoner could not be indicted in one county for an offence which took place in another. There was practical and substantial justice in this, as a poor man might be unable to bear the expense of bringing his witnesses from a distance. But after a time the difficulty was removed by an Act of Parliament, which provided, that it should be sufficient if it were proved that the crime occurred within 500 yards of the boundary between the two counties.

The amount of punishment by death was awful ; horse-stealing, burglary, and highway-robbery were all capital offences, and even smaller crimes, such as trying to injure animals. Daniel Dawson was a rider at Newmarket. He was tried before Judge Heath for poisoning the water of which some horses, intended for the races, drank. There was a drinking-trough for them on the race-course, and in order to prevent an injury of this kind it was enclosed and locked. Dawson bored a hole, and poured in some injurious liquid intended to make them ill. It so happened that the horses did not drink as he expected they would, and he added more and more, supposing that he had not made it strong enough. When, at last, the cover *was* taken off, the water was so poisoned that one of the horses who drank of it died. I heard him tried. He was found guilty and actually executed[1].

Passing flash notes was another capital offence. A man named Bird was tried for offering one to a woman at Coton, Cambs., in payment for a looking-glass, which he pretended to have taken a fancy for, receiving the change ; and he was executed. A man could suffer death for stealing from a dwelling-house any article worth 40s., or from a shop worth 5s. In a robbery at Nottingham, where two men entered a hosiery warehouse and stole £70 worth of goods, it was made a capital offence, because a door communicated between the warehouse and the dwelling, which was ruled to make it a burglary. They were convicted and sentenced to death. One of them had committed two or three slight offences previously ; the other was quite a young man of seventeen years, and this was his first offence, but the judge made no distinction. Such distinctions were, however, afterwards made when public opinion changed, because a man so committed might have been previously guilty of other offences. On one occasion when five men were tried for a serious crime, I was counsel for the prosecution. All were found guilty. Garrow, who was a very humane man, reprieved two of them, and consulted me as to whether he should sentence three or one of the rest. Of course I was in favour of mercy ; and only the worst, who appeared to have been the chief instigator of the others, suffered death.

---

[1] "A case of poisoning a race-horse came before the Recorder of Barnstaple last week. The prisoner, *George Woolacott*, groom, was indicted for administering poison to a mare called ' Little Sally,' before the Barnstaple races. Immediately after the prisoner left the mare she grew very sick and vomited, dying in great agony on the morning of the race-day. The jury found him guilty, and the Recorder said he could not pass a lighter sentence than penal servitude for five years."— *Guardian*, July 8, 1868.

I remember an instance of Richardson's humanity. A man was tried at Cambridge before him, and sentenced to seven years' transportation. Immediately were heard shrieks and cries which proceeded from his wife, who was present. The judge enquiring from whence they came, observed to her, " You are well rid of such a man." " My Lord," she said vehemently, "he was always a kind and good husband to me." "Well," replied Richardson, "there is some good in him then." A sentence is never irrevocable while the judge remains in the assize town. The next day R. said in court that he had looked over the depositions, and on re-consideration should change the punishment to two years' imprisonment with hard labour.

Romilly and others endeavoured to soften the penal code, and very wisely attacked only one or two of its severest enactments, as for instance, the law which inflicted capital punishment for stealing goods of the value of five shillings from a shop. When Romilly tried to repeal this, Lord Ellenborough effectually opposed it in the House of Lords.

While I am upon the subject of trials I will mention a few more which also came within my own knowledge, and turned upon circumstantial evidence, which is not always to be depended upon. I will give an instance of this related to me some time ago by a magistrate in Bucks., and confirmed by another, both having been present at the investigation. A woman disappeared from a village, and about ten days after a body was found murdered in a wood not far off. Decomposition had begun ; yet there was form enough left in the features to point them out, together with the clothing and general appearance, as those of the missing woman. But all doubt was set at rest by a peculiar transverse scar on one arm which she was known to have had. A man was taken into custody, and evidence was given that he had been seen walking with the deceased on the London road, and towards this wood, on the day of her being missed. He was on the point of being committed by the Coroner for wilful murder, when a villager came forward and said, "That is not the body of ——," naming her, "for she is still alive and in London." When asked how he could prove it, he answered, "Give me some money for the journey and I'll go and fetch her." The inquest was adjourned, the real woman produced, and it was never discovered who the one murdered was.

I remember also a curious trial at Norwich when Parke was judge. A highway robbery had been committed, and two weavers were accused of the crime. They were remarkable looking persons of different height. The prosecutor who had been robbed, and several witnesses who had met them near the spot, swore to them ; the jury, however, acquitted them, and the judge said that they left the court with unimpeachable characters. The explanation is this. There were two more weavers, exactly resembling the others in appearance and relative height and dress, who had really been the robbers, and the guiltless couple were proved to have been only walking near the spot, and within an hour or two of the time when the robbery was committed.

There was a clergyman named Waterhouse, of St Catharine's College, Cambridge, who held the living of Little Stukeley, Hunts. His servants were, one day, all out in the field, and he was murdered in his own house in open day-light. A man was apprehended and condemned to death on circumstantial evidence. He had been seen to cross the Huntingdon road by a tunnel, through which a watercourse ran, soon after the murder, and in his possession was found a bill-hook with some blood and snow-white woolly hairs upon it. The deceased was remarkable for snow-white woolly hair. The judge, Garrow, told us at the dinner at Bury St Edmund's, that he was not quite satisfied with the evidence, and had sent a fortnight's respite. At that time the execution of a murderer took place on the third day after sentence was passed ; the more dreadful the offence the less time given to repent of it[1]. When the respite reached the under-sheriff (Mr Margetts), a curious circumstance had happened, and with his, what I call, strong and accurate sense, he told the gaoler not to inform the man of the respite. He then himself set off to tell the judge what had occurred. The prisoner being taken by the turnkeys to walk in the prison yard, and looking up while there, saw at a window another man, confined for debt, a man with snow-white hair, and so much resembling Mr Waterhouse that he believed it was his ghost, and immediately confessed his crime. When Garrow heard of this he decided that the respite, having been granted, should continue, but that the culprit should be executed at its termination. The remarkable fact, as bearing on circumstantial evidence was, that in his confession he said that he did not commit the murder with the bill, but with a sword belonging to Mr W., which he threw away in a wood near the house, and that the blood and white hairs were those of a sheep ! On searching the wood the sword was found as he had described.

I never knew a criminal executed for murder who was afterwards found to be innocent, but I remember hearing of a man who suffered capital punishment at York about thirty years ago, and that it was afterwards supposed to be a case of mistaken identity. It is a fashion now to excuse criminals

---

[1] *Sentence of Death.* An Act passed, July 14, 1836, repealing those parts of the Statute which ordered execution in three days, the pronouncing of the sentence immediately after conviction, and the feeding of the culprit on bread and water only.

on account of madness.   I believe that this is often simulated.
I remember a man being tried for the murder of his wife.
He was acquitted on the ground of insanity, and confined
as a lunatic.   My own opinion at the time was that the
lunacy was assumed.   Some years after, in a trial in which
I was engaged as counsel, I had occasion to call this *very*
man as a witness.   I said to the keeper, in whose charge
he was, " How lately has he shown symptoms of insanity ? "
and he answered me, " Never since the trial."

[I asked my father who was the best Judge he ever knew?
After some consideration, he said,]

Richardson was most to my mind.   Heath was severe,
but inclining to admit technical objections.   Lord Tenterden
was a very able judge.   He came our circuit as Mr Justice
Abbot, and I saw a good deal of him at Thetford, which is,
curiously enough, at the very edge of the county, so that
a few houses are not in Norfolk at all.   Only one judge came
there, and remained a week, from Saturday to Saturday.   On
these occasions Abbot would ask some of us to dine at his
lodgings ; the parties were of six, and after dinner we played
two rubbers each, and sat out two.   He afterwards succeeded
Lord Ellenborough as Chief Justice of the King's Bench.
He was a classical scholar, and had obtained the only two
prizes given at that time at Oxford.

[My father added to me, " I have a grateful recollection of him,
for he paid me a high compliment once in the Court of King's
Bench.   I had gone up to argue some case, which had been transferred to it from the Norfolk Circuit.   Scarlett was first, and did not
say much ; I followed, and Parke, who was my junior, was next proceeding to say, 'after the case has been ably argued by Mr Pryme,' when
Lord Tenterden interposed, '*very* ably argued'."

I hope I may be excused adding this testimony to my father's ability as a lawyer, which, with many other gratifying circumstances, it never occurred to him to dictate himself. My father lived in the times of fourteen Chancellors, commencing with Lord Thurlow and ending with Lord Cairns. Three of them were twice over in office, and Lord Eldon held the great seal more than twenty-four years. I asked him which of them he considered the best? He said, " Eldon would have been but for his indecision." He was inclined to think Pepys (Lord Cottenham) the best, but doubted between him and Wilde (Lord Truro)[1]." "It was against Erskine that he had not prac-tised in Chancery. I heard him often, both as counsel and Chancellor. Once in an appeal he showed his surprise at an act of bankruptcy having been declared differently before the masters and before the commissioners. 'Can this be so?' he said, and he had to be assured that it was the practice[2]."

My father then mentioned some humorous lines on the deriva-tion of the word Chancellor, quoting the four last. I have met with a copy among his papers and will give them all.]

THE DERIVATION OF CHANCELLOR.

The Chancellor, so says Lord Coke[3],
His *title* from CANCELLO took ;
And every cause before him tried
It was his duty to *decide*.
Lord Eldon, hesitating ever,
Takes it from CHANCELER, to *waver*,
And thinks, as this may bear him out,
His bounden duty is to *doubt*.

On the Northern Circuit there was an appointment of a poet laureate, who was expected to make and recite an-

[1] Lord Kingsdown says, in his *Recollections of the Bar*, that " Lord Cottenham was certainly as long as I remained at the Bar one of the best Judges I ever saw on the Bench."

[2] " Lords Erskine, Lyndhurst, Brougham, and Campbell, all under-took the highest judicial office in Chancery, without ever having had the slightest practice there."—*Edinburgh Review*, No. 263.

[3] 4 Inst. 88.

nually, at the barristers' dinner, a set of verses connected
with matters interesting to the Bar; and also of an Attorney-
General, who was to bring forward any transgressions of the
understood rules of the society.  This plan was adopted on
the Norfolk Circuit, and I was appointed poet laureate, which
office I retained for many years, and on my resignation of
it Mr Raymond was elected.  The small pieces were collected
and written in a volume.  I cannot quote any of them, for I
lent it to Mackworth Praed, who was a member, and after
his death I tried, but in vain, to get it back.

[Barristers on circuit were thrown together in those days for a
much longer time than at present, and consequently there was a
greater necessity for intimacies between those whose tastes were in
accordance, and of courteous civility towards others.  My father
made many pleasant acquaintances in this way, of whom, I regret to
say, he has only left a solitary record.  The names of Sergeants
Blosset and Storks, of West, Maltby, Andrews, and Austin, all recall
the friendliness of days gone by.]

Among my brother circuiteers was Henry Crabb Robinson,
who came to the bar when he was nearly forty years old.
We made a permanent compact for travelling together in
my carriage with post-horses, the expense of which we
shared.  He showed considerable powers of mind in his addresses to juries.  He told me that when he had augmented
his small private property to a certain amount he should
quit the profession and return to a literary life.  Some of
our brother barristers thought it good in intention but impro-
bable in execution.  He acquainted me every year with his
progress towards this intellectual enjoyment, and so strictly
did he adhere to his resolution that when he had attained his
point he abandoned his practice in the middle of a circuit.
He is now (1865), at the age of 90, indulging his social and

literary tastes. He had the rare good fortune of being intimate with Goethe, Wordsworth, Coleridge, Lamb, and Southey.

In 1814 the frost was so sharp and the scarcity of coals so great, there being no land-carriage for them, and the rivers all frozen, that some of the trees in St John's College were cut down for firing, and at all the colleges two or three men sat together in one room. I gave a very high price for a sack of coals, to fetch which I sent a man and horse to Bottisham.

We were still at war with France, though the end was approaching. The splendid victories of Lord Wellesley in Spain, Nelson's battles, and now the allied armies, were all against Napoleon. I differ from Burke about France. His writings, which I have been lately re-reading, advised nothing less than its complete subjugation. I think it may be said of him, and others who supported his policy of interminable war with France, "Dum obstare vellent promovebant." Sir James Mackintosh took the other side, in a book called *Vindiciæ Gallicæ.* In his views of America and India I concur. With judicious policy I think we might have kept the former as we have kept Canada; but would this have been expedient or permanent?

The speeches of Burke would not be endured now, they are so diffuse; there is not one of them which might not have been spoken in half the words. They fill two thick octavo volumes, and show the justice of those lines in Goldsmith's *Retaliation :*

\*   \*   \*   \*   \*   " He went on refining,
And thought of convincing while they thought of dining."

He was a man of splendid talents, and had a command of fine language, but was wanting in judgment; that passage in his speech about Marie Antoinette, that in the age

8

of chivalry a thousand swords would have leapt from their scabbards to avenge even a look that had offered her insult, is splendid nonsense, unworthy of a college declamation[1]. There is a traditional anecdote in the House of Commons that Burke, in making a speech in favour of economy and retrenchment, quoted against Lord North the line of Tacitus, " Magnum vectigal parsimonia est." Lord North interrupted him to say, "The honourable member should have pronounced it vectigal ;" whereupon Burke continued, " I thank the noble Lord for his correction, as it gives me the opportunity of repeating the line ' Magnum vectigal parsimonia est'."

Lord North was minister when I was born. He had a refined taste in literature, but was hardly of the calibre for a Prime Minister, and did not manage the American war well. He had a habit of sleeping in the house ; a member making a dull speech against the government, thought to give point to it by saying, "and there is its head fast asleep on the treasury bench." Lord N., who was not really asleep, roused himself and said, "Would that I were."

Burke died before I went to town[2]. He was the conductor of the impeachment of Warren Hastings. He had a pension in the latter part of his life, and it was thought that he was never so independent afterwards.

[Of Hastings my father said, " There could be no doubt whatever that Hastings acted in a very tyrannical manner, and the only excuse, if excuse there could be, was that he might mean to support the British government." Cowper thus defends him :

"While young humane, conversable and kind ;
Nor can I well believe thee, gentle then,
Now grown a villain, and the worst of men."]

---

[1] Burke was told by Sir Philip Francis that the celebrated passage in his *Reflections* in praise of Marie Antoinette was "pure foppery," and urged by him to suppress its publication.

[2] July 8th, 1797.

1815. In February I lost a relative and intimate friend in Smithson Tennant, M.D., F.R.S., Professor of Chemistry at Cambridge. He was known throughout Europe by several important discoveries, among others that the diamond is the purest form of carbon, which he explained in the *Philosophical Transactions.* He was killed at Boulogne as he was riding over a drawbridge in company of General Bulow, having been to see Buonaparte's Pillar. General B. was only a little hurt, as he had nearly crossed the drawbridge, which was insecurely fastened, before it fell, having called out to his friend when he saw the danger, but in vain, to bid him stop. He died in half-an-hour, having fallen into the trench below and fractured his skull. General B. soon recovered, and afterwards commanded a detachment of the Prussian army at Waterloo. Prof. Tennant's desk and papers were immediately seized and put under seal by the French police. Enquiries were made in England for his relatives by Messrs Adams, bankers at Boulogne. We believed that he died intestate, and before letters of administration could be obtained the news arrived of Buonaparte's landing from Elba and again making himself Emperor of France. We urged the sending over his papers, &c. lest war should break out, and were informed by Messrs Adams that they could not be obtained before administration was granted, but that the delay was immaterial, as in *any* case his effects would be sent over to us. We accordingly received them, after war had been declared, by a neutral vessel, without any charge being made by the police. I mention this circumstance to show the gradual progress of liberality in the Law of Nations. Tennant was buried in the cemetery at Boulogne. Hayes, a Lay Fellow of Trinity, wrote his epitaph in Latin, and Whishaw revised it. Whishaw was of Trinity, a great friend of Tennant, and a very learned man ; he had a private fortune, and therefore did not sit for a fellow-ship. He wrote a short Biographical Memoir of Tennant, which was privately printed for distribution. A copy is in the University Library.

[Mr Whishaw was of the Chancery Bar, and one of the commis-sioners for auditing the public accounts. Francis Horner speaks of him as " a very particular friend of mine, a most excellent critic and accurate in his opinions of characters." If so, there may be some value attachable to his description of a very distinguished woman, which I have found in a letter from him to Professor Tennant, preserved among my father's papers. "Since I wrote last I have seen Madame de Stael several times. She has seen and read a good deal, and is very lively and flowing in her conversation. ' Satis eloquentiæ, *sapi-entiæ parum.*' She is about to publish a Pamphlet on Suicide, a trite, common-place subject, fit only for a College exercise, or a sermon; and afterwards some letters on the manners and literature of Germany."

In my father's library is a miniature copy of BOETHIUS, a Dutch edition, date clɔlɔcxxxiii. In it is written "Smithson Tennant's Book given to him for reading the first Chapter of St John's Gospel out of English into Greek 1769, when he was eight years and one month old."]

Henry Warburton, M.P. for Bridport, was also a great friend of Tennant. He said that he should do what the administrators could not do, *i.e.* buy some of his valuable books and present them to his friends, which he was sure he would have wished done.

S. T. had a farm of 500 acres at Cheddar, in Somerset-shire, where he experimented in connexion with agriculture. He was very well read in Political Economy, and we used to discuss that subject before I gave my lectures; for we were, besides being relations, so intimate that he used to say when I came to town, "There is always breakfast at nine o'clock" (at his chambers in the Temple), and we also, when not otherwise engaged, dined together at the Grecian Coffee-House in the Strand. I often met in his company a learned chemist, with whom he shared the expense of certain great experiments. I also had the advantage of meeting scientific men at the house of my wife's relative, Major Rennell, F.R.S., among others Sir Humphry Davy. It shows the necessity of not disregarding slight discoveries, that the fact of D.'s ascertaining that gas would not ignite through a tube was at first laughed at. When he came to determine what length the tube must be, he found the safety lamp (1816). Tennant was succeeded in his Professorship at Cambridge by Cumming; a kind as well as truly learned man, who but for weak health and want of ambition might have been in the foremost rank of discoverers.

June 18, for ever memorable as the day on which the battle of Waterloo was fought. I was in London when the news came. An address was voted by the University.

In my early days the "Cambridge Union" did not exist. The only clubs that I can recollect were "The True Blue," said traditionally to have existed from the time of the revolution of 1688, and to have taken its colour in opposition to the Orange of King William. An especial dress, including a blue coat, was worn by the members, who were few in number, and it was confined to Trinity College. It was reputed to be a hard-drinking club. The other, called "The Speculative," after a great debating society at Edinburgh, met once a week in term time, and consisted of twenty members; Pattison (afterwards Judge), Sumner (Bp. of Winchester), and Pearson (afterwards Archdeacon, and son of the eminent surgeon of that name), and I, belonged to it. The present "Union" was formed in 1815, as its name implies, by the junction of two rival societies. It first met in a small room at the back of the Red Lion Inn,

and afterwards removed to premises in Green Street, which
had been formerly used as a dissenting chapel. Dr Wood,
Master of St John's, when Vice-Chancellor, in 1817, came
(like Cromwell to the House of Commons,) with his two
Proctors to the "Union," and commanded its dissolution on
the ground that it was political. One of these told me that
he did not like it, but felt obliged to obey orders. Some
years later (1820), when Dr Wordsworth, Master of Trinity,
was Vice-Chancellor, he sent for two or three of the leading
men of the dissolved "Union," and proposed that if they
would frame a set of rules prohibiting discussion on the
character of any living politician, or debates on modern
politics, and submit these to him, they should be permitted
to re-assemble. This was accordingly done. Modern politics
are now allowed.

[How are times changed! This Society, which at its origin was
contained in a small room, now numbers between 4 and 5,000 sub-
scribers, and possesses a valuable library of about 8,000 volumes.
It moved into a new building behind St Sepulchre's church on Oct.
30, 1866, which was opened by the Earl of Powis. There was a
debate on that evening; the subject being, "that this house views
with regret the late substitution of a Conservative for a Liberal
Government." After putting *satisfaction* for *regret*, the motion was
carried by a majority of 120. Dr Wood, were he living, might
reasonably complain now of discussions concerning, not the politics,
but the *manners* of the *period*.]

I was invited to become one of the members of the
Cambridge County Club, and I have remained so for more
than fifty years, being now (Oct. 1868) the senior member[1].
The number was at *that* time limited to forty members,
who met at a social dinner five times a year at the Red

[1] His Royal Highness the Prince of Wales (while residing at Mading-
ley) was elected an Honorary Member, April 1861.

Lion Inn; it was understood that political discussion was
excluded. Such clubs formerly existed in every county,
but now survive in only two or three. We were a most
harmonious body, though including men of very different
opinions in religion and politics. It consisted of the principal gentlemen and clergy of the county, two among the
former being Roman Catholics; and such was the kindly
feeling, that it was intimated to them that, if *they* would
wish it, the day should be changed when it fell upon a
Friday to some other; but they declined this, saying that
there was always an abundance of fish and such things as
they might eat.

[The members of this club enjoyed the feast of reason as well as
that other excellent one which "mine host" of the Red Lion proverbially sets before his guests. One of them wrote down for my
father, during dinner, these lines, which may be new to some; they
were made by the Chancellor, Lord Hardwicke, on sending a hare
to a friend who was a poet:

"Mitto tibi leporem—vestros mihi mitte lepores,
    Sal mea commendat munera—vestra sales—."]

# CHAPTER VII.

## 1816.

1816. BEFORE I left college I meditated giving a course of lectures on Political Economy, and had continued my reading in reference to this object, for I deeply felt the importance of making that science, which has since influenced to so great a degree the legislation of Great Britain and its treaties with other countries, a part of a liberal education. Hitherto no lectures had been given upon it in any University of the United Kingdom; but Dugald Stewart, Professor of Moral Philosophy at Edinburgh, had in 1806 added to his own lectures for two or three years a supernumerary, supplemental course on that study, and Professor Smyth, in his lectures on Modern History, had explained some points regarding it. I apprehended considerable opposition to so novel an attempt, and I waited till Dr Kaye, master of Christ's College, and afterwards bishop of Lincoln, became Vice-chancellor in 1815. I knew that he was a man of generally liberal views, for he had been private secretary to Lord Henry Petty, when Chancellor of the Exchequer. He expressed himself at the first

mention of my wishes highly favourable to them, but said
he wished to consult the Heads. A few days afterwards
he sent for me, and stated that on mentioning it to them
they granted my request, but expressed a wish, which he
thought reasonable, that I should not give my lectures at
an earlier hour than twelve o'clock, lest they should interfere with college lectures, to which I instantly assented.
Dr Kaye added, "some of them wished me to withhold my
consent altogether; I of course treated such a suggestion
as it deserved."

I am reminded here of a change which Professor
Smyth effected. His predecessor in the chair of modern
history, Symonds, had been restricted in the number of his
pupils by the Heads, who were afraid of any interference
with the regular studies of the University, to twenty-six
(I speak from memory only), nominated by themselves.
When Smyth was appointed by the Crown, he refused to
abide by this plan, and admitted all who chose to come.

I now set myself to compose a course of lectures in my
leisure hours, which I commenced delivering in March 1816.
They were elementary and eclectic, but contained somewhat
not exactly to be found in any books. [Those at Oxford,
which were not commenced till long afterwards, were on a
totally different plan.]

["They attempted to analyse the original and efficient causes
of national prosperity—to shew by what measures of the legislature,
and by what conduct of individuals in private life, it is augmented
or diminished—and to assist the reader of history in explaining
the phænomena of the strength or weakness, the rise or fall, of
States. They were of an elementary and popular nature, requiring
no previous knowledge of the subject. They were intended to
facilitate the study of a science hitherto inaccessible without the
most arduous perseverance; to simplify the order, explain the

obscurities, and point out the errors of Adam Smith's *Enquiry into the Wealth of Nations;* to combine with his discoveries what the experience of subsequent events, and the researches of subsequent authors have taught, and to place some part of the subject in a point of view different from what any writer had done. Their plan was—first, to trace the history of national wealth from the rudest to the richest state of society, and to examine each change as it naturally arises in the progress of opulence and civilization; secondly, briefly to explain the systems of the ancients, of Dr Paley, of the French Economists, and what is called the commercial system; and thirdly, to explain the principles of taxation and finance[1]." The science had in fact at that time to be made, to be culled from different authors, and arranged in one comprehensive and, as far as could be, popular scheme. And this my father did for his Cambridge Lectures, collecting a quantity of books in different languages on Currency, Commerce, Manufactures, Population, Prices, &c., extracting their information, and harmonising it into a whole, with the addition of his own views[2].]

My first audience consisted of about 45 persons, some of whom were graduates and fellows of colleges. I give *their* names as showing their liberality, and out of gratitude to them that they assisted me by their presence in this first introduction of the new science to the University of Cambridge.

| | |
|---|---|
| Professor Monk, M.A. | Trinity. |
| Rev. R. Jefferson, M.A. | Sidney. |
| Professor Clarke, LL.D. | Jesus. |
| Rev. P. P. Dobree, M.A. | Trinity. |
| Professor Smyth, M.A. | Peterhouse. |
| — Graham, | Trinity. |
| Rev. G. C. Renouard, M.A. | Sidney |

(prevented from attending by illness).

[1] *Camb. Calendar,* 1862.

[2] These books (more than 700) are bequeathed to the University Library at Cambridge, for the use of his successors.

| | |
|---|---|
| Rev. J. Brown, M.A. | Trinity. |
| Mr Hodgson, | Trinity. |
| Sir R. Ferguson, | Trinity. |
| H. Gunning, M.A. | Christ's. |
| G. Stevenson, B.A. | Trinity. |
| F. Thackeray, M.B. | Emmanuel. |
| Mr F. P. Montague, | Peterhouse. |
| Samuel Grove Price, A.B. | Downing. |
| — Sperling, | Trinity. |
| Rev. J. D. Hustler, M.A. | Trinity. |
| Marchese di Spineto, | Cambridge. |
| Rev. T. Bradburne, M.A. | Christ's. |
| — Crowther, | Trinity. |
| Thomas Jas. Thackeray, | John's. |
| Charles Finch, | Cambridge. |
| Martin Thackeray, M.A. | King's. |
| E. Valentine Blomfield, M.A. | Emmanuel. |

One of my auditors in later years was Wm. Makepeace Thackeray, and I have the syllabus which he used, with some of his pencilled sketches in it. Then, and ever after, I carefully abstained from any political allusions, and had the gratification of being told by Mr Price of Downing College, afterwards M.P. for Harwich, with whom I was well acquainted, a man of extreme tory opinions, that he had tried in vain to discover any indication of a political bias; that he thought that he certainly should do so when I came to the concluding subject of taxation, but that he had watched in vain[1].

---

[1] "It was hard to prevent those to whom the science was new from imagining that it had something to do with party politics, which, in his own words, had about as much to do with Political Economy as *they* had with manufactures or agriculture."—*Life of Archbishop Whately*, Vol. I. p. 143.

In my early courses I vindicated Brutus from an accusation of an usurious transaction preferred against him by Adam Smith in his *Wealth of Nations.* On its being suggested to me that *this* might induce a supposition of political bias on my part, I expunged the passage. I may here mention that the whole of the French economists who flourished in the beginning and middle of the 18th century, expressed themselves in their works as adverse to any restriction on the power of the Sovereign. Sir James Stuart and Adam Smith, the only eminent English writers on the subject at the time I commenced my lectures, were, the one an exiled Jacobite, the other an extreme tory.

It was the French economists who first traced the natural progress of industry in civilised society, taught us what were the objects in which wealth consisted, and demonstrated the superior value of agriculture, the advantages of internal over foreign commerce, the mischief of restraints on the freedom of trade, and the necessary connection which subsists between the prosperity of states and the liberty of the subject.

The great business of the political economist is to ascertain on what the general riches and prosperity of a country depend, and what laws and lawgivers can do to promote it. It is taken for granted that in doing so they will promote its happiness at the same time.

Moralists and divines have sometimes thought otherwise, but the fact seems to be that their labours and those of the political economist must assist each other. Men are not in fact capable of moral and religious instruction when they are only anxious how to provide the necessaries of life for themselves and their families ; and they seem best fitted, perhaps only fitted, for intellectual improvement, while not merely the necessaries but the comforts of life are enjoyed.

[In this place I may not inopportunely insert a letter from a French Economist.]

"J. B. SAY *to* G. PRYME, ESQ.

" MONSIEUR,

"J'ai reçu il y a seulement une quinzaine des jours votre *Syllabus* et l'obligeante lettre dont il était accompagné. Quoique je n'y sois nommé qu'une seule fois, j'ai vu avec plaisir dans l'analyse des leçons, que vous aviez adopté quelques parties essentielles de ma doctrine.

"Vous me demandez si j'ai fait un *Syllabus* dans le genre du vôtre : non, Monsieur, parcequ'il n'y a encore en France aucune école publique où l'Economie politique soit enseignée. Il peut être remplacée jusqu'à un certain point par *l'Epitome* que j'ai placé à la fin de mon Traité, et qui a été très perfectionné dans l'édition qui va paraitre.

"Notre gouvernement parait avoir enfin sentir l'importance de cette étude. Il a fondé dernièrement une chaire d'Economie politique à la Faculté de Droit. Le Ministère m'ayant fait demander avant de la créer, si je consentirais à remplir cette chaire, il est possible quelle me soit destinée. Je me flatte que cet enseignement fera des rapide progrès en tous lieux; et ce n'est pas avec une médiocre satisfaction que j'ai vu qu'il avait pénétré dans une des vieilles Universités d'Angleterre. Il est impossible qu'Oxford ne suive pas bientôt l'exemple donné par Cambridge. Chez nous cette science est moins généralement comme que dans votre ile; cependant à voir la manière dont elle se propage, on peut predire que dans un petit nombre d'années, personne n'osera se montrer dans la carrière administrative et judiciaire, sans en posséder au moins les élémens. Et comme de semblables progrès se font partout en même tems, l'influence qui en résultera sur la politique en l'administration des États, est veritablement incalculable.

" Je m'occupe en ce moment de la publication de la 4ᵉ édition de mon ' Traité.' Elle sera plus ample, et j'espère qu'on la trouvera plus complète et mieux liée que toutes les précédentes. Les critiques de M. Ricardo m'ont été fort utiles. Elles m'ont obligé à approfondir la doctrine des valeurs comme mesure des richesses, et à résoudre, parmi beaucoups d'autres, cette importante question : *Comment le bas prix des produits fait il la Richesse des Nations?* J'ai fait mon possible pour que l'Economie politique ne présentât aucune difficulté qui ne peut être resolue à l'aide de cette 4ᵐᵉ Edition.

" J'attends avec impatience le Traité élémentaire depuis longtems annoncé par M. Malthus. Agréez, Monsieur, en même tems que mes remercimens pour votre interessante programme, l'assurance de ma haute consideration et l'expression de mon désir sincère de cultiver vôtre honorable amitié.

" J. B. SAY."

" PARIS. *Rue du Faubourg St Martin, Nʳˢ 92.*
" *le 27 Août 1819.*"

[A curious foretaste of the readiness of the French government to co-operate with us in relaxation of restrictions is to be found in the following extract from the *Star*, which my father has dated January, 1818. "Some weeks ago we announced that the French merchants had presented memorials to the government, recommending the establishment of a system of free-trade, and that the French Cabinet had taken the proposed measure into serious consideration; we have every reason to believe that such are the enlightened views entertained by that cabinet on the subject, that the impediments which seem to prevent its adoption are considered as matters of great regret. The desire of the French merchants to establish a free transit of goods, is founded in wisdom. Let us hope it will be listened to, and that all governments will bend their labours towards the establishment of a general system of free-trade as speedily as possible." Colonel Torrens says, " It is for the economist to propound principles true in abstract—it is for the statesman to propose measures attainable in practice[1]." A letter from a Scotch Economist may fitly close this portion of the volume.]

"35, FRITH STREET, SOHO,
LONDON, 26 *May*, 1823.

" SIR,

"An inflammatory sore throat has kept me from visiting this place three weeks longer than I intended. On my arrival here I found your letter, and perceiving you were to be here so early as the thirtieth, I do not think it worth while to send you the article on Political Economy, in the expectation that I should be able to give it to you personally when here.

"From the statements in your letter I have the satisfaction to perceive that we very nearly agree on the principal points of Political Economy. My Lectures were pretty well attended, at least I had about sixty effective students. This I consider a good beginning; but whether it will be supported time must decide. I should think that the growing importance of the science would secure you a constant increase of Students. The time cannot be far distant when a knowledge, or at least some little attention to, Political Economy will be considered as necessary for a legislator as a knowledge of Greek.

" I shall be most happy to receive your Introductory Lecture and Syllabus, from the perusal of which I promise myself great pleasure.

" I return you many thanks for your kind invitation to

---

[1] Torrens' *Financial Tracts*, 1—20.

visit you in Cambridge. I should like much to see an English University, but in this case I am afraid that I must take the straightest road home to Edinburgh.

"I hope you will have the goodness to call on me when you are here, and that you will allow me the pleasure of making your acquaintance.

"I am, with much respect,

"Very faithfully yours,

"J. R. M<sup>c</sup>Culloch."

*"To G. Pryme, Esq."*

# CHAPTER VIII.

## 1817—1824.

1817. WHILE on a visit to London this year I heard Dr Chalmers preach at Rowland Hill's Chapel. It was for the benefit of the Scottish Hospital, and such was his celebrity and the desire to hear him, that it was fixed for eleven o'clock on a Thursday (May 22), lest the concourse of a Sunday congregation should be too numerous; each governor of the Scottish Hospital was allowed to take in a friend, and Mr Clason, who was one, took me. We went early, before ten o'clock. When the doors were opened every seat and nearly the whole of the standing room was immediately occupied. The text was, "It is more blessed to give than to receive." He preached extempore. When

9

Dr Chalmers had finished the first part of his discourse (the giving), he said, "I am exhausted, sing a few verses of a hymn." Rowland Hill stepped forward from his seat beside him in the pulpit and gave one out, after which Dr C. went on with the other portion of his sermon. The whole of it lasted an hour and three quarters, and my only feeling was a regret at its termination. Clason told me that on the Sunday following, when Dr Chalmers preached at the Scotch Church, Mr Wilberforce came too late, and being a slight man, was taken in at an open window, and so got to a seat reserved for him.

[Another person speaking of *this* sermon says, "Probably no congregation since the days of Massillon ever had their attention more completely fixed, their understandings more enlightened, their passions more agitated, and their hearts more improved[1].]

I was staying at this time with my friend Vincent Thompson, in his chambers at Lincoln's Inn, and he wished to take me one evening with him when he was going to Mr Wilberforce's house at Kensington, but I declined, partly because I had voted against him (a plumper for Lord Milton) at the Yorkshire election. But it was a needless and over-strained feeling on my part, for he was not the man to have considered that.

[I have read a remark in Mr Wilberforce's life exactly confirming this estimate of him. Some years later my father must have taken an interest in a bill which Mr Wilberforce was concerned in, and have sent him some *agenda*, for I find this note respecting it; which also shows how kindly he would have been received at the ever-hospitable Gore House, had he availed himself of his friend's proposal[2].]

---

[1] Quoted in *Memoirs of T. Chalmers, D.D., LL.D.*, by the Rev. Wm. Hanna, LL.D.

[2] Afterwards Mr Serjeant Thompson, of Upper Belgrave Street. He

"KENSINGTON GORE,
7 *Mar.* 1821.

"DEAR SIR,

"I return you many thanks for your obliging communication, on the subject of which however I need not trouble you, as the bill in question is withdrawn. I will only therefore express the pleasure with which I correspond with the descendant of an old Hull friend, and I remain,

"Dear Sir,

"Your faithful Servant,

"W. WILBERFORCE."

"*To G. Pryme, Esq.*"

Curran died this year. He was one of those men of genius who, from time to time, have been conspicuous in Ireland. His eloquence was remarkable. In one of his speeches he pointed at Lord Clare, who had been most arbitrary, in his very presence, but the allusion was so carefully veiled that it could not be called a libel. C. was an insignificant looking man and dressed shabbily, so that he was not always recognised as a gentleman. On one occasion, just before starting in a stage-coach, he was accosted in the inn-yard by one of the passengers, who asked him to brush his coat for him, and offered him sixpence to do it well. Curran brushed the coat, took the money, and then, to the surprise of his fellow-traveller, assumed his place inside the coach. Presently he said, "I shan't return you the sixpence, for I did the work, but I shall give it to the first beggar I see."

and his brother, General Perronet Thompson, were my father's early and intimate friends. They were sons of Thomas Thompson, Esq. F.A.S. of Cottingham Castle, near Kingston upon Hull, and both Fellows of Queens' College, Cambridge. Mr V. Thompson was a man of cultivated mind and great kindliness. He had a fine taste in art, of which he was a liberal patron.

[The Princess Charlotte died Nov. 6, 1817. The lamentation throughout the country was extreme—induced by pity, regret, and even political ambition, as the following extract from a letter will show. It was written by the same gentleman, afterwards Mr Thorold, who told my father the anecdote of Sheridan and Mr Alley.]

"BENJAMIN HART, Esq. *to* MR PRYME.

" *      * I am told that all the friends of reform are genuine mourners of the Princess. They expected much from her principles when she came into power, not recollecting that power more frequently changes former principles than *they* regulate power. You, I hope, are not inconsolable. In that wish

"I remain,

"Truly yours,

"B. HART."

1818. I was present in the Court of King's Bench this year, and heard the argument before Lord Ellenborough and the other judges on a very singular case. A man had been tried for murder at Warwick assizes and acquitted, as all thought, improperly. A culprit cannot be tried again for the same offence, but in cases of murder certain near relations had the power to "appeal the murder." The brother of the deceased, William Ashford, did so. Abraham Thornton was again arrested and tried in the Court of King's Bench in Nov. 1817. When asked by the officers of the court whether he were guilty or not guilty? he answered, "Not guilty, and this I will prove by my body:" as he said this, he threw down a gauntlet on the floor. The brother would have taken it up, but was prevented by his friends, he being a man very inferior in strength to his adversary. Mr Reader was the counsel for the prosecution, and said, "Can this obsolete proceeding be allowed in the nineteenth century?" To which Lord Ellenborough answered, "It is the law of the land." It was then suggested that in cases where the proof was very strong against a prisoner, the trial by "wager of battel" could not be allowed, and it was the argument on this which I heard in the following spring, when it was decided that, though obsolete, this mode of trial must be permitted[1].

[Mr Crabb Robinson when he was 91 years of age told me that he had been present *when* the prisoner was *appealed*, and that he saw him "put his hand in the breast-pocket of his coat and draw forth a gauntlet, which he flung down at the feet of the brother. The king's-ancient serjeant called out, 'What! would you add the murder of the brother to that of the sister?' Lord Ellenborough gravely rebuked him, saying, 'What the law permits cannot be murder.' The gauntlet was taken up, and the case was argued, and all manner of curiosities of law produced from term to term, till at last it was got rid of. But had the court decided it otherwise, the lists would have been put up in Westminster, and the Judges of the Court of Common Pleas must have been present to witness the battle, and if the brother could have escaped being killed till sun-down then the prisoner would have been hanged." Mr Crabb Robinson added, "You will find the whole account of this barbaric custom in Shakespeare's King Richard II."]

I received a letter one day from the editor of the *Courier*, an ultra-tory and chief paper, asking permission to reprint in its columns a small pamphlet which I had written in answer to a protest by Archdeacon Thomas, against the formation of a Church Missionary Society at Bath. Mine was entitled *The Counter-Protest of a Layman*. I did not belong to the Church Missionary Society at that time, but I could

---

[1] In 1774 Edmund Burke defended this Law of Appeal. In 1819 Lord Eldon proposed and carried a Bill to abolish *Trial by Battle* and Appeals of Murder.

not help writing to defend it from such a violent attack upon
it. The pamphlet went through three editions, besides its
circulation in the *Courier*.

[A copy of the *Christian Observer* for this month, August 1869,
has been sent me by a friend just as this book is going to press, in
order that I might see what is said, concerning my father's protest,
in an article entitled " Fifty Years Ago." I venture to transcribe a
portion of it.

"At a meeting, under the presidency of the Hon. and Right Rev.
the Lord Bishop of Gloucester, the Archdeacon pulled out a roll of
paper and read his protest. * * 'As ARCHDEACON OF BATH, in the
name of the Lord Bishop of this diocese—in my own name—in the
name of the rectors of Bath, and in the name of nineteen-twentieths
of the clergy in my jurisdiction, I protest against the formation of
such Society in this city.'

"Such a performance of 'archidiaconal functions' did not, even
in those days, pass without animadversion. From Bath in the west,
to Cambridge in the east, and Yorkshire in the north, the conflict
raged. It is a curious sign of those times, that the late Professor of
Political Economy at Cambridge, a Fellow of Trinity, who took part
in the controversy, thought it well to state that during the sixteen
years he had resided in the University, he had only been four times
in the church frequented by Evangelical Christians, and that he was
not a member of the Church Missionary Society, and had no present
intention of becoming one. Having thus purged himself of all com-
plicity with fanaticism, the keen lawyer proceeded to dissect the
Archdeacon's protest. He could not see how 'compassing sea and
land to gain proselytes' applied in such a case, for on referring
to Matt. xxiii. 15, he found the answer directed against those who
made a man 'twofold more the child of hell than themselves.' 'Was
then the conversion of a heathen to any sect of Christianity to
make him the child of hell?' Nor could he see that if one half
of Bath subscribed for missions, and the other did not, this would
*necessarily* create discord any more than if one half should subscribe
to the Bath Infirmary, and the other should not. Upon the charge
against the Society, of calling forth the contribution of small sums

from the lower classes, the future Professor of Political Economy could discern that 'it elevates while it softens the heart of the donor. A man feels that it is more blessed to give than to receive, and beginning to save (which he never thought of before) a penny for the Society, he saves perhaps a shilling for himself, and becomes more economical, prudent and moral.' How amply this remark has been justified by the annals of our religious societies, time and space would fail to tell."

It may not be uninteresting to add that the *Courier* of that time, which I found among my father's papers, was just about the size (the whole of it) of one page of *our* present *Times*, and that the price was sevenpence (the stamp being fourpence).]

The Woodwardian Professorship of Geology became vacant this year by the marriage of Professor Hailstone. There were two candidates for it, Mr Gorham of Queens', and Adam Sedgwick of Trinity. The latter professed to know nothing of the subject, but pledged himself, if elected, to master it, and to resign the assistant tutorship in order that he might give the more complete attention to it. Some of his friends however, myself among the number, voted for Mr Gorham, feeling that it was only just to do so, as he had been studying Geology for a long time. I need hardly say that Sedgwick, who was elected, completely redeemed his promise, and that his eloquent Lectures have been the delight of all who have heard them. Mr Gorham's fate was different. He took a curacy, and was afterwards famous for his controversy with the bishop of Exeter (Philpotts).

About this time I received a visit from Dr Parr. He said to me frankly, "I don't know you, and I don't know your wife, but I owe a great deal to her grandfather, and therefore I have called upon you." He was the son of an apothecary at Harrow, and Dr Thackeray, head master of Harrow school, perceiving his great talent, urged his father, who meant him for his own business, to send him to college, which he very reluctantly agreed to. Parr was a pedant, but then he was what all pedants are not, a very learned man, and of considerable natural talent. He edited a Latin book, written in the Mediæval times, and with peculiar idiomatic elegance called *Bellendenus de statu*, &c. He added to it a long Latin preface, in which he gave an eulogy on the characters of Burke, Pitt, and Lord North, with a sort of apology for the latter. He speaks thus of him in reference to the American war, " Bellum Americanum spe lentius gessisse." Pitt, Sheridan, Wilkes, Lansdowne, and Richmond are also alluded to. It was very good modern Latin, and every classical scholar in my day read it. The undergraduates who were trying for honours also used to read it, thinking it likely to be given in examination.

[The exact title of the book, which is scarce, is *Guglielmi Bellendeni magistri supplicium Libellorum Augusti Regis Magnæ Britanniæ, &c. de statu, libri tres*, 1787. My father's copy has the addenda to the preface, which many have not. The first piece in the book itself is an Epithalamium on the most august nuptials of Charles I. and his queen. It is adorned with prints of Burke, Lord North, and Charles James Fox.]

Dr Parr was particular about pronunciation, and hearing Monk once say " eloquentia," pronouncing the *t* as *sh*, he called out, " Monk, Monk, ever say *eloquentïa*," sounding the *t* as in tear. Our perverseness in pronunciation is odd, we making some Latin words longer than the original, as St Helēna, and some shorter, as academīa and Alexandrīa. Parr, and Maltby (who had been his pupil) were once in the company of ——, a clever man whom Parr disliked. —— enquired how *Samaria* should be pronounced? Parr answered, " Ned (meaning Maltby) and I call it Samarïa, but *you* may as well go on calling it Samarïa." Dr Maltby was a pupil of Dr Parr. He was examining chaplain to Tomline, bishop of Lincoln, who though of different politics, Maltby being an avowed whig, gave him the living of Buckden in Hunts. Lord Grey, who had never seen him, made him bishop of Chichester, from whence he was translated to Durham. He was very hospitable, and I and two or three other barristers often dined with him at Buckden when on circuit. This place was *then* in the diocese of Lincoln, which at one time extended from the Humber to the Thames, including a part of Herts. An alteration of the law has since taken the county of Hunts. from it, and given it to Ely. The bishop's palace was formerly at Buckden[1]; there are remains of an old palace at Lincoln, instead of restoring which, the ecclesiastical commissioners made the mistake of buying a country house some miles from the city, and so separating the bishop from his Cathedral and his clergy.

1820. Early in this year King George III., after long bodily as well as mental illness, died. A University Address being voted to George IV., I attended with it. The King's manner seemed to me more reserved and less easy than that of his father. The levee was held at Carlton House, on the south side of Pall Mall, now Carlton Gardens.

An unpleasant event soon occurred in the Cato Street conspiracy. A number of men bound themselves together against the arbitrary proceedings amounting almost to tyranny of the Castlereagh administration, during which prosecutions and arrests were made, and the Habeas Corpus Act suspended. One evening there was a cabinet dinner at Lord Harrowby's. A man presented himself at the door and said, "I must see Lord Castlereagh." The servants refused admittance until he exclaimed, "Life and

---

[1] "The Bishop's (Sanderson) chief house at Buckden, in the Co. of Huntingdon, the usual residence of his predecessors,—for it stands about the midst of his Diocese" (temp. 1660).—Izaak Walton's *Lives.*

death depend upon my seeing him." Lord C. saw the man, who said, " I belong to the Cato Street Confederacy, but I cannot go the length of murder; there is a plan to attack this house to-night, and kill you and all the cabinet ministers." Prompt measures were taken, and police accompanied by soldiers were conducted by this man to the place where the plotters were assembled. The ringleaders were taken into custody, tried, found guilty, and some of them hung. The informer was indicted as belonging to them, but no evidence was forthcoming, and he received an acquittal. It was thought best *thus* to free him from the chances of any future prosecution. I do not know how he was rewarded[1].

Informers were employed very much at one time when plots and treason were apprehended. One instance I have given in another place, in the anecdote of Lord Nelson's fleet capturing and detaining the Danish fleet. £10,000 a year is (or was) allowed for secret service money, and Lord Melville, on his trial, said that nothing should ever induce him to divulge how that money had been spent, though he could say that it had been spent on the public service.

A dissolution of Parliament following on the old King's death, occasioned an event which I must preface by some account of the mode in which the borough of Cambridge was at that time represented. The election for Members had been confined to the freemen, about eighty in number, most of whom were resident, and who, up to the year 1780

---

[1] Thomas Haydon Green, who murdered his landlord and then committed suicide (Oct. 1869), was stated by his wife at the inquest to have originally kept a milk-shop in Cato Street. The accounts say that he it was who betrayed the conspirators. The Government rewarded him with a place in Somerset House, and a retiring pension, and he changed his name from Edwards.

inclusive, had usually returned two of the neighbouring country gentlemen. Soame Jenyns, author of the *Internal Evidences of Christianity*, had been one of them. He was elected in 1774. Soon afterwards Mr Mortlock, a banker in the town, prevailed upon the freemen, who had the power of adding to their number, to bestow the freedom upon about fifty of the tenants and friends of the Duke of Rutland. One of these latter was Crabbe, the poet, whom I saw for the first time in the year 1818, on occasion of a vain attempt of Mr Adeane, of Babraham, to oppose the Rutland interest[1]. At the general election in 1784 two friends of the Duke, General Manners and the Hon. General Finch, were returned, and sat for many years. These were succeeded in 1820 by Mr Madrille Cheere of Papworth, Cambridgeshire, and Colonel Trench of Co. Limerick, Ireland. This new influence of the Duke of Rutland had caused great dissatisfaction, even among persons of the same politics as himself, especially as he had no property within twelve miles of Cambridge. The two leaders of a little party among the freemen hostile to his interference were Mr John Finch, a private gentleman of moderate means, and Alderman Bottomley, both of avowed tory principles.

After the unsuccessful attempt of Mr Adeane in 1818, the Rutland party attempted to introduce another batch of freemen, about half of whom were non-residents; the reforming party were strong enough then to reject the non-residents, but they admitted the others. At the time of the general election, after the king's death, it was resolved, though success seemed hopeless, to keep alive the feeling of independence which I have spoken of as arising among the

---

[1] Crabbe was appointed, through the influence of Mr Burke, domestic chaplain to the Duke.

freemen of Cambridge, by the nomination of Mr Adeane and myself for the borough. The numbers were for Trench and Cheere 37 each, Adeane 18, Pryme 16.

[The householders of Cambridge were beginning to move towards a reform of the old and exclusive system, for thirty-two most respectable men sent at this time a requisition to the Mayor requesting him " to call a public meeting of the householders for the purpose of taking into consideration the general state of the Borough, and for the discussion of the question relative to the right of *Voting;* which right we believe to be vested in the householders of the said Borough of Cambridge."

In consequence of the Mayor declining to call a meeting, the householders were requested to assemble at the Shire-Hall to consider the subjects mentioned in the requisition.

Three years afterwards my father wrote and printed "*A Letter to the Freemen and Inhabitants of the Town of Cambridge on the state of the Borough.*" In this he took a survey of the charters and records of the corporation from the time of Henry I. to that at which he was writing, and of the gradual loss of freedom under its different masters. He commended the manly feeling of independence lately shown by the corporation in the choice of Mayors, and in resisting the introduction of strangers among them; and reminded them that steady perseverance " must succeed and bring the corporate rights to be vested in those hands where alone they ought to be, in a numerous and respectable body of inhabitants of the town."]

1820. In the spring of this year I purchased and went to reside in a house in Sidney Street, opposite Trinity Church. It was a large remnant of the Trinity Hostel, which, with many others of the like kind, were superseded by colleges. In making considerable alterations I preserved as much as I could the remains of the internal arrangement, keeping one long low room for my library, which now amounted to several thousand volumes. At first it seemed as if it would be impossible to remain there, for our servants believed in a rumour that the house was haunted, and for some time we had a difficulty in persuading them to remain, till at length the ghost was laid by ourselves occupying the room in which "the black lady" was said to walk.

[The foundation of the belief was that a skeleton had been dug up in former years in the garden, but this was easily accounted for by the fact of the house having been once occupied by Sir Busick Harwood, Professor of Anatomy.]

I now attended Trinity Church, in which parish my house was situate. Mr Simeon, the vicar, called upon us, and sometimes invited us to his rooms in King's College. He was a celebrated extempore preacher, and was the founder and head of the Evangelical party at Cambridge. I entertained similar views on some points of doctrine which I had learnt from Dr Milner, but I ventured to differ from him as to the impropriety of theatrical entertainments and card-playing, which latter was then still a general custom. He candidly argued the matter with me; I maintained them to be objectionable only in their abuse, when the play was immoral or the stakes were high. Mr Simeon's opinions on one point have been, I think, imperfectly understood. He positively disclaimed to me a belief in *particular predestination* as understood by Calvinists. I cannot give my own views on that point more conclusively than is expressed in the second collect of our Morning Service. Prof. Lee had not then shown in one of his sermons that the words in the New Testament implying *predestination*, applied to congregations of early Christians, not to individuals.

In 1822 a vacancy occurred in the representation of the University. There was a contest between William John Bankes, Esq., an anti-catholic tory, Lord Harvey, a pro-

catholic tory, and James Scarlett, a whig, of whose committee at Cambridge I was chairman. He polled only 219,
and Bankes 419 votes. The whig cause appeared *then* so
hopeless that Lords Tavistock and Althorp withdrew their
names from the boards of Trinity College in consequence,
and thereby lost their right of voting. That we ought never
to despair of future success in political affairs was shown
by the fact that within eight years from that time two whigs
were returned for the University, Lord Palmerston and Mr
Cavendish.

Scarlett was an eminently successful barrister. He told
me that one reason of his great success in addressing juries
was his habit of watching their countenances, and if he found
that the topic which he was urging did not make the impression he wished, he proceeded to other points of the case, and
then returned to it again, and argued it from a somewhat
different point of view. His quickness and clearness in acquiring a knowledge of a case were also remarkable. In
one to be argued in the King's Bench, Mr Fitzroy Kelly and
I, having been engaged in it on the Norfolk circuit, were
his juniors. He appointed a consultation on the morning
for which the argument was fixed. When we met he said
that he had not had time to read his brief, and requested
K. and myself to state our respective views of the case.
A few hours later, during which he had been otherwise occupied, it was called on; he showed himself completely
master of the subject, and had almost exhausted it when
we followed. In private life I found him kind and hospitable, and possessed of great conversational powers[1].

In the summer of 1823 the first stone was laid by Mr
Manners Sutton of the new court of Trinity College, which

[1] Afterwards created Lord Abinger. He died April 7, 1844, during the
Assizes at Bury St Edmunds.

was built, partly by subscription, on ground formerly occupied by the dwelling-houses of the college baker and cook.
There was a large baking-office there also, at which all the
college bread was baked, a custom now disused.

The court was intended to be of stone, but when it was
partly built a fire consumed it, and the money (£40,000)
destined to complete it, was much of it spent in repairing
the losses thus caused. So it was finished off shabbily with
stucco, except the river front, which is of stone. The name
of *King's Court* was given to it by the then Master, Dr
Wordsworth, but Professor Sedgwick wished for *St Michael's
Court.* It is nothing more now than New Court.

[1824. With a view to interest the University in the movement
of sympathy with the Greek patriots, a committee had been formed
at Cambridge, holding its meetings—to save expense—at my father's
house. This summer he invited, through Mr Hobhouse, the Greek
Deputies, who had come over to England for the purpose of obtaining a loan, to stay with him at the Commencement in July[1].
Their cause had been supported by Lord Erskine in a letter to
Lord Liverpool, and Lord Byron had himself gone to Greece
"with considerable resources of his own, and was willing to lend
himself to the cause with all his energy." But his death at Misso-
longhi in this year (April 19), was a heavy blow to the sanguine
hopes which had been formed of his presence effecting a change.
Committees were formed in London and elsewhere, and above
5,000*l.* was collected. Lords Lansdowne and Fitzwilliam, and Mr
Wilberforce, gave largely. The "Society of Friends" also raised a
handsome subscription. My father took great interest in these efforts,
and not only subscribed, but purchased some of their bonds, which
he kept as long as there was a hope of their being serviceable to
the cause.

[1] Sir John Cam Hobhouse, afterwards Lord Broughton, born June
27, 1786, died June 3, 1869. "A persevering advocate of Parliamentary
Reform half a century back."

None, my mother says, could be more agreeable than these Greeks. Many guests were invited to meet them, of whom, I believe, Lord Berners and Professor Sedgwick alone survive. Orlando was extremely stout, and Luriottis slender. They wore black frock coats, richly braided with silk, and a small crimson cap (not a *fez*). They were very abstemious, and when offered cake and wine at bed-time preferred black-currant jelly dissolved in water, as they said, the most refreshing drink in summer.]

In this year I was elected one of the Conservators of the Bedford Level Corporation. It was instituted in the time of Charles I. for the drainage of the fens in Cambridgeshire and adjacent counties, but went almost to ruin during the wars of the Commonwealth. It was revived by Act of Parliament in the reign of Charles II., and took its name from the then Earl of Bedford, who was the earnest promoter of it, and by far the largest proprietor. Its operations extended over nearly 300,000 acres of fen, out of which rose occasional elevations, on the largest of which the city of Ely, with its fine cathedral, stands. The Isle of Ely was separated in the time of King Henry I. from any county, and was literally an island, being inaccessible except by water. It often formed a secure retreat for the defeated party in civil war. There is a tradition which was related to me by the late Mr Bevill, registrar to the Bedford Level Corporation, of the time when many of the Saxons took refuge there after the Norman Conquest. The army of King William I. attempted to pursue the fugitives by making a causeway through the waters to the N.W. of Ely, on a foundation of dry sedge, and in order to defend it, engaged a witch of great celebrity to prevent by her incantations the attacks of the besieged on it. But the Islemen contrived to come in their boats and set fire to the sedge, and she was literally burnt without the formality of a trial. Possibly the names of Witch-ford and Witch-ham are derived from this incident[1].

The Corporation consisted of a Governor, (to which office a Duke of Bedford was always elected,) six Bailiffs, and twenty Conservators, who all met at Ely twice a-year for a few days. These were elected by every person who was the owner of 100 acres. It had been decided that the word "person" applied to women as well as men, and the former voted when a poll took place. The first Adventurers, as they were called in the Act, were recompensed by the allot-ment of one-third of the fen land, which was also burthened with an annual tax for the requisite repairs of the works. They made several cuts or artificial rivers from 16 to 100 feet wide, with strong banks, into which the water from the land was thrown by windmills (many of which have since been removed as unnecessary), and of late in some parts by steam. Two subsequent Acts of Parliament for additional works have rendered the drainage so complete that this Cor-poration has now but little to do, and the Adventurers' tax has ceased.

At the first board-meeting after I was elected a Conser-vator we made a voyage by the river Ouse from Ely to Littleport. It was ten miles in length, whereas the road by land was only five miles. The tract through which it passed, called the *Padnals*, was one swamp, on which there was no building except two cottages, for the foundation of which

---

[1] Macaulay describes the state of this part of the country in 1689, as "a vast and desolate fen, saturated with the moisture of thirteen counties, and overhung during the greater part of the year by a low grey mist, high above which rose, visible for many miles, the magnificent tower of Ely. In that dreary region, covered by vast flights of wild fowl, a half-savage population, known by the name of the *Breedlings*, then led an amphibious life, sometimes wading, and sometimes rowing from one islet of firm ground to another."—*History of England*, Vol. III. p. 41.

earth had been carried thither by boats; and the inhabitants of them gained their livelihood, as many others did at that time, by catching fish in the summer, and wild-fowl in the winter. One of these men who was examined as a witness at Cambridge assizes being asked, as usual, what he was? said, " I follow fowling and fishing." On another occasion a poor man, a witness in court, said in answer to the same question, "a banker." The judge, I think it was Alderson, remarked, "We cannot have any absurdity." The man replied, "I *am* a banker, my lord." He was a man who repaired the banks of the dykes, so peculiar were the local callings. The result of our "view" was the making a new bed to the river Ouse by cutting off a great part of the bend, and this tract of barren acres now produces excellent crops of corn instead of reeds and rushes.

The surface of the fens consists of peat, beneath which, at a depth of from five to ten feet, is the clay, with rare intervals of gravel, on the top of which lower stratum have been found the horns of deer, prostrate trees quite black, and in one part a gravel road, a portion of a boat, and other marks of human habitation.

It has been supposed that some irruption of waters deluged these low lands, on which the peat was gradually formed from the decay of moss and aquatic plants. A similar formation of peat is found in most of the hollows of the rocky hills in the North of England. I was cautioned against it when shooting grouse, and told that where I saw a green spot I should be up to the knees.

[The following interesting statement is from one who is a great authority in the botany and geology of the fens[1].

---

[1] William Marshall, Esq. of Ely.

"'The changes which the fen country has undergone since the first serious attempt at drainage by the Adventurers, now two hundred years ago, must have been very great, but they have chiefly occurred within the last half century. It should never be forgotten that the original scheme of drainage was simply to shut out the highland waters and the tides by means of banks and sluices, and then to drain off the fen waters by *gravitation only*. Windmills for lifting of the fen waters from a lower to a higher level came in afterwards, and were at first regarded (indeed they were indicted) as nuisances, and it is a question whether (notwithstanding the vast expenses which had been incurred), the Bedford Level, 100, or even 150 years after the general drainage, was not in nearly as bad a state as at the commencement. Three causes only have produced the vast change which has come over the fen country within the last fifty years, viz. the improvement of the outfall by the making of the Eau Brink Cut (opened in 1821), the substitution of the certain help of steam for the uncertain aid of the fickle wind (which it was notorious refrained from blowing during great falls of rain), and the practice of claying the land. It should be obvious that the last two causes of improvement were substantially dependent on the first, and it is therefore to the improvement of the outfall that the present results are mainly attributable. Windmills have now nearly disappeared, and the complete control over the water which steam has given the fensman (aided by claying) has enabled him to substitute wheat for oats, and made the Bedford Level the granary of England. Indeed the drainage of the land has been carried so far that *forecasting* fenmen look forward with anxiety to the consequences which may hereafter ensue from the subsidence of the surface, the wasting of the vegetable soil, and a want of water in summer-time. The drainage of the fens has necessarily produced a vast destruction of the indigenous marsh plants and of the insects which fed upon them, and many plants which were once very common have now become rare, others linger only in small patches of primitive fen, as yet innocent of the labours of the drainer, while a few are probably extinct[1]."]

[1] A list of 49 plants classed under the above heads is given in the Appendix.

The Isle of Ely had a separate jurisdiction under the Bishop of Ely, who had power as a Lord Lieutenant over everything except the militia. He appointed the magistrates absolutely, instead of the Lord Chancellor. The assizes were holden at Ely in the spring, and at Wisbeach in the summer, and presided over by a Chief Justice, appointed by the Bishop, who had his trumpeters and little state. The Quarter-sessions were also divided between the aforenamed two places. I remember Christian, the Downing Professor of Laws, and subsequently Serjeant Storks, being Chief Justices. Ely was the last place in the kingdom where a man was hung on a gibbet—the very man who was tried for murdering a brother poacher, and who had nearly got off owing to the doubt about the boundary[1].

During the time of Lord Melbourne's administration a Bill passed to take this great civil power from the Bishop on the first vacancy. The assizes were given up and amalgamated with those at Cambridge. The sessions also would probably have been lost to the Isle too ; for, strange to say, the County members took no part, but I (being then in the House) moved an amendment, which was carried, " that the sessions remain as heretofore."

They were very pleased at this in the Isle, and I received soon after, through the Clerk of the Peace, a vote of thanks for the part which I had taken. In place of transferring the power of appointing the magistrates hitherto wielded by the Bishop to the Lord Lieutenant of Cambridgeshire, as had been suggested, it was proposed to have a Custos Rotulorum of the Isle itself, and the Marquis of Tavistock was appointed to be the first.

The Soke of Peterborough, being in some respects an

---

[1] Above, page 104.

exclusive jurisdiction from the rest of Northamptonshire, has also a Custos Rotulorum. When William IV. was to be proclaimed at Peterborough, the County magistrates &c. being all assembled for the ceremonial, the late Lord Fitzwilliam entered the room. As for political reasons he had not been invited, the company were rather taken aback, and the Chairman began to apologise for there having been no place appointed for him. "There is no difficulty about it," he replied with that dignity which belonged to him, "the Custos Rotulorum of the Soke of Peterborough knows his *own* place: follow me." Then, turning to the Clerk of the Peace, he said, "Give *me* the proclamation," took it in his hand, led the way, and read it to the public.

# CHAPTER IX.

## 1825—1828.

1825.　IN the latter end of September the Greek Professor, Peter Paul Dobree, died in College after a short illness.　I had formerly, when a resident fellow, been with him almost constantly during a similar attack, in which his life had been despaired of by Dr Davy and Mr Okes, but from which he completely recovered.　In this illness, when his death was hourly expected, I passed the last night with him.　Dr Bayne, who had just graduated in medicine and was then a resident fellow, kindly volunteered to sit up with me, which I accepted.　Professor Dobree expired the next forenoon; he had requested me to be his executor.　He bequeathed his MSS. and books containing MS. notes to the University, directing that Dr Hollingworth, the Norrisian Professor of Divinity, and I should use a discretionary power in cancelling whatever passages we chose. Also he left a thousand volumes to the library of Trinity College, and the remainder to his nephew, Mr Peter Carey of Guernsey. Dr Hollingworth and I availed ourselves of the power thus given us, and we cancelled any severe or sarcastic observations on living authors.

Professor Dobree was a native of Guernsey, and was educated at the grammar school of Reading, the head master of which was that eminent Greek scholar, Dr Valpy. He had there acquired a taste for Greek criticism, and applied it chiefly to adjusting the doubtful readings of those authors, the MSS. of whose works varied. When he came to the University he gave much attention to this line of study, somewhat neglecting that which was more connected with college examinations, resisting the arguments of myself and other friends, who urged him, after taking his B.A. degree, to compete for the Chancellor's Medal or some other classical honour. He however obtained a fellowship, which he thought desirable, not merely for its emoluments but for the opportunities which a college residence afforded him of pursuing his researches.

He and Porson had a taste for any neat mathematical problem which their limited knowledge (both having been Senior Optimes) enabled them to appreciate. I recollect Dobree showing me some curious little problem that Porson had devised[1].

On the death of Porson, Dobree was a candidate for the Greek Professorship, but the seven electors bestowed it upon Monk, who had graduated in the same year and had obtained one of the Chancellor's medals. Dobree now suffered for his omission to compete for one of them, and Dr

[1] For an Algebraical problem and its solution by Prof. Porson, see Appendix to the *Reminiscences of Charles Butler*, Esq. Vol. I. Note 3.

Barnes, Master of Peterhouse, alleged this as a reason for
withholding *his* vote from him. Dobree soon afterwards
most ably edited some of Porson's MSS., entitled *Ricardi
Porsoni Aristophanica*, which so completely established his
reputation for Greek scholarship, that when Monk resigned
the professorship, on being appointed Dean of Peterborough,
he was elected to it without any one venturing to oppose
him. He meditated an edition of Demosthenes, and left
remarks on many other Greek authors which were afterwards
edited in a work entitled *Dobræi Adversaria*, by Professor
Scholefield, his successor.

In addition to this deeper learning he possessed much
general knowledge, which he often manifested in humorous
remarks. His acquaintance was very limited, as he preferred
the society of a small number of intimate friends. He was
buried in the chapel, Oct. 3rd.

[I can remember my awe, as a child, at seeing. for the only time
in my life, my Father weep. Dr Jeremie has since told me that
at the funeral he was quite overpowered and wept like a child,
and that his great emotion left a deep impression on *his* mind.
Dr Jeremie has given Professor Dobree's portraiture more at length
in one of his Commemoration Sermons, from which he has permitted
me to borrow the following portion. " I would pause for a moment
at the name of him who filled the chair of Porson, and who now
rests by the side of his grave—similar, alike, in his affections and
pursuits; in the peculiar cast and power of his genius; in the nobler
features of his moral character; and but too similar in his untimely
death. The memorial which adorns these walls .was traced by a
friendly hand; but with singular precision and fidelity. It has
touched upon his distinguishing qualities—his modesty, his candour,
his gentleness, his inflexible love of truth. his unfeigned contempt for
all which bordered upon artifice and meanness, and, above all, that
childlike simplicity of heart, of which ' the noblest natures are ever
found to have the largest share.' If ever it could be said of any

man, it might indeed be said of him, that he loved learning *for itself* [1]."]

It was by Professor Dobree's introduction that I became acquainted with Mr James Amiraux Jeremie, now the Regius Professor of Divinity. He was also from Guernsey. We were much brought together in Dobree's illness, during which he shewed great kindness and tenderness of heart, and we have been real friends ever since. I cannot let this opportunity pass without some mention of his amiability and learning and eloquence, as exemplified by his constancy as a friend, his excellence as a professor, his admirable sermons as a preacher.

We two were the last, or nearly so, of the Dons who regularly attended the Sunday morning sermon at Great St Mary's, since given up, where we sat together in the place, which, now that the church has entirely lost its peculiar and dignified arrangement, shall know us no more. I voted in a small minority in the Senate-House in favour of retaining it, and also, equally in vain, against the abolition of the morning sermon.

[My father lamented the removal of the gallery in which the Vice-Chancellor sat, facing the pulpit, supported on either side by the Heads, Doctors, and Professors. Dr Whewell deprecated the change also, and printed some reasons against it.

Yet he was not so wedded to old usages but that he could say, " I highly approve of the division now made in the services in our chapel on Sunday morning. Their exceeding length had a very bad effect on my mind when an undergraduate; and Lord Derby once intimated the same thing respecting those at Oxford to me in conversation in the House. I quite agreed with Bishop Thirlwall in the view he took in his letter to the master (Wordsworth) on the subject when he was resident Fellow of Trinity."]

[1] Dr Jeremie's Sermon preached in Trin. Coll. Chapel, Dec. 16, 1834.

In the same autumn the greatest monetary panic and run
on banks that was ever known took place. This was occasioned partly by a great number of wild schemes for joint-
stock speculations, as stage-coach, washing, tea-companies,
&c., &c. One bank had actually been lately commenced
by a mercantile firm at a time when they knew themselves
to be insolvent. The extensive issue of one- and two-pound
bank-notes had facilitated such speculations. After the
panic became general the legislature of that day forbad
the future issue of notes below £5, but permitted those
already in existence to be circulated for three years longer.
I then acted as Commissioner of Bankruptcy, the number
of which occupied me so much that on being asked to give
two consecutive days in Bedfordshire for the winding up
of an old bankruptcy, I was unable to do so till nearly three
months afterwards. Among them were two banks, Messrs
Hollick and Nash of Cambridge, and, Messrs Rix and Gorham of St Neots, who stopped payment on account of some
imprudent advances which they could not immediately meet ;
but they paid 20s. in the pound[1].

---

[1] So little was this Panic of 1825 foreseen, that in the King's Speech
of that year his Majesty said "there never was a period in the history of
the Country when all the great interests of Society were at the same
time in so thriving a condition."

Mr Nassau Senior has given so graphic a description of the consequences which might have ensued that perhaps I shall be pardoned for
transcribing it : "Then followed that dreadful week which has been
called 'the panic,' in which the question every morning was not who
has fallen? but who stands? in which nearly 70 banks suspended their
payments, a state of things which if it had continued only 48 hours
longer, would, according to Mr Huskisson, have put a stop to all dealings
between man and man, except by barter; in which, in fact, nothing but
the unexpected arrival of about 200,000 sovereigns from France, the
discovery, in the cellars of the Bank of England, of 800,000 one pound
notes, long before condemned to be burnt, and the intervention of a

In passing through Peterborough on my way to one of those Bankruptcy Commissions I dined with the Bishop, Dr Herbert Marsh, from whom I had a general invitation. He took me into his garden, and showed me a tortoise which had been there beyond the memory of man; and said that he supposed him to be about 200 years old. Though we differed widely in political sentiments, and with regard to the Bible and Church Missionary Societies, to the Committees of which I *now* belonged, yet our friendly relations remained the same as when he had been fellow of St John's College. He had previously filled the See of Llandaff (a very poor bishoprick), and I remember his calling just afterwards and saying, in answer to my congratulations, "You had better call me Bishop of Aff, for the land is gone." His amiability and benevolence in private life attracted the admiration of all who had opportunites of observing him. When he was elected Lady Margaret's Professor of Divinity, so many persons were desirous of hearing his early Lectures, that he obtained leave to give them from the pulpit of Great St Mary's, and his audience, including some ladies, nearly filled the church[1]. One of his theological works was severely assailed in the *Critical Review*, and it was proposed at the Masters of Arts' reading-room to discontinue taking in that periodical, but Professor Monk said that there was every rea-

Sunday, prevented the manifest failure of an establishment which we have been accustomed almost to consider a part of the constitution." *Lecture on the Mercantile Theory of Wealth* by William Nassau Senior.

[1] Among my Father's papers I find this Epigram.
*On three Preachers of St. Mary's in Cambridge attacking Calvin.*
  \*  \*  \*  \*  \*
  "*Butler* in clearness and in force surpass'd :
  *Maltby* with sweetness spoke of ages past :
  Whilst *Marsh* himself, who scarce could further go,
  With criticism's fetters bound the foe."

son for the contrary, as unless we saw what was written against the Church, we should be unable to answer it; and his enlightened view obtained the assent of all.

This Master of Arts' reading-room was a kind of Club, which was holden at a private house in Green Street, where tea and coffee might be had, and newspapers and pamphlets were taken in. Members were elected by ballot. The institution of the Philosophical Society, which may be said to have been formed upon it, occasioned it gradually to die a natural death. Previously to its being in Green Street, it was held at a house in Sidney Street, opposite to Sidney College; it was called familiarly "the Drum."

1826. The old Parliament having nearly expired, a Dissolution took place in this year. The Election for Cambridge Borough was fixed for May 6th, when a similar attempt to that in 1820 was made to open it. The numbers were, Marquis of Graham, eldest son of the Duke of Montrose, 24, Trench 23, Pryme 4. I must account for the falling off in my votes by saying that the resident freemen on *our* side were not requested to vote, and we agreed not to bring in non-resident voters, as the form of an opposition and the opportunity of speeches were all that was required.

There was a sharp contest for the County of Huntingdon. As there had been no one of the Duke of Manchester's family ready to be a Candidate in 1820, they had allowed Lord John Russell, who was related to them, to be returned without opposition; but Lord Mandeville, the eldest son of the Duke, having now attained his majority, appeared as a Candidate, along with Mr Fellowes of Ramsey Abbey, who had sat during the three preceding Parliaments. This caused a contested election, and Lord John lost his seat, being in a minority of 53. I took a very active part in this Election, and was one of the Counsel for

Lord John[1]. The late Mr Dover was the other. Mr Dover was a barrister, a friend of Lord Byron, of Mr Adeane, and of Sir Robert Rolfe, afterwards Lord Cranworth. At that time, and previously to Parliamentary Reform, there was no registration of Electors, and votes were objected to at the hustings by the Agents of the Candidates, and sent to the Sheriff's room, where the Assessor sat to decide, and the Counsel examined witnesses, and argued on the validity of the votes. This lasted several days. Previously to the Polling day at Huntingdon I went down to Nottingham, the freedom of which Borough had been voted to me, to record my vote for Lord Rancliffe and Mr Birch. This was my last opportunity of doing so, as the Reform Bill disfranchised those who did not reside within seven miles of a Borough.

Besides the political interest which induced me to take this prominent part in the Huntingdonshire election, I had recently acquired a right to do so by the purchase of property in the County.

While the Country was in the fervour of Election, my friend Mr Daniel Sykes, of whom I have before incidentally spoken, passed some days with me at Cambridge, a place which he delighted frequently to visit, and to revive his Academical recollections. It is time I should speak of one with whom I had an intimate and most valuable friendship.

[At this point something occurred to hinder my Father dictating any more, and a return to the subject was postponed until too late. I therefore make a few extracts instead from a little memoir which he wrote of this very dear friend[2]. Mr and Mrs Sykes used fre-

---

[1] My Father refused the Fee, which was probably 200 guineas, as I find that sum marked on a Retainer for Counsel at another Hunts Election (1830), on which my Father has written "Retainer accepted but fee refused".

[2] Memoir of the Life of Daniel Sykes Esq., M.A. and M.P. by George Pryme Esq., M.A. and M.P. &c. 8vo, 1834.

quently to visit us either on their way to or from London. Both were delightful people. He dignified, clever, sincere; one whose every word and look bespoke the upright man.]

"Mr Sykes, after being 14th Wrangler in 1788, became a Candidate for a Fellowship (at Trinity). As his health was then very indifferent, his Father, who was not only a wealthy Merchant but a Classical Scholar, wished him to desist, and offered to make up to him the pecuniary advantage which he might sacrifice. His answer was, 'Ten thousand pounds a year would not make it up to me.' He persevered and was elected. He was called to the Bar in 1793, was Recorder of Hull, and then its Member, residing near it at Raywell, a beautiful domain, where he exercised great hospitality. He was the friend of Henry Brougham and William Wilberforce. In the House of Commons he was listened to with great attention; his speeches being sometimes marked by keen irony, and strong, though not illnatured, sarcasm. He had the rare quality of viewing a subject in all its bearings before he formed an opinion or drew an inference. His knowledge of Classical and modern literature was considerable, and he was well acquainted with the best authors of France and Italy, where he had travelled much. He was fond of English poetry, the reading and discussion of which formed part of the evening's amusement at Raywell. Of the abstract and experimental Sciences he had that general knowledge which marks the well-educated man; but on the Moral Sciences, especially Political Economy and Modern History, he had bestowed deep attention, and formed comprehensive views.

"He had a great abhorrence of anything bordering on meanness or insincerity, and would only just tolerate the society of those in whom he noticed such defects. This feeling, together with his desire of deriving from social intercourse something more than mere amusement, made him cautious in forming intimacies, and somewhat difficult of access, beyond what the courtesies of life required. He may be classed among those who hide beneath a cold exterior the strong glow of feeling, and a heart warm with affection. But the magic circle once passed, there was no man with whom friends were more at ease, and might be more familiar without fear of offence. It was with difficulty he could be induced to think less favourably of those whom he had once liked. He viewed their errors with sorrow; their foibles with good nature; and apologised for them when others condemned or ridiculed."

1827. This Parliament was marked by incidents and measures, the full bearing of which were not then distinctly seen. When the broken health of Lord Liverpool occasioned his retirement from office in the Spring, Mr Canning became Premier. Many of his Tory coadjutors declined to act under him: the Cabinet was broken up, and a new one was formed, composed of the more liberal part of his late colleagues, and of some of the more aristocratic Whigs. A different course of foreign and domestic policy was now pursued. Many of the Tory statesmen went into opposition; while most of the Whigs, though declining to hold office, hailed the change as, on the whole, beneficial, and took their places on the ministerial benches. Some of them however still doubted as to this course, and expressed their belief that the new Premier was in heart the same as when, in 1819, he spoke against Reform. Mr Sykes was inclined to adopt the former course, and thus wrote:

"I cannot make up my mind on the late changes. I believe that I must go with the rest of my friends; but still my old opposition feelings stick to me; and strongly disliking Canning, I cannot cordially support his administration. However there are cases in which what is strictly right must give way to what is strongly expedient. * * * At Wentworth there seemed to be a good deal of diversity of opinion between the bending and the unbending Whigs. I incline to think that the former are right, though if my personal convenience only were consulted, I should greatly prefer being in opposition. What you say about the effect of education is quite agreeable to my own views, and I am convinced that we cannot spread liberal opinions more widely, or inculcate them more strongly, than by encouraging the literary education of the mass of mankind. In confirmation of this, I was pleased to hear from a very intelligent friend of mine, who has lately been visiting me after a tour through the populous parts of Lancashire and Yorkshire, that whatever diversity of opinion existed on other points, he met few well instructed persons who were not anti-tories. Blessed with the light of knowledge, they are opposed to those who would shut it from their eyes."

In April a vacancy in the representation of the University took place by Sir John Copley's being created Lord Chancellor. He was succeeded by Sir Nicholas Tindal, afterwards Chief Justice of the Common Pleas, who was returned by a majority of 101 votes over Mr Wm. J. Bankes, a former member.

[The style of Sir N. Tindal's address is so unlike that of one which a candidate for the University would now send forth, that I print it as a curiosity. He gratefully refers all his success to Alma Mater, and does not promise to alter and reform her.]

" BEDFORD SQUARE,
19th *April*, 1827.

" SIR,

"I take the liberty of offering myself to your Notice as a Candidate for the high and distinguished Honor of representing the University of Cambridge in Parliament, on occasion of the Vacancy in that Representation, made by the appointment of Sir John Copley to an important office in the State.

"Having been educated in that University, and feeling that I owe all that I enjoy in life, to the Habits of thinking and acting which I formed, and to the Studies which I began, under the discipline of that learned Body, I shall feel it no less a Debt of Gratitude, than the impulse of my Inclination, to watch over, and to promote the Interests of the University of Cambridge to the utmost of my power.

"I beg to assure you, Sir, that the Principles upon which I have hitherto acted, and to which I shall adhere through Life, in all questions of Religion and of Policy, are those which have placed, and which I doubt not will ever preserve, the present Illustrious Family, on the Throne of these Realms.

"I trust I shall have the Honor of your support at the ensuing Election, and I beg to assure you that I remain, Sir,

"Your very faithful

"and obedient Servant,

"N. C. TINDAL."

"*G. Pryme, Esq.*"

Tindal had been fellow of Trinity College, and, when called to the Bar, chose the Northern Circuit. Not having seen a mountainous country before, he walked with a guide from Newcastle-upon-Tyne to Carlisle. His foot slipped on a hill-side, he fell but was not much hurt, and asked his guide the name of the hill, who answered, *Tynedale Fell.* He thought the guide was jeering him, but no, it was the real name. *Fell* in the North means a high hill. The poet laureate of the Circuit in his next Ode mentioned

"The way which Tindal came,
And by his falling gave the Fell a name."

I never knew any one on the Circuit ride it on horseback, as was formerly the custom, but Tindal and some other Judges had their groom with two horses, and rode, except in and out of Circuit towns, for which they entered the Sheriff's carriages. Tindal once, when thus riding, talked with a woman at a turnpike-gate, who expressed a great desire to see the Judge, and asked for a description so that she might know him when he passed through; soon after the Sheriff's carriage came up, into which he entered, saying to her, " Now you have not only seen, but talked with a Judge."

I may here mention regarding Sir John Copley, that partly by his instrumentality an annual dinner of the members of Trinity College had been established in London. It was attended by many of the eminent men who had been educated at the College, but after some years it languished, and finally ceased to exist.

About this time I spent a few days with Dr Davy, Master of Caius College, at his country house at Heacham in Norfolk. He had been a fellow of Caius College, and a physician in extensive practice, which he relinquished on being made master. His acute mind led him to give much attention to metaphysics. On this and other literary subjects he had written a good deal, but he directed in his will, and with almost his dying words earnestly requested, that all his MSS. should be destroyed[1]. I have reason to believe

---

[1] We happened to be visiting Caius College on the day on which the destruction took place. It was done by boiling them in the great copper of the College kitchen, as the most effectual mode.

that he had been sceptical up to middle age, and afterwards becoming, as I know, a sincere believer, dreaded lest there should be some taint of his former opinions in his writings which might be injurious to others. As an instance of his remarkable acumen I would mention that he contended, when the news of the battle of the Nile (Aug. 1st, 1798) arrived, that the English ships ought to have been placed not parallel with, but obliquely to the French ships which were anchored in Aboukir Bay. This notion was thought so presumptuous in the University that his acquaintances sometimes amused themselves with alluding to the subject in his presence that they might draw out his theory. Some years afterwards a Biography, with numerous letters of Lord Nelson was published, from which it appeared that he *had* directed the ships to be stationed in this manner, but that through a mistake of those to whom he gave the directions they were not properly placed.

Dr Davy was fond of discovering meanings for curious signs, and he told me some of his interpretations. "The Green Man and Still," he considered was the green-man, or one who sold herbs for the distiller. Formerly gamekeepers were dressed in green; I have seen one so dressed myself at Bunny, and Dr D. supposed that in the sign such an one was represented, the original meaning being lost sight of. On Lincoln Heath there was a small inn called the *Green Man*, and doubtless it had reference to a gamekeeper or ranger[1]. This reminds me that Lincoln Heath was in my younger days a large tract of unenclosed land, chiefly rabbit-warrens. I have passed over it since in a mail-coach, and

---

[1] This explanation differs from those given in Hotten's entertaining book on *Signboards*, nor are the other two signs which my Father goes on to describe mentioned in the latest edition (the fifth) I have met with.

found the desolate waste I knew to be fields waving with corn.

I have seen a singular sign in Wisbeach at a public-house called "The Three Goats;" we may be certain that no goat was ever naturally in that part of the country. Mr Jackson of Wisbeach, who was something of an antiquary, told me that *gote* was in that part of the country a word for an outlet, a corruption of *go-out*, and that there were three outlets, or, so to speak, sluices there for the water, and thence the name. I remember seeing an Inn with this device : in place of the usual painting on a board at the top of a post, there was a small gate, and on the four bars were painted these lines :

> " This gate hangs well,
> And hinders none,
> Refresh and pay
> And then pass on."

1828. HAVING given a course of Lectures for twelve successive years, with three exceptions, caused by illness and unavoidable professional engagements, which had been attended not only by students but by several M.A.'s, a grace was proposed in the Senate (May 21st, 1828) to confer upon me the title of Professor of Political Economy. It was opposed by that class of persons who are averse from any thing new. Dr Johnson observes that "there are some men of narrow views and grovelling conceptions, who without the instigation of personal malice, treat every new attempt as wild and chimerical; and look upon every endeavour to depart from the beaten track as the rash effort of a warm imagination, or the glittering speculation of an exalted mind, that may please and dazzle for the time, but can produce no real or lasting advantage. Such have been the most formidable enemies of the great benefactors to mankind; for their notions and discourse are so agreeable to the lazy, the envious, and the timorous, that they seldom fail of becoming popular and directing the opinions of mankind."

The Caput of this year was composed of

Martin Davy, D.D., Caius . . . . . . . . Vice-Chancellor,
John Lamb, D.D., Corpus . . . . . . . . Divinity,
William Frere, D.C.L., Downing . . . . Law,
Fred. Thackeray, M.D., Emman. . . . . Physic,
Thos. Musgrave, M.A., Trin. . . . . . . . Senior non-regent,
Hamnet Holditch, M.A., Caius . . . . . Senior regent;

any one of whom might have rejected the grace, but did not. After passing this ordeal it was offered to the Senate :

"Cum Georgius Pryme, M.A., Collegii S.S. Trinitatis nuper Socius, publicas Lectiones de principiis Œconomiæ Politicæ instituerit, et per multos annos perlegerit : Placeat vobis, ut idem Georgius Pryme titulo Professoris Œconomiæ Politicæ vestris suffragiis cohonestetur."

Placets 18, non-placets 9, in black-hood house[1].

I was not, of course present, but the gratifying news was brought to me immediately by George Peacock, after-wards Dean of Ely. It was like one of his fine acts. I must add that he was soon followed by Musgrave, who became in after years Archbishop of York. I was very intimate with both. I had perhaps done Peacock a little service when he was a young man. I was one of the examiners in his first year at Trinity ; I sent for him afterwards, and

---

[1] "It was at Naples that the first Professorship of Political Economy in Europe was established in 1754, by the munificence of the Fiorentini Intieri."

Mr Nassau Senior was appointed first Professor of Political Economy at Oxford in 1826. It was founded by Mr Drummond of Albury, Surrey, and is only retained for a few years.

Dr Whately founded that at Dublin in 1832.

told him that he ought to try and make his handwriting more easily legible, that I and the other examiners had made it out because our time was not limited, but that it would not be so when he should go up for his degree in the Senate-House, and his papers might be thrown aside as illegible. He thanked me and profited by the hint, as I observed to him in the next year's examination. At the time of his degree Herschel was Senior Wrangler, and he, Peacock, was bracketed with Fallows of St John's. They were of course examined again, and Peacock was second wrangler. The Trinity undergraduates were so pleased that they chaired him round the great court at night; Mansel, hearing the noise, opened his window and enquired the reason of it, on being told he said, "Well, well, I'm very glad to hear it, but make a little less noise." I was in the Court at the time.

[Another College friend, Mr Parke, was congratulated this year on his promotion by my Father, and as they were rivals in academic distinction, it is pleasant to record how friendly were their relations towards each other, in a letter which does honour to both of them.]

"LONDON, *Nov.* 25, 1828.

"MY DEAR PRYME,

"Many thanks to you for your kind congratulations on my promotion: which however I cannot persuade myself to attribute to anything but my good fortune. Though circumstances have disabled you from joining in the race, where I have been a winner, you have had the advantage of being free from its anxieties, and have hitherto enjoyed and I hope will long continue to enjoy, a happy life, uniting with those studies which have almost absorbed my attention, the successful pursuit of other sciences. I think your condition by no means unenviable.

"I have now had my office a week, and feel tolerably comfortable, but have much to learn.

"I doubt whether I shall be able to come to Cambridge soon: but I hope I shall, and shall, of course, see you.

"With my kind remembrances to Mrs Pryme, in which Mrs Parke unites, believe me,

"My dear Pryme,

"Yours very sincerely,

"J. PARKE."

1829. In June of this year a vacancy occurred in the representation of the University by the promotion of Sir Nicholas Tindal to the Chief Justiceship of the Common Pleas. The candidates were Wm. Cavendish, Esq., present Duke of Devonshire, and Mr George Bankes; the former was returned by a majority of 147. He was selected as a candidate on account of his having been recently (1829) second wrangler, a thing unusual for one who was heir presumptive to a peerage. This election was remarkable as returning a whig member for the first time since Lord H. Petty's defeat in 1807, which might be partly attributed to the academical distinction won by Mr Cavendish, and partly to the political re-action which was taking place here as elsewhere. At the general election in the following year he was again returned with Lord Palmerston, who had gradually come to embrace whig principles. Later on, in 1831, at the dissolution upon the question of Parliamentary Re-

---

[1] He succeeded Mr Justice Holroyd in the Court of King's Bench, being previously called to the degree of Sergeant, and giving rings with the motto "*Justitiæ tenax*."

form, both were defeated by a large majority, and replaced by Messrs Goulburn and Yates Peel.

In the autumn of this year Robert Hall, the celebrated Baptist preacher of Leicester, came to Cambridge, where he had formerly ministered. On a previous visit I had requested Mr Ebenezer Foster (Senr.), at whose house he was staying, to introduce me to him. At that time the Test Act had not been repealed. His first words to me were, "Mr Pryme, is this true which I have heard of you, that for some years you held an office which required conformity to the Test Act, and though a member of the Church of England you would not conform?" I answered, "Certainly, I did not comply technically, though substantially, with its provisions." As a fellow of Trinity I was in the habit of receiving the Sacrament, and on my call to the Bar I had taken the oaths at Westminster which the Test Act required, but did not present a certificate of having received it, and thereby subjected myself to a penalty. This was from dissatisfaction, though I was then a Tory, with the intolerant enactments of the Test Act, which extended not merely to the fellowships of colleges, but also to the most trifling offices under government, custom-house officers, &c.

This Act was passed in the 25th Charles II., and was entitled "An Act for preventing dangers which may happen from Popish Recusants." It required any one holding any office, or receiving any pay, salary, or fee, by reason of any patent or grant from his Majesty, or from any of his Majesty's predecessors (which Parke considered to include a fellowship at Trinity College), and residing within thirty miles' distance from Westminster, should receive the Sacrament of the Lord's Supper in some parish-church, and deliver a certificate of it under the hands of the respective minister and churchwarden, and bring two credible witnesses to prove it on oath, under several penalties for neglect or refusal, among which were, being unable to be guardian to any child, or executor or administrator of any person, or to receive any legacy or deed of gift, or to bear any office, and the forfeiture of £500.    Barnewall, afterwards writer with Alderson of *The Reports*, was called on the same day as I was, and said, " I take a different oath."    Charles Butler was the first Roman Catholic called to the Bar under the relaxation of the act.

[Miss Berry, writing in 1810, speaks of 300 Communicants at St James's church, Piccadilly, "accounted for by the number of people obliged to qualify, as it is called, for offices, and commonly doing so at this church[1]."

Lord John Russell brought a Bill into the House of Commons in the Session of 1828 to repeal the Test Act, by which the Sacramental Test was exchanged for a Declaration.   The Duke of Wellington supported it in the House of Lords, where it passed by a majority of 102.   Bishop Blomfield and all his Episcopal brethren were in favour of the repeal of the Test and Corporation Acts, maintaining "these exclusive measures to have been defensible at the time of their enactment, but that they had failed of the object for which they were intended, had become unnecessary in an altered state of things, and tended to bring religion and the Church into discredit by the profanation involved in the use of the Sacramental Test[2]."]

On this latter visit of Mr Hall to Cambridge he said to me, " I rejoice that the Test Act has been repealed, because its enactments pressed grievously on many of my religious friends, but I believe it (the repeal) has been injurious to the dissenting cause, for it has removed a bond of union among different classes of dissenters which the grievance had cemented."

[1] Miss Berry's *Journal*, Vol. II. p. 412.
[2] Bishop Blomfield's *Life* by his Son, Vol. I. p. 137.

The powerful impression left by Mr Hall's preaching was not the result of an uninterrupted eloquence, for at the commencement of his sermons a considerable hesitation was apparent, till, as he gradually became animated with his subject, it disappeared in the resistless flow of his forcible language, aided by his fervid manner[1].

He published a sermon in the year 1800, upon the French Revolution and the atrocities which followed upon it. It was much admired, even by men whose religious principles were most opposed to his; and he was personally complimented on it by the Vice-Chancellor. Like some other men of intellectual eminence, he did not disbelieve in apparitions, and I once heard him distinctly say that he felt confident he had seen one[2].

While on the subject of eminent preachers I may mention two or three others, Churchmen, with whom I had personal acquaintance. Christopher Benson had obtained celebrity at Newcastle-upon-Tyne, and was therefore invited to become one of the select monthly preachers at St Mary's Church, Cambridge. He had been little known while at Trinity College, as bad health and deficient energy consequent thereon, had prevented his distinguishing himself then. His manner was mild, persuasive, and impressive, and he had a way of looking very much to his audience. In one of his sermons he addressed the students, strenuously urging

---

[1] It was a frequent remark of Bishop Blomfield's that the Divine whose style of composition he should most like to have was Robert Hall. In him, he used to say, "there was the force of Johnson without his stiffness, and the richness of Burke without his redundance."

Bishop Blomfield's *Life* by his Son, Vol. II. p. 193.

[2] Izaak Walton relates with every circumstance of truth in his life of Dr John Donne the apparition to him in Paris of his wife who was in England at that time and very ill.

the useful employment of their time while in the University,
and closed the subject by saying, "for myself, I can only
speak the language of regret." As he said so he paused for
a minute, during a dead silence of the congregation, and the
effect upon their minds was, I believe, far more complete
than if he had been known to have obtained academic
distinction. He afterwards became Master of the Temple,
where his excellence as a preacher attracted a congregation
much more numerous than the one naturally belonging to the
Temple Church[1].

Hugh Rose's sermons and manner of preaching resem-
bled Benson's; he had obtained high University honours.
I had the pleasure of his intimate acquaintance, and I recall
some delightful parties at the rooms of Professor Dobree,
which never exceeded the number of eight, where he and other
friends met, and at which he showed his great social and intellectual qualities. But there was a more peculiar charm
in his *tête-à-tête* conversations, which I sometimes enjoyed at
my own house. One monthly course of his sermons, which
he afterwards published, was devoted to an examination of
the German Neology, then first attracting attention, and
was deemed by all who heard him a triumphant refutation
of it. An asthmatic complaint terminated in middle age
his efforts, at a time when the Church apparently most

[1] "The time was when his name was a household word in the
country and in London; when the scholars at the Universities, and
the magnates in the Metropolis, were to be seen in crowds, both at
St Mary's and at the Temple, to hear one of the most impressive and
effective preachers that had been known within the memory of man.
* * * We would remark in passing that he whose memory is forgotten, who flits from us like any other man, was, in 1825, well known
to our Statesmen, and well reputed of in the Church, and though now
passing away in silence, would then have been generally mourned as
a great man falling in our land." *St James's Magazine*, May 1868.

needed them. It is difficult to convey the full effect of his eloquence to those who never heard his sweet deep-toned voice, or saw his tall and dignified figure, his calm yet earnest manner[1].

Dr Mill, on his return from India, where he had been head of the College of Calcutta, answered Strauss in a course of learned and abstruse Sermons, which were therefore not so popular as Rose's. He was a man remarkable for his great simplicity of mind and manners as well as for his great learning; and was on the next vacancy after his arrival in England elected Professor of Hebrew. I had been one of the examiners at the annual examinations of Trinity College in his first year. He was first in his year. One of the subjects was the sixth book of Herodotus, which recounted the expedition of Xerxes King of Persia into Greece. I gave the following among the printed questions, "State what account the native Persian historians give of their wars with Greece." I myself knew not the language, and expected no one to answer it, but thought it desirable to call attention to the subject, which might be found treated of in the Universal Ancient History. Mill gave a complete answer. I asked him if he had at all studied Oriental languages. He answered that he had begun to do so, but that he had got *this* information from the Universal Ancient History.

[Dr Mill was 6th Wrangler in 1813. He turned his Oriental learning to good account. He accompanied Bishop Wilson in one of his Indian journeys, who relates of him that "his knowledge of Sanskrit served him well. The delight of the native priests on hear-

---

[1] Rev. Hugh James Rose, born 1795, died 1839.—First Chancellor's Medallist, 14th Wrangler, Editor of the *British Magazine*, Principal of King's College, London. Christian Advocate at Cambridge in 1829. Domestic Chaplain to Dr Howley, Archbishop of Canterbury.

ing him converse in it was indescribable[1]." He also says, "Dr Mill's Sanskrit work, called the *Christa Sangita*, is an epic poem in Sanskrit verse, containing the History of Christianity, and the evidences on which it rests. It is a wonderful proof of genius and learning, and a most valuable gift and legacy to India. So much were these learned Brahmins struck with the poem, as the pundit read it, that they continually asked for more and more; and it was not till day dawned, and the camp began to move, that they released him[2]." Dr Mill had attended Daily Service all his life. First at Trinity College Chapel, then at the College in India, again during his residence at Cambridge in his own parish Church, afterwards at his living of Brasted, Kent, and lastly during his canonical residence at Ely. There he lies buried, and a recumbent statue with folded hands, placed in it by his friends, gives some idea of one who had the most saintly countenance I ever beheld.]

While on the subject of Sermons I may mention some curious texts which were, and were not, preached upon. When a new Master of Trinity is chosen, the custom is to close the gates at the time when he arrives to take possession. He knocks, and is admitted. Dr Bentley of St John's was so unpopular with the Fellows of Trinity that when promoted to be their Head the gates were kept shut against him. The tradition is that he got into the Lodge by means of a wall which divided its garden from St John's, and that he preached his first sermon from the text, "With the help of my God I shall leap over the wall[3]." But the fact is that he merely replied to a friend's congratulation in the words of the Psalmist.

It was said jocularly on Mr Hailstone's succeeding Mr Raine, head master of the Charter House School, as vicar of Trumpington, he ought to preach on, "He gave them hailstones for rain."

[1] Bateman's *Life of Dr Wilson*, Vol. I. p. 413.
[2] Ibid, Vol. II. p. 121.
[3] 18th Psalm, 29th verse.

Mr Pitt became Premier in his 24th year; he usually when he came down to Cambridge had a Deanery or some preferment in his pocket. Paley the philosopher remarked on one of these occasions, "If I were to preach before him I think I should select for my text, 'There is a lad here which hath five barley loaves and two small fishes, but what are they among so many?'" A story grows by going, and it has been said that he *did* so. Sterne was fond of choosing singular texts. I have heard that he once preached on "Is there any taste in the white of an egg[1]?"

Robertson, the historian, wrote a Sermon on the appropriate and prepared locality of Palestine for our Lord's coming, and showed that had he come to the Greeks or Heathens they could not have received him, as did the Jews, who had been taught to expect a Messiah. This was the only Sermon that he ever published.

[The title of this sermon is, "The situation of the World at the time of Christ's appearance, and its connection with the success of his Religion considered." Edinburgh, 1818. It was preached in the year 1755, before the Society for Promoting Christian Knowledge. Mr Dugald Stewart, writing in 1801, says of it, "This Sermon, the only one he ever published, has long been ranked, in both parts of the Island, among the best models of pulpit eloquence in our language. It has undergone five editions; and is well known in some parts of the Continent in the German translation of Mr Ebeling."]

[1] 6th Chapter of Job, 6th verse.

# CHAPTER XI.

## 1830—1832.

1830.　ON June 26 George IV. died, and was succeeded by the Duke of Clarence as William the Fourth. He kept for a while the existing Ministry under the Duke of Wellington. A dissolution of course took place (July 24th) and in most of the Counties and open Boroughs members in some degree favourable to Parliamentary Reform were returned. There was an Autumn Session, and on the 15th Nov. Ministers were left in a minority on a question connected with the Civil List, and immediately resigned. Well do I remember dining at the annual Philosophical dinner at Cambridge on the 16th Nov., and Peacock coming in and saying to me, "Ministers have resigned, and now we shall have the whigs in." The King sent for Earl Grey, who was considered the leader of the whig party, to form an Administration, and he undertook to do so, but only on the principles of "Peace, Reform, and Retrenchment." Lord Palmerston became Foreign Secretary. This of course vacated his seat. When he came down to Cambridge for re-election he called upon me to ask me to join his committee, and we had a long conversation.

I expressed to him some surprise at the late Ministry going out on so slight a question. He said it was believed in the House that they would be in a minority on Parliamentary Reform, which might afford a prestige to that measure, and they therefore preferred to be in a minority on a question of less importance, and made no effort to secure the attendance of their usual supporters. Lord Palmerston had gradually adopted whig principles, and it has been said that he was more years in office under various Administrations than political consistency allowed. It is true that he passed most of his life in some office of Administration, and on that account his political change was concluded by persons of hasty judgment to have been the result of interested motives. I have through life carefully watched his conduct, and am convinced that it was quite the reverse. His first avowed change was in favour of Roman Catholic Emancipation, which lost him, as might have been expected, the representation of the University at the next election. His next avowed change was while he was a member of the Duke of Wellington's administration, when he gave an anti-ministerial vote in the House of Commons on the disfranchisement of the Borough of Grampound, and sent in his resignation the next morning.

I think I may say that there was a general desire for Reform throughout the country. A slight measure had already

12

been attempted by Mr Hobhouse. An unexpected payment from Austria of a debt incurred on a subsidy during the last war with France somewhat perplexed the Parliament as to the mode of its disposal. A small portion of the money was applied to the improvement of Carlton House with its garden, the palace of George IV. Mr Hobhouse proposed to purchase close Boroughs, which were frequently sold, vest the funds in the hands of trustees, and transfer the franchise to some of the great unrepresented towns; but the proposal for the appropriation of the rest was rejected with somewhat of derision. Had it been carried out many of the great towns might have petitioned in favour of further reform, but most probably would not have joined in that vehement agitation which carried so abrupt and extensive a change as the measure of 1832.

[Mr Hobhouse's plan was not new. In 1785, Mr Pitt, being Prime Minister, made a third and last attempt to amend the representation. His plan was to purchase from thirty-six boroughs of small population their right of sending members, and to transfer the seats thus acquired to counties or populous places. It was rejected by 248 to 174. The really radical reformers were, after all, the old tories, who unfortunately resisted *all* change, even when rendered necessary by the progress of time, proposed by such a Minister as Mr Pitt, and supported by such a citizen as Mr Wilberforce.]

Great corruption having been proved in the Borough of Grampound, it was proposed to disfranchise it, and transfer its members to Leeds. This plan was successfully opposed by Lord Liverpool's Government, and instead of that, two members were added to the two alone representing Yorkshire up to 1826. This was like putting a dam across a river to make it flow back; the only consequence of which would be that the accumulation of waters would at length burst the barrier and deluge the country around. Spring Rice told me that it was said on *that* occasion among a few of his friends, "Reform is *now* carried."

[Lord Palmerston, speaking 20 years later, describes as revolutionists, "men who, animated by antiquated prejudices, dam up the current of human improvement until the irresistible operation of accumulated discontent breaks down the opposing barriers and overturns and levels to the earth those very institutions which the timely application of renovating means would render strong and wholesome [1]."]

I have seen an advertisement, before Grampound was disfranchised, offering a Borough for sale (Westbury), as not only to be sold, but to be sold by order of the Court of Chancery. A short time before the Reform Bill Lord Monson paid £100,000 for Gatton, which contained about twenty-five houses, and rather more than one hundred inhabitants.

Mr Aubrey, fellow-commoner of Trinity College, and nephew of Sir J. Aubrey, told me that his uncle, whose heir he was, thought that he could not spend £1000 a year more pleasantly than in buying a borough and sitting in Parliament. He sat for Aldborough in Yorkshire, by arrangement with its proprietor, Mr De Crespigny, and on the understanding that he was to vote as he pleased [2]. He did not pay £1000 annually for the privilege, but calculated that it cost him that. £5000 was the sum usually paid for a seat.

Previously to the Reform Bill of 1832 pecuniary influence had operated upon the electors of many boroughs to

[1] Lord Palmerston's Speech on Mr Roebuck's Motion on Foreign Policy June 25, 1850.

[2] Sir John Aubrey, Bart., M.P. for Wallingford 1768. Lord of the Treasury 1783. Lord of the Admiralty 1802.

an extent scarcely now to be imagined[1]. At Hull and
Beverley, and probably at many other places, it was customary after the election to give four guineas for a single
vote or two for a divided one. At Hedon, a small Borough
and sea-port on the Humber, now disfranchised, it was
usual to give twenty guineas for a single vote, and ten for
a divided one. Before an election there was no actual promise made, but the voter would say on being canvassed,
"You will do what is usual after the election, Sir, I suppose,"
and the candidate would reply in the affirmative. Many
of the *poor* electors did not wait for an election but borrowed of the member sums of money, for which they gave
a promissory note. When an election came ten or twenty
guineas was receipted upon the note, the residue of which
still gave the candidate a hold upon the elector for a future
occasion. This was told to me by Mr Chaytor, of Spenni-
thorne, in Wensleydale, who long represented the Borough.

To show the extent to which corruption prevailed, I may
mention that when the Reform Bill was spoken of to some
electors in Stafford, they expressed their pleasure at it, and
hoped that there would be introduced into it some plan for
the better payment of poor voters! St Alban's was on the
Great North Road, which gave the town prosperity by its
posting; and it was said of its inhabitants, when the great
Inn was given up, that they remarked, "We have nothing
now left to sell but our votes."

1831. On Jan. 31st a Town-meeting was held at Cambridge, to petition for Parliamentary Reform, at which I
attended and took an active part. The new cabinet arranged a plan of parliamentary reform, and to Lord J.

---

[1] This was written some few years before the late Bribery Commissions were thought of.

Russell, though not then a Cabinet minister, its introduction was committed (on March 1st), because he had been chairman of the election committee which had occasioned the disfranchisement of the little corrupt borough of Grampound.

The Measure now proposed took every one by surprise by its extent and thoroughness. It is true that what would have contented the reformers of a preceding generation would not have satisfied them in this, yet even the radicals had formed no notion of the sweeping clauses which would be introduced. Many people objected to it as going too far, and so did I; but I thought it a choice between that and revolution.

This Bill was not to affect Ireland. I remember the Irish Parliament, and the sensation caused by the Union in 1801, which may be said to have been a commencement of Parliamentary Reform. It had been composed of 300 Members. Some Boroughs were disfranchised, some that had previously sent two were reduced to one member. In this way the members were compressed into one hundred, and those who were excluded received compensation in money. Twenty-eight representative Peers were elected for life by the others.

The Scottish Parliament came to an end in Queen Anne's reign, and members were elected ever after to serve in the English Parliament. On the old system (that is since the union) the voting was confined to the Corporations. Forty-five places sent members, and there was this anomaly in counties, that no one could vote who did not hold lands from the Crown, so that a man might have had thousands a year in landed property, and have no voice in the representation. The Boroughs were arranged in classes of four or five, each of which elected a delegate, and these met and elected the member. Much of this was now to be altered; borough members were no longer to be elected by town-councillors or delegates, but by £10 householders, and the qualification for voting in counties was to consist in owner-ship of land or houses worth £10 a year with residence, or holding as tenant in actual possession. Several Counties were to be joined together, and the rest (22) to return one member each.

The second reading of the Reform Bill passed on the 22nd of March by a majority of one. General Gascoyne, M.P. for Liverpool, moved, on April 18, an Amendment adverse to the proposed reduction of the numbers (upwards of 90), and on a division put Ministers in a minority of eight. This occasioned a ·dissolution of Parliament on the 22nd of April. There was now a general cry throughout the country of " The Bill, the whole Bill, and nothing but the Bill." Such was the feeling that only seven County members were returned who were adverse to Reform, and General Gascoyne was rejected by his constituents.

[I have heard my Father relate an amusing anecdote in refer-ence to this. A friend of his, a barrister, was dining alone at a country inn. The waiter, an intelligent man, was so interested in politics that while attending to the guest he could not refrain from discussing the events of the time. " And," said he by way of climax, " what I say, Sir, is the bill, the whole bill, and nothing but the bill." When the reckoning was brought the visitor paid it, but gave nothing to the waiter. He demurred to this, and was met by the answer, " Why you yourself told me you was in favour of the bill, the whole bill, and nothing but the bill." The "village politician," however, was not unwilling to accept an amendment to his bill.

Mr Sykes in one of his letters, wrote, " It is quite gratifying to me, an old reformer, to hear no other cry but 'reform, reform' from London to Barton."

But while rejoicing over this success he was not hastening his own election. Though he had received invitations from various parts of the West Riding to stand for the County, he declined, saying, " There is a time for all things, and the time is come when I ought to retire."

My father now received a requisition to stand for Huntingdon, which he thought proper to decline, and thence this letter in answer to one he wrote to an old college friend, and which he has given me permission to insert.]

*Wednesday, May* 4, 1831.

" MY DEAR PRYME,

" I cannot pass through Cambridge without endeavouring to see you—but as I am unsuccessful—I beg in this way to express my thanks for your note. I am glad (with you) that we were not opposed to each other—but with you I feel that the present occasion is one where great duties may interfere with private sentiments. I shall be most happy to see you in town. I am going there in haste, and remain,

" Sincerely yours,

" FRED. POLLOCK."

In the new Parliament, which met June 21, a Bill with some alterations, but leaving the numbers of the House as they were, was again introduced, and with a few changes passed the Commons by a large majority (109) in September. But it was known that a majority of the House of Lords was still adverse to it, and accordingly it was rejected by them on Oct. 8th by a majority of 41. Parliament was prorogued on the 20th, to re-assemble on the 6th of Dec. A fresh Bill was brought forward in the Commons, and passed on March 23rd. But there was still the opposition in the Upper House to be overcome. Lord Grey proposed to the King to create a number of new Peers, which he was unwilling to do.

The second reading passed by only nine, a majority insufficient to secure success in the third reading. This, with the result of Lord Lyndhurst's hostile motion on May 7, caused Lord Grey to tender his resignation. The King tried to form another Administration, but such was the state of agitation throughout the country that no statesman would attempt it. As a proof of the excitement, many persons informed the tax-gatherer that they declined payment, and one of the great whig noblemen stated in his place in Parliament that he had done the same. Lord Grey was of course recalled by the King, who instructed his private secretary to intimate to several of the Peers the expediency of their absenting themselves from the House of Lords. They did so, the Bill passed, with some amendments to which the House of Commons agreed, on June 4th, 106 Peers voting for it and 22 against it, and the Royal Assent was given by commission on the 7th.

Besides the vast changes comprehended in the transference of representative power from small and close Boroughs to the large centres of industry, as Manchester, Birmingham, Leeds, Sheffield, &c., the Act of Parliamentary Reform altered the whole system within the towns which retained the franchise, and gave it to every occupier of a ten-pound house, continuing it to the freemen of the Corporation who resided within seven miles of the town-hall. This last was an addition of the Lords, to which the Commons assented.

Among the benefits conferred by the Reform Bill was the shortening the duration of elections. The time for keeping the poll open in Boroughs was unlimited. I remember Lord Milton's contest with Lascelles in 1807. The polling lasted 15 days. Lord M. was in a minority for some days (Wilberforce heading the poll), but then he gradually gained, and at 3 o'clock on the 15th day was elected by a majority of 188.

Above 23,000 persons voted. Lord Fitzwilliam's steward informed me that that election cost upwards of £90,000. Wilberforce's expences were subscribed for and were above £40,000. There were but two members for Yorkshire then, and York was the only polling place. Some voters had to go 90 miles. To those who could not afford the journey *mileage* was given[1].

In June 1832, a general meeting of the electors of the Borough of Cambridge was called, at which a requisition was adopted and signed, inviting me to become a candidate for the representation. I accepted the proposed honour and issued the following Address.

"TO THE ELECTORS OF THE TOWN OF CAMBRIDGE.

"GENTLEMEN,

"The return of any real Representatives of the Town of CAMBRIDGE will soon, for the first time, take place. But the Enfranchisement which has just been accomplished does not so much confer benefits on the nation as give it the means of obtaining them. The work is yet to be done. It remains with the next Parliament to plan, to discuss, and to adopt such temperate measures as may gradually remedy our present evils. It remains for the Electors to send to the House of Commons men who may execute this task carefully, impartially, and honestly.

"I have been called forth by a Requisition numerously signed by my fellow-townsmen, to assist in this difficult

---

[1] The contest for the Westminster Election (1784) lasted 40 days and ended in a majority of 235 in favour of Mr Fox. A scrutiny was demanded by Sir Cecil Wray and lasted through part of two sessions till it was quashed and Mr Fox declared to be elected.

task, and I obey that call, unconnected with any other candidate. Whether I possess the qualities requisite for this purpose or not you have had full opportunities of observing during the twenty years which I have passed among you. The course, which I should pursue in Parliament, if honoured by your choice, may be judged of by that, which I have hitherto taken in public affairs, better than by any declaration which I now could make. But my sentiments about West India Slavery may not be so well known, though I expressed them some time since at a Town Meeting holden for that purpose. I have ever been anxious for measures to improve the condition of the Slave, with a view to the early and complete abolition of Slavery. I regret that my duties at Ely, as a Member of the Bedford Level Board, must prevent my waiting immediately upon each of the Electors, but I shall take the earliest opportunity of doing so.

> "I am, Gentlemen,
>
> "Your obedient, faithful servant,
>
> "GEORGE PRYME."

"*Cambridge*, 11th *June*, 1832."


Some doubt was entertained as to who should be the other Whig candidate. Mr Edward Ellice, one of the secretaries to the Treasury, was applied to. He declined, saying that he felt secure of his re-election at Coventry, but that his colleague at the Treasury, Mr Spring Rice, would be willing to exchange his seat at Limerick for one at Cambridge, as he was uncomfortably situated at the former place on account of the agitation for the Repeal of the Union. This selection was very agreeable to me.

Mr Spring Rice had been a fellow-commoner of Trinity College while I was a resident fellow, and we had had much social intercourse. When he first came down to Cambridge on this invitation, he had, previously to accepting it, asked me in the kindest terms whether his being a candidate would interfere with my probable success, and said that if I thought it would do so, he should immediately retire. And during the seven years of our parliamentary connection I ever experienced from him the greatest courtesy and kindness[1]. Our opponent in the tory interest was to be Sir Edward Burtenshaw Sugden, now Lord St Leonards. One day we accidentally met, when he said to me, "Suppose we forget our electioneering, and that you let me drink tea with you and talk over old times?" To this I gladly acceded, and I asked him in our evening's *tête-à-tête* if he remembered my suggestion about his practice as a conveyancer? He answered that he had often thought of it, and of the change in his career which he had then so little anticipated.

I was sometimes asked during my canvass to pledge myself to a particular question. I positively refused to do so, and answered that my promise would render a debate useless, but that I would tell them what was my present opinion[2]. I and many of my constituents endeavoured to conduct the Election on principles of perfect purity. Four solicitors offered their gratuitous services on my committee. After the election a tradesman who had acted as a check-clerk called on me to inform me that payment had been offered to him for his services which he had refused with indignation, and he said that many like himself would willingly have acted

---

[1] Mr Thomas Spring Rice, afterwards Baron Monteagle.

[2] Dr Johnson says that "a true Patriot is no lavish promiser; he undertakes not to shorten Parliaments; to repeal Laws; or to change the mode of representation transmitted by our Ancestors. He knows that futurity is not in his power, and that all times are not alike favourable to change."

gratuitously if the opportunity had been given them. My whole expenses were under £400.

At my two subsequent contests there was a subscription towards the expenses of myself and my colleague, the amount and application of which I never knew, and to which each of us contributed.

The dissolution which was to give effect to the Reform Bill took place in December. The two late members, the Marquis of Graham and Lieut.-Colonel Trench, retired from the representation of Cambridge, and the latter was returned, under the altered state of things, for Scarborough, where his friend the Duke of Rutland had much political influence.

The election took place December 13th, and the numbers were,

> Pryme.........979
> Rice...........799
> Sugden .......540

[The Chairing took place the next day, and it may be worth describing as the first variation in Cambridge from the literal *carrying* out of the term. I can remember, when a child, seeing from a window Lord Francis Godolphin Osborne[1] and Mr Adeane borne down St Andrew's Street, sitting on wooden chairs, which were fastened to poles and supported on men's shoulders. The chairs were covered with bows of orange, and green and white satin ribbon —the colours of the two members. Every now and then, when the populace pleased, the procession stopped, and the chairs were tossed up as high as the bearers could reach, amid loud huzzas. I recollect the look of discomfort at such times on Lord F. Osborne's face, as he sat in his peculiar, stiff, stately manner, dressed in a green coat and top boots.

On *this* occasion the two members were seated in a handsome car covered with blue silk, and adorned with rosettes of crimson and blue and buff, their respective colours. It was drawn by six grey

---

[1] Afterwards Duke of Leeds.

horses, ridden by postilions dressed in blue silk jackets and caps. This cortége, headed by a marshal and three trumpeters on horse-back, and followed by a band of music and a numerous cavalcade of horsemen, had a most imposing effect, and paraded the town (Barn-well included) for many hours. Mr Spring Rice, with that perfect courtesy which marked all his actions, insisted on my father's taking the place of honour, and handed to him first the silver goblets of copas and mulled wine which, as they passed by some of the col-leges, were generously brought out to refresh the members, who sat, bareheaded, through a long winter's day to receive the congratula-tions of the delighted people. I doubt if such a thing occurred again, and certainly there is no ceremony now.

As may be supposed, my Father was intensely gratified by the position of trust and honour in which he was placed by his fellow-townsmen, and he looked forward with pleasure to a future sphere of usefulness and mental activity in the House of Commons. But there is always something to remind us that these earthly triumphs are incomplete. He felt it keenly that the friend with whom he was accustomed to "take sweet counsel," and who would have rejoiced in his rejoicing, was gone, "and never must return[1]."]

[1] Mr Sykes of Raywell died in January of this year.

CHAPTER XII.

1833.

1833. THE Reformed Parliament met on the 5th of
February. Our first business was the election
of Speaker, Joseph Hume having proposed Mr Lyttelton
in opposition to Mr Manners Sutton, who had occupied that
position during many years. The ministers, though ap-
proving personally of Mr L. and differing from Mr M. S.
politically, yet supported *him*, thinking that his experience,
combined with that courtesy and tact for which he was
remarkable, would be better able to regulate the probable
turbulence of an assembly containing so many new members.

I found in the house several of my old college acquaintances—Messrs Rolfe, Ralph Bernal, Hon. George Lamb,
Henry Warburton, Sir Fred. Pollock and Mr Stuart Mack-

enzie. I did not remember this latter when he said, "Won't you recognise an old college acquaintance?" till he told me his name. Among those who kindly welcomed me was the Chancellor of the Exchequer (Lord Althorp). He came down from his place, and said, "Mr Pryme, you and I have met before at Trinity." Shortly after he asked me to dinner. I soon made many more acquaintances, the usage being that no personal introduction is requisite between members *in* the house.

Petitions were in this first session very numerous, as if every grievance could at once be remedied, and every reform or improvement immediately effected. It was at first almost impossible to transact business, as five or six members would start up to speak on almost every petition. At that time any member might speak to a petition, but it was soon found in a reformed parliament, that the mass of them was so great that the custom interfered with business, and therefore a standing order was made, that no one should speak to a petition except the person who presented it, and that he should merely describe from whence it came and its purport[1].

For myself, I made it an inflexible rule never to give the slightest interruption to a speaker, never to assist in counting out the house, and never when present at a debate to abstain from voting, or, as I termed it, pair off with myself, merely because there seemed to be reason on both sides of the question. I remember once on an important motion, respecting the affairs of Greenwich, feeling uncertain how to vote, being unacquainted with the place. I consulted

---

[1] The late Sir Robert Heron, M.P., complains in his "notes" that "there are men who waste time day after day till 8, 9, or even 10 o'clock P.M. in foolish speeches on petitions, often without any general importance." This was in the Session of 1836.

a Tory admiral (Lord Hardwicke) and a Whig one. They both took the same view, and I therefore voted in accordance with it, and was surprised to receive from the Mayor and Corporation of that town a vote of thanks for my conduct in supporting the bill.

I attended constantly in my place, securing it after prayers, and carefully observed the various traits of character in leading men on minor as well as on great occasions. The Ministers introduced only two measures of importance, one of which was for the abolition of West Indian slavery. Before its introduction I attended a meeting (such as is usual on great occasions) of members favourable to the Government, which was convened by a private circular, to be held in the great room in the Foreign Office; Mr Stanley, late Lord Derby, and then a Cabinet minister, propounded the heads of the measure. Several observations were made and alterations suggested, some of which he adopted when he afterwards brought forward the Bill, which with various emendations passed into law. The planters were to receive as compensation twenty millions sterling.

The other Measure, called the Irish Temporalities Bill, passed at the close of the Session. It abolished several Irish Bishoprics, imposed a per-centage tax upon the larger benefices, took the whole revenue from those livings where no Protestants resided, and provided for the building and repairs of churches and glebe-houses, by abolishing the church cess, which had been a great grievance both to the Roman Catholic and Presbyterian portion of the population; but previously to this measure the Irish Coercion Bill was introduced in restraint of the turbulence of meetings which had been frequent in Ireland, notwithstanding Roman Catholic Emancipation. I first heard Lord Macaulay, then M.P. for Leeds, speak on this question, which seemed to tax his ingenuity in vindicating it[1]. One of his arguments was that the very severity of some of its enactments made it the less likely to be drawn into a precedent. I had met him a few days before at Lord Althorp's (Feb. 23). He was personally known but to few of the company, and a murmur of "Who is he?" ran round among the rest, who were struck by the powers of his conversation.

Macaulay held the office of Secretary to the Board of Commissioners for the affairs of India, not having a seat in the Cabinet, and spoke frequently in support of Ministerial measures. His eloquence had the fluency and clearness of Burke without his exceeding diffuseness. His judgment was rapid, I would not call it hasty, though his quickness in grasping at results might sometimes make it appear so. The following is an instance: in a speech (made some years after the time I am speaking of) in opposition to Serjeant Talfourd's Copyright Bill, which nearly tended to perpetuate copyright in the family of an author, he urged that the fancies of his descendants might induce them to suppress works of general estimation, and he instanced as a *fact*, that the grandson of Richardson (the novelist) would not suffer his novels to be read in his family. In the year 1851, while I was travelling on the Continent, I was mentioning this argument in conversation, when a gentleman, Rev. Mr Temple, who overheard me, apologised for interfering, but wished to state that he was the son of that grandson, and that his father had excluded *only Clarissa Harlowe*, the details of which he thought, and so must every careful father think, unfit for his daughters to read.

---

[1] "Sixty murders, or attempts at murder, and not less than 600 burglaries, or attempts at burglaries committed in one County alone, and in comparatively a few weeks! Why this was far worse than Civil war – a loss of life and property equal to the sacking of three or four Towns."

Macaulay accepted a judicial office in India, partly with
a view of improving the administration of justice, in which
to a certain extent he succeeded. On his return he began
to write his *History of England.* I am possessed of an
exceedingly rare volume, *The Memoirs of Captain Peter
Drake*, Dublin, 1755, which had been suppressed, and was
so scarce that Thorp, the noted bookseller of Bedford Street,
Covent Garden, who dealt chiefly in old books, had never
heard but of one other copy. It contains an account of
many strange and surprising incidents which happened to
him through a period of sixty years and upwards, many
of them connected with King William's and Queen Anne's
wars with Louis XIV. of France[1]. I offered Macaulay the
perusal of it upon condition that he *personally* returned it
into my own hands.

He called on me in London with it on the third day
afterwards. I asked, as he returned it so early, if he had
not found it worthy of his attention? He told me that
he had read through it, and extracted all that he thought
might be useful to him for his history.

[My Father had at one time designed writing a History of England himself in continuation of Smollett, who he said was "a very
good annalist, but very little of a philosophic historian." For this
purpose he had made a valuable collection of pamphlets and tracts;
but, business of all kinds pressing on him, he gave up his intention.
He told me that he offered the use of them to another writer who
was engaged on an English history, but he declined borrowing them,
as he was writing for his booksellers and against time. Macaulay

---

[1] This person, my Father told me, is supposed to be the original of
Captain Dalgetty in the *Legend of Montrose.* The name gave rise to a
pleasant *mot* by Baron Alderson which should not be forgotten. He and
Lord Campbell were differing at a dinner party about its pronunciation;
the latter saying Dālgetty. It was settled by Baron Alderson remarking,
"I thought that you Scotsmen always laid the emphasis on *get*."

lost no opportunity of increasing his stores. A friend of mine told me, at the time it happened, that M. met a boy in St Giles' singing, and with a collection of ballads, all of which he bought for a shilling. Turning round after a time he saw the boy following him, and asking him why he did so, was answered, "I wanted to hear how you would sing them."]

"ALBANY, LONDON,
*Nov.* 4, 1848.

"MY DEAR SIR,

"I am much obliged to you for your kind suggestion, of which I will hereafter avail myself. The two volumes which I am now about to publish must, I am afraid, stand as they are.

"I hope and believe that few important pamphlets relating to the times of which I have hitherto treated have escaped me. I have rummaged the British Museum, and the Pepysian Library, and have during some years carefully examined the catalogues of those booksellers who deal in such works. The greater part however of my materials has never yet been printed.

"I occasionally see Mr Hartwell Horne. I will speak to him about the Queens' College Collection.

"Believe me,

"My dear Sir,

"Yours very faithfully,

"T. B. MACAULAY."

Lord Palmerston also invited me two or three times to dine with him at his house in Hertford Street. I fancy it must have been owing to College recollections. At these parties the guests were expected to go punctually at the hour named, and there was a pleasant talk on rather higher subjects than mere dinner conversation for twenty minutes or half-an-hour before dinner was announced.

[Speaking of Lord Palmerston at another time, my Father said,]

His capacity of mental labour was great: one night after a very late division we were walking up Parliament Street together, when just opposite Downing Street he said to me. "I must leave you here, for I have a dispatch to revise at the Foreign Office." I expressed some surprise at his continuing his labours so far into the night, and he replied that he frequently did so.

One of the measures much petitioned for and really required was Municipal Reform. The Ministers thought it too difficult and important a thing to be undertaken without careful enquiry, and proposed a select Committee to investigate the subject by examination of witnesses, &c. Of this Committee I had the honour to be nominated a member. We selected for our examination Boroughs of wholly distinct characters. While we were still sitting it was found difficult to make our enquiries sufficiently extensive, and that it would be desirable to send Commissioners to enquire on the spot into the state of every Corporation, so that it was not till two years afterwards that the present Act was passed.

The first speech which I made in Parliament was on occasion of a petition being presented (Feb. 14th) by a member in favour of some men who were imprisoned for selling works written against the Christian religion. I said that I rose as a member of two missionary societies to protest against our legally prosecuting such men; that they were only doing in *their* way what we were doing in *our* way in heathen countries, and that the Christian religion had in itself its own defence, and did not require to be supported by force. This speech was much cheered from all parts of the House, and a Roman Catholic member came up to me and thanked me.

Dr Watson, Bishop of Llandaff, wrote in answer to Tom Paine's *Age of Reason* the *Apology for the Bible*. Scholars are aware that *apology* means in this sense vindication. George III. said of it, "Apology for the Bible! I didn't know that it needed one." I think that the Bishop mistook the true line of defence, for he quoted from the Bible, in which Tom Paine did not believe, to verify the truths which he had assailed[1]. I began to write an answer myself, taking another mode. Paine disbelieved the Pentateuch, saying that it professed to be written by Moses, and yet contained an account of his death, which he could not have described himself. I would have quoted from a Greek book, the name of which I now forget, a similar relation, where the death is, as in the Pentateuch, added by another. Again, to T. P.'s objection that Moses always speaks in the third person, I should have urged that Xenophon in his *Anabasis* speaks likewise of himself as "Xenophon." Cæsar does the same in his *Commentaries*. But before I could finish the little pamphlet, Hone and others were tried and imprisoned, and there was an end of the matter.

A great change for the better gradually took place in the mode of arranging Committees on local bills. Formerly Members went in and out of any Committee, and sat and voted or not as they liked. I remember being for a short time on a Brighton railway committee, and leaving it to attend a Cambridge one, which I was bound to do as its representative. One day whilst sitting on this latter, I received a pencilled note from a great London merchant, saying, "We are just going to a division, come and vote." I

[1] Mr Charles Knight says in his *Passages of a Working Life*, "I fear that I acquired a sceptical humour from such defences of the faith as Watson's *Apology for the Bible*, and Lyttelton's *Conversion of St Paul*. They attempted to prove too much to satisfy my reason, which they addressed exclusively."

wrote back, "Not having heard the evidence I should not know how to vote." The old feeling of favouritism was not quite extinct. Since the Reform Bill a Committee of selection has been appointed which regulates the others.

I said to Sir R. Inglis, M.P. for Oxford, who was Chairman of it in my time, "If you think of putting me on any Committee, I wish you would choose one where a knowledge of Civil engineering or mathematics would be useful." He answered that he should be very glad to do so as those were subjects that members generally avoided. I was accordingly placed on one about the navigation of the Severn[1]. It so happened that a question of pure mathematics arose. Godson, M.P. for Kidderminster, (a Wrangler) of Caius College, Cambridge, and a Scotch member who was a good mathematician were, as well as myself, requested to discuss it, and the Committee agreed to abide by our decision, so impartial were they.

Lord Ashley, now Lord Shaftesbury, introduced his Bill for regulating the hours of employment in factories, and when the details of the Bill were to be considered, moved that I should take the Chair in the Committee of the whole House. The discussion occupied some hours, and a division took place on one point. It passed into law, and was perhaps hardly less important in its humanity than the abolition of slavery. It forbad children under nine years old being employed at all, and provided that no child should work more than nine hours a day. It has been sometimes termed "the nine hours Bill." After this, during my stay in the House, I was

---

[1] The Severn Navigation Improvement Association passed a special resolution expressing "the deep obligation they are under to George Pryme, Esq. for his unremitted attendance in the Committee on the Bill." Mr James, M.P. for Carlisle, told me that my Father was esteemed in the House to be the best Chairman of Committees.

frequently placed in the same position on Bills introduced by private members; and on one occasion I gave the casting vote. On a clause of the Highway Act, prohibiting the ploughing up of any footpath which ran across a cultivated field, it was moved to omit it. On a division the votes were equal. I, as Chairman of the Committee, had to give the casting vote, and I gave it *against* the clause, stating my reasons, as is usual. They were, that as such footpaths often run diagonally across a field, if left untouched by the plough, every ridge and furrow (*land* is the technical term) must have been interrupted, and a space left waste and divided unequally, whereas if ploughed, the track would soon be restored by persons passing along it. This will be apparent to every practical agriculturist. For those Bills which were proposed by Government there was a regular Chairman of ways and means, with an annual vote of £1200 per annum. Mr Bernal, M.P. for Rochester, held that position in our first Parliament, and for many succeeding ones.

One day Lord John Russell called me aside and told me that he had been requested to introduce a Bill to enable a new religious sect, called Separatists, *to affirm*, as the Quakers might, instead of taking an oath; he said that his position and official duties prevented his doing so, and as he knew that I was a friend to Religious Liberty he asked me to undertake it, and said that he would give me what assistance he could. I assented, and he added, "I'll send the deputation to you." They stated to me many practical grievances, one of which was that a member of their persuasion was then in prison for a contempt of the Court of Chancery, because he could not, according to his tenets, put in his answer upon oath. I introduced a Bill to relieve them, and after a deal of tedious and vexatious opposition succeeded in getting it passed to the Lords. One of its opponents in the

House of Commons was my esteemed friend, Mr Goulburn, who afterwards shewed his great financial judgment as Chancellor of the Exchequer. He objected to granting a privilege to so small a sect to save them from the consequences of their own perverseness. I answered that the advantage was not merely to the witness, and asked if my Right Hon. friend was a party in a cause which could only be established by the evidence of a Separatist, which of them would suffer the greatest grievance by the exclusion of the testimony? to which answer the house showed its approbation. It met with very little opposition in the Upper House, where it was expected to be thrown out, and became the law of the land. I was present in the Lords as a spectator at its introduction there. The Duke of Wellington immediately rose and spoke in its favour, which probably occasioned its success. After all my pains I received no thanks from any of these Separatists, except a most fervent letter from a surgeon in Ireland[1].

The Duke's manner was dignified and stately, and his speeches concise and clear. He was a very independent man, and the value of this was felt when a late nobleman, having had a dispute with the Lord Chancellor respecting the appointment of some magistrates who were dissenters, wrote some angry letters, and in consequence was informed that the King had no further occasion for his services as Lord Lieutenant. He intended bringing the matter before the House of Lords, but refrained from doing so when it was intimated to him that if he did, the Duke of Wellington would support the Lord Chancellor. It was curious that the first time I heard Lord Grey speak, he mentioned

---

[1] On some other occasion the Wesleyans sent my Father their thanks for Parliamentary services he had rendered them accompanied by a Life of Wesley, with a special inscription to him engraved on the cover.

me by name as supporting the removal of some disabilities under which the Jews were at that time labouring.

In April of this year, Mr Grote, M.P. for London, commenced his annual motions for election by Ballot. The Ballot was first proposed in 1795 by Major Cartwright; he was a retired officer on half-pay, and I sometimes met him when I dined out as a boy with my uncle in Nottinghamshire. He seemed to my childish views a man of considerable ability, but I have since thought that his ideas were chimerical. I thrice voted against the Ballot, but being gradually convinced by the speeches of two or three members of its affording some remedy against bribery and intimidation, I with ten other members, also formerly adverse, voted three times for it. But since I have talked with those likely to know how it would work, and reconsidered it, I am again opposed to it. I had thought *then* only of its effect in Protestant Great Britain, but I have been told by a Roman Catholic gentleman possessing large estates in Ireland, that he believed that if the Ballot were introduced into that country, the priests, who have immense influence over the people, would use it to return members.

In regard to Counties I think it would be of little avail; the landlord would still ask the tenant the questions if he would vote, and if he had voted for so and so? In Boroughs it might be better, but the tradesmen would be still under political influences. I will give an instance that occurred in one of my own canvassings. I called on a tradesman, and said, "I know what your former vote was; I don't ask you to vote for me now, but that you would not vote at all." He answered, "I dare not; I have been looking over my books, and I find my returns are £1,500 a year; about £1,200 is from Tory customers. They do not ask me to vote for their Candidate, but if I were not to do so, I know that they would withdraw their custom." A higher tone of moral feeling is gradually diminishing those evils which it was thought the Ballot would remedy. I have always wished my own tenants to vote according to their conscientious opinions, and during a contested election for the County of Huntingdon I published a letter with my name, condemning any coercion as contrary to this maxim in the New Testament, " Do unto others as you would they should do unto you."

[My Father's candour in mentioning the fluctuations of his views on the Ballot are borne out by the remarks of the late Lord Fitzwilliam. I am kindly permitted by his son to insert two letters in this volume, which exhibit his high principles and excellent judgment. Speaking of one whom he calls " the neophyte," he says,]

"Gradual changes of opinion upon particular questions are what may, I had almost said, must, take place in the mind of every man who *thinks;* but sudden changes with respect to the whole course of politics, and the relations which men bear to one another in public, do not very much recommend the turner to the favour of those who reflect and observe.

"With respect to Ballot, I have no *political* objection, but my *moral* objection is invincible—if your electors are not sufficiently independent, the true remedy is not in *secresy*, a very near relation to *falsehood;*—but in striking off the dependent or corrupt classes—corrupt and dependent electors there will always be ; but when they are in such numbers as to amount to *classes*, amputation is the true remedy.

" Believe me,

"Yours most faithfully,

" FITZWILLIAM.

" *To G. Pryme, Esq.*

" I hope we shall see you at Milton in the winter.

" WENTWORTH, *Sep.* 14, 1839."

Cobbett sat in the first Reformed Parliament for Oldham. He looked like a better sort of farmer; he had been, I believe, a common soldier, and lived a good deal in America. He was a very able man, but his career in the House was a complete failure. Though bold in public assemblies he was timid and overawed in Parliament, and was never able to say more than a few sentences.

One of his chief objects was to abolish corporal punishment in the army. He had been tried for a libel on this subject and imprisoned. It is probable that every one would now agree with him. At that time 500 lashes were sometimes given, and even 1000, though not all at once. If, by the advice of the surgeon present, the flogging was stayed before the due number had been given, then the rest were inflicted at a future time[1]. The first modification was made by the Duke of Wellington, as Commander-in-chief, who made the rule that no more than 50 lashes should be given. I was deeply impressed with the dreadfulness of this punishment when a boy, by meeting a soldier sobbing bitterly, supported by two women. I asked them how it was? and they told me what he had undergone. This merciful change in flogging, and his wise rules about duelling, were the two great features of the Duke's policy while Commander-in-chief: had he tried to *abolish* either he might have failed, but his great tact and wisdom made him stop short of this, and enabled him to effect a very great reform in both[2].

Cobbett was said to have "a good face for a grievance." I remember one trait which shows it. He moved to bring in a Bill to modify the Stamp Act, more especially that part of

[1] Such a sentence was ordered in 1811, and 750 administered.

[2] *March* 26, 1868. In Committee on the Mutiny Bill a motion was carried prohibiting corporal punishment in the Army in the time of Peace.

it which obliged every one to give a twopenny stamp on payment of any sum between £2 and £5. Lord Althorp said that it would require great time for modification, and that it should be taken into consideration, but that meantime the Member for Oldham might, if he liked, have that particular grievance of the twopenny stamp redressed at once. We all who were opposite to him were amused to observe that Cobbett looked quite disappointed, as if feeling that the sting was taken out of his complaints. Mr Orde, one of the Lords of the Treasury, set to work to do all the rest, and so assiduously that it impaired his health, and he died.

The House adjourned on the 24th of August.

# CHAPTER XIII.

## 1834.

IN the Session of 1834 several useful and economical Acts of minor importance were passed, among others the consolidation of different Boards of Revenue. But the only measure of public importance was the New Poor Law Act, introduced by Lord Althorp. The chief griev- ance of the old poor law was that the usual rate of wages was so low that able-bodied men had parish relief ac- cording to the number of their families; and the certainty of this assistance occasioned a careless habit of working, and an indifference towards their employers. In some parishes if able-bodied men had no work they were set by the overseers to the most frivolous employment, as emptying water from one pond into another, and then taking it back again. There was also a great parochial expenditure in poor-law removals and appeals to the Quarter Sessions thereon. In the year 1833 a Commission of Inquiry into the Poor-laws had been appointed, of which Mr Nassau Senior was Chief Commissioner. It was a subject which interested him more than any other. He issued questions to me and many other persons who were known to care about it, as the best means for obtaining useful information. The Report, written entirely by him, was delivered in 1834, and on this was founded the Bill.

Lord Althorp privately showed some of the details of this Bill to a few men whom he thought were practically acquainted with the subject. Among them were Mr Miles, M.P. for Somersetshire (Tory), Sir Edward Knatchbull, M.P. for Kent (Tory), Dr Whately, afterwards Archbishop of Dublin, and one of the Chairmen of Quarter Sessions in Notts.[1], Mr Nassau Senior, and myself. Mr Nassau Senior was the first Professor of Political Economy at Oxford. He was the chief of us all in his energy and practical acquaintance with the subject, and knew all that passed in the Cabinet Councils respecting it. I breakfasted with him two or three times that we might have a conference together. The Measure met with great opposition, chiefly from the Tories and Radicals, but passed by great majorities in both houses. Three Commissioners were appointed to carry this Act into execution, Mr J. Frankland Lewis, Mr J. G. S. Lefevre and Mr George Nicholls.

---

[1] Most likely the Rev. J. Becher, of Southwell. "He was noted for his knowledge of, and work in Benefit Societies and Clubs. Valuable suggestions were derived also from the Rev. R. Lowe (father of the present Chancellor of the Exchequer), Rector of Bingham, who had introduced very successfully the workhouse test into his own large parish."—*Extract from a private letter.*

It may be remembered that I have described a conflict between a Pressgang and the crew of a Greenland Whaler which took place in 1797, in the Humber. Mr Silk Buckingham, M.P. for Sheffield, on introducing a Bill to prevent naval impressment, alluded to that occasion and stated the fact that several of the impressers had been wounded and one of them killed. Sir James Graham, then First Lord of the Admiralty shook his head and said, " No, no," on which Mr B. replied that there was a Member present who saw it, and appealed to me, and I arose and said, "I and Colonel Thompson saw that very conflict." How little did I foresee when, as a boy, I beheld that encounter, that I should be called upon to speak of it thirty-seven years later as a Member of the House of Commons.

[Sir James Graham probably only doubted for the sake of eliciting truth. He could have had no hostility to a measure of relief, or, if he had, his candour and readiness to acknowledge himself mistaken, if he were so, showed itself in his carrying an Impressment Bill in the Session of 1835. As a boy he exhibited the future bent of his life. When other boys were choosing what they would be, he would say, " I will be a Statesman." A stone is still shown in the village on which the youthful politician stood and harangued his playmates.]

Sir James Graham was a man of great abilities, but perhaps too hasty. After he quitted office he brought in a Bill for the better regulation of the Medical Profession. Wakley had one also. I carefully compared the two, and was convinced that Sir James Graham's Bill was the better. When we voted he expressed to me his pleasure at seeing me on his side, and asked me to be Chairman in Committee.

Sir James Graham was one of the celebrated seceders

on the Irish Church Temporalities measure, which had been recommended in the King's Speech of this year. After the Bill had been amended both by Lords and Commons, Mr Ward moved a resolution which proposed appropriating a part of the sequestered funds of the Irish Church to purposes of education. This not being opposed by the Ministry, occasioned the secession (May 27) of Lord Stanley, Sir James Graham, the Duke of Richmond, and the Earl of Ripon from the Cabinet, and nothing more was enacted on that subject during this Session.

There is a complete collection of H. B.'s caricatures in the upper library of the Reform Club. One of the cleverest was *The Derby Dilly.* O'Connell had repeated the two lines from the *Anti-Jacobin,* which had parodied Darwin's rather far-fetched illustrations in his *Loves of the Plants:*

> "So down thy vale, romantic Ashbourne, glides
> The Derby Dilly with its three insides."

O'Connell altered it to six insides to suit Lord Stanley and his adherents. The *Derby Dilly* alluded to was a chaise holding three persons inside, called a *diligence,* which in former days was established in country towns, and in which your place was booked as in a Coach.

Dr Darwin was a writer of the most harmonious verse of any poet, more so even than Pope, but there is a good deal of twaddle in his poems. He began life as a Physician at Lichfield, and afterwards removed to Derby. He and Dr Storer of Nottingham, and Dr Vaughan[1] of Leicester, were three famous Doctors who were sent for to great distances. Darwin was a Jacobin, and the writers in the *Anti-Jacobin* Newspaper parodied his similes. He is said to have

---

[1] Father of Sir Henry Halford, who changed his name.

composed his poetry as he went to his more distant patients, and that for this purpose he built a carriage, the first of its kind, to hold only one person, in order that he might not be expected to ask any one to go with him. It was nick-named a sulky[1].

At the end of the Session, Lord Grey feeling himself unequal to the fatigues of the Premiership, and the great object of his life—Parliamentary Reform—having been accomplished, recommended the King to send for Lord Melbourne, who had held Office under him, and who now succeeded him as Prime Minister.

In the autumn of this year the hasty burning of the Exchequer tallies occasioned a fire in the palace of Westminster, and destroyed St Stephen's Chapel, where the House of Commons sat, the interior of the House of Lords, and the Speaker's residence. Against the meeting of the Parliament next session, the House of Lords was fitted up for the use of the Commons, and the Peers assembled in the Painted Chamber, where they sat till the present buildings were ready.

[Only the lower half of St Stephen's Chapel had been used by the Commons. The upper part, with its vaulted roof and unglazed windows, was a large vacant chamber. In the centre of this was a wooden lantern called "the ventilator." This had eight small openings in it, just large enough to admit a head, and was surrounded by a circular bench. By this means ladies who were privileged to go there could catch a glimpse of speakers within a certain radius. When tired of peering through these pigeon-holes we roamed about our prison, and it was very refreshing to look out on a summer's evening upon the Thames. We were locked up, and every now and then our custodian came to tell us who was " on his

---

[1] Sterne speaks of a carriage in France to hold one, called a *Désobligeante.*

legs." Sometimes members came up; Mr Stanley, now Lord
Derby, often when Mrs Stanley was there. The present gilded
cage which is so complained of is a paradise to the draughty
dusty room I speak of, but we liked it nevertheless, and it was
a great treat to have tea in a Committee-room. I remember
Mr T. B. Macaulay joining our party there on one of the evenings
of an anti-slavery debate.]

When the Reform Bill passed, the Earl of Winchelsea,
who had been the vehement and sincere opponent of it,
and also of Roman Catholic emancipation, uttered a prophecy, that within ten years there would be neither King,
nor House of Lords, and that Mass would be sung in Westminster Abbey. This prophecy was fulfilled in every point,
though not exactly in the sense in which he had intended
it. Within the time specified there was no House of Lords,
for the interior of it was burnt; no King, for a Queen
occupied the throne; and Mozart's Requiem was sung in
the Abbey[1].

Lord Spencer died in November, and Lord Althorp
succeeded to his title. He could of course be no longer
Chancellor of the Exchequer, and Leader of the House of
Commons. The King availed himself of this circumstance
to dismiss the Ministry, and sent for Sir Robert Peel to
form one on Tory principles.

[Miss Berry gives the following account of the change of
Ministry. "It seems that when Lord Melbourne was with the King
at Brighton, and began to propose talking of affairs, the King
stopped him, saying, 'Come, we are going to dinner, and won't
talk of business till afterwards.' When the 'afterwards' came, and
Lord Melbourne wished to take his orders about filling up Lord
Althorp's place, he cut him short by saying that he, Lord Mel-

---

[1] On occasion of a Musical Festival held there while the decorations
for the Coronation remained.

bourne, had always told him that it was impossible the Government
could go on without Lord Althorp in the Commons; that therefore
he considered it dissolved by Lord Spencer's death, and they had
better all resign." The messenger, Mr Hudson, who was sent for
the new Premier, was twelve days in reaching Rome.]

I would wish to say a few words here in reference to Lord
Althorp as Chancellor of the Exchequer, in which office he
propounded most ably, and clearly, and candidly his measures of finance, without much eloquence or embellishment of
language. His calmness and sagacity were of the greatest
use in breaking the force and subduing the impetuosity of
those reformers who, in the excitement of the times, and the
energy of their newly-found power, would have made, perhaps, dangerous financial alterations. He reduced the stamp
duty on newspapers from $3\frac{1}{2}d.$ to $1d.$, and the advertisement
duty from $4s.$ $6d.$, and so much more for each line beyond
a certain number, to $2s.$ $6d.$ and no more. The manufacture
of paper made from hemp was liable to only half the duty
($1\frac{1}{2}d.$ the lb. weight) for that upon the sort made from linen
and other materials. This difference had frequently given
rise to disputes between the manufacturers and the Excise
officers. Lord Althorp reduced the duty to $1\frac{1}{2}d.$ for *all* kinds.
The tax on the tanning of skins rendered it necessary, for
the prevention of fraud, to require their being not less
than a certain time in the tanpit, which injured the quality
of many of them; this tax he abolished. I give these three
instances out of many wise alterations which he proposed
and carried[1].

Lord Althorp was of the same year and under the same
College tutor as myself. From his answers in the lecture-

[1] He died, Oct. 1, 1845.

rooms, both classical and mathematical, we anticipated that he would distinguish himself at the College examinations at the close of each academical year, and he was accordingly in the first class of both. At that time noblemen could not compete for University honours (they might have got a Browne's Medal, but they never did), and obtained their degree without examination, under an erroneous view of the letters of King James I. This mistake has since been remedied, and the privilege requested by him is now held to relate only to the number of terms to be kept, and that Noblemen and eldest sons of Baronets should have their M.A. degree at the end of six terms. The same restriction had formerly extended to Fellow-Commoners. Sir James Scarlett (B.A. 1790) told me that he had, when a Fellow-Commoner of Trinity College, paid much attention to mathematics, and was desirous to compete for honours in the Tripos, but that the authorities of that time objected so strongly that he felt obliged to relinquish the intention. The present Duke of Wellington was, I believe, the first Nobleman obliged to undergo examination.

Lord A. soon came into Parliament, where he fully justified any expectations which had been formed of him. Sitting next his nephew (Lord Althorp) in the hall of Trinity one day we talked about his deceased uncle, and he was astonished to find that he had been in the first class. I took pains to get a copy of the list[1] for the year 1801, and sent it

[1] The names are arranged alphabetically (the usual method at this College, Trinity), without any regard to their superiority of merit.

JUNIOR SOPHS.

| | |
|---|---|
| Lord Althorp | Parke |
| Brandreth | Pryme |
| Hon. H. Cust | Rose |
| Garratt | Wiles |

*Cambridge Calendar for* 1802.

to him, and he expressed himself to me afterwards as much gratified by it.

During the Ministerial interregnum the Duke of Wellington took the seals of several Offices. H. B., the celebrated caricaturist of the time, published a sketch of the different Ministers sitting in consultation round a table, every one of whom bore a slight variation of the Duke's features.

On Sir Robert Peel's return to England, he was asked what course he would pursue? he answered, "I am sent for, like the doctor to a patient, and I must make myself fully acquainted with the symptoms before I can prescribe."

Peel's intellectual vision seemed to me clear and powerful, but confined to what lay immediately before him, instead of taking in large views of future consequences. This was strongly the case with regard to Roman Catholic Emancipation, and the Repeal of the Corn Laws, which had long been imminent to the minds of others before the light flashed upon his own. But when he at last resolved on those measures he carried them through with energy and sincerity. This is fully shown by the two volumes of posthumous correspondence published by Lord Mahon. I have read them, and they confirmed my previous impressions. His subsequent measures on Paper Currency seemed to indicate the same limitation of views. In Oct. 1844 he brought in a Bill which passed into law, familiarly called "Peel's Bank Act." To explain the necessity for this I must go back to the year 1797, when the demand for payments in gold out of the country occasioned such a diminution of metallic currency, and such an extensive issue of Bank of England notes for supplying the deficiency, that the Bank was unable to meet the great demand of those who required payments in coin, and stopped payment. This was owing to two causes, political disturbance and scarcity of money. Adam Smith said a Banker need keep only a fourth part of the money for which he is answerable in gold ready to meet demands.

The Government of that day ventured upon giving a temporary order for suspending the compulsory payment of notes by gold, which was afterwards prolonged by Act of Parliament, for a time practically indefinite, and this depreciation continued till a Bank-note was worth only three-fourths of its nominal amount in gold. This might have proceeded to an utter depreciation, like the Assignat for a Louis d'or, which passed in common currency for a franc, as a friend of mine who was in Paris in the days of the Revolution of 1789 told me. But this tendency was somewhat checked in England by the Government taking Bank-notes in payment of taxes, and by the Bank of England being obliged to receive them in payment of the bills of exchange for which they had issued them. After the Peace with France there was a less necessity for the exportation of gold, and a general anxiety to return to cash payments, and this was secured by legislation in 1819. Peel's subsequent Act of 1844 limited the Bank of England's issue to the sum (about fourteen millions) which it had previously lent to the Government, and to the amount of gold in its coffers; and that of country Bank-notes to their *then* existing amount. It seems to me that the compulsory diminution of Bank of England notes, as the quantity of bullion in its vaults should diminish, would contract the currency of the country precisely at the time when the exportation of gold and silver would require a supply of paper money to fill the vacuum. The inconvenience of this must become more aggravated on the gradual diminution of local Bank-notes, which another branch of the same measure is occasioning.

[In a book of extracts which my father has made I find a remark of his against one from Lord Lytton. "'While a writer should be in advance of his time, a Statesman should content himself with marching by its side. A nation could not be ripened, like an exotic, by artificial means; it must be developed only by natural influences.' Most Statesmen lag after their time through not making themselves acquainted with the feelings and thoughts of the people. G. P."]

Sir Robert Peel was once exceedingly taken by surprise at a majority in favour of a motion for the Repeal of the Test Act, which had been formerly passed for the purpose of excluding Dissenters from place and power under severe penalties. Many Tories, partly from religious motives, voted for it, among others, Lord Mandeville told me that he did so. An Opposition Member (who afterwards became a Cabinet Minister) said to me, that he never saw consternation so visibly depicted in any human countenance as in Peel's, when the Tellers announced the numbers on the division. Instead of staying, as usual, to move the adjournment of the House when the business should be concluded, he requested another Member to do it for him. It was said, that he drove immediately to the Duke of Wellington, who was at his own house waiting to hear the result, and enquired of him what should be done? and that the Duke, with that military calmness and prompt decision which he ever showed, said, "Our course is obvious; we must take it out of their hands, and you must state to-morrow that, as you unexpectedly found the feeling to be so extensive, you will introduce a Bill for the desired relief." He did so, and it passed into law.

Parliament was dissolved Dec. 30. I was again returned with Mr Spring Rice for Cambridge, but by a majority of five votes only over Mr J. L. Knight, afterwards Sir J. L. Knight Bruce, Vice-Chancellor of England. I had twenty-one Tory split votes, one of which was given me by a man named Preston, a retired publican and rate-collector, with whom I had occasionally some good-humoured talk. When I called upon him I found him sitting by the fire reading the Bible with his wife and daughter. He said, "As long as you offer, Mr Pryme, I have always one vote for my politics, and one for you."

I had offended some of my constituents by my vote on the motion of Mr Daniel Whittle Harvey for the revision of Pensions from the Crown, some of which were alleged by him to have been granted to improper persons. But I and many others considered ourselves bound in good faith to maintain the List, as it was part of the usual compact on the accession of a Sovereign, who gave up to the nation some of his hereditary revenues. The Radicals voted with Mr Harvey. He was of course in a minority; but later Mr Edward Strutt, M.P. for Derby, brought forward, with the consent of Government, a measure which diminished the pensions by one half as persons died off; and, which was of more importance, required that it should be stated annually to the House of Commons on what grounds any new ones were granted.

In consequence of that vote I was hard run at this election, and with one man I argued for an hour, trying to make him understand my view of it as a matter of good faith, and as a bargain with the new King, but I could not; and instead of voting for me, as he had done previously, he only abstained from voting against me.

Some instances of bribery on the part of my opponents were afterwards proved at the Cambridge Assizes, and more were suspected.

# CHAPTER XIV.

## 1835.

ON the Meeting of the New Parliament (Feb. 19), the
Right Hon. James Abercromby, M.P. for Edinburgh,
was proposed as Speaker in opposition to Sir C. Manners
Sutton, and chosen by a majority of 10 in a House of
622 Members.

A Meeting of Members friendly to the late Administration
was convened at a large room lent by the Earl of Lichfield
in his house. Lord John Russell proposed to move an
Amendment to the Address, in answer to the King's speech,
gently censuring the late dissolution of Parliament as unnecessary. Joseph Hume objected to it as being a feeble
(the term was "milk-and-water") proposition, and proposed
one more spirited, to which it was answered that Hume's
Amendment was certainly the better of the two, but that

as there was no probability of its succeeding, it was better
to adopt the milder one.   Hume and his supporters gave
way, and the result showed the wisdom of this course, as
the Amendment of Lord John was only carried by a majority
of 7.   I am not aware of any Amendment in answer to a
Sovereign's Speech being carried since the time of King
William the Third.

[My Father said to me, in speaking of Mr Hume's Amendment,
that he was always going too far, and that the wisdom of other men
who succeeded better, lay in the moderation of their reforms.]

The Address was presented, as usual, by Members of
the House in a body.   His Majesty on his Throne received
it with calm dignity, but his countenance evidently shewed
a feeling of mortification.

The Mover and Seconder of the Address in answer to
the King's speech, always appeared in Court-dress, but the
rest stood in a semicircle before the Throne in their ordinary
morning dress.   On this occasion one honourable Member
chose to appear in Court-dress, and seeing himself, when we
were assembled previously, differently habited from the
others, enquired if he were correct? to which the Speaker
answered, "*Singularly* correct, Sir[1]."

---

[1] It is said in Timbs's *Century of Anecdotes*, that Members wore in
1782 Court-dress in the House, but no authority is given.   I am indebted
to a friend well acquainted with the traditions of former etiquette for the
following : "With respect to the costume of Members of Parliament, I
have always understood that they were in Court, that is, I believe more
properly speaking, full dress, bag-wig and sword, at that time worn by all
gentlemen.   An anecdote which confirms it is told of David Hartley, the
dinner-bell of the House, getting up to speak.   Sir Robert Walpole took
the opportunity of taking his ride, and went home, changed his dress for
riding costume, rode to Hampstead, returned, put on full dress and came
down to the House, when he found D. Hartley still on his legs, not having
finished his speech."

Barristers often appeared in the house in wig and gown, and Members in uniform or Court-dress on the nights of state parties. There were three Members who wore top-boots and leather breeches, Colonel Windham, Mr Byng and another, whose name I forget[1]. It had been the fashionable morning dress thirty years before. Sir R. W. Vaughan, an old Welsh baronet and Country gentleman, wore shorts and gaiters.

There was formerly a singular privilege regarding the dress of County Members. An anecdote concerning it which I have heard from one to whom Lord Leicester related it, affords besides a curious illustration of the men and manners of an older time. "Of all political subjects the one on which Lord Leicester most prided himself was the part he took in the debates on the American War. He told me that on nearly the last occasion when it was debated in the House of Commons, and when the resolution for an Address to the King to make peace was carried by the Opposition by a very small majority[2], in a very excited House, he called out to Sir George Saville (Member for Yorkshire), to move that the Address be carried up to the Throne by the whole House, thinking that they should be strong enough to carry that motion by the same number as had just voted; and that he (Lord Leicester) undertook to stand at the door of the House, so as to prevent any of the Members leaving it while the motion was rapidly made, which was carried by the barest possible majority. It was well known to the Opposition that this would be very disagreeable to the King, and in order to mark their sense of the treatment they had been receiving from the Court, the County Members went

---

[1] Probably Sir Francis Burdett, who always wore them.

[2] Feb. 22, 1782. An Address hostile to the Government was moved by General Conway, and carried by *one* vote.

up to the Throne—according to their privilege—in leather-breeches and top-boots, instead of Court-dress, a privilege of course very seldom exerc'sed.   Lord L. said that this was the then temper of the Opposition on this sore subject; and the Court was not behind hand with them; for as a marked and well understood insult to the Opposition, General Arnold was placed conspicuously on the King's right-hand, where he was visible to the whole body of the Members[1]."

A curious difficulty occurred in last Session which I omitted to mention.   A Quaker (J. Pease, Junr.) was returned in 1832 as the Whig member for the Southern division of Durham.   When he came to the table to be sworn, previously to taking his seat, he claimed to *affirm* instead of taking the oaths.   The Speaker requested him to withdraw, and Lord Althorp moved that a Committee be appointed to consider whether the Act of Parliament permitting affirmation in certain cases extended to this one.   Their Report, presented a few days after, was in favour of it, and the motion was agreed to unanimously.   But another difficulty presented itself.   It was a rule that the hat might be kept on when a Member remained sitting, but must be taken off when moving in the House, and this dilemma was certain to occur daily.   Some friend of Mr Pease, to obviate this, instructed the door-keeper gently to remove his hat and retain it till he quitted the House.   In the course of a year or two he put it on and off for himself.   It might have been thought that an individual of these peculiar habits would not have felt at home in such an Assembly, but this was not the case, and the feeling of *bonhommie* which generally prevailed in this "best and pleasantest Club," as my friend Hope Vere designated it, placed him perfectly at his ease.   As a

[1] General Arnold came to England a short time previously.

proof of it I will relate the following anecdote. After the termination of Peel's short Administration, when several of us were in the library of the House, writing letters or conversing on the formation of Lord Melbourne's Ministry, one of those present jocosely asked Mr Pease what place *he* was to have? he answered, "There is but one place that I could think of taking, and it has not been offered to me." "What is that?" we exclaimed, and he replied, "Of course the Secretary at War."

To return to Hume, he had been a surgeon in India, and had made a fortune. He had an office and kept a clerk at his own cost, in order to examine the Estimates and accounts of public monies, and to prepare his statements and facts; and by his attention to economy effected a considerable reduction in the National Expenditure. He had his faults, which produced political errors, for he looked rather to what in his mind was desirable than to what was practicable. That kind of feeling predominated throughout. He suggested even the smallest economics.

Gilt-edged paper was, I take it, given up in consequence of his observation on the extravagance of using it for Parliamentary notices. Parker, Secretary to the Treasury, brought up some reports. Hume remarked, "I think that splendid gilt-paper is unnecessary." P., nettled at this, replied, "Perhaps the honourable Member may think the margins are too wide;" but it had its effect, and in a short time the paper in the library and writing-rooms, as well as all the future reports, had no gilt edges. Soon after it went out of fashion altogether. This reminds me of a little anecdote of Monk. I had a dislike to books being printed on hot-pressed paper, and I advised him not to have his Æschylus so published. Shortly afterwards he presented me with a copy on *plain* paper, saying he had ordered the printer to have *one* so printed on purpose that he might give it me. It was partly done as a little quiz, and partly to please me.

March 28. I attended a dinner which was given to Lord John Russell in honour of his public conduct by a large number of Members who voted in the two majorities on the Speakership and the Amendment.

Mr Sheil was distinguished, like O'Connell, by his advocacy of a Repeal of the Union, and was one of the most eloquent and impressive speakers in this Parliament. On a motion respecting Ireland, during this short Administration, he said, that the grievances of that country had been fatal to several Governments, and "even now," pointing with bended form to that space of the floor which lies before the Treasury Bench, "have dug the grave that is yawning before the present one." The sensation which his action and his figure created was so intense that we were almost tempted to look if there were not a chasm in the place he pointed to. He spoke with prophetic lore; for not long after the three Resolutions respecting Irish Education completed the list of minorities with which, as in the case of the Election for Speaker and the Amendment to the Address, the Peel Administration had begun. Mr Stanley and Sir James Graham had kept aloof from it, and did not take Office for a long time afterwards.

March 26. The Ministerial dinner at the Mansion House took place. The Lord Mayor was Mr W. T. Copeland, and he did me the favour of sending an invitation, which I accepted.

[This preceded by a very few days the Ministerial defeat. "On Monday, the 30th of March 1835, Lord John Russell in his place in the House of Commons moved, 'That this House resolves itself into a Committee of the whole House, to consider the Temporalities of the Church of Ireland ;' and a little before three o'clock in the morning of the following Saturday the motion was carried by 322 against 289 votes[1]."]

On the accession of Lord Melbourne to Office (April 8th) Lord John Russell became the Ministerial Leader of the House of Commons. The proposal of this was not palatable to several of the supporters of Government with whom I usually acted, and I was deputed to represent our objections to the Right Hon. Edward Ellice, formerly Secretary to the Treasury, who in some degree admitted the force of them, but showed that he was less objectionable than some others whom he named to me. Lord J. R.'s manners were cold and indifferent and the exceeding self-confidence which he manifested rendered him unwilling to consult the opinions of others. This was more strongly shown after he was Leader, by his not calling together the supporters of Government previously to the introduction of *important* Parliamentary measures, which had been usual. One instance was on the proposal for a grant to Railways in Ireland. Some of the supporters of Government disapproved of this application of the public money; but, not having been consulted about it, had no opportunity of representing their objections. When Lord John explained his measure in the House many independent Members withdrew. Soon after I rose from my seat behind the Treasury Bench, and was retiring for a time, when the Secretary to the Treasury, Mr John Parker, M.P. for Sheffield, whispered to me his hope that we would not by our absence incur the risk of leaving the Ministers in a mi-

---

[1] *Times* Nov. 30th, 1868. "On the 30th of March 1868, after an interval of precisely 33 years, or more than the lifetime of a generation, Mr Gladstone rose to propose a motion almost identical in its terms with that of Lord J. Russell in 1835 ; * * and it is not a little remarkable that the leader of the attack on this occasion both voted and spoke against Lord Russell's earlier motion."—*Idem.*

nority.   Acceding to this I joined the others in the Library,
and we agreed to return to the House, and vote with the
Government for the introduction of the Bill, but that we
should beg them to understand that we should vote against
it in its future progress.   By so doing Ministers had a small
majority on that occasion, and nothing more was heard of
the intended Bill.   Had a preliminary meeting of Members
taken place, Ministers would have been spared the mortification of bringing forward a measure, which they were obliged
to abandon.

[In speaking thus of Lord John Russell it is of the course of action
which he chose to take as a *Minister*.   As a patriot and a man of
letters my Father always admired him, as will be seen elsewhere.]

Brougham was not made Chancellor again, and when the
reason for it was privately questioned among a few members
in the House, I heard Lord —— give, "his flighty conduct."
Brougham was a man of splendid talents, and vehement feelings, but injudicious.   His speech at Liverpool was much
admired.   Aubrey came to me one day—it was at Brighton—
with a newspaper in his pocket containing it, and read it to
me with admiration, saying, "What do *you* think of it?"   I
remember the passage which was thought so magnificent,
spoken as it was, before the *real* cause of the burning of
Moscow was known; Mr Canning had been praising Mr Pitt,
calling him "the immortal statesman."

[My Father then repeated to me, with all the animation of his
younger days, several sentences of this speech commencing, " Immortal in the misery of his devoted country !   Immortal in the
wounds of her bleeding liberties !   Immortal in the cruel wars which
sprang from his cold, miscalculating ambition !   Immortal in the
intolerable taxes, the countless loads of debt which those wars have
flung upon us, and which the youngest man among us will not live

to see the end of! Immortal in the triumphs of our enemies, and
the ruin of our allies—the costly purchase of so much blood and
treasure! Immortal in the afflictions of England, and the humilia-
tion of her friends, through the whole results of his twenty years'
reign, from the first rays of favour with which a delighted Court
gilded his early apostasy to the deadly glare which is at this instant
cast upon his name by the burning metropolis of our last ally. But
may no such immortality ever fall to my lot! Let me rather live
innocent and inglorious, and when at last I cease to serve you, and
to feel for your wrongs, may I have an humble monument in some
nameless stone, to tell that beneath it there rests from his labours
in your service, an enemy of 'the immortal statesman,' a friend of
peace and of the people."

It is only just to Lord B.'s memory to say that 23 years after
the above speech was delivered, when he was Ex-chancellor,
being again at Liverpool, he admitted with an admirable candour,
that Mr Pitt was a great Minister, a great Orator, and a man of
unsullied public virtue, as far as freedom from mean, sordid, despic-
able views could make him such.]

Brougham was very witty. Some Barristers on one occasion wished, rather unnecessarily, to be made Serjeants,
and it being usual on taking the Coif to present rings with a
motto on them to the Queen and Lord Chancellor, Brougham
was asked what it should be? and answered, "Oh! nothing
can be more appropriate than the old legal word *Scilicet.*"
He must be nearly ninety years old now; for I remember
that when I first saw him he was leaving the *Academical* as I
was entering it, and that I thought him much older than myself, and I am now eighty-five.

In consequence of this change of Ministry taking place in
the middle of the Parliamentary Session, little progress could
be made in practical reforms. The only measure of this kind
introduced was one for regulating English and Welsh Corporations, founded on the results of the Commission which I
have before mentioned. It displaced the whole of the exist-

15

ing Corporations, and replaced them with persons elected by popular suffrage.

It was in this year that Mr Greene (Tory), M.P. for Lancaster, moved to introduce a Bill for substituting Declarations in lieu of Oaths in certain cases, some of which he mentioned. I rose to express the hope that he would include oaths on admission to the freedom of a Corporation, and said that I had sometimes been present at Huntingdon when the quaint words of the oath, among which was that of swearing to "be *buxom* to the Mayor," invariably occasioned a laugh among the persons present[1]. Mr G. answered that he intended it, and then came across the House to ask me if I would second the motion, in which request I willingly acquiesced. The Bill passed into a law. Parliament sat late this year, and was not prorogued till Sept. 9.

I knew Walter, the Editor of the *Times*, and he invited me to pay him a visit this Summer during some "interval of business" at his country house, Bearwood, Berks. He described to me the cause of the large extension in the circulation of that Journal. He was the first to establish a Foreign Correspondent. This was Mr Henry Crabb Robinson, whom I have previously mentioned, at a salary of £300 a year, which though not amply remunerative to him, sufficed, as he wished to reside in Germany. Mr Walter also established local reporters, instead of copying from Country papers. His Father doubted the wisdom of such a large Expenditure, but the Son prophesied a gradual and certain success, which has been realised. I can remember the *Times* occupying only four pages, and those of a size much smaller than at present[2].

---

[1] Buxom (= Germ. biegsam), from Sax. buzan, to bend. John de Trevisa, a clergyman, tells his patron that he is "obedient and *buxom* to all his commands."

[2] The first publication of the *Times* with *that* name was on Jan. 1st,

I remember seeing it when a Schoolboy, and that I was rebuked for calling it "Ti-mes." I said, in answer, " *Timeo,
ti-mes,*" not knowing better. When I was a young man there
were only three or four daily Papers—the *Times* and
*Morning Post* among them. Monk and I took in together
the latter, there being at that time no reading room for
Undergraduates. We afterwards changed it for the *British
Press*. The *Anti-Jacobin* was a weekly Paper, and the predecessor of *John Bull*[1]. It was said that it did no good,
as it was taken in only by those who were of the same
opinions; but the Newspaper must have been serviceable, as
other people seeing it lie on a table would occasionally read
it. Canning was a great contributor to it. The verses were
collected together in one volume, called *The Poetry of the
Anti-Jacobin.*

1788. A writer in the *Leisure Hour* calculates that a copy *now* with its
supplement is equal to an 8vo volume of 500 pages.

[1] " The celebrated *Anti-Jacobin*, the object of which was to ridicule
and refute the theories of religion, government, and social economy, propounded by the revolutionary leaders in France. Its first appearance was
on Nov. 7, 1797, its last on July 9, 1798."—*Cornhill Magazine* for 1867.

# CHAPTER XV.

## 1836.

1836.  PARLIAMENT met Feb. 4th.   Among the practical Reforms in this Session was that for the Commutation of Tithes in England and Wales, in adjusting the details of which I took an active part as it passed through the House.   The exaction of Tithes in kind, whether actually, or by annual valuation, or sometimes by a Lease on the Incumbency, which might be cut short by its termination at any moment, had been a practical grievance, and a check to Agricultural improvement ; for the Farmer who might expend any sum upon improving his land was only entitled to nine-tenths of the additional produce occasioned by his outlay.   This pressed so strongly on the minds of occupiers of land as to influence materially their conduct at County Elections.   In those of Cambridgeshire, where there was a numerous body of Yeomen who owned no

Landlord, the grievance was predominant, and they had looked to Parliamentary Reform as the only means of effecting a Commutation of Tithes. In some few Parishes indeed this had taken place on the passing of an Enclosure Bill, by giving to the Incumbent an allotment of land instead of the Tithes in kind. At a Cambridgeshire Election in the year 1826, the Tory member, the Honourable Charles Yorke, who had vacated his seat by taking a sinecure Office, came down for re-election. A Whig Candidate, Lord Francis G. Osborne, though supported by only two of the County Gentlemen, had so decided a support of the Yeomanry that the original Member retired without coming to the poll, and at the election in 1830 two Whig Candidates were returned.

The Bill, which passed into Law, enacted that the right to Tithes in kind should be commuted for a money payment which should fluctuate according to the average prices of corn for the seven years preceding the payment. A Board of Tithe-Commissioners was instituted, to whom there was to be an appeal when the Parson and the Landowners could not agree on the precise terms. The change was disliked at first by the majority of the Clergy, but a feeling of satisfaction has since prevailed among them by the removal of a great source of discord with their parishioners.

Among minor Bills proposed this Session I moved for leave to introduce a Bill for the abolition of Grand Juries. Their function had been useful, perhaps necessary, before the power of committal was given to Justices of the Peace by the Statute of Philip and Mary. I had observed in my professional practice that Grand Juries, who heard in their own room witnesses for the Prosecution *only*, sometimes, through their deficiency of legal knowledge, occasioned a failure in justice, and, at the best, intervened superfluously between the committing Magistrate and the judicial

trial. I will give one among many instances. Two men
were indicted as principals for the crime of arson. I was
Counsel for the prosecution. The Grand Jury threw out
the Bill against one of them, considering him to be, not a
principal but an accessory. I learnt this through the Clerk
of the Arraigns. One of the Judges at Westminster had
said in a former case—a case of Burglary in which two
men were actively concerned, and the third stood at the
corner of the street where the house was, in order to give
an alarm if necessary—that "it was as good as if his arm
had been in the house"—so the point had been already
decided as between accessory and principal, only the Grand
Jury had not read the Law Reports, and did not know
of it. I then sent up a bill against the prisoner as accessory, which they found. At the trial, when the nature of
his participation in the offence appeared in evidence, the
Judge interposed, and asked me if I could contend from
these facts that the prisoner was not a principal but an
accessory? I, of course, felt the insuperable difficulty; the
Judge directed an immediate acquittal, and the man escaped
with impunity, though the proof of his guilt was indis-
putable.

It might have been expected that many Members of the
House of Commons who were usually summoned as Grand
Jurymen in their Counties would be unwilling to lose that
dignity, and that the general reluctance which Englishmen
feel to interfere with ancient institutions would be fatal to
my motion, and it was accordingly negatived.

In Scotland a Petty Jury is composed of fifteen men,
twelve of whom make a majority. I talked with Campbell
and other Lawyers on the subject, and suggested that in our
Juries composed of twelve men nine should make a majority.
I suppose it is a made story that a man said he had served

on many Juries and always found that there were eleven obstinate men.

I had frequent opportunities of conversing with O'Connell, both in the House and at the Reform Club. He agitated for the Repeal of the Union, but he once said to me, " I am not anxious so much for Repeal in itself, but I feel that the agitation about it may be the means of obtaining a good and mild Government for Ireland." And I think they had a large share of it in lesser taxation. As an instance of this the Salt-tax was then 15*s.* a bushel in England, 6*s.* in Scotland, and only 2*s.* in Ireland. That country was also exempt from Income-tax.

He shewed me in the library of the House of Commons, as an illustration of the name of Tory, an Irish Act of Parliament for the suppression of " Rapparees, Tories, and other Robbers." The appellation of Whig as well as Tory was also a nickname, and given by the opposite party in allusion to sour milk.

On one occasion I was engaged with O'Connell and Jeffrey and Warburton in earnest talk in the Library of the House. Peacock told me not long after, that we had been observed, and that some persons in Cambridge to whom an eye-witness mentioned it, were uneasy at *my* being one of the party. I related to him the subject of our conversation, at which he was much amused. We were arguing whether the Gaelic Language had a Scottish or Irish origin, and trying to settle its migrations. Jeffrey held that Ireland was peopled from the North of Scotland. I also am inclined to this view.

I had known Warburton (M.P. for Bridport) when we were Undergraduates together. I remember Lord John Russell, at a dinner at his own house gently rallying W. on his having been called by the *Examiner*, "the Nestor of the

Radical camp;" and he *was that;* for though he was far more
Radical than any of us Whigs, there was a kind of temper
and judgment about him which moderated what otherwise
might have been extravagant in his views. When some one
moved for a Committee to enquire into a point, "What," said
Warburton, "is there not a Committee of inquiry always
sitting—his Majesty's Government?" On another occasion
he made the best speech I ever heard in the House on
*that* subject; it was on my friend Sir Andrew Agnew's wild
Bill for the better Observance of the Lord's Day. Warburton
urged the necessity of a day of rest of body and mind for
the artisan and labourer, and observed what a *national* advantage, apart from any religious view, a day of entire
relaxation would be. I once said to Sir A. A. "How can a
man of your good sense bring in such a Bill?" He answered,
"It's not mine, but I am in the hands of a body of religious
men who wish it." "Why then," I replied, "don't you eman-
cipate yourself?" He said, "I quite agree with you as to
the absurdity of some of the enactments, but it is the Bill of
'the Society for the better Observance of the Sabbath,' and
I can't help it." It was lost of course, because it went too
far, but the discussion produced great good throughout the
kingdom in leading people of all classes to attend to the subject, and improve the observance of the Lord's Day. The last
time that Sir A. Agnew brought forward his Bill, Mr B.
Hawes M.P. for Lambeth and two or three other members
succeeded in, I may say, quizzing it out of the House. We
were in Committee of the whole House, and I was in the
Chair. When we came to that clause which enacted that
it should be unlawful for any Cab or public Carriage to be
let out upon a Sunday, Hawes moved as an Amendment, "or
for any private carriage to be used." Before putting it to the
vote Sir A. A. appealed to me not to do so. I answered

that as it had been moved and seconded gravely, I had no option. The clause was carried by a majority, and no more was heard of the Bill.

But to return to O'Connell. He was not sufficiently guarded in his language when speaking of other men, and on one occasion some one opposite to him said " Such language might provoke a duel." "Oh no," remarked O'C., pointing to one of his hands with the other, "there's too much blood upon this hand already." I heard him say this, and the effect, as he suited the action to the word, was very great. I was told by a medical man who attended me as well as him during a prevailing Influenza that he took the Sacrament every week, and was a sincerely religious Roman Catholic.

I remember Mr Silk Buckingham bringing in a Bill to prevent duelling. It was very impracticable in its enactments, and a small Committee was formed, of which I, and Gronow, and O'Connell were members, to try if we could shape it into a good measure. We found such great difficulties in the way that we could not, and it was given up. O'C. and G., who had both fought fatal duels, spoke, but without mentioning themselves, as earnestly as possible against the practice.

Gronow sat only in one Parliament, for the Borough of Stafford. I had frequent conversations with him, and found him an extremely pleasant man. I have heard the account of his concern in a singular duel from my friend Mr Henry Crabb Robinson, and I will give it as nearly as I can in his words. "I was travelling after the Peace in 1814 in the South of France, towards the Pyrenees, and I rested at Toulouse. A gentleman at the Hotel there said to me, 'I advise you not to go to the Pyrenees, the country people there are very superstitious, and a circumstance has happened

lately which makes it unsafe for the English to go to ——,
naming one of the famous watering places.' He then told
me that there had been a French Officer there, who, conscious of his own skill in arms, insulted every Englishman
who came in his way, and never failed in killing whosoever
challenged him.   Gronow heard of this and resolved to
check his insolence.   He (Gronow) had the knack of shooting without raising his arm ; had the Frenchman shot first
G. must have been killed, so certain was his aim, but, as
he did not, it made the difference of about two seconds,
and G. shot *him* dead."

Mr Fox was once engaged in a duel, which had a pleasant
termination given to it by his good humour.   He had made
a violent attack in the House upon the Ordnance Department, in consequence of some severe calamities which had
occurred to a body of our troops, arising from the scan-
dalous badness of the ammunition supplied to them.   Mr
Fox imputed not merely jobbery in the Department, and
gross misconduct in the Contractors, but insinuated something like corruption in the Master-General, and made also
a personal attack on Mr Adam.   He was in the House,
and after replying to Mr Fox, thought it incumbent on him
to send him a challenge.   They were to fight next morning
in Kensington Gravel Pits—now, like duels themselves, a
thing of the past—Mr Fox with the Duke of Devonshire and
Lord Leicester, who related the anecdote to my informant,
played cards at Brookes's until it was time for the meeting.
Mr Fox fired a second time and in the air, but his antagonist's bullet hit him on the edge of his waistband, and lodged
without much mischief to him in the belt of his thick lea-
thern breeches.   Mr Fox immediately turned round to his
opponent and said with an indescribable smile, "By Jove,
if you had not used Ordnance Powder, I should have been

a dead man." The effect was irresistible, his adversary immediately tendered his hand to Mr Fox, and in later life they were excellent friends[1].

Duelling was a capital crime; the severity of the law, as is usual, had counteracted its punishment, and jurors declined to bring in "wilful murder." The only conviction which I can recollect was of a man named Fitzgerald, who was thought not to have been quite honourable towards his antagonist.

Lord Byron's great uncle fought a duel with Miss Chaworth's grandfather, and killed him. That was supposed to be one of the reasons which impeded the Poet's suit. The quarrel originated at a dinner of the Nottinghamshire Club, holden at the Star and Garter Tavern, Pall Mall. All gentlemen then wore swords. They withdrew into a private room without seconds, and Mr Chaworth was immediately killed[2]. The thrust which caused the fatal wound being found upwards, it was conjectured that there had not been fair play, and that Lord B. had grappled with his opponent. He was tried by his Peers in Westminster Hall, and found guilty of manslaughter; he however claimed the benefit of the Statute of Edward VI., and was discharged on paying his fees.

Lord Camelford's death in a duel[3] made a great sensation, the more so that he was considered the best shot in England. In connexion with that reputation I remember an anecdote. He was in a Coffee House and while sitting

[1] A duel was fought between Mr C. J. Fox and Mr Adam, Nov. 30th, 1779.

[2] Jan. 26, 1765. The duel is said to have originated in a dispute whether Mr Chaworth who preserved his game, or Lord Byron who did not, had more game on their estates.

[3] Mar. 10th, 1804.

at one of the tables reading, a stranger entered, seated himself at the next table, and took the candle from Lord C.'s,
calling out in an affected tone, "Waiter, bring me ——."
Lord C. directly said, imitating the accent, "Waiter, bring
me a pair of snuffers;" and when brought he rose up and
snuffed out the candle that had been removed; the stranger,
very much ruffled, said, "Waiter, who is that?"   "Lord
Camelford, Sir," was the answer, whereupon he demanded
his bill and got off as quickly as he could.

There were two duels in the old Borough times between
Candidates.  One of them was prevented by a slight noise
in the wood near which it was to take place.  It turned out
to be only a pheasant.  Soon after there appeared in one
of the periodicals of the day a letter signed "The Cock
Pheasant," against Duelling, and saying that for *his* part he
disliked to be shot at.

[I remember when I was a child my Father passing a whole night
away from home.  He had been dining in the Hall of one of the
Colleges, and a quarrel had arisen between two of the party, which
led to a Challenge.  Towards morning he came back for a few
minutes to relieve my Mother's anxiety, and then returned, and did
not leave the persons till they were fully reconciled.  Mr Wilberforce
enumerated among his blessings of every kind, " My never having
been disgraced for refusing to fight a duel [1]."]

The Duke of Wellington's wise order, as Commander-in-
Chief, that before any Challenge could be accepted by one
Officer from another, the causes which led to it should be
investigated, checked duelling in the Army, and led to its
discontinuance elsewhere.

Lord Camelford once took a freak to cross in a boat from

---

[1] Wilberforce's *Life*, Vol. v. p. 113.

Dover to Calais, while we were at war with France. The police, hearing of his design, apprehended him. Mr Pitt, who was his kinsman, instituted an enquiry, and in a few days ordered his release. Lord C. was so angry at his not giving, on hearing who it was that had been arrested, an instant order for his discharge, that he said to Horne Tooke, with whom he was well acquainted, " How can I avenge myself?" He answered, that he could do it very well by putting his black servant, Mungo, into his Borough of Old Sarum. Lord C. agreed; but the next day thought better of it, and told Horne Tooke so; "Well," said he, "then the next best thing you can do is to put *me* in." This was done, and H. T., who had in early life taken holy orders, sat till the end of that Parliament. Addington, then Prime Minister, timidly dreading his eloquent attacks, to get rid of him had a Bill brought in to prevent Clergymen being returned as Representatives.

In one Session (1834), thinking it a hardship that Clergymen without cure of souls, might not be in the House when there was the grievous inequality of Dissenting Ministers and Roman Catholic Priests being admitted, I moved a repeal of Addington's Bill, and Baring, afterwards Lord Ashburton, seconded it. I forget if it went to a division; but the majority against it was so great, that if not, I withdrew it. I thought that many men were hardly kept out of the House, such, for instance, as younger sons who had taken orders, ˙and then succeeded to their family estates. My own friend, Mr Jolliffe, of Ammerdown Park, Somersetshire, was such an one, Le Grice, of Cornwall, was another. While I was in Parliament a Dissenting Minister, named Fox, sat for Oldham. He was a very eloquent man, and Hope Vere took me once to hear him preach. It was said, too, that there was a Monk in the House named Romaine[1].

---

[1] Five or six Clergymen have seats at present (1869) in the House of Lords, and one, Lord O'Neill, "came not to his place by accident;" but was created, being previously the Rev. Wm. O'Neill.

# CHAPTER XVI.

## 1836.

1836.   THIS Summer I paid a visit to my Brother-in-law, Dr Thackeray of Chester.   When there I went to see his Welsh farm and woods in Flintshire.   He had purchased a barren waste in 1804 many years before and planted it, chiefly with Oak and Larch, and he lived to see a forest arise, chiefly from acorns which he himself had sown.   His method of thinning and pruning was so excellent that he three times obtained the thirty guinea gold medal of the Society of Arts, for planting Forest Trees.   Curiously enough, his friends had all thought him mistaken in planting Larch, a tree for which there was no demand at such a distance from land or water carriage, but the event proved him accidentally, if not intentionally wise.   The Railroads came, and Larch was in such request for the Sleepers, that many of the trees soon found their way from the Welsh Mountains.   His woods were the admiration of the neighbourhood, and Professor Lindley came all the way from Town to inspect them. His mode of training was to select a leading shoot in each tree, when about two or three feet high; he then cut off with a sharp knife, and as close to the tree as possible, four or five of the shoots immediately *below* those he had pruned the year before—thus beginning at the top, and contrary to the usual practice, working downwards. He also paid great attention to draining his woods deeply.

[In order to see the plantations we drove to Nerquis, and then mounted ponies. The cottage where they were waiting for us was inhabited by a tenant of my Uncle's, and she afforded us a specimen of genuine Welsh sentiment. We noticed a very simple barometer which the country people use—an inverted phial. The inside of it was beaded, as if with dew-drops. "Ah!" said the good woman in Welsh, "they are the tears of the morning." The tears were soon dried however, for we had a charming sunshiny day on the Mountain, which was carpeted in the open spaces with gorse and heather in full bloom; and amidst all the soft blue forms around us *Möel Vamma*, the *Mother of Mountains*, was conspicuous.]

Dr Thackeray was a great benefactor to the Hospital and Charity Schools of Chester. The Townspeople presented him, through the Marquis of Westminster, with the freedom of the City, and erected, after his decease, a fine monument to his memory in the Cemetery; he having previously had a Public Funeral when he was buried in the Cathedral[1].

Having a few days to spare I accompanied the Rev. Elias Thackeray, Vicar of Dundalk, on his return to Ireland; my object being to get more accurate and practical knowledge of the state of that country than I could collect from books and

---

[1] William Makepeace Thackeray, M.D. Cantab. born at Cambridge 1769. Died at Chester 1849.

speeches. We landed at Kingstown, and proceeded in a jaunting Car to Dublin, along a road studded with pretty Country Houses, and passed a few days at the Gresham Hotel in Sackville Street. To my surprise we were less assailed by beggars than in London. I looked of course at and into the fine public buildings, but felt a far deeper interest in exploring the ruinous district behind the Castle. It abounds with roofless houses, the upper floors of which were unoccupied, and the lower ones, pervious, of course, to the rain, were inhabited by people in a most destitute condition. I conversed with many of them, and with the little shop-keepers in the neighbourhood, all of whom readily gave me what information they could. Want of employment, and their own disregard of appearances, were the prevailing causes of their wretchedness.

I wished to hear while at Dublin some Criminal trials, and I had enquired the time of holding the Sessions of Mr Shaw[1], the Recorder and Member for the University, with whom I was on courteous terms, notwithstanding the wide difference in our politics, he being an Extreme Tory and Orangeman. Mr Thackeray took me into Court, and introduced me to one of the Sheriffs, who placed me beside him, and to several of the Corporation. The Recorder in the first interval of business beckoned to me, and entering into conversation, invited me to name a day to dine with him at his Country Seat.

I observed in the Irish Court a usage different from that in an English one. The witness, instead of standing in a box, was seated on a Chair in the middle of the central table, which conspicuous situation seemed to me more likely

---

[1] Sir Frederick Shaw (Recorder of Dublin), though an old man, made "an eloquent and effective speech," which was loudly cheered at the Great Conference of the "Irish branch of the united Church of England and Ireland" held in 1869.

to impress his mind with the responsibility of giving correct
testimony than being in the witness box in our English
Courts; and on the whole I thought Justice was as admirably
administered as I had ever seen it.

From Mr Shaw's evident friendship towards me I found
it was supposed that my Politics were in accordance with
those of the Orangemen. In Dublin and elsewhere I listened
quietly to political remarks, deeming that controversy would
be useless, and wishing not to argue but to observe accurately
the feelings and sentiments of the people I was amongst.

We next proceeded to Drogheda, a neat Seaport Town,
where we stayed all night and part of the next day. I found
there a curious instance of manufacturing process in the fabrication of that article (pins), which Adam Smith instances as
an illustration of the division of Labour at the beginning of
his work on the *Wealth of Nations.* Some of the intermediate stages of the manufacture require very little manual
strength, it was therefore found profitable to send unfinished
pins from a manufactory in Lancashire to Drogheda, where
rent and labour were cheaper, and to have these intermediate
processes performed there by young girls. The pins, still
unfinished, were sent back to be completed in Lancashire.

Thence we proceeded to Dundalk, of which place my
Brother-in-law was Vicar[1]. We visited the School where
Children of all religious beliefs were being educated together.
Portions of scripture, agreed upon by both Protestant and
Roman Catholic Clergy (of whom Archbp. Whately was
one), were printed on separate slips, and read aloud by the
several classes. Instruction in the respective tenets of Roman

[1] In the Irish Sketch Book, Vol. II. p. 187, Mr Thackeray has
drawn his kind and venerable cousin to the life, and in another work
he alludes to him as "the gentle Elias." The Primate of Ireland
(Lord John Beresford) had such regard for him that he held his Pall.

Catholicism, the Church of England, and Presbyterianism was left to their several Pastors.

We went to see the burying-ground of the Parish, where I observed a crowd of persons. I enquired of the Vicar what it was, and he said he believed it was a Roman Catholic funeral. I asked if such took place in the same ground as the Protestants? he seemed rather surprised at the question, and answered that of course they did. It appeared in another conversation with him that his man-servant was a Roman Catholic. I asked how it was that he attended the family prayers? He answered that when the man first came into his service it was mentioned to him that he need not join in their devotions, but he said, "I'll come and see," and afterwards, finding nothing to offend him, continued to attend.

Having shown me the habitations and modes of life of some of his own Protestant parishioners, the Vicar then introduced me to the Priest, Mr Marmion, a courteous intelligent man, and left me with him. He said to me, "Now what do you wish to see?" I requested him to take me to some of the best and some of the worst dwellings of his own poor. In the former we found a very neatly-furnished cottage of a brother and sister, who by their industry maintained their bed-ridden Father, and who expressed their satisfaction at being able to do so without any charitable assistance. We then visited one abode where dirt and discomfort were obvious, and the furniture was scanty and broken. I enquired of Mr Marmion if he thought that intemperance was the cause of the disorder of this home and of others like it, and he said that he believed that it was.

I found the state of Agriculture in Ireland for the most part very indifferent, so far at least as regarded the abundance of weeds, especially that large succulent plant called the Ragwort, which the small occupiers seemed too indolent to eradicate. There were some exceptions. A Farm about a mile from Dundalk was in excellent condition, but then the Farmer (named Campbell) was a Scotchman. I was invited to pass a day with Mr Booth, the owner and occupier of a Farm about three miles from Dundalk on the road to Louth, in order that I might inspect it, and I thought it superior both in cultivation, and in plain useful buildings, to anything I had seen in the (at that time) few well-cultivated districts of England. The day after I left Dundalk (to my regret) a circumstance occurred which showed the liberal Irish hospitality. My Brother-in-law received a letter from the Archbishop of Armagh, saying that he had heard that an English Member of Parliament was his guest, and inviting him to bring him on a visit of some days to the Palace.

On my return to Chester I visited Liverpool and travelled from thence, for curiosity, a few miles towards Manchester on that then novel mode of conveyance, a Railroad. It seems to me extraordinary that it had not been discovered long before. While I was at School tramways were used at Hull between the Docks and Warehouses, whereby one horse drawing a cart did the work of three or four. Within a mile of them were steam Engines for grinding wheat, or crushing seed for oil, and yet no one till nearly 40 years afterwards thought of combining the two. Dr Darwin predicted a change, both in prose and verse. "There is reason to believe it (the *Steam Engine*) may in time be applied to the rowing of barges, and the moving of carriages along the Road[1]."

> "Soon shall thine arm, unconquered Steam, afar
> Drag the slow barge, or drive the rapid car."

[1] Darwin's *Economy of Vegetation*, Vol. 1. p. 31, 4th Ed. 1799.

Stuart Mill says, "hitherto it is a question if all the inventions yet made have lightened the day's toil of any human being." Perhaps so; but then men for their toil get greater comforts which are the result of such inventions.

This was the first and then the only railway in existence. It had been formally opened by Ministers Sept. 15th, 1830, at Liverpool. One of the party, Mr Huskisson, lost his life by getting out of the train too hastily. My friend Daniel Sykes was with him, and told me the particulars.

Mr Huskisson made early efforts in the cause of Free-trade, and had a triumphant success about the Silk-trade. No manufactured silk was admitted into this Country, not even from India, and as the heat of that climate renders the silk more pliable it was much sought after, and people were thankful to obtain in some *indirect* way a few India handkerchiefs. At the time Mr Huskisson mooted the subject there was an absolute prohibition against importing French silks. He obtained an alteration of the Law, and they came in, as well as the raw silk, at a duty of 30 per cent. Even with this the English manufacturer contrived to improve upon them, so that ours were in time made superior to the Foreign. Fox, who understood nothing of Political Economy, opposed the commercial treaty which Pitt had made with France previous to the Revolution, and which as far as it went was favourable to Free-trade[1].

I have a high opinion of Cobden. He had clear ideas of Political Economy when he effected the treaty of Commerce between France and England; and he proved his disinterestedness by declining office, as if he wished to show that he had only his Country's good at heart, not his own aggrandisement.

[1] "Of that generation of Statesmen (Erskine, Sheridan, Grey and Fox) Pitt alone had studied Adam Smith."

I found at Chester an old friend in one of the Canons, Archdeacon Wrangham. He was a native of East York- shire, and one of the many excellent scholars educated by Joseph Milner. He came up to Magdalene College in 1786, and in October of the following year, on the suggestion of Dr Jowett, then, I believe, Fellow and Tutor of Trinity Hall, removed thither, as holding out far better academical prospects. He obtained one of the Browne's Medals for the Greek and Latin Epigrams, was 3rd Wrangler, 2nd Mathe- matical Prizeman, and 1st Classical Medallist, though the distinguished Tweddell was his competitor. After this extraordinary career of eminence in University honours, his election to a clerical fellowship, to which a share in the tuition was usually attached, seemed a matter of course in itself, and of great importance to the prosperity of the College. A vacancy soon occurred, he was rejected, and a Mr Vickers, who had been 4th Wrangler, but was in every way inferior in talents and attainments to Wrangham, was brought from another College to supplant him. The astonishment of the University was great. A sufficient, or any real reason, was in vain sought for. No moral objection was alleged or existed; nothing was suggested except dis- pleasure at a severe epigram (which he did not write about a garden made by Dr Jowett) and his political opinions. Young Wrangham was a Whig, and therefore, according to the usage of those troubled times, was accused of being a favourer of the bloody excesses of the French Revolution. He had put up in his rooms the table of the French Revo- lutionary Calendar. This was quoted as a proof of his approbation of their whole proceedings, while the motto which he had written upon it was not mentioned or thought of:

"utinam his potius nugis tota illa dedissent
Tempora sævitiæ[1]."

(Would in such trifles they had spent that time
Disgrac'd by bloodshed and ferocious crime.)

His prospects at his College were now closed; he shook
the dust from off his feet against its walls, and migrated,
previously to taking his M.A. degree, to Trinity College,
not with any hope of a fellowship, to which he was not then
eligible, but from admiration of its literary character and
of its high-minded exemption from the taint of political
prejudice in the disposal of its offices and emoluments.

"Thebes did his rude unknowing youth engage;
He chooses Athens in his riper age."

But his merits were appreciated elsewhere. The valuable
rectory of Hunmanby, on the East coast of Yorkshire,
was given to him by the Osbaldiston family, and the
Archbishop of York appointed him his examining Chaplain,
gave him a Prebendal Stall in that Cathedral, the Arch-
deaconry of Cleveland in 1820, and that of the East Riding
in 1828.

A few years after this visit of mine to Chester he made
a gift to Trinity College of one thousand volumes, containing
from 8 to 10,000 tracts. The Archdeacon amid his severe
studies and laborious duties made the formation of a large
library his chief amusement. Sydney Smith when on a
visit to him at Hunmanby, once said to Mrs Wrangham,
"If there be a room which you wish to preserve from being
completely surrounded with books, let me advise you not
to suffer a single shelf to be placed in it, for they will
creep around you like an Erysipelas till they have covered
the whole."

[1] Juv. *Sat.* IV. 150.

The Epigram was made on Dr Jowett's fencing in a small angle of the College from the public way and converting it into a garden. I give the correct version :

> "A little garden little Jowett made,
> And fenced it with a little Palisade;
> A little taste hath little Dr Jowett,
> This little garden doth a little show it !"

Wrangham told me at Chester that he did not write these lines, but only, thinking them clever, repeated them. They have been also attributed to Porson, as composed extempore. Jowett having turned the little garden into a gravelled plot, the author, whoever he was, added two more lines by way of P. S. :

> " Because this garden made a little talk,
> He changed it to a little gravel walk."

[I remember Archdeacon Wrangham and my Father talking together in the Summer of 1836. The former was much interested in Lord Prudhoe's account of the magic he had lately seen practised at Cairo. He told us that Lord P. asked the boy, who was the *clairvoyant* and who held some ink within the hollow of his hand, to describe Archdeacon Wrangham. The boy contemplated the dark mirror for awhile, and then said, " I see a mild (or gentle) looking Frank, walking in a garden, reading on a little book." This was a true description both of his person and his habit, and the Archdeacon was so pleased with it that he was inclined to believe a little in the sorcery. He was a most courteous refined gentleman, as well as an elegant Scholar. I asked him to write something in my Album, and he returned it to me with some lines which would fill a corner in the *Arundines Cami.* I have placed them in the Appendix, unwilling that such graceful verse should perish.]

Soon after my return to Cambridge, I attended in King's College Chapel the funeral of the Rev. Charles Simeon, the celebrated Evangelical Preacher, who had ministered for more than fifty years in the Church of the Holy Trinity. The procession assembled in the Quadrangle of King's College, and included nearly all the Heads of Colleges and leading Members of the University, who were desirous of showing respect to the deceased. And this was the man whose early ministry had met with such vehement opposition, who could with difficulty draw a congregation, and whose first Administration of the Sacrament was attended by only four persons!

["Nearly 700 members of the University assembled to join in the solemnity. The whole Town throughout the day partook of the general feeling; the shops were closed, and a silent awe pervaded the streets." Mr Simeon had lived down all hostility, had gained the devoted regard of his adherents, the respect even of his opponents, and now "Honour's voice" would "provoke his silent dust," but

> "All life long his homage rose
> To far other shrines than those;
> And the Prize he sought and won
> Was the Crown for duty done."]

# CHAPTER XVI.

## 1837.

1837.  PARLIAMENT met Jan. 31st, and the Session was opened by Commission. Reform continued to progress, though not in any extensive measure. Some improvements in the Law had taken place already. The mitigation of the Penal Code was effected step by step through many Sessions. In this year the punishment of Death was abolished for Forgery and the uttering of forged notes, and for several other offences, thereby preventing acquittals from a reluctance in juries to inflict the severest penalty. In some cases punishment might take place where guilt was doubtful; the having forged bank-notes in possession with the intent of uttering was punishable with transportation. The Bank of England generally offered a culprit to abstain from the charge of uttering if he would plead to the minor offence, and it was thought that some persons who really had not a guilty intent accepted this compromise from the dread of an ignominious death.

The disposal of Landed Property by Will required three Witnesses; that of personal property did not even require one. Lord Langdale, in the House of Peers, was the author of an Act requiring two witnesses, and two only, for the testamentary disposal of any property whatever. Various other valuable emendations of the Laws respecting Wills were included in this Act, which passed the lower House all but unopposed.

Several Acts also passed in Amendment of Scottish Law. The Right Hon. John Archibald Murray, M.P. for Leith, twice previously Lord Advocate of Scotland, and afterwards a Judge under the title of Lord Murray[1], was the only Scottish Lawyer on the Ministerial side. Having, of course, opened the debate at each stage of the proceedings he was not, by the rules of the House, permitted to reply to the objections of Sir George Clerk and other Scotsmen. I had formerly acquired a popular knowledge of Scottish Law in order to compare it with the English; and Mr Murray generally instructed me in the merits of the particular measure which enabled me, though an Englishman, to give some answer to his opponents. I can recollect at this moment the surprise of Sir G. Clerk when I first did so. Mr Murray was the friend of Francis Horner, and a most delightful person in private life. I met at his house the famous Pole, Czartorysky.

---

[1] "John Archibald Murray who was so beloved by Francis Horner, and by a multitude of persons who never saw him, for Horner's sake. Various honours fell to him in the course of his life, but the highest was unquestionably the place he fills in Horner's *Memoirs*." He was born in 1780. Died in 1859.

In this Session I brought forward a motion for appointing a Commission to enquire into the state of the Universities of Oxford and Cambridge. Among the errors of the then existing state of things that always pressed strongly on my mind was the limitation of some of the Fellowships in every College in Cambridge, except Trinity and King's, to particular Counties or Districts, which often amounted to exclusion, as in some Colleges there could not be more than one or two born in a particular County eligible to Fellowships. It might have been reasonable Centuries ago, when there was much less travelling intercourse between different parts of the Kingdom, and a kind of Clanship arose which might gradually have excluded all Candidates for Fellowships except those born in a particular neighbourhood. But this could not possibly happen in the 19th Century. As an instance of the evils of exclusion I may mention that Mr Inman of St John's College, Cambridge, who was Senior Wrangler in the year 1800, could never obtain a Fellowship, being born at Sedbergh in Yorkshire, and educated at its School, to which two Fellowships were attached; these and two others of that County *generally* were filled by men of far inferior merit. The whole of Wales also was considered as one County. This was a great hardship.

Dr Wood, Master of St John's, Cambridge, was the author of one good thing. He opened the Foundation Fellowships. This reform did not, of course, affect such as had been founded by Bequest. The celibacy of Fellows, arising chiefly from the slow succession to livings, was another evil of the older Statutes which I wished to see abolished, as regarded those who did *not* hold any College office.

[Although the Motion made by my Father for a University Commission was many years in advance of that which was eventually issued, and was deemed by the then Administration premature, yet, whether it were really so or not, it was received with sympathy and approval by many, and represented the feeling of others as well as his own. Prof. Sedgwick wrote to him in 1833, "Our University wants a Visitation," and Mr Spring Rice told the presenter of a Petition on this subject in 1837 (this very year), that "those bodies and their whole system required a searching investigation." Many letters were written to my Father pointing out *gravamina* of which the writers were specially cognisant, among them the following may justify insertion. I have retained the Capitals wherever Dr Arnold wrote them after the German custom.]

DR ARNOLD *to* PROFESSOR PRYME.

Rugby, *March 8th*, 1837.

" SIR,

"I thank you much for your Letter. I had regarded your intended Motion respecting the Universities with the deepest Interest, and feel therefore Extremely obliged to you for allowing me to express some of my Views on the Matter to you. As to the great Question of all, the Admission of Dissenters, it is so mixed up with the still greater Question of the Church, that I hardly know how to separate them;—and besides I imagine that nothing on this Point could be carried now. But there are three points at Oxford, which, though of very different Importance, might all I think be noticed with Advantage.

"First, the System of Fines; I do not mean as regards the Tenant, but as regards those Members of the College Foundations who do not belong to the governing Body. It is the Practice, I believe, to divide the Corn Rents either equally, or in certain fixed Proportions, fixed by the Founder, among all the Members of the Foundation; but the Fines, which form always a large Proportion of the gross

Income of the College, are divided exclusively by the go-
verning Body amongst themselves. Where this governing
Body includes all the Fellows, as at Oriel, Corpus, and New
College, then those who do not share the Fines are only
the Scholars and Probationer Fellows: but where it consists
of what is called a Seniority,—seven or whatever number it
be, of the senior Fellows,—then all the Fellows not on the
Seniority are excluded; and this is the case at Brazenose.
Now the Question is,—whether this is according to the
Founder's Intentions, or whether it has been legalised by
any subsequent Statute,—of the Realm, I mean, not of the
University. The Fines originally were a direct Bribe, paid
by the Tenant to the Bursar or Treasurer of the College, for
letting him renew on favourable Terms: subsequently the
Bursars were not allowed to keep it all to themselves, but it
was shared by all those with whom lay the Power of either
granting or refusing the Renewal. But still if the College
Property be notoriously underlet, because a great part of
the Rent is paid in the Shape of Fines, those who are entitled to a certain Share in the Proceeds are manifestly de-
frauded, if they are not allowed their Proportion of the
Fines also. This Question only affects the Members of the
several Foundations as Individuals; still it has always struck
me as a great Unfitness, that a System should go on with
such a primâ Facie Look of direct Fraud about it.

"Secondly,—All Members of Foundations are required to
take an Oath to maintain the Rights of the College, &c.;
and, amongst other things, they swear that if expelled by
the College, they will not appeal to any Court of Law.
This Oath is imposed at Winchester College, or was in my
Time, on every Boy as soon as he was fifteen. I object
utterly on Principle, to any private Society administering an
Oath to its Members at all. Still more so to Boys: but even

if it were a Promise or Engagement, the Promise of not appealing to the King's Courts is monstrous, and savours completely of the Spirit of secret Societies, who regard the Law as their worst Enemy. The University has lately repealed some of its Oaths; but it still retains far too many.

"Thirdly,—The University should be restored,—that is, the Monopoly of the Colleges should be taken away,—by allowing any Master of Arts, according to the old Practice of Oxford, to open a Hall for the Reception of Students. The present Practice dates, I think, from the Age of Elizabeth, when the old Halls had fallen into Decay; and then the Gift of the Headship of the existing Halls was placed in the Chancellor's Hands, and every Member of the University was required to be a Member of some College, or of one of these recognised Halls. The Evils of the present System, combined with a Statute passed, I believe, within the present Century, obliging every Undergraduate under three years' Standing to sleep in College, are very great. The number of Members at a College is regulated therefore by the Size of its Buildings, and thus some of the very worst Colleges have the greatest number of Votes in Convocation, and consequently the greatest Influence in the Decisions of the University. I am obliged to be brief; but this Point is, I am sure, of the greatest Importance, and might open the Door to much Good. I am not at all able to answer for all the Details of the Matters which I have mentioned, and you know how readily the Enemy would exult if he can detect the slightest Inaccuracy in Detail, and how gladly he will avail himself of such a Triumph to lead away Men's minds from the real Question. But I think all the three Points which I have named are of Importance. I am delighted that you take up this Question. No man ought to meddle with the Universities who does not know them well and love them well; they are great and noble

Places, and I am sure that no Man in England has a deeper affection for Oxford than I have, or more appreciates its inimitable advantages. And therefore I wish it improved and reformed; though this is a *therefore* which men are exceedingly slow to understand.

"Will you thank Mr Robinson for his Letter, which I hope to answer by Mr Wordsworth, who is now staying with us. I think he has not quite understood my meaning; he may be assured that I shall not hastily leave the London University,—though I do not wish it to be in all Things the Antipodes of Oxford,—I would far rather of the two that it should be its exact Counterpart; and yet I am very far from wishing that.

"Believe me, to remain, with very sincere Respect and Esteem,

"Your very faithful and obedient Servant,

"T. ARNOLD."

After a short debate on my Motion, it was privately intimated to me that Lord John Russell wished me to withdraw it, thinking that the time for it was not yet come, and saying, that *he* would bring it forward as soon as he thought he could do so with a probability of success. It was not till thirteen years afterwards that the Cambridge Commission was issued[1].

It was during this year that Mr Monckton Milnes, afterwards created Baron Houghton, entered the House as Mem-

---

[1] Lord Palmerston said on one occasion, "The great mistake made by all Governments, not only in this country, but everywhere, is to be too late in the measures which they adopt. Government comes down with its measure when the time of proposing it with effect is gone by, and a measure which may be the result of conviction and the spontaneous offering of modified opinions, and a concession to a sense of justice wears to the public all the appearance of a surrender to fear."

ber for Pontefract. I remember his Grandfather being M.P.
for Yorkshire. His Father, who was a great friend of, and
contemporary with, Lord Palmerston, was a first Classman in
College Examinations. He represented Pontefract, and made
an admirable speech on the Address, in favour of continuing the war against France. He was between twenty-
three and twenty-four years of age when Mr Perceval, in
forming his Administration, offered him either the Chancel-
lorship of the Exchequer, or (if he preferred not to have a
seat in the Cabinet) the Secretaryship for War. On his declining to take Office, from a dislike to giving up his political
and social independence, the same offer was made to Lord
Palmerston, and he accepted the latter place, Mr Perceval
himself retaining the former. Not long afterwards Mr Milnes
retired into the private life of a Country Gentleman. At a
later period he was offered a Peerage by Lord Palmerston,
which he declined.

Mr Monckton Milnes had not .published his Poems when
he entered the House. But without that *prestige* his speeches
were listened to respectfully, and he was usually much
cheered. He once introduced Baron Bunsen to me at Cambridge, and we had half an hour's talk on Political Economy.
Though I admired Bunsen's fine intellect, I did not think
his views on that Science very enlightened. He advocated
Free Trade in Germany, but only between the different
States.

It was an understood rule in the House of Commons
to give a patient and attentive hearing to the maiden speech
of a new Member. On the other hand it was expected that
he should comport himself modestly. I remember but two
exceptions. One was the case of Mr D'Israeli, who entered
Parliament as the Tory Member for Maidstone in this year.
It was said that he had formerly professed Radical principles,

but this, I think, by itself would not have occasioned an unfavourable reception, had not his too confident and presumptuous manner offended his audience. When he found that he could not get a hearing, he threw himself down on the Bench behind him, exclaiming with vehemence, "The time will come when you *shall* hear me."

[My Father saw this prediction *more* than verified. He said to me while dictating the preceding passage, "I see him in my mind's eye now. I remember once paying him a compliment for which he gave me a smile and a bow. He had remarked in a speech, 'Although the honourable member for Cambridge thinks slightingly of my plan,' I rose for a moment and said, 'I never could have thought slightingly of anything said by the Author of *Vivian Grey.*'"]

This was an exceeding contrast to the graceful, harmonious, modest, and almost timid maiden speech of Mr W. E. Gladstone[1]; a manner that I never saw excelled except by Lord Derby's when he was in the House of Commons. The speaking of these two was like a stream pouring forth; or it might be described as if they were reading from a book. I have heard Pitt, Fox, and other great speakers, but never any to equal Lord Derby, when Mr Stanley, for elegance and sweetness of expression. His manner was most graceful and his voice harmonious. I never missed a debate, and observed his speeches and his conduct on every occasion; and I could not help thinking rather that his object was to become Prime Minister than that he was actuated by any definite political principle. Of Mr Gladstone

---

[1] "A foreigner once remarked that until he had heard Mr Gladstone speak some few years ago, he never believed that the English was a musical language; but that after hearing him he was convinced that it was one of the most *melodious* of all living tongues."—*Times*, Jan. 28, 1867.

we all agreed in saying, "This is a young man of great promise."

On the 20th of June Queen Victoria succeeded to the Throne by the decease of her Uncle, William IV. We took the Oath of Allegiance to her that afternoon by her baptismal name of Alexandrina Victoria. A few days afterwards she consulted some of her Cabinet Ministers (I had it from one of them) individually, who recommended the more euphonious name of Victoria to be used only.

Parliament, by the Statute of William III., dies a natural death at the end of six months after the decease of a Sovereign, the reason for which I never could comprehend. The Dissolution took place, however, sooner than it need have done, and the third and last Parliament of William IV. was prorogued by the youthful Queen in person, July 17. The silvery tones of her voice as she read her speech were peculiarly attractive.

Mr Spring Rice, then Chancellor of the Exchequer, and I were again returned for the Borough of Cambridge ; I by a majority of 64 over my former opponent, Mr J. L. Knight. The Hon. H. T. Manners Sutton was now the second Candidate on the Tory side.

[There was a short Autumnal Session in November, which was opened by her Majesty. The Address was carried in the Lords without a division, and in the Commons by a majority of 509 to 20. The only debates of any importance were on the Pension List, and on the Affairs of Lower Canada. A great dinner was given at Cambridge in December to the Whig Members, at which 450 persons were present.]

# CHAPTER XVII.

## 1838.

1838. THE new Parliament re-assembled on Jan. 16,
and the Debates on Canada were renewed with
increased animation on account of the recent Insurrection
there; but the interest felt in them is now become a thing
of the past, and it would be as useless as impossible for me
to follow in detail the work of each Session step by step.
One great measure passed in this is one entitled to special
notice; it was the Act to abridge Pluralities, and to make
better provision for the residence of the Clergy. This was
greatly needed, for Beneficed Clergy frequently held two
or three Livings. I have heard my Uncle speak of one
who held eleven pieces of preferment. Curates also were

pluralists, having often two or three Curacies to serve, and they passed the Sunday in riding about from one to the other. In a village near Cambridge there is an Obelisk (whose history I could never learn), and it is related that the Parish Clerk stood by it on a Sunday and waved a handkerchief if there was a congregation in the Church; if not, the Curate rode on. Most of the Curacies in that neighbourhood were served by Fellows of Colleges, and so much the custom was it, that there was a Curate's Club formed, in order that they might sup at each other's rooms after the labours of the day. Three out of the four Chaplains at Trinity College never resided in my time, but engaged the fourth to take their share of the service for them. He was called *Pontius Pilate*, because he was said to offer to give any man as far as that name in the Service and beat him!

Dr Parr had a Curacy in Warwickshire, and resided on it, although his living was in Huntingdonshire. On a visit to Cambridge he once said, " There happened to be a County Election as I came along, and so I dropped a vote at Huntingdon[1]."

In my younger days some of the Bishops even did not reside in their Dioceses. Dr Mansel, Master of Trinity, was Bishop of Bristol, and usually resided at his Lodge, visiting his Diocese occasionally. It was a small Bishoprick. He told

---

[1] Dr Parr was however a good Churchman. His friend Mr Basil Montagu and his step-daughter were on a visit to Hatton. On the Sunday when the Creed was being said Dr P. noticing that Mr B. M. did not rise with the rest of the congregation, called to him from the reading desk " Basil, stand up." It was not that Mr B. M. was disinclined to do so, but rather that he was in a reverie, and had not noticed when the others stood up. Dr Parr said to him afterwards " You know I could not have a fine Lawyer like you coming down from Town and setting my poor people a bad example."

me that when he had deducted all necessary expenses, and those charities which he felt obliged to support, his net income was only £800 per annum.

Dr Watson, Bishop of Llandaff, also resided in Cambridge, and towards the end of his life had a country-house at the Lakes, and lived there entirely. He kept his Regius Professorship of Divinity, appointing, with the consent of the University, a Deputy with a salary of £200 per annum. Drs Kipling and Ramsden were successively his Deputies, both learned men. He was said to have had thirteen pieces of preferment, and not to have lived within a hundred miles of any one of them. Certainly he never resided in his Diocese during an Episcopate of thirty-four years. The Bishop of Elphin had a house at the Hills, near Cambridge. Attending a Levee one day, George III. said to him, " I think, my Lord, your Bishoprick is in Ireland." " Yes, your Majesty." " You are very often in England," was the royal rejoinder. The Bishop took the hint, and retired to his Diocese[1].

The Clergy had, generally speaking, no schools to superintend; the Village children went to a Dame-School, paying 3d. a week. The Clergyman's time was only occupied by the Sunday Services, and by visiting his Parishioners, if sent for, when they were sick or dying; they therefore followed their own tastes in their pursuits, and shooting was one of these[2]. I can relate an anecdote of a circumstance which happened within my own knowledge. When a boy at Mr Beetham's in Nottinghamshire, a funeral was to take place

---

[1] Episcopal non-residence was an admitted fact, for we read in Lord Colchester's Diary "A Bishop wanted amongst the Heads of Houses at Cambridge, Mansel is recommended."

[2] Sydney Smith in a Visitation Sermon in 1817 advised the Clergy not to devote too much time to shooting and hunting!

in a village close by, the Clergyman of which was from home. They sent to the next Parish, but the Vicar was out shooting, and the messenger followed him. He agreed to perform the Service, shot up to the Church, put his gun in a corner, donned the Surplice, and after the interment continued his day's sport. John Wesley's preaching effected the first change, and stirred up men to greater earnestness.

Forty miles was the distance within which two livings could be held. There was some doubt whether it meant as the crow flies, or by the road. I have been told that Milner, Dean of Carlisle, maintained that the former was the true interpretation, but it was ruled to mean forty miles by the nearest passable road.

By this Act of 1838 no person having preferment in one Cathedral could hold any in another, and not more than two preferments could be held together; nor two benefices, unless within ten miles of each other, nor if the population of one of the two were more than 3,000, or if the united yearly value was more than £1,000. Non-residence was to incur the forfeiture of a portion of the income according to its duration. Bishops could enforce residence, appoint Curates in case of the non-resident Clergyman not doing so, order two services on Sundays, and require a curate where the population should exceed 2,000.

Several Acts improving our English Law were passed, one of which abolished the creditor's power to arrest any person who owed him money to any amount which he chose to specify, and consigned the supposed debtor to a prison, unless he could find securities to a much larger amount. This power of arrest is now confined to cases where there is good ground for alleging that the debtor is intending to quit the Kingdom, which must be done before a Judge, and his fiat obtained.

The Irish Poor Law Act passed in this Session, and one for carrying the Mails by Railways.

On the Accession of a new Sovereign a fresh presentation at the Levee is requisite. I was presented to Queen Victoria on the 23rd of May by the Chancellor of the Exchequer (the Right Hon. T. S. Rice), with whom I had dined on her birthday (the 17th May). Although at this time only 56 years of age, this was the fourth Sovereign at whose Court I had been. I could not help contrasting the girlish gracefulness of the young Queen with the venerable appearance of her Grandfather. A few days after this I had the honour of meeting her at an evening party given by His Royal Highness the Duke of Sussex at Kensington Palace.

I had met the Duke once previously at a party of five or six at Mr George Adam Browne's rooms at Trinity. All smoked, in compliment to him, but myself. He noticed it, but in courteous terms. He was a Freemason, and so was G. A. B., and their intimacy arose, I fancy, from an acquaintance formed at one of the Lodge Festivals.

Freemasonry was very useful in the dark ages, and even in late years it has been of some advantage. I have read an anecdote of one of our Officers being wounded in the Peninsular War, and lying on the field of battle. A French Officer passed him, and the Englishman made the *sign* on the chance of his being a Freemason like himself, and was relieved and taken care of by the other, who understood it.

[I add an account of the party, which I have found since my Father's decease, in a letter written to me by him on May 31, 1838. " I arrived at Kensington Palace soon after 10, the hour fixed on account of Epsom, and joined the gay crowd; which slowly moved on through long suites of apartments, part of them galleries full of books. When we got near the presence the rapidity was occasionally checked by two servants joining hands across a doorway. We then reached the Duke's room : he was splendidly dressed in a uniform, with a black skull cap. As everyone passed before him, he bowed or spoke. I heard him say to O'Connell, " Ah, my friend Dan." Three rooms further on was the Queen. She stood with ladies on each side, a little advanced from the circle, handsomely but simply attired in white muslin and lace. She bowed or spoke to each one as they passed. To two ladies she went up and shook hands, and looked very pleasing and interesting. After staying a few minutes in a circle or line opposite we passed on, and found we had got round to the former rooms. A large one was now open, as is usual at routs, with servants behind a counter serving tea, coffee, lemonade, wine, cake, and ices. Strawberries, cherries, peaches, and magnificent grapes were in abundance. We came down to the entrance, but waited long for our carriage, and got home at half-past two. There were, I hear, 1500 persons, chiefly Whigs, a small sprinkling of Tories, the magnates of the land, and all in Court-dresses. It was indeed a splendid scene. I spoke or talked with about 100 whom I knew. I enjoyed it much at the time, and am glad to have seen it."]

The Coronation did not take place till June 28th, 1838. The intense anxiety to witness it caused many who had obtained tickets of admission to Westminster Abbey to be there as early as 4 or 5 o'Clock in the morning. The House of Commons assembled at 10 o'Clock, when a ballot for the names of Counties took place. As any one was drawn, the Members thereof, including the Boroughs within it, crossed the Street, between ranks of Police, to the Abbey, where a portion of a commodious gallery afforded them an excellent sight of the Pageant. I had the good fortune to sit next to Sir James Graham, who knew, and took pleasure in pointing out to those around him, the distinguished persons who were present. " There is Prince Esterhazy," said he, as he passed, his robes adorned with Jewels; " he walks half a million;"

and so on[1]. We saw the whole of the proceedings, except the taking of the Sacrament by the Queen, for which she passed under our gallery to the Communion Table. The only undignified part of the proceeding was the scramble for Coronation medals, which were thrown down while the Lords did homage. Queen Victoria's demeanour on this, as on all other occasions when I saw her, was easy and dignified without formality.

[An anecdote illustrating this remark, and also her kindness of heart, must not be omitted. An aged peer, Lord Rolle, fell on going up the steps to do homage. The young Queen instantly went towards him and held out her hand to assist him, an action which was appreciated by all who saw it. One who was there told me that *this* was the most affecting incident, and that the most striking one was when at the moment of the Queen's being crowned, all the Peers and Peeresses put on their coronets amid a cry of " God save the Queen." The House of Commons joined for the first time in the ceremony by nine loud and hearty cheers after the homage of the Peers.]

Each of the Members of Parliament received a gold medal the next day on signing a declaration of having been present at the ceremonial in the place assigned to him. One of the County Members expressed to me his disappointment in not obtaining the medal by reason of his having accompanied a party of Ladies instead of being with the other Members.

[1] The Esterhazy Jewels, chiefly brilliants, were sold in 1867, by Christie and Manson. "These fashioned into the most extraordinary ornaments and sewed over uniforms till the fabric was literally stiff and cumbrous with their weight, were worn by Prince Nicholas and Prince Paul at the Coronations of Francis II., of Geo. IV., of Wm. IV., and of Victoria." The gem of the collection was a magnificent single stone, 17 carats, which ornamented a sword belt, and fetched £4,000. The Hungarian uniform embroidered in every part with costly pearls sold for more than £2,000.

During this Season I had the honour of an invitation to one of the Queen's State Balls, and saw her dance in a Quadrille with Lord Canning. Parliament was prorogued August 16.

Nov. 5th. I went on a visit to Lord Hardwicke at Wimpole to see his farms. They were in excellent order, and he had a very fine kind of wheat growing on them, imported by himself from Le Couteur, some of which he obligingly permitted me to purchase for the farm which I had in my own occupation. Lord H. had been a Naval Officer previously to coming to the title, which was of great advantage to him, for he is a prompt man of business both in and out of Parliament.

[In this winter my Father published a little volume of verse, "Jephthah and other poems," the recreation of his few leisure hours. He gave the greater part of the edition away to his friends. This is not the age for simply didactic poetry, as the *Athenæum* in a kind review of the little volume well said. "The seeming incongruity of the pursuits of poetry and Political Economy prepossessed us in favour of these elegant relaxations of an enlightened and well disciplined mind. The correct rhythm and select phraseology in which the results of research and reflection, informed by genuine feeling, are conveyed, give pleasure in the perusal ; though the images are not so vivid, nor is the passion so deep, or the impulse so strong, as to manifest the afflatus of creative genius. Poetry—that in a time when the appetite for reading was less vivacious, and the intellectual palate less habitually stimulated—would have delighted the select few, is now laid aside as insipid ; nothing but the highest or the lowest will now attract readers[1]."]

[1] *Athenæum.* December 24, 1838.

# CHAPTER XVIII.

## 1839.

1839.  PARLIAMENT met Feb. 5th; the Queen coming in person to open it. In this Session an Act was passed which affected the domestic life of every family in the United Kingdom. The Postage price of letters had been gradually increased during Mr Pitt's administration, and now varied, according to distance, from 4*d.* to 1*s.* 6*d.*[1] If there was one enclosure in the letter the postage was doubled, if two trebled, which occasioned frequent disputes with the Postmasters. Members of the two Houses had formerly the privilege of franking, by merely writing their name at the corner of the direction, and without any date.

---

[1] It may be interesting as relating to Foreign Posts, to notice that a letter to my Father from Lausanne written in the year 1821, cost 2*s.* 2*d.*; and though posted on the 20th of November did not reach London till December 3rd.

This was afterwards limited by requiring the date of time and place of posting to be added, and lastly by restricting the number to be sent to ten daily, and that of those to be received to fifteen, which was fixed by Mr Pitt on information given him by Mr Samuel Thornton, M.P. for Hull, who noted, by his request, the number which passed between him and his Constituents.

Mr Rowland Hill had previously published a plan for reducing all postages to one penny if within half-an-ounce. More Petitions than I remember in favour of this scheme, numerously signed, were now sent from all parts of the Country. The Government yielded to this general request contrary to their own opinion, as one of the Cabinet informed me, and they introduced an Act for regulating Postage Duties, and authorizing the Lords of the Treasury to carry out the measure, for which I and many other members voted under a similar feeling. By way of making the transition less difficult to the Postmasters, a uniform rate of fourpence was at first tried, and was followed in the next year by the present rate, the privilege of franking being still continued. It occasioned an immediate annual loss of more than two millions of Revenue, and of course required the levying of a tax to that amount on some other article. It has since been inconsiderately said, that such loss has been constantly diminishing, because the Revenue from the penny postage has been constantly increasing till it has more than reached the original amount. True, but such reasoners forget that the increasing population and Commerce of the Country must have proportionately augmented the Revenue therefrom if the old rates of postage had continued[1].

---

[1] The new Postage Law by which the uniform rate of 4d. per letter

After Easter the Right Hon. James Abercomby resigned the Speakership, feeling himself unequal to sustain the fatigues of his office. He was the son of Sir Ralph Abercromby, who commanded our forces in Egypt, to which the French army, deserted by Napoleon, had surrendered. He was a Barrister, and had practised at the English Bar with success. He united much courtesy with that plainness of manner which we often see in Scottish gentlemen, and his judicious and impartial conduct as Speaker had secured for him a general admiration. He was called, as is usual, to the House of Lords by the title of Baron Dunfermline, and was succeeded in his office by Mr Charles Shaw Lefevre.

An Act was also passed in this Session for further improving the Metropolitan Police. A separate one was provided for the City with similar clauses as to regulations, officers, &c., but with a Commissioner appointed by the Common Council, and some different provisions. The very imperfect state of the old Metropolitan Police, if Police it could be called, and the confused state of our criminal Law, forced itself upon Sir Robert Peel's attention, when he became Secretary of State for the Home Department, under the Duke of Wellington, in 1828. He has not perhaps had all the credit due to him for his introduction of the New Police, but one reason for it is, that crime has increased with the increasing population, and therefore the benefit is not so obvious; but it is a great improvement on the old system, especially at night, when a few superannuated men, who cost less than younger ones, called watchmen, were

was tried as an experiment, came into operation Dec. 5, 1839, the uniform rate of 1*d*., Jan. 10, 1840.

1839. Last year of the heavy postage, £2,522,495.
1840. First year of the low rate £471,000.
*Haydn's Dict. of Dates.*

appointed and paid by the Parishes to saunter through the streets with a lantern and staff. They disturbed the rest of the inhabitants by proclaiming aloud the hour, that it might be known that they were at their duty:

> "Past one o'Clock, and almost two,
> My Masters all, good day to you[1]!"

They had a little box to retire to in bad weather, and were supposed to be often in collusion with thieves[2]. Sir Wm. Pepys had his house (in Gloucester Place, Portman Square) robbed. The Burglar entered Sir William's room. After the trial he had an interview with him. A Culprit would often tell particulars in hope of mitigating his punishment. Sir Wm. Pepys, who on the night of the robbery had been ill and was lying awake, asked the man how it was that he had not heard the ladder put against the window-sill? he answered that he could not, for the Watch knew of it and called the hour at that precise moment. This I had from Sir William's son, the late Bishop of Worcester.

In addition to these old men, a few officers of higher grade were attached to the Bow Street Office, and known by the name of "Bow Street Runners;" they exercised a general superintendence, visiting occasionally the houses of resort frequented by thieves, and holding some intercourse with them. It was understood between them that a thief when wanted was to offer no resistance, and in return was

---

[1] *Herrick.*

[2] Capt. Gronow speaking of George IV.'s Coronation says "There was no police in those days, and, with the exception of a few constables and some soldiers, there was no force to prevent the Metropolis from being burnt to the ground, if it had pleased the mob to have set it on fire." The Metropolitan Police Force in 1866 comprised 6882 persons.

not to be treated with any violence, or unnecessary restraint.
Many of these Runners showed great ingenuity in detecting
the perpetrators of offences. A friend of mine, a Barrister,
told me that he had the following relation from Townshend,
who was one of the most noted among them. A robbery
was committed at a country-house in Essex, and one of these
men (I think it was Townshend himself) was sent for. He
detected on the drive near the house a little hay, which
convinced him that a Hackney Coach had been there. He
went to the nearest turnpike and enquired if one had passed
through it about such a time? The man said, "Yes," but
could not remember the number. "It was 45," said a boy
at play near; "I'm certain of it, for I shouted as it passed,
Wilkes and Liberty[1]." The Runner immediately returned
to Town, found out No. 45, and summoned the Driver of it
before a Magistrate. The man acknowledged that he had
been out of Town, but asserted that it was elsewhere that
he had gone. The Magistrate said, "Turn down his sleeves,"
knowing the custom of these men to place the turnpike
tickets there, and that there was just the chance that he
might not have given up the one that freed him back. It
was so, and the ticket proved to be for the Essex route.
The man peached and the other robbers were taken.

The same friend told me another curious anecdote of
the ingenuity of these Detectives of former days. A friend
of his was invited one evening to meet M*r*Manus, who had

---

[1] The mob required Gentlemen and Ladies of all ranks as they
passed in their carriages to shout these words. An old writer says,
"This day, July 23, 1772, paid my maidservant her wages, and would
not let her lodge in my house as she refused to stay with me till Michaelmas, though very inconvenient to me, as I don't know where to provide
myself of one in her room; but 'Wilkes and Liberty' have brought
things to that pass, that ere long we shall get no one to serve us."—
Cole's *Register de Vicaria de Spalding*, p. 335.

gone down to the North on business, and from his own lips he had the following recital. He (M<sup>c</sup>M.) was sent for to inspect a house which had been entered by Burglars. After careful examination of the locks he pronounced that it was so cleverly done, that it could only have been effected by one of three or four men who were skilled in such work. Thereupon he returned to Town, and visited one of the houses where thieves resort. Entering into conversation with those he found there, he asked casually, "Where's such a man?" and "I don't see ——," and presently it came out that one man, whom he knew by name, had not been seen since the day of the robbery. His next step was to visit the different Coach-offices, and after some enquiries made in vain, he at last discovered that a man, like the one in question, had gone down with luggage to Oxford the day after the robbery. He took his place for the next day, and when arrived at Oxford set about tracing him in this way. He dressed himself very shabbily and visited the different little Inns in the outskirts of the Town, saying at each, "I want a pot of beer for ——," naming the man he wished to find. He was met with, "We dont know such a person here," to which he replied, "Oh! its a mistake then, no matter," and so on, till at last the answer was, "We'll send it." "No," says he, "that wont do, he's in a hurry, and I'm to go with you." He went, and found his man, and some of the stolen property in his possession.

A very perfect system of Police had been instituted in Paris during the latter part of the reign of the Bourbons (previous to the Revolution), of which a description has been given in an interesting work on the Police of our Metropolis, by one of its Magistrates, Patrick Colquhoun, though some of the details were said to be exaggerated.

Sir R. Peel proposed, in 1829, and carried into effect the

present system of Police, which is too well known to render
any description requisite. There is another boon which we
owe to him. By his "Six Acts" of Parliament he simplified
and adapted to the altered state of society several departments of criminal Law.

On the renewal or extension of the Metropolitan Police
Act, which included a circuit of ten miles from Whitehall,
I moved for altering the hours of closing Public Houses on
Sundays. They had hitherto been shut during Divine
Service in the morning, i.e. from eleven till one o'Clock.
I proposed that they should not be opened on Sundays till
one o'Clock. One of the Middlesex Magistrates had sug-
gested it to me, and I advised that a formal resolution to
that effect should be passed at a meeting of Magistrates.
It was done and placed in my hands, which so strengthened
my argument that the motion was agreed to, and the rule
found to work so well that it has since been extended to the
Kingdom generally.

Some little time after I met with a person who, having
no idea of my being connected with the matter, told me
what a remarkable change as to drunkenness that particular
clause had effected in his District ; for practically (which the
Publicans could hardly understand at first) it closed their
houses at midnight on Saturday.

At Whitsuntide I went on a visit to Dr Goodall, Provost
of Eton College. I was connected by marriage with his wife,
and beyond this family tie, there was the pleasure of enjoying his company as a Scholar. He won the Browne's Medals
for the Greek Ode and Epigrams in 1781, the year of my
birth, and also in 1782. Among the latter was one of the
shortest ever written, and it was very happy. Vestris was at
that time attracting great audiences by pirouetting on one
foot, while the other was raised at a right angle to the

body. The Vice-Chancellor, somewhat oddly I think, chose for the subject of the Epigrams, "*Stans pede in uno.*" Goodall took for his own motto part of a line of Horace, "Sumite materiam Vestris." The Epigram ran thus :

"IN STATUAM MERCURII.

"Sum tibi Mercurius. Quæris cur sto pede in uno?
Scilicet hoc hodie contigit esse lucrum."

In the Greek he turned it thus. To a person boasting of his skill in standing on one leg, another replies, "There is nothing in that, for any goose of my flock can do the same."

I alluded in this visit to these epigrams, and, old man as Goodall was, he was gratified by my praise.

[I can remember Dr G.'s fine and portly form entering my Father's Library, a long, low room filled with books, some of which were always in use and scattered on tables, chairs, sofas, even the floor. "Well Mr Professor," said the Provost of Eton after the first greetings, "this is a literary, I won't say a littered, room." Mr D'Israeli has described him in *Coningsby* as "the courtly Provost, the benignant Goodall[1]."]

The Epigrams of the Ancients were sententious rather than witty, and were more properly Inscriptions. Porson was constantly consulted about the Browne's Medals. In my year, when Gretton was Vice-Chancellor, who was no Scholar, it was so. I myself have been called in twice to help to decide upon them. The late Provost of King's (Thackeray) once consulted me as to a case of conscience, whether a man who had sent in several Epigrams on the same sheet of paper to select from, instead of only one pair, should be

---

[1] He died March 25, 1840.

entitled to the prize; I advised that a man is not the best judge of his own composition, as for instance in my own case when I had sent in two pair, and those which I had thought inferior were selected. The subject of mine was "*Nugæ Canoræ*," sounding trifles. For one of them I took my own Epigram. It is but a trifle, but if I gain the prize it will be a sounding trifle. They are now separated, and a prize may be given for each to two different men. In the debate which occurred in the Schools previously to the Grace to that effect passing (Sept. 1865) I took a part, and spoke against their division.

Mr Serj. Frere, late Master of Downing College, Cambridge, gained the Epigrams twice (in 1796 and 1797). They were excellent, and the Greek was beautiful.

"*Quæ doctus Roscius egit*," part of a line from Horace of the Augustan age, was the subject once given for the Epigrams (1805), and, as I think, very improperly. It was at the time of, and in allusion to the celebrated actor, Master Betty, the young Roscius, who at the age of twelve years played the most celebrated tragic characters in imitation of Garrick, who had himself been called the English Roscius[1]. Churchill, who was esteemed a fine satiric writer, wrote a poem called the *Rosciad*, which praised Garrick, and abused all other actors. I have read his poems lately, and was much disappointed. Instead of Satire I found little but virulent abuse. A few of the lines are impressive, as those two which Monk used to quote:

"With that low cunning which in fools supplies,
And amply too, the place of being wise."

I fancy that his fame partly arose from delineations of the

---

[1] Horat. Ep. II. I. 82. Master Betty when not quite thirteen got 100 guineas for each of 25 nights.

principal Dramatic Actors in his first work (*The Rosciad*), of which we cannot now judge[1].

While on the subject of Epigrams I may add a few of local interest. The following was told me by Selwyn (Father of the Professor), as one written by Gray the Poet, on Smith (Master of Trinity before Postlethwaite), who had published a celebrated book on Optics, when nearly blind, and cut down a row of Chestnut-trees:

> " Do you ask why old Focus Sylvanus defies,
> And wont suffer a Chestnut in being?
> 'Tis not for the prospect, because he's no eyes,
> But because he has writ about seeing."

ON THE MARRIAGE OF DR WEBB AND MISS GOULD.

> " Tela fuit simplex ; cupiens decus addere Telæ,
> Fecit Hymen geminam, puroque intexuit Auro."

> " Single no more, a double Webb behold,
> Hymen embroidered it with Virgin Gould."

Englished by the Author, the Rev. James Chartres, of King's College, Cambridge.

EPIGRAM.

> Poetis nos lætamur tribus :
> Si vis, amice, scire quibus?
> Pye, Peter Pindar, parvus Pybus
> Et forsan si ulterius pergis
> Habemus etiam James Bland Burgess.

STATUE OF CERES SPEAKS.

> " Nay flout not, Girls, 'tis not more strange than true,
> I once was lovely and admired as you.
> Transported now to Beauty's happier shore,
> I feel abashed, and show my face no more."

[1] My Father wrote this in 1862.

This was written by Mr Lambert, Senior Fellow of Trinity, on the fragment of a colossal Statue of Ceres, presented by Dr Edward Daniel Clarke to the University of Cambridge, of which, though the head and bust remain, the whole surface of the face is completely cut or worn away. Dr Clarke received ten guineas a sheet, free of all deductions, for his *Travels*, an instance of fleeting celebrity.

[He was the first of modern Travellers, who went abroad in the short time of the Peace, and described what he saw in Countries all but inaccessible at that time.]

On Spray, a bad singing man in Trinity College Chapel, appointed by Bishop Hinchliffe, because he had a vote in the County of Northampton[1]:

> "A singing-man and yet not sing!
>     You ill requite your Patron's bounty."
> "Excuse me, you mistake the thing,
>     My voice is in another County!"

Attributed to Bishop Mansel.

[1] This Epigram was communicated by one of the Seniors of Trinity. My Father thought it likely that the man had been recommended by the old Lord Sandwich, and that the vote was in the County of Huntingdon. Another version is that the man was "deaf and dumb," and made a lay-Clerk of Ely because he voted for the Rutland interest in Cambridgeshire, but I have reason to believe that the former of these two accounts is the right one. A friend suggests that he remembers hearing it, and that the second and third lines ran

> "Come, justify your patron's bounty."
> "Excuse me, Sir : that's quite another thing!"
>         &c.         &c.

# CHAPTER XIX.

## 1840.

1840.  PARLIAMENT met Jan. 16, the Queen reading her Speech, in which she announced to us
her "intention of allying" herself "in marriage with Prince
Albert of Saxe Coburg and Gotha." It now became the
Country to provide an income befitting her future husband.
A motion was made by Ministers for a grant of £50,000
per annum to the Prince. An amendment was moved by
Mr Hume, proposing £21,000 as amply sufficing[1]. This
being almost unanimously rejected by a large majority,
Colonel Sibthorp, a Tory, M.P. for the City of Lincoln,
moved an Amendment for £30,000, which was carried by

---

[1] Mr Hume said, "The noble Lord (J. Russell) must know the danger
of setting a young man down in London with so much money in his
pockets."

a majority. I voted for the larger sum, partly because it was the same as had been given to Prince George of Denmark when he married Queen Anne, when, too, money was more valuable, and would buy more of the necessaries of life. As we went into the Lobby, I said to the Secretary of the Treasury, "Why have you forced us to this?" and he answered, "We could not help ourselves." I expected that my vote would have been unpleasing to my Constituents, but on subsequent enquiry was told that it had been generally approved.

I was travelling soon afterwards outside the Mail-coach to Yorkshire, and I enquired of the Coachman, who lived in Lincoln and was a Freeholder of the County, if Colonel Sibthorp had not gained in popularity with the Electors by his motion. He answered, "Quite the contrary, they thought it a shabby act." I am convinced that the love of Royalty is deeply rooted in the lower middle classes, and this story is a proof of it. How little did those who thus reduced the Prince's income foresee the admirable manner in which he would spend it, by encouraging Arts and Manufactures, and Agriculture.

The marriage took place on the tenth of February. I had two tickets sent me for the Colonnade in St James's Palace, through which the Processions passed, but I did not care to go as my wife was away. Every thing was done on a magnificent scale, and all went well, but the day was unfortunately extremely wet. The Sun came out, however, just as the Queen and Prince started for Windsor Castle, in time to fulfil the good old adage, "Happy is the Bride that the Sun shines on." The Queen held her first Levee afterward on March 6; I went to it, and saw Prince Albert for the first time. He stood on her Majesty's left side, and was of course quite passive. All that one could *then* say of him was that he was a man of graceful form and pleasing countenance.

[Two important measures were suggested by the Speech this Session. One had regard to the Municipal Corporations in Ireland, the other—the result of the Ecclesiastical Commission which had been appointed during Sir Robert Peel's short Administration in 1835 —was a proposal for modifying the constitution of Chapters, reducing the revenues of Cathedral Establishments to a large amount —nearly £300,000 a year—and applying this surplus to the augmentation of small livings, and provision of additional Churches and resident clergymen. This latter measure was introduced by Lord John Russell, and cordially supported by Sir Robert Peel, the Archbishop of Canterbury (Howley), and the Bishop of London (Blomfield). My Father took an active part in this Bill, but has only left the following short comment on it.]

It equalised the incomes of all the Bishops except those of London, Durham, Ely, and Winchester. It abolished some of the Canonries, and appropriated, and placed the surplus revenues of these last, and of the larger Bishoprics, in the hands of an Ecclesiastical Commission in aid of small Endowments. I was asked to present a petition from the Minor Canons of Canterbury, by one of them. My answer induced him to request that I would become the advocate of the claims of the Minor Canons *generally*, and I had communications with, and deputations from, other Cathedral Cities. I succeeded in establishing, on discussion of the Clauses, a claim on their part to be presented to certain Benefices in the Patronage of the Chapter, which might not be tenable by any of the Canons, and which had often previously been given to their relations and even to strangers; also to the houses *not* occupied by the remaining Canons, or by the Chancellor of the Diocese. This Act did not extend to Ireland. It was opposed by Sir Robert Inglis and Mr Gladstone.

Sir R. Inglis was a thorough Churchman, and had such a repugnance to Dissent that he longed for *none* to exist. He was very good-humoured, so much so, that once when he had spoken, objecting to a certain line of Railway, that "there were so many *dissenters* from it," I made an Epigram, and asked him if he would look at it. The turn of it was that it was strange to hear him advocating the cause of the Dissenters, and he enjoyed the joke as much as any of those to whom I. showed it.

Inglis being a religious man, felt that Lotteries, which tempted all sorts of people to speculate in them, led to loss of health and a love of gambling, he therefore brought in a Bill which procured their *final* abolition.

[Sir R. Inglis was an elegant Classic Scholar, and according to Mr D'Israeli "a man of very ceremonious manner, and an English Gentleman." From a note which I have found from him, it would seem that it was my Father who called his attention to the subject, and that at a period later than the date of the present Chapter. It is pleasant to observe in it the writer's thoughtful care not to lead others into temptation.]

SIR ROBERT INGLIS *to* PROFESSOR PRYME.

7, BEDFORD SQ.
2 *March*, 1847.

" DEAR Mr PRYME,

" I am very glad to have the pleasure of agreeing with you; and trust that such pleasure is not confined to our condemnation of Lotteries, the immediate subject of the letter with which you have favoured me by this morning's

Post. I have myself received several letters similar to that which you enclosed to me :—lest they should tempt our servants by lying about, I have always at once destroyed them ; but have done no more. I will now however speak to the Solicitor-General about the matter.

"Believe me, Dear Mr Pryme,

"Very faithfully yours,

"ROBERT H. INGLIS."

Pitt, who had been at his wit's end to carry on the war for which the taxes did not suffice, had availed himself of them. The Shares were £10 each, and the Government sold them to a Contractor, Bish, for £2 or £3 more. He again sold them to the Public for £17. By this means the Exchequer was enriched to the amount of two or three hundred thousand pounds each year. Dr Mansel, Master of Trinity College, gained a Prize of £1250; Mr Beales, a Merchant in Cambridge, won £10,000, which stimulated many others to try. The Drawing was conducted very impartially ; and to assure the public of this, two Christ's Hospital Boys were selected to draw the numbers from one wheel and the prizes and blanks from the other. There were many private Lotteries. I can just remember Snow Hill, where the Branghtons in *Evelina* lived. It being so narrow as scarcely to allow two carriages to pass, it was pulled down and widened and converted into Skinner Street (1802). The houses in it were apportioned as Prizes in a Lottery, and people took shares[1].

[1] I have seen a Scheme which offered six prizes of more than £20,000 each ; £337,760 to be distributed among 17,000 members, no blanks, and every number to have £6 at least.

Sir Fitzroy Kelly attempted to introduce in this Session a Bill for confining capital punishment to Murder and High Treason. The minds of many others besides my own were not then prepared for so great a change, and his motion was negatived. My vote on that occasion was one of three erroneous ones which I consider that I gave in the House of Commons. The gradual consideration of the subject would long since have induced me to assent to such a proposition, and the practice of the present time (1865) has for a good while been in accordance with it.

[In his speeches, Mr Kelly said, that within the recollection of many Members there had been nearly 200 capital offences, and in the early part of the last Century nearly 300. The Bill went through the usual stages, till on the third reading it was thrown out by a majority of 27, or 78 against 51. In the following year Mr Kelly again introduced the Bill, but it did not get beyond the Committee, for on some unfavourable divisions he withdrew it. Twenty years after the Criminal law consolidation Acts passed, leaving treason and wilful murder as the only offences punishable by death. Both Lord John Russell and Sir Robert Peel abolished capital punishment in a great number of cases.]

June 10. Addresses were voted in both Houses of Parliament on occasion of the attempted Assassination of the Queen by a young man named Oxford[1]. A form of thanksgiving was also used at all the Churches.

[I was in London at the time, and the excitement was immense. Everyone was delighted with the Queen's presence of mind and ten-

---

[1] Edward Oxford, who had been a servant in a public-house, discharged two pistols at Queen Victoria and Prince Albert as they were proceeding up Constitution Hill in an open Phaeton from Buckingham Palace, June 11, 1840. He stood within a few yards of the carriage, but fortunately neither her Majesty nor the Prince was injured. He was adjudged insane and sent to Bethlehem."—*Annual Register*, 1840.

derness in going instantly to her Mother to re-assure her, lest she should hear of it before she could be certain of her daughter's safety. The next day we were walking up Constitution Hill and met her near the same spot where the attempt was made. She sat with Prince Albert beside her in a light open carriage holding only two. The courage of the Guelphs is proverbial. I have heard the perfect self-possession of the Queen's Grandfather on a similar occasion graphically related to my Father by one of his intimate friends, who from his family connexions had the best means of knowing the details. "When George the 3rd," he said, "was shot at by Hadfield in Drury Lane Theatre, the Prince of Wales was dining with Lord Melbourne. The news was brought there in haste[1]. The Prince said to Lord M., 'What should I do, William?' Lord Melbourne answered, 'As your Royal Highness asks my advice, I should recommend that you take a Hackney Coach and go to the Theatre.' It must have been a fine sight to see old George with his courage, first turning to his wife, and saying, 'Its only a squib, Charlotte,' then bending forward to show himself unhurt to the people, directing how the man should be dealt with; and, finally, the curtain drawing up, all the Princes of the blood present, and the National Anthem sung[2]. Hadfield was only mad on that subject. He had property and lived under surveillance with every comfort, and his friends were allowed to visit him. No one could have told that he was a lunatic, unless the King was mentioned, when he would put his hand to his head and say, 'the Crown is here[3].'"]

[1] By Mr Jefferys, M.P. for Coventry, who instantly left the Theatre, to inform the Prince of the King's safety.

[2] "The following stanza (originally composed *impromptu* at Quebec) was sung as the concluding verse :

'From ev'ry latent foe,
From the Assassin's blow,
      God shield the King :
O'er him Thine arm extend,
For Britain's sake defend
Our Father, Prince, and Friend :
      God save the King !'"

[3] Hadfield died Jan. 23, 1841.

During my Parliamentary residence in Town I frequently dined by invitation at the Political Economy Club, of which the Oxford Professor of that Science and I were Honorary Members. It was instituted on a plan proposed by Ricardo, who wrote a work on Political Economy, propounding some new points. It consisted of a limited number of members, who dined together several times a year, and discussed afterwards, somewhat on the plan of a debate, subjects connected with the Science, of which previous notice had been given. For instance :

1.  To what extent are considerations of justice and morality admissible in the discussions of questions of Political Economy ?—Lord Overstone.

2.  Was Ricardo correct in stating that " The same rule which regulates the relative values of commodities in one country, does not regulate the relative value of the commodities exchanged between two or more countries ?"— Colonel Torrens.

I was well acquainted with this last debater, and he told me the origin of his introduction to the Science ; that being appointed to the command of some lonely place, he took with him the *Wealth of Nations*, and a few other books on Political Economy, and there mastered the subject.

Sydney Smith became a member of this Club in the latter part of his life, and sometimes took an active part in the debate ; though not profound, he argued with his usual witty force and novelty of illustration. I was so fortunate as frequently to hear and converse with one whom I had so much admired as the author of *Peter Plymley's Letters*. There also I used to see Lord Lansdowne, M. Van der Weyer, and Count Pollon. This latter presented me with an Italian work, " *Dell' Economiste Politice del Medio Evo, da Luigi Cibrario.*"

[I have found the note that accompanied the present from the Sardinian Ambassador, who was equally sanguine, with M. Say and Mr M'Culloch, of the final triumph of the new Science.]

COUNT POLLON *to* PROFESSOR PRYME.

11, GROSVENOR ST.
*March* 21, 1844.

" DEAR SIR,

" I hasten to acknowledge the receipt of your note of yesterday's date. I have read with much pleasure and infinite interest the copy of your letter on the subject of the Corn Laws, which you were pleased to forward to me inclosed. The principles you set forth and maintain therein with a most prudent and becoming moderation, must, like all other truths, prevail generally in the end, and I hope soon.

" I send *this day* the Italian Book I mentioned to you, and remain, dear Sir,

" Yours truly,

" POLLON."

[My Father dictated to me an account of the origin of the Reform Club, but unfortunately that leaf of my MS. is missing. He pointed out to me a mistake in Mr Tom Duncombe's life, which he was anxious to rectify. He said that the Club in Great George Street, Westminster, had nothing to do (as said *there*) with it. The one was a Radical Club, and died a natural death about the same time that the other came into existence. Some, however, of its members were invited to belong to "the Reform Club," which had its first beginning at Gwydir House, Whitehall, in 1834. The present House in Pall Mall was built for it in the Italian style by Sir Charles Barry, the Architect of the House of Commons, and cost, with its furniture and fittings, above £93,000. While speaking of this Club in its political aspect as a *réunion* of Whigs, and *something more*, I suggested to my Father the word " Liberal." " No," said he, " it is an offensive expression, as if the Tories were not liberal. The only thing in politics in which Serjeant Frere and I agreed was, in a preference for the words Whig and Tory."]

The Great Western Railway was opened this Summer[1]. As a curious contrast I may mention that little more than 100 years ago (1734), a Coach was advertised to go from Gloucester to Bristol in one day, and from Bristol to Bath on the second day, "if God permit[2]."

[1] Two thousand pounds is said to have been taken on the first day.

[2] A new line was opened in 1867, by which Bath is reached in an hour and a half from Gloucester.

# CHAPTER XX.

## 1841.

1841.  IN January of this year I went on one of my occasional visits to Lord Fitzwilliam at Milton.
I mention it because a rather curious thing occurred. There
was in every week, during Lord F.'s residence, a Public day,
on which any of the neighbouring gentry, who chose, came
to dinner without invitation ; one occurred while I was there
at this time, and Dr Davys, Bishop of Peterborough, was
one of the company.  I said to him in the course of the
evening, " Do you remember our reading in the *Anti-Jacobin* about *Bawb-adara* in your rooms at Christ's ? "  " To
be sure I do," he answered.  " Well," replied I, " there he
is !"  He was much interested, and said, " Is that indeed
the *real* Bawb ? "  One of the pieces in the *Anti-Jacobin*
was on Sir Robert Adair.  To hide his name a little, and

19

in allusion to his having been in India, he was called *Bawb-adara*. He was one of the visitors in the house, and was very old (78); but he was active and cheerful, and took the part of a Robin-Redbreast in some Charades which the Ladies Fitzwilliam kindly acted for our amusement one evening.

He was in no way ridiculous as the *Anti-Jacobin* endeavoured to make him out, but on the contrary, when the Whig Ministry went out while he was at Vienna, and, according to custom, the Embassies changed hands, *he* was the only exception to the rule. The Tories asked him to remain, and his answer was, "I am the Ambassador of the Country and not of the Ministry, and I shall be happy to stay and do my best." He made no great show of talent, but conducted the diplomatic affairs committed to him with considerable ability.

[It is singular that it was Mr Canning himself who selected Mr Adair, the intimate friend of Mr Fox, as "the fittest person to unravel the tangled web of our diplomatic relations with the Ottoman Court[1]." At the termination of his successful mission there he was made G.C.B. He wrote the account of his Embassy to Vienna in consequence of an attack on his conduct. The present Lady Albemarle asked him how long he had taken to compose his book? He answered, "Three months." "How quickly you wrote it!" she said. "Quickly," he replied; "it was time to write quickly, for I was 80 when I began it." He died in 1865 at the great age of 92.]

On my return home I visited the Palace at Peterborough. I found the same old tortoise that Bishop Marsh had introduced to me fifteen years previously, but now transferred from the garden to a glass-case in the Hall[2]. Dr Davys was

[1] My Father once spoke of Mr Canning as having "a deep and master knowledge of human nature and affairs."

[2] Having died in 1831. He was "believed to be 220 years old."

Tutor to the Princess Victoria, and had so excellently fulfilled his office that he was not only promoted to a Bishopric after her Accession to the Throne, but his eldest daughter
was made Resident Woman of the Bedchamber; an office
created in order to include her in her Majesty's Household.
It is said that he was the first to inform the Princess of the
future greatness which awaited her.

[I have learnt on good authority that this is not quite correct,
and I am enabled, by the kindness of my informant, to give the true
version of a circumstance which, like everything else pertaining to
the history of our Queen and Royal Family, has a peculiar interest
for her subjects. The Princess, in studying the Peerage, found out
by herself her grand future, and told her discovery to the Baroness
Lehzen. *She* quietly took the first opportunity of mentioning the
fact to the Duchess of Kent—who acknowledged to her daughter
the truth of the discovery, and pointed out the great responsibility
of such an office—and how diligent and careful the Princess should
be, in qualifying herself for such a position. Bishop Davys had the
highest opinion of Baroness L., and used to say that he thought the
Princess derived very great good from her instructions; and as for
the Duchess of Kent, he thought her the best and wisest and most
judicious person and Mother in existence.]

Parliament met on Jan. 26 in this year. Several minor
measures of legal and commercial reform were brought
forward, and most of them passed into Law. I took part
in the details of a Bill for rendering Release alone effectual
to convey Freehold Estates. Previously conveyances of
Land could only be made, according to the practice of
Feudal times, by feoffment, which required the personal
attendance of Seller and Purchaser upon the land in the
presence of two witnesses, who made a written memorandum
thereon. To avoid this inconvenience, the course had been
generally adopted of granting a Lease of a year to the

Purchaser, which legally put him in possession ; and then a deed, dated the following day, which released for ever the possession of the Land.    It was now enacted that the Lease for a year need not be made, but that the Deed of Convey- ance should be liable to both Stamp duties.

I don't know who first mentioned the subject to the other, but Lord Worsley, M.P. for North Lincolnshire, and I agreed in the desirableness of enfranchising *all* Copyhold tenures.    We were aware that there was not the slightest probability of so comprehensive a Measure passing through either House of Parliament ; but we hoped by degrees a change might be effected.    Lord W., who was well ac- quainted with Lord Redesdale, then the Chairman of Com- mittees in the House of Lords, conferred with him as to the kind of Bill which there was a reasonable probability of passing into a law, and we did not venture to propose more than *this ;* which was that a certain large proportion both in number and value should bind the remainder for an enfranchisement of all within the Manor, by consent of its Lord.    That the Trustee or Guardian of Infants should be able to consent for them, and that the Committee of a Lunatic might do the like.    This passed both Houses without a division.    It remained, as we expected, nearly a dead letter on the Statute-Book, yet still we felt that the thin end of the wedge was inserted.    Subsequently (after I ceased to be in Parliament) two other steps were taken towards the same object, enabling either party, the Lord or the Copyholder, on a succession or sale, to compel the other to immediate enfranchisement, and providing that if they could not agree on the pecuniary terms, Valuers should be called in to decide[1].

[1]  15 and 16 V. c. 11.—21 and 22 V. c. xciv.    All these Acts may be properly described as "the Copyhold Acts."

Another Bill, with which I had much concern, was entitled, "An Act to commute certain Manorial rights as to Copyhold, &c." It related to the last unrepealed restriction of Feudal times upon Landed Property. The powers of the Lord of the Manor in former times over the owners of any land was excessive. An instance of which is, that on the death of one such leaving Children under age, he became their Guardian, and received their rents to his own use, providing only their maintenance and education out of them. Even to their marriage his consent was requisite.

May 25. I saw Mr T. Duncombe's monster petition presented ; it was so large that it was wheeled up to the table on a kind of barrow. It was said to be signed by 1,300,000 people, praying for the adoption of the People's Charter, a document then beginning to be talked about, which proposed Universal Suffrage, Vote by Ballot, Annual Parliaments, the abolition of all Property Qualifications by Members, and their payment instead. From this arose the name of "Chartists," not yet quite extinct.

During this Session, and in several following years, I attended the Soirées given by the Marquis of Northampton, as President of the Royal Society, to which he invited me, though not an F.R.S. We had known each other at Trinity College; he came up to it as Lord Compton, in Oct. 1808, just when I returned into residence as a Fellow. The College Prize Essay on King William III., for Bachelors of Arts, was in that year awarded to C. J. Blomfield (afterwards Bishop of London), and recited in the College Chapel on the 4th of November. Lord Compton, who had been brought up in extreme Tory principles, expressed afterwards, during the dinner in Hall, some surprise at the Whig opinions which that Essay displayed ; when, to his astonishment, Mr Lambert, the venerable Senior Fellow, said, " I observed no sentiments therein which did not seem to me perfectly constitutional." After taking his degree, Lord Compton travelled for some time on the Continent; on his return he said that he had observed the state of things under the absolute Governments of the Countries which he had visited, and that in consequence, although he left England a Tory, he came back a Whig. He paid much attention to Scientific pursuits, and when the British Association met at Cambridge for the first time in the year 1833, he was its President.

May 22nd. I went with the Bishop of Lichfield (Bowstead) to one of the Archbishop of Canterbury's Public dinners, several of which were given in each year, according to custom, previously to the diminution of the Archiepiscopal income occasioned by one of the Ecclesiastical Reform Bills. We assembled in Court-dress, and had a short service in the Chapel, which opens out of the Lollard's Tower, read by the Chaplain, the Rev. Wm. Mill, of whom I have previously spoken. We then passed through a gallery hung with portraits of former Archbishops to the dining-room, where we were waited upon solely by his Grace's numerous retinue of Servants. The dinners of the Speaker, to which each M.P. was annually invited, were on a similar plan, though not equal in stateliness and magnificence to those given in Lambeth Palace. Although it was only Spring-time there were at the dessert Peaches and Nectarines in abundance.

[In a letter, bearing date 23 May, 1841, my Father described to me more in detail this grand Archiepiscopal hospitality, which, though small compared to Wolsey's in his age, has passed away as *too large* for ours. " Yesterday I dined at Lambeth Palace. The Dukes of Cambridge and Rutland were present, Lord Normanby, four Bishops, Sedgwick, French, Mill, &c., in all about 65. I sat between Sir Frederick Pollock and a College contemporary whom I slightly knew, Colonel Sir Hercules Pakenham. Prayers, *i. e.* Litany, were read in Chapel by Dr Mill. The effect of this just previous to dinner is good. Turtle and excellent dinner—wines ditto—Dessert, superb—Ices, strawberries, peaches, nectarines, grapes, &c., and everything handed. Coffee, tea, and liqueurs. We dispersed about 10. The Palace is venerably magnificent, and the Archbishop kind and gentlemanly. Yet I could not help thinking it too much for a Minister of the Gospel."]

Bishop Bowstead had been preferred by a Whig Ministry to Sodor and Man, and was translated a few years afterwards to Lichfield. We missed him much from his place at Cambridge (he was Fellow and Tutor of Corpus Christi College), for his mildness and excellence and consistent character had endeared him to every one. He lived but a few years after his removal to Lichfield.

In Parliament nothing important occurred till in the month of June, when the Government was left in a minority of *one* on Sir R. Peel's motion of want of confidence. According to the modern Parliamentary usage, a resignation of Office or a Dissolution would take place. The intention of Ministers to adopt the latter course became immediately obvious by their hastening the requisite measures of financial arrangement. The habit of resigning, on the defeat of a measure, takes away from the supporters of the Government, unless they have been previously called together and consulted upon it, the power of forming and acting upon their own opinions, and renders them the mere registers of the Premier's.

It now was with me a matter of doubt whether I should contest the Borough of Cambridge for a fourth time. My health was beginning to suffer under the strain of a constant attendance, for I very seldom left the House till it rose, nor ever omitted a division on any subject of importance. My Family urged upon me the necessity of retiring if I would not absolutely shorten my life, and I therefore yielded, though unwillingly, to this consideration.

The Tory interest at Cambridge had latterly become more predominant. I know not how it would have been had I as a Townsman stood, but as it was, Sir Alexander Cray Grant and Mr Manners Sutton were returned by a majority over the two Whig Candidates when the Election took place at the end of June. Sir A. C. Grant had latterly been my colleague, having been elected on a single vacancy when Mr Spring Rice was called up in 1839 to the House of Lords, by the title of Baron Monteagle. Mr Milner Gibson, who had retired from Ipswich, was the unsuccessful Whig Candidate on that occasion.

The Ministry met the New Parliament, but not for long; while I was at Harrogate in September I heard of Lord Melbourne's resignation in consequence of a hostile vote on the Address. Sir Robert Peel then became again Prime Minister, and remained in Office five years.

# CHAPTER XXI.

## 1842—1846.

1842. I NOW enter on a period of my life which has in it but little that is eventful to record; but I shall note down anything of more than private interest which took place during the remainder of my days, and which my memory may suggest. I partially resumed my Profession, and still continued to attend two or three of the principal Assize Towns. I had a general Retainer from the Mint, and had been nominated by the Attorney-General Counsel for the Bank of England. This was an excuse for continuing on the Norfolk Circuit, but my real object was that I might be enabled, as a Barrister still practising, to plead exemption from being High Sheriff for Hunts, which office would have involved an expense and trouble that I should have greatly disliked.

When my age released me from this liability, I retired from a Society which had brought me into pleasant intercourse with the Judges, some of whom, as Pollock, Coltman, Parke, had been my College friends, and in which I had passed many happy hours with a variety of clever and genial companions.

I continued to interest myself in the affairs both of the Town and University, and I also paid frequent visits to my Farms. I had long since studied a little of Chemistry, which I now applied to the culture of my land.

Mr Coke was the first improver of Agriculture. He was followed by Mr Pelham, (afterwards Lord Yarborough), by Lord Spencer, and others. Mr Coke was also the first to introduce turnips as a food for Cattle. Hitherto they had been cultivated in gardens only[1]. He adopted drill-husbandry, and he waged war against weeds. It seems almost fabulous to say that I have more than once seen samples of wheat sworn to in Court by witnesses recognising amongst them the seed of a peculiar weed that grew in the same field. Mr C. was so well known that he was always called Mr Coke of Norfolk, not of Holkham ; I met him in the House before he was created Earl of Leicester. Lord Erskine was on a visit at Holkham when he saw a field of wheat sown by the new method of drilling. He mistook the young wheat in blossom, standing up in regular rows, for lavender, and on being told that it was the new mode

---

[1] "We saw a turnip-field for the first time. These farms (near Ramsey, Hunts), seemed to be cultivated in the Norfolk method of husbandry." Lord Orford's *Voyage round the Fens in* 1774.

of Drill-husbandry, he wrote some lines, which may perhaps be found in a book called *The Spirit of the Public Journals*[1]. This was a reprint of the political squibs and jeux d'esprit which appeared in the public papers in the early part of the century, and was published annually in a Duodecimo volume. Jekyll was the Editor.

[I am indebted to the kindness of Lord Erskine (Grandson of the Chancellor) for a copy of these verses, which I sought for in vain in many collections of *Ephemera*. They are transcribed by himself from his Grandfather's original MS., and he reminds me that it must be remembered, as partly accounting for the mistake, that the stamens of wheat at the time of flowering have a purple hue somewhat resembling Lavender. The mistake was both natural and fortunate, since it served to exhibit Lord Erskine's geniality, and his versatility in transforming it into a subject of amusing interest to his friends.]

COPY OF VERSES, BY THOMAS, FIRST LORD ERSKINE, (the Chancellor), AT THE HOLKHAM SHEEP-SHEARING.

TO THOS. WILLIAM COKE, ESQ.

LAVENDER, OR THE WONDERS OF THE DRILL.

When first in Holkham's rich domain
My eyes explored the verdant plain,
'Twas strange, I thought, that in my view
Not e'en one blade of corn there grew,

---

[1] Lord Campbell relates this story in his *Lives of the Chancellors*, Vol. VI. p. 619, giving the words " What a beautiful piece of Lavender !!!" but not the verses. In Vol. VIII. p. 547, the anecdote is transferred to Lord Brougham, in apparent forgetfulness of its having been related before of Erskine. After the lapse of nine years Lord C.'s *memory* was probably failing, and perhaps this little circumstance may account for some other notices that were thought strange in that last volume.

And thus to Holkham's Lord I spoke,
Much moved and far too sad to joke :
" Why with such skill and amplest room
Is all here wasted on perfume,
For man or beast no provender,
Nor aught around but *Lavender?*"
In vain I waited for reply,
Loud bursts of laughter shook the sky,
From the whole world of husbandry.
The cause was plain—'Twas wheat I saw,
In leaf the same, by Nature's law,
But sown and reared with matchless skill,
Transformed by wonders of *the Drill.*
Just so in human kind we see
Some clumsy lout with bended knee,
And shoulders round and neck awry;
But set up straight with chin on high,
By Serjeant's cane at breast and toe,
No man alive this lout could know.
Fathers and mothers stare in vain,
To find their shapeless cub again ;
The lad is Tony Lumpkin still,
Transformed by wonders of *the Drill.*
Go on, Great Teacher of us all,
Repeal the curse of Adam's fall,
Awake in Earth long dormant powers
To glad our hearts with fruits or flowers,
And corn, until we scarce believe
The Applish prank of Mother Eve.

ERSKINE, *July* 11, 1819.

In July of this year the Duke of Northumberland came
to Cambridge for his Installation as Chancellor (succeed-

ing Lord Camden), and was a guest at St John's Lodge, being a member of that College. A magnificent Fête was given to him in its grounds, which were temporarily connected with those of Trinity by a rustic-bridge built across the intervening stream. A grand dinner in the Hall of Trinity the next day was followed by a Ball (of which I was a Steward), in the new Fitzwilliam Museum, which was then only just completed, and to which the collection of Pictures, &c., from the old Museum in Free-School Lane was not yet transferred.

1843. In October of this year (the 25th) the Queen visited Cambridge ; she was of course accompanied by Prince Albert. This was the first visit of a reigning Sovereign since that of Queen Anne. The Heads of Colleges presented Addresses, but there was no great ceremonial or pomp exhibited. The heartiness and simplicity of Queen Victoria's reception formed a remarkable contrast to the elaborate magnificence and cold pedantry of Elizabeth's[1].

Dr Whewell was Vice-Chancellor, and the Queen was of course at the Lodge of Trinity, which always is a Royal Residence for the time being. Among other buildings visited the next day by the Queen was the University Library ; I was one of a few selected from the Library Syndicate,

---

[1] Queen Anne came over for the day from Ely. But Queen Elizabeth (in 1564) paid a much longer visit. She rode in on horseback, dressed in a black velvet habit, from Haslingfield, and went directly to King's College Chapel, which she entered "under a canopy borne by the 4 Senior Doctors in Divinity ; and the Provost met her arrayed in a rich Cope of needlework and began the 'Te Deum,' after which Even-song was solemnly sung, every man standing in his Cope." She was afterwards entertained with plays in the same Chapel, the Provost himself acting ; and with Latin Disputations in Great St Mary's Church. Before taking leave she visited the various Colleges on horseback, and talked with divers scholars in Latin. See Cooper's *Annals of Cambridge*.

and appointed to conduct her over it. We had much to show that was valuable and curious, especially the MS. of the Gospels, known as the *Codex Beza*[1], and an Anglo-Saxon MS. of the Gospels. Prince Albert lingered over these with great interest.

The Queen went on to Wimpole, the seat of Lord Hardwicke, where she passed two nights. A Ball was given there on the 27th, at which I was present, with many other guests from Cambridge.

[Repeal of the Corn Laws now began to be extensively agitated. An Anti-Corn-Law League had been formed at the close of the year 1838 in Manchester. Edinburgh took the lead in holding a Meeting, which was presided over by the Lord Provost. In Parliament, Lord Brougham proposed that all petitions for abolition of these laws should be referred to a Committee of the whole House, and that evidence should be heard at the Bar. This was negatived without a division; and Mr Villiers's annual motion in the Commons on the subject was defeated by a majority of 371 to 172. Mr Cobden took a part, and made an address to a Conference of 700 Clergy at Manchester who approved of the abolition. It could not in point of fact be called a Radical scheme, for the Chartists certainly opposed it at first, and interrupted several meetings by their hostility. It was not till 1842 that Legislation commenced. Sir Robert Peel then proposed to the House of Commons a sliding scale, commencing with a duty of 20s. and descending to one of 1s., which passed in 1842, notwithstanding an Amendment to the contrary by Lord John Russell. But this was not acceptable to the Anti-Corn-Law Delegates, who were determined on nothing less than total Repeal. Lord Melbourne proposed a resolution asserting the principle of a fixed duty instead of a fluctuating one, but this was defeated by a large majority. Meanwhile the League went on with its agitation, and resolved to raise £100,000 to pay Lecturers on the subject;

---

[1] This is the MS. usually known in the Greek Testament Collations as D; it was printed in fac-simile type at the expense of the University by Dr Kipling in 1793.

and the *Times* in 1843 declared it to be a great fact, and urged concession. In that year a County Meeting was held at Huntingdon,
at which my Father took a part; but before describing it he dictated
to me a short dissertation on the whole subject, which I trust I may
not have written down inaccurately.]

This Country had in the last Century grown more wheat
than was required for our own consumption, and as an encouragement to the Farmer, a bounty of 5s. a quarter was
given by Government to the exporter.

In the time of the great scarcity (a kind of disease having
attacked the wheat being one cause of it) the Pitt Ministry
issued a Proclamation withholding this bounty, and when
Parliament met obtained without difficulty a Bill of Indem-
nity. We had been at war with France since the Spring
of 1793, which occasioned a much higher freightage (from
the risk of capture both by Privateers and ships of war) on
exportation and importation of all commodities. The population of the Country was gradually increasing, and the price
of wheat rose greatly, so that the old bounty was never
re-imposed, and died a natural death. This state of things
continued till the Peace with France in 1815, when, from
the freedom of importation, the price of wheat became exceedingly reduced. The Corn Laws were then enacted, but
by the dilatoriness of the Government of that time in not
pressing immediately forward some measure of Agricultural
protection, vast quantities of corn were imported on the
speculation of a rise in price, which of course contributed to
a great depression, and many persons were ruined[1].

The duty on its importation varied almost inversely as
the price, estimated by the averages of the principal markets

[1] Mr Robinson's Act passed in 1815 permitting importation when
wheat should be 80s. per quarter. Serious Riots took place at this time.

of the Kingdom. It was therefore the interest of the Importers to have the grain released from the Bond-warehouses at a low duty, and fictitious sales at a fabulous price were arranged to affect the averages. One method was told me by a leading merchant who knew it well, though he was too conscientious to practise it himself. *A* in London sold a large quantity of wheat to *B* in Hull by letter at an enormously high price; *B* resold it to *C* at Wakefield, who sold it back to *A* in London, where it was quietly lying all that time in warehouses, of which the Custom-House officers had a key as well as the owners. Each of these transfers being returned to the Inspectors, thereby raised the nominal averages, and of course reduced the duty on the Foreign Corn on its release for Consumption.

At the time when the Corn Laws were repealed, and for some years before and afterwards, I held in my own occupation about 500 acres of my Huntingdonshire property. In every year I realised a profit beyond the estimated Rent and interest of Capital, except in the two immediately following the Repeal, which I attributed to the abruptness of that extreme measure.

[In answer to a correspondent in a local journal (in 1852) on the subject of Free Trade, my Father preferred "the *general* interest of the kingdom" to private consideration, and said, "Suppose that my farming balance-sheets for the last year or two were unfavourable, this would no more show the expediency of restraining or taxing the importation of the food of the people, than the unfavourable balance-sheets of manufacturers seven or eight years ago, would have shown the expediency of laws artificially raising the price of manufactured commodities."]

I had always thought that certain burthens (the Poor and Highway Rates, &c.) falling exclusively upon land required, according to the strictest principles of Free Trade, some compensating duty on the import of Foreign Corn, and when in Parliament made a speech to that effect, which I published. Joseph Hume's motion, made some years previously, of a 12s. duty, diminishing 1s. every year, which was indignantly negatived by the Landed Gentry, would doubtless have prevented any sudden loss to the Farmers, and Lord Derby's proposal of a fixed duty of 5s. a quarter would have sufficiently compensated the Home-grower, whereas the present duty of 1s. per quarter does little more than effect a record of our importations.

Previous to the Repeal a County Meeting to petition in favour of Protection was called at Huntingdon. It was numerously attended, and four dissentients only, of whom I was one, appeared. One of us thought that it would be useless to address the meeting, but the others considered that it would do some little good to our cause if the mass of Protectionists refused to hear us. Lord Fitzwilliam made the first attempt, but his voice was soon lost in clamour. I and the Rev. E. Baines (Rector of a large Parish in the County) followed, and met the same fate. This latter published soon after a little pamphlet entitled "A Speech which was *not* permitted to be spoken."

Lord Fitzwilliam had always advocated immediate repeal without any countervailing duty, as I well knew from frequent correspondence and conversations when visiting him at Milton. His very large estates in Ireland, Yorkshire, Northamptonshire, and Huntingdonshire, never made him swerve in that or any other course from what he thought for the interest of the Country.

·

[I insert here a letter which is not only interesting as shewing the commencement of a popular word, but also as evidencing

20

the private charities of one whose whole life and bearing exhibited
the true meaning of the word nobleman.    Happily there are *still*
many such.]

"LORD FITZWILLIAM *to* PROFESSOR PRYME.

"MILTON, *Feb.* 28, 1844.

"MY DEAR SIR,

"I will write on the other side a draft for £20, which
I see has hitherto been my contribution towards our poor old
friend's support—I hope the present arrangement is sufficient
to provide amply for his comfort, but, if not, I shall willingly
add to it.    I see you are in town, so I do not propose a visit
here now, but perhaps at Easter I may have the pleasure of
seeing you.    I am glad to see you have been giving your
mind to the *protectionists* as they are now called, though I
do not think it a good name to have given them, as I fear it
will be rather a popular title.

"Believe me,

"Yours very faithfully,

"FITZWILLIAM."

[Feb. 17, 1844.    A Society was established "for the Protection
of Agriculture," in order to counteract the Anti-Corn Law League.
The Duke of Richmond was chosen Chairman.    Petitions against
repeal were presented to Parliament in great numbers.    I have before
me a copy of one, and of the printed address that accompanied
it when sent for signature, which says, "For while the prowling
wolves from the Cotton Forests are howling around us, and our timid
shepherd, 'Sir Robert,' has left us to our fate, it behoves us to come
forward firmly, fearlessly, and energetically, to resist a bill fraught
with so much mischief to the agriculturist and the country in general."
Towards the close of 1845 the failure of the potato crop and the
prevailing distress assisted the Anti-Corn Law movement, and in June
1846 the Seven Years' war against Protection was ended.    Sir Robert

Peel's second measure, by which the duty was reduced to 4s., when corn was imported at or above 53s. until Feb. 1849, after which 1s. per qr. only was to be levied, went further even than Mr Hume's, and was supported, though unwillingly, by the Duke of Welling-ton. It was the old story of the Sibyl's books over again.]

1844. After much local agitation a measure was sub-mitted to Parliament for greatly improving the Drainage and Navigation of the Middle Level. I being no longer a Member of the House of Commons was able to act as one of the Counsel for the Bill. Numerous were the parties interested, and various were the grounds of opposition to this comprehensive measure. We had days of strenuous contest before the Parliamentary Committee. But we suc-ceeded in obtaining the important Act for the Middle Level. There then existed near Whittlesea a Mere of about 1500 acres in extent[1]. This was so completely drained soon after this Act passed that we (the Committee of Management) were able on one of our *Views* to take luncheon in a tent erected in the middle of it. The soil was exceedingly fertile, being the alluvium of ages from rivers and streams which flowed into it. But an unexpected difficulty in its cultivation arose. The wide and deep fissures which took place, as it became dry, at first rendered it dangerous for horses to plough.

["These cracks resulted merely from the desiccation of the soft soil, and are renewed in dry seasons to some extent. But another

---

[1] A Fleet of 7 vessels was fitted out by Lord Orford in 1774, which was able to anchor here. A journal kept during the voyage says, "Whittlesey Meer is somewhat more than two miles from the points we sailed between. The water rolls with great force, and in high winds the waves swell five or six feet high, being very much exposed by the lowness of the neighbouring grounds, which afford no defence against them." See Lord Orford's *Voyage round the Fens in* 1774. Edited in 1860 by J. Walbanke Childers, Esq. Published by Edwin White, Doncaster.

phenomenon is the subsidence of the soil. This has been very great, and is gradually going on—a circumstance which adds of course to the difficulty of draining the land, the water being lifted from 7 to 12 feet by a centrifugal pump (worked by steam power) into the higher level of the Rivers which convey it to the Outfall near Lynn. Within a few hundred yards of the Mere, the boggy soil has gone down upwards of 7 feet from its original level, and the bed of the Mere has also subsided in a great degree, although not quite to the same extent. Many curious things were found in the Mere. Among them was a beautiful relic, a 'Thurible' of the middle ages— or what is popularly known as a Censer for burning Incense. The vessel was of silver gilt, and of most elaborate workmanship of the date of the 14th century. Attached to it was a massive silver chain by which it was swung. With it was found a vessel for containing the Incense called a ' Navis,' also of silver with gold chasings, and the figure of a Ram's head at each end. This latter emblem clearly indicates that the vessels belonged to the monks of Ramsey. There were also some plates and other articles bearing the same insignia. When found all these relics were encrusted over with bivalve shells, which no doubt had tended to preserve them from the corroding action of the water. They are in possession of Wm. Wells, Esq. M.P. Lord of the Manor of Holme, and owner of four-fifths of the Mere[1]."]

Before quitting the subject of these Levels I may mention a kindred one, the Norfolk Estuary. My practical acquaintance with *them* drew my attention to the possibility of reclaiming a large tract of land in the wide Estuary between the Counties of Lincoln and Norfolk, through which the river Ouse falling in at Wisbeach, and the Cam at Lynn, found their devious course to the Sea. Sir William Foulkes and Mr Hamond of Westacre, who both had large estates in Norfolk, and three or four other gentlemen, entertained the same idea, and we met in London in 1846, and resolved

[1] For this information I am indebted to John Laurence, Esq., of Elton, Hunts.

on endeavouring to obtain an Act of Parliament for the purpose. A much smaller tract of land than we proposed to obtain had been successfully embanked from a curve in the Humber, of which the Government was sole proprietor ; for the Sovereign claims to be the owner of the Sea-shores. But this Norfolk Estuary Scheme of adding so large a portion of Land to our Island seemed so beneficial to the country that the right was conceded on the payment of five per cent. on the outlay of drainage. The Scheme involved a large expense beside, as we had to give considerable compensation to the owners of frontages, who claimed the right of gradually extending them as the Sea receded. We began by embanking a channel in the middle of the Estuary of two miles in length, and then making small embankments from the land extending nearly to the other, leaving a small orifice through which the high-water tide flowed, and, being thus made stagnant, left a deposit of soil when it retired.

This Channel has improved the navigation to Lynn, for which the Shipowners are obliged by the Act to pay a small tonnage on each voyage of their ships. It was questioned at a Middle Level meeting upon whom this small payment should fall ? whether on the owners of the Ship or of the freight ? It was answered by me in a letter in the Cambridge paper, signed " Paul Progress," that the Shipowner should pay for the saving caused by the diminished risk of the navigation, upon the same principle that a hosier gives £10 for a stocking-loom to enable him to *undersell* those who knit stockings with a set of needles costing 10*d.*

Speaking of the Great Level, King James is reported to have said, "that he would not suffer any longer the land to be abandoned to the use of the waters." A Royal speech, but there is no royal road to these great works. The reclamation has proceeded very slowly. Some of the land is now very good pasture, but it is feared that it will by no means repay what has been expended on it[1].

1845. The British Association visited Cambridge this Summer for the second time—Lord Northampton was the President. I read a paper in the Statistical Section, of which I was one of the Vice-Presidents, "on the different methods employed to estimate the amount of Population." Lord Sandon, Sir Charles Lemon and Colonel Sykes were the other Vice-Presidents.

Soon after the Railway from London to Cambridge was opened I went by it in October to Town to be present at the opening by the Queen of our new Hall in Lincoln's Inn. I was one of the four senior Barristers who were presented to the Queen in the Library. A Grand Banquet which was honoured by her presence took place before three o'clock. The Society had now become very rich owing to the expiration of the long building Leases of a range of houses in the neighbourhood, and it applied a part of its increased revenues to building a new and splendid Hall. The old one was very small, and as a proof of it there was only room for a Bar-table of six messes, (each mess consisting of four) besides the Benchers' table. The new Hall has two Bar tables which accommodate sixteen messes. Wine is now given to the Students in addition to beer.

Prince Albert was elected a Member of our Society

---

[1] "Last year the Norfolk Estuary Company handed over to the Prince of Wales a tract of 90 acres of reclaimed Wash-land; this the Prince determined upon farming himself, and it was sown with oats. Without any assistance from artificial or other manures it has yielded a very prolific crop." *Morning Post*, Dec. 1869.

on this "opening day." He was called to the Bar a month after, and to the Bench in January following.

[1846. In March of this year my Father, whose activity and energy were unabated, though he was approaching seventy years, offered to give a course of four Lectures to the Cambridgeshire Mechanics' Institute "On the Progress of Nations from rudeness and poverty towards civilization and opulence." This was accepted, and a kind vote of thanks sent to him through the Honorary Secretary, Mr Hemington Harris.]

June 10. Prince Albert dined with us at Lincoln's Inn as a Bencher on Grand Day. I was present, and with two or three others of the Senior Barristers who were not Benchers, honoured by an invitation to join the party at the high table.

[My Father always regretted that the rules of his Inn prevented his being a Bencher, as he would have been, had he belonged to the Temple. He lived to be the Senior Member of Lincoln's Inn, yet it was only by invitation that he could join the higher table. It was well and kindly said after his decease, "Perhaps the mistaken policy of the Benchers of that society, in conferring the honours in their gift almost exclusively on those who, whether by accident or otherwise, had been appointed Queen's Counsel, is at once illustrated in the case of Mr Pryme, who was condemned year after year to see those who might have been his children elevated to positions of dignity and honour, while he remained seated in the lower and less noble place[1]."]

While in Town I attended two of Babbage's Saturday evening réunions, to which he had kindly given me a general invitation. There I found again my former friend, Lord Murray, who happened to be in London—our pleasure on meeting was, I think, mutual.

On these occasional visits to London, I enjoyed ex-

[1] *Daily News, Dec.* 10th, 1868.

tremely the hospitality of a few old friends—Lord Wensleydale, Sir George Rose, Kenyon, &c.  At the house of the
last I met Wordsworth.  We were both staying in Park
Street, Westminster, he at Mr Joshua Watson's, and we
agreed to walk together to the dinner in Harley Place.
As we went along I mentioned Scott's poetical eminence.
Wordsworth simply remarked, " Scott's eminence is in description."

[I remember my Father pointing out Lord Murray to me, and
their gratification at meeting.  He was a fine portly man, with a
handsome, genial face.  His last words to my Father were, " You
must come and see me in Scotland," but they never met again.
These Soirées were charming—unique—the rooms so well lighted,
and apparently multiplied by a *semi*-magical Lamp of Mr Babbage's
own invention—the Host so clever, and so kind to his guests, and
they the finest company in London.  Of Sir George Rose's witty
sayings I can only relate two.  A third, which my Father repeated to me, I have since seen in print.  Some one was going
up in a balloon, on a peculiarly hazardous ascent.  He was a rich
man, and his friends, who knew he had not made a Will, play-
fully speculated on what would become of his property if any accident happened to him.  " Of course," said Sir George Rose, " his
heirs would take it by descent."  He was entertaining a party when
one of the Servants in carrying out a tray full of glass let it fall.
Sir G. R., seeing his wife look uneasy, remarked to her, " Don't distress yourself, Dame ; its only the Coachman gone out with the
*Break.*"

December 22.  The Ter-centenary of the foundation of
Trinity College was kept as a great Festival.  The Commemoration Service with a Sermon preached by Dr Jeremie
took place in the Chapel at four o'clock[1].  I dined in Hall

---

[1] In this eloquent Sermon a contrast was drawn between the close of
each Century.  The first ending with an imprisoned Monarch, and his
people at variance,— the shadow of a still greater calamity advancing.

as one of the numerous guests, and spent the evening at
the Master's Lodge after leaving the Combination Room.
Our College has long been celebrated for the number of
eminent men whom it has produced, and these have generally appeared—as elsewhere in all departments, in all Countries—in clusters, with intervening periods of rest. The
cause of this was given as a subject for the Prize Essay
of Bachelors of Arts in 1801 ; when H. Vincent Bailey obtained the first Prize, and printed a few copies of his admirable essay on the subject. We boast the names of Lord
Bacon, Sir Isaac Newton, Dr Barrow, Dr Bentley, Roger
Cotes, and John Dryden—luminaries of a former age. After
a gloomy interval the splendid light again dawned upon us,
and within my own time I remember Blomfield, who in
learning was nearly equal to Bentley, and Monk, who was
his Biographer ; Porson, Sedgwick, Airy, Whewell, Bishop
Thirlwall, and Babbage.

The second while the country was in anarchy, and divided between the
love and hatred of a lost dynasty. The third happily concluding in Peace
and Plenty.

1847—1851.

1847. FEB. 25. The Duke of Northumberland, our Chancellor, having died, Prince Albert was proposed as his Successor. The Johnians persuaded the Earl of Powis to contest the election. He had opposed the amalgamation of two Welsh Sees, Bangor and St Asaph, and was in consequence much supported by the Clergy; he had also manifested on several occasions extreme High Church opinions, which induced many electors to withhold their votes from him, although he had been a Student and Graduate of the University, which Prince Albert was not. I doubted between the two, and ultimately voted for the Prince, who had a great majority.

In the Spring of this year I went to reside at Wistow in Huntingdonshire. I wished to lead a more tranquil life than I could do in Cambridge, and to look more after my property. I therefore added to one of my Farm-houses such additional rooms as I and my wife required, and resided there henceforth, except when I returned annually to Cambridge in order to give my Lectures during the Lent Term. I thus fell into an altered way of life, not less busy perhaps, but certainly less exciting, and could truly say when settled in this simple abode where I could calmly pass away my age,

"O blest retirement, friend to life's decline[1]."

I became a Magistrate for the County, and was glad to bring my legal knowledge to the assistance of my Brother Justices.

There is much that is interesting in this County, both in natural features and in old associations. It is well wooded, indeed there was once a vast Forest of many miles in extent, traces of which still remain in various woods, and in the names of villages—Woodwalton, Upwood, Woodhurst, Old Hurst, Warboys (bois)[2].

The name of Huntingdon denotes still the same sylvan character. It is now a pretty small country Town, but was in the time of King Edward I. a place of some importance with its Castle and a mansion within its precincts; with its 274 Burgesses paying dues to the King and the Abbot of Ramsey. It is said to have had fifteen Churches,

---

[1] Cowley's desire was to be " Master at last of a small house and large gardens, and there dedicate the remainder of his life only to the culture of them, and the study of nature."

[2] It appears to have been a Forest till Henry II. Leland says, " Huntingdonshire in old times was much more woddy than it is now, and the dere resortid to the fennys: it is full long sins it was deforestid." *Itinerary*, Vol. IV. p. 31. fol. 48.

but now they are reduced to two[1]. It is celebrated as the
birth-place of Oliver Cromwell. Cowper the Poet resided
here for two years; the house he lived in is now a School,
and for many years it was advertised as "Cowper's House."
I remember reading his *Task*, which now seems so completely a thing of the past, a very few years after it first
came out. There is a curious trait of him which I met
with long ago in a Cambridge Paper. Among his earlier
poems were some strong lines against the Roman Catholics.
He went afterwards to live in Berkshire, and became friendly
with the Throckmortons. From regard to their hospitality
and kindness he omitted these lines in the later editions of
his poems.

[My Father had the lines, but of course he would not quote
them, as he said, "not to do what Cowper wished undone." Since
then I have seen the lines published, and a different version of the
suppression given as an excuse for doing so, namely, that Cowper
probably cancelled them on account of a wish not to aid in rekind-
ling the flames of the Gordon riots.]

A fine group of old trees is visible from the high road
near Somersham; they stand alone in a wide plain and excite
attention by their solitariness. Here there was a Summer
Palace of the Bishop of Ely[2].

Warboys wood is one of those I spoke of. The hand-

---

[1] Huntandene in the old Saxon chronicle; "surpassing all the neighbouring towns both in pleasantness of situation, beauty of buildings,
nearness to the fens, and plenty of game and fish." Henry de Huntingdon,
Archdeacon and Historian.

[2] It was a turreted mansion, and there are many traces of what it has
been, but no buildings are left. Bp. Stanley, brother to the then Lord
Derby, lived there. Bp. Heater made a bargain with Q. Elizabeth and
gave it up to her. It was a part of Henrietta Maria's dowry, and Colonel
Waller, the Regicide, got it after Charles the First's death. It was pulled
down later because it was being used for granaries and pigsties. "The
Mayor and Corporation of Cambridge visited Nicholas West, Bp. of Ely,

some spire of its church is a landmark for many miles around. "The Witches of Warboys" are traditionally known for bewitching, as was supposed, the families of Mr Throckmorton and Sir Henry Cromwell, in the 16th Century. A Father, Mother, and daughter named Samwell, were found guilty (the mother confessing, the others maintaining their innocence) and executed. In years long past a Sermon was preached annually at Huntingdon against the sin of witchcraft by a member of Queens' College, Cambridge, but it has long been discontinued[1]. Within this century the belief as far as Hunts is concerned partially remained. An old woman, supposed to be a witch, was tormented in consequence, and finally ducked in a pond. Sinking or swimming was one of the *ordeals* of witchcraft, but *that* was probably forgotten though the custom remained. The rude assaulters were to be prosecuted, and the trial must of necessity be in the County where the offence was committed, but such was the prevalence of the superstition in Hunts that affidavits were sent up to the King's Bench, and sufficient cause was shown that there could not be an impartial Jury. The Judges were satisfied and changed the place of trial, or "venue" as it is technically called, from the old Norman French. The men were found guilty and sentenced to imprisonment. I had this relation from Mr William Hunt, a Barrister on the Norfolk Circuit[2].

at Somersham, in 1518, when they presented him with a salmon, six capons, and a gallon of Ipocras." *Annals of Cambridge*, by C. H. Cooper.

[1] Sir Henry Cromwell, Grandfather of Oliver, being Lord of the Manor of Warboys, received the forfeiture of the Samwell goods; "But he, unwilling to possess himself of them, gave them to the Corporation of Huntingdon conditionally on a Sermon being preached every anniversary of the Annunciation of the B. V." Noble's *Crom.* Vol. 1. p. 25—6.

[2] About the year 1825 there was a woman at Great Paxton, Hunts, Nanny Izzard, whom the people tormented for a witch by sticking pins into her.

Warboys is about two miles from Wistow, and has pleasant associations for me. I have the gratification of being intimate with the Rev. William Finch, its Rector, and, I may say, Squire, for there is no other. His father was a younger son of the 3rd Earl of Aylesford. I was once mentioning to him the Statue of the Duke of Somerset in the Senate-House at Cambridge (he himself is an Oxonian), when he quietly added, " my great Grandfather[1]." His literary knowledge is extensive, and his conversation abounds in acute remarks on men and manners, and agreeable anecdotes. We agree upon almost every topic except Politics, on which we widely differ, and only mention them occasionally in a playful hit at each other.

Abbeys and religious houses were numerous. Besides two principal Towns dedicated to Saints (St Ives and St Neots), we have the remains of a Monastery of the Dominican order at Ramsey, or Ramesey, as it was spelt This is a small cheerful Town about three miles distant from Wistow. It had a Mere once, which was navigable as well as Whittlesea, though on a smaller scale. The Abbot of Ramsey sat in the House of Lords, and had also a residence at Broughton. The remains of the Abbey have been modernised, and are inhabited by Mr Fellowes, who has large estates in this County, which he represents, as well as in Norfolk[2]. His judicious activity as a Magistrate and Country

---

[1] Charles, 6th Duke, K.G., commonly called "The proud Duke of Somerset," was present at the Coronation of James II., William and Mary, Anne, George I., and George II. He filled high offices in the Courts of Charles II., William III., and Queen Anne.

[2] Very old and curious muniments are still preserved in the Abbey. Quite lately the Duke of Manchester sent experts to examine them in reference to a dispute about the Tolls on a quaint old bridge at St Ives which belongs to him.

gentleman, and his estimable private character, have made him valued by all parties. Of his kindness as a neighbour, though our politics differ, I must speak with gratitude; and it has always been with regret that I have felt obliged to vote against him.

No Abbey-lands, indeed no Church-lands, pay tithes. There are fifty acres on a farm of mine at Sawtry that pay no tithe; thence I infer that there was an Abbot there, for the maxim in law is

"Ecclesia non solvit Decimas Ecclesiæ."

[On reference to old books I find that there was a Monastery of the Cistercian order at Sawtry St Judith. There are old moats still remaining, and it is said that the bye road to the Farm spoken of above was made of stones from the Abbey. The Monks of Sawtry, or Saltrey as it was anciently spelt, were very charitable, as some old rhymes which have been repeated to me tell:

"Ramsey the rich, and Peterborough the proud;
Little Saltrey, a poor Abbaye,
Gave more alms than them all awaye."]

I must now speak of my own little village, which lies quite in a hollow beneath a hill which retains the ancient name of Schilhow[1]. From it, on a fine clear day, are plainly discernible the Cathedrals of Peterborough and Ely, the great tower of the latter looming far above the distant horizon. These, together with the fine spires of Yaxley and Whittle-sea, carry the eye over an area of vast extent. The sunsets in these level plains are of remarkable beauty.

Oliver Cromwell was Lord of the Manor of Wistow, and conveyed his property to the Pedley family, one of whom was a Fellow of Trinity in my time. I have heard that a

---

[1] *Howe* signifies a hill (the German *höhe*).

part of my land belonged to Oliver Cromwell, but it is only traditional.

Although the village lies low and in such a sheltered spot it is extremely healthy. We have few deaths, and in one year had none; and it has been noticed in the Registrar's returns for this happy infrequency. A portion of my land is in the Fens, or lowlands, once liable to inundations, but now artificially drained[1]. The drainage of the Middle Level has made them almost too dry. At the depth of several feet in Wistow Fen, of peat formation, were found prostrate trees (the wood of which was black), bones and horns of deer.

July 1st. I went to Cambridge to be present at the Installation of Prince Albert. The Queen and Chancellor arrived on Monday July the 5th, received the Address of the University in the Hall of Trinity, and dined with the Vice-Chancellor (Dr Philpott). The next day the Ceremony of Installing took place in the Senate-House, her Majesty being present. Wordsworth, as Poet Laureate, wrote the Installation Ode. A grand banquet was given at 6 o'Clock in the Hall of Trinity, at which Ladies were present; afterwards the Queen held a Reception at Trinity Lodge, when all the chief University Officers, their wives and daughters, were presented to her. They entered by the great staircase into what is called King Henry the 8th's Drawing Room, and passed out by a Turret stair—through a private entrance which had been made by Bishop Mansel—into the Great Court.

---

[1] There were many objections formerly made against the draining of the fens. "The *savans* of Cambridge urged that the Cam would have its stream dried up by it, and as Cambridge is concerned in its river, so the well-being of the whole country, yea, of the whole kingdom, is concerned in Cambridge and its University, and the stream of knowledge would be dried up with the stream of the Cam."

On the 7th the Chancellor received the Heads, Doctors, and Professors, at a Levee at 9 A.M. at Trinity Lodge.

[1847. There was a general Election in this Summer. The Candidates for Cambridge University were The Hon. Charles Ewan Law, Mr Goulburn, and Mr Shaw Lefevre. My Father voted on this occasion for the two latter. Mr Goulburn said to him laughingly, " I know you only vote for me because you consider me the least bad;" and he was very near the truth. My Father had a very great regard for Mr Goulburn, which was returned, as I find by several letters addressed to him by Mr G. I once asked him this question, " Do you think he was as good a Chancellor of the Exchequer as Gladstone?" The answer was, " I have no hesitation in saying he was better, though I think Gladstone exceedingly good." In reference to this general Election Colonel Perronet Thompson wrote my Father a letter which I have selected out of many, all characteristic of his great ability, his energy, his genial humour, and his advanced politics. To these last I may here say there were bounds. He took his stand last year on the Irish Church, when his faculties were as perfect, and his political insight as keen as ever. The Country may possibly have cause to lament some day that there are younger Politicians who only commence their race starting from the goal at which the older ones think it wise to stop.]

" BLACKHEATH, 9 *Aug.* 1847.

" DEAR PRYME,

" At the time you were voting for Goulburn and Lefevre, I was engaged in the course of dinners, &c. which accompany an election as a sort of *accomplices after the fact.* We were on the whole very fortunate, seeing that a fortnight before we were all broken in pieces by the effect of running against one of those walls which the Whigs are proverbially said to build up for themselves to run against—to wit the Education question. Without this, there would have been no contest; and it is odds whether the Tories would have presented themselves at all.

"*Les choses marchent*, and you Whigs will end in being carried like St Peter in your old age whither you would not. It was observable that at Bradford scarcely a word was said about either Corn Laws or Free Trade.

"The leading questions brought forward were the 'Dissenters,' and the necessity of extending the suffrage. This last question walks in good clothes at Bradford; even the Tories being obliged to admit upon the Hustings that they were ready to extend the Suffrage when the people were fit for it.

"With kind remembrances to all,

"believe me,

"Yours very truly and sincerely,

"T. Perronet Thompson."

"*G. Pryme, Esq.*"

[I regret that my Father, who was much attached to General Thompson as well as to his brother Vincent, left no distinct notice of this his oldest and well-loved friend. But the mutual regard that existed between these political veterans, who agreed in differing, will be evident from many passages. Colonel Thompson had written in 1842, "the desire is strong upon me, to be allowed to ask your acceptance of a publication somewhat of the nature of ' *Works*'.'[1] Though I cannot expect to carry with me your approval in all things, I have a sort of satisfaction in thinking you will find some matters therein redolent of ancient community of scenes," to which my Father replied, "Your *Works* are more voluminous than I expected. So much the better, there is a raciness and spirit about all you write which delights me even when I differ in opinion. I had read several papers in the *Westminster Review*, some which I knew to be yours, and others which I recognised by their style, as I do S. S. in the *Edinburgh*. My views on the Corn Laws *tend* to a total re-

---

[1] *Exercises, Political and others.* 6 vols. Published by Effingham Wilson in 1842.

peal *by degrees*, coupled with relief from those burthens which press on the production of Corn. Your plans are more imposing and splendid. I deem mine more practicable."

There was a third Brother, who would have been also a distinguished man if he had lived. In speaking of General Thompson's recent decease, the Journals stated that he and his two Brothers were all fellows of Queens' College, Cambridge. This is incorrect; the two who have been spoken of by my Father were so, but the third, Charles William, only graduated there. He became a soldier, and was killed in action with the French, near St Jean de Luz and Bidart, and was buried, with two others, in the garden of the country-house of the Mayor of Biarritz. A Tombstone was erected over them by some kind and unknown hand. It bore this Inscription :

Ci + Gisent

Le Lieut<sup>e</sup> Colonel J. C. Martin,

Les Capitaines Thompson et Watson,

De la Garde Royale De S. M. Britannique,

Tués sur le Champ de Bataille

le 12 Decembre 1813.

Mrs Opie, who was intimate with the Thompson family, wrote some lines on the sad event, beginning

"Weep *not*, he died as heroes die,"

which, after she became a Quaker, she toned down into

"Weep, *though* he died as heroes die."]

1848. In February of this year another phase of the old French Revolution occurred. Louis Philippe was obliged to abdicate in consequence of a tumult produced by his preventing a popular meeting. Nearly every Monarchy in Europe was shaken to its centre by Revolutionary outbreaks. Some years ago I went over again the History of the first Revolution, and also read collateral evidence, and I feel convinced that had Louis taken the advice of Necker and Lafayette the only Revolution would have been his summoning a Convention of the States, an old Institution reduced to a shadow and a name, and that he would have died quietly on his Throne. He did summon it, but too late, and it fell, at discord within itself, whether it should be one Chamber or three.

The three great grievances were, (1) the different rates of taxes on salt, so as to require a Cordon of Revenue Officers in some Provinces which created a vast expense. (2) The farming of the Revenue, and (3) the exemption of the Nobles from all taxation. The invasion of the Western side of France by Austria and Prussia on an understanding with Louis, was intended to support his absolute power. Necker wanted to be in the Cabinet, but he was a Protestant, and not liked by the Catholic party, and was sent away. Within a year he was recalled as Prime Minister, but it was then too late. Lord Chesterfield foretold the French Revolution many years before it happened in a passage of his works which is little remembered[1].

Louis Philippe had always professed liberality towards the people, but he became more and more absolute till the French would no longer endure it. I foresaw clearly in my own mind the Revolution of 1848, and acted on it, and persuaded two other men to act on it. I was left with them, in June 1847, Co-trustee to a large Property, and by the direction of the Will every portion of it was

---

[1] This is probably the passage, " By the last account of the present state of France, the domestic discords are so great, and promise to be so much greater. The King is both hated and despised, which seldom happens to the same man. The Clergy are implacable, upon account of what he has done; and the Parliament is exasperated because he will not do more. A spirit of licentiousness as to all matters of religion and government is spread throughout the whole kingdom. If the neighbours of France are wise, they will be quiet, and let these seeds of discord germinate, as they certainly will do, if no foreign object checks their growth, and unites all parties in a common cause. May 19, O. S. 1752."

within a year to be vested in Consols. There was a good deal of it in the French Funds, and seeing, as I thought, a cloud in the horizon, I urged our selling *that at once;* rather against the wishes of one of them, who regretted the loss of the higher interest.

We sold out in July or August. In February following came the outbreak in Paris, and my Co-trustee had the candour to tell me that he had calculated that though we had lost some interest we had saved £10,000 of the principal[1].

[" How fortunate," said I to my Father as I wrote down this, "that you saw the shadow of the coming event!" "Yes," he answered, "how fine are those lines of Campbell which express the foresight that age may bring:

'"Tis the sunset of life gives me mystical lore,
     And coming events cast their shadows before.'"

"Without forethought there is no foresight," a learned Judge remarked to me lately, in lamenting the many mistakes and mishaps arising from the want of it.]

I have said that nearly every throne in Europe was shaken by the events then happening in France. Hanover was an exception, and England. But we were not without our alarms. In April of this year the Chartists decided to send a deputation to the House of Commons with a monster petition[2]. Every preparation was made by the

---

[1] Speaking of Lord Brougham's visit to Paris only one month before the Revolution (Jan. 1848), Lord Campbell says, "Paris was a little agitated by the coming political banquets which the Government had prohibited; but although there was a considerable outcry about the Spanish marriages, no serious apprehension was entertained, and the Orleans dynasty seemed firmly fixed upon the throne of France."

[2] It was said to be signed by five millions, which on Examination proved to be less than two, and among the names were those of the

Government to prevent a disturbance of the peace. The Duke of Wellington was consulted, and his wise counsels probably averted the danger. Special Constables were sworn in. Gentlemen—among whom was Louis Napoleon—offered themselves in great numbers as such, and were concealed on the day (the 10th), in places from whence they could easily be summoned. Soldiers and Cannon were stationed out of sight near London and Westminster Bridges, and the deputation attended by thousands of people began their march from Kennington Common. Dissension with each other had however weakened their strength, and the whole affair passed off without any vehement demonstrations. People in the country who trembled for the issue were rejoiced to hear next morning that all was quiet.

["A Memorial praying for a Royal Commission of Enquiry into the best methods of securing the Improvement of the Universities of Oxford and Cambridge," signed by nearly 300 Graduates and former Members of those Universities, was presented to Lord John Russell in Downing Street, on the 10th of July. Lord J. R., in reply, stated "that he would take the subject into his serious consideration, that his attention had been already drawn to it,—and that he found that a great variety of opinions were entertained as to the best method of effecting reforms, but that he agreed with the Memorialists as to the existence of defects in the present system." My Father did not sign this Memorial, and his reason is shown in the following letter, written two days before the Memorial was presented.]

Queen, Prince Albert, Duke of Wellington and Sir Robert Peel; besides imaginary and absurd names.

PROFESSOR PRYME *to* THE RIGHT HONOURABLE LORD JOHN RUSSELL.

REFORM CLUB, 8 *July*, 1848.

MY LORD,

I am informed that a Memorial from Members of the Universities of Oxford and Cambridge, praying for a Commission of Inquiry, is to be presented to your Lordship on Monday. It will probably be in your recollection that I made a motion in the House of Commons (4 May, 1837) on the same subject, which after a debate I withdrew on the Chancellor of the Exchequer (Mr Spring Rice) expressing a wish to have the measure left to the consideration of the Government.

As my wish for such Commission is unchanged, I think it right to state why I have declined signing this Memorial. It is because the first paragraph contains a charge against the Universities, which I think is incorrect.

That Cambridge has been steadily endeavouring to improve its courses of study and examinations, I know to be the case from forty years' residence there; and I believe that Oxford has in some degree done the same. But there are many and great defects, some of which I then stated to the House, beyond their internal power to remedy. Some of these were not originally inherent, but introduced in consequence of a Royal Commission during the reign of Queen Elizabeth, and I beg leave to state my strong opinion in favour of such a Commission, though I could not sign a Memorial so worded.

I have the honour to be

Your Lordship's

Faithful Servant,

GEORGE PRYME.

In the Autumn I went, as I occasionally did, to Harrogate; not the gay place of former years when no German Spas were accessible, yet still having its Balls and Coteries. Here I usually met some old Parliamentary friends, among which this year was Sir Frederic Trench, who gave me the startling news of Lord George Bentinck's strange death. Colonel Trench was a most polished and amiable man. He was the original author of the plan for embanking the North side of the Thames, which he illustrated by a book of engravings, privately distributed among his friends. Referring to the date of the one he gave to me—though I was his political opponent—I find it to have been in 1825, so that it has taken nearly forty years to convince the public of the desirability of such an undertaking[1].

One day we made an excursion to Bolton Abbey, a few miles distant, the fine ruins of which are kept in preservation by the Duke of Devonshire, who owns the greater part of the small valley in which it is situated. "The stately Priory was reared" by a Mother whose Son failed in the leap.

> "And Wharfe as he moved along,
>     To matins joined a mournful voice,
>     Nor failed at Even-song."

The course of Wharfe which runs down to it is obstructed by two rocks, between which the channel is so narrow that it has been leaped over by adventurous visitors, despite its sad tradition[2].

---

[1] Mr Crabbe Robinson says in his Diary, "Feb. 11th, 1825, went to Covent Garden Theatre. A Panoramic view of the projected improvement of the Thames, by the erection of a terrace on arches along the Northern shore, is a pleasing anticipation of a splendid dream, which not even in this projecting age can become a reality."

[2] "The famous Strid" where the boy is said to have been drowned is not so named from its being possible to 'stride' across it, but from the A.-S. *Stryth*, tumult. *Quarterly Review*, Oct. 1868.

"This striding place is called the Strid,
A name that it took of yore;
A thousand years hath it borne that name,
And shall a thousand more."

Not far off dwelt a curiosity, a Centenarian. This man had been a Gamekeeper, but had many years retired hither, the Duke, in whose service he had been, still giving him the liberty of shooting. The old man had his faculties quite perfect, except some feebleness of sight. He said to me, "I can't see your features, but I can see you're a man and have shoes on."

From Harrogate I went to Wensleydale to visit some relations who were still living there. One, recently deceased, had bequeathed a small property to me, which linked me again with this charming valley.

[In October of this year a Grace was passed which effected a very important change in the Studies at Cambridge. The University Commission was not issued until two years later, so that this change was not recommended from without, but entirely proceeded from within. A Syndicate, appointed in the beginning of the year, had recommended certain Regulations tending to this, and these had been favourably reviewed by Dr Philpott[1] in a pamphlet. In it he also vindicated the dignity, and at the same the progress of the University, which, said he, "has not been accustomed to shew itself backward in exhibiting a proper regard for the preservation of existing systems, and in watching with a careful and scrutinizing eye the proposals which have been made for alteration of them. But neither, it must be said on the other hand, has the University shewn itself indisposed to accept suggestions for improvements, or to carry into effect with hearty good will the changes of its system, which its judgment has approved. It would be an unjust reproach to our Senate to assert that it has the inclination to reject proposals for change, either without examination altogether, or without the full and candid consideration which the desire of improvement dictates. Experience has abundantly proved that its attachment to ex-

---

[1] Then Master of St Catharine's College.

isting systems is not of that blind character which prevents its perceiving the difference between the rash proposals resulting from a restless desire of change, and the well-considered measures devised in a friendly and cautious spirit for enlarging the sphere of its usefulness, and adding to its influence. During the last quarter of a century, the history of the University records an almost continued succession of improvements introduced with the best effect into our course of studies." My Father entirely approved of the proposed alteration, and under the signature which he sometimes used of " Ex-Socius," examined and commended Dr Philpott's pamphlet in the Cambridge paper thus: "A Senior Wrangler cannot be supposed to be averse or indifferent to mathematical studies; nor would he support further encroachments than the Classical Tripos has made upon their exclusive reign, unless potent reasons had forced conviction upon his mind. The advocacy of a measure introducing new studies into our academical career comes, therefore, with peculiar force from such an individual. Prejudice would naturally bias his mind to a different direction, instead of taking, as he has done, a calm, comprehensive, and statesman-like view of the proposed infringements on mathematical monopoly."

By the Grace alluded to all Candidates for the ordinary B.A. Degree were required to have attended the Lectures of certain Professors, including Political Economy, and to produce a Certificate of having passed an Examination by one of them. Thus were the Moral and Natural Science Triposes established. Alluding to this change my Father says:]

I still gave my Lectures annually to an audience much increased by the alterations which had taken place in the studies and regulations of the University. In the yearly examinations I was now assisted—as were other Professors in their departments—by one whose ability and kindness were of great use to me, and with whom, whether in the Schools or in Society, association was always pleasurable. Mr Birkbeck, who is the son of the late Dr Birkbeck, a Physician well known for his philanthropy and as the Founder of Mechanics' Institutes, has since been chosen to be the Downing Professor of the Laws of England.

# CHAPTER XXIII.

## 1850—1860.

1850. July 20. I DINED at the Reform Club with a large party who had invited Lord Palmerston to a splendid dinner. It was given to celebrate his recent triumph in the House of Commons, where in defending his foreign Policy he had spoken for five hours : an oration which Sir Robert Peel in speaking for the last time (a few days before his fatal accident) characterized, although he took the opposite side, as "a speech which made us all proud of the man who delivered it."

Oct. 29. I attended the funeral (in the Chapel) of my wife's relative Dr George Thackeray, Provost of King's College. His handsome person, genial disposition, and great powers of conversation made his company delightful. He took particular interest in the text of Shakespeare's plays,

and the derivation of words used in them.   He added many
learned and ingenious MS. notes to *Nares's Glossary*,
which have been useful in a recent edition (the Globe)
of Shakespeare.   He was also a naturalist, and M. Audubon,
with whom he was intimate, said that his collection of stuffed
birds at King's Lodge was "one of the finest he had ever
seen."

1851, Feb. 8.   A Moral Science Tripos meeting at Trinity
Lodge.   Whewell, though a Conservative, was ever foremost
in advocating *real* improvements for his College and University.   We had had many Professorial meetings at the
Lodge to discuss the range of our new examinations, and
much correspondence with him on the subject.   I examined
him when a Freshman at the annual College Examinations,
and he was the best in his year, which did not appear on the
list, as each class is arranged alphabetically.   I soon became
well acquainted with him, and my admiration of his powerful
mind and extensive knowledge was blended with a strong
feeling of personal regard.   It is to be regretted that from
the paucity of his publications the full extent of his knowledge was not revealed.   Among them I would name a
quarto pamphlet on the application of Algebra to Political
Economy, and two excellent ones on the Cambridge studies.

The Professorship of Casuistry, now usually called that of
Moral Theology, was of small value, and always given as
a sinecure.   Dr Whewell was the first who gave Lectures
on the subject, which he continued after he became Master of
Trinity College till he ascertained that he could have an
active successor in Mr Grote.   They both ignored the principles of Moral Philosophy, laid down by Paley in his work on
that subject, which had been adopted as an Examination
book throughout the University, and built anew a system
founded on the existence of a moral sense, as supposed by

Bishop Butler, author of the *Analogy*. If that foundation be
granted his (Whewell's) published treatise is clear and forcible, and powerfully expressed, but there is no attempt at
a refutation of Paley's principle of general expediency; and
I never yet met with any one who could tell me where
such an attempted refutation was to be found. I put the
question to Whewell and to his successor, Professor Grote;
the latter candidly answered that he knew of none, and
Whewell referred me to an edition of Butler's four Sermons
with *his* notes. I read them, and found that he *assumed* the
existence of the moral sense without attempting to prove it.
I then pressed him for a further proof, but he never gave me
one, and it therefore rests, if I may coin the word, on their
*ipse dixitism* [1].

1851. Having a little spare time this Summer I went
in August with my Family by way of Antwerp, to visit
Ypres, whence my Father's family had come. It was with
deep interest that I approached the old fortified town, and
crossed its drawbridge. It is of considerable size, and has
a clean and airy appearance from its wide and paved streets.
The Hotel de Ville is one of exceeding beauty, with a tower
in the centre. I had got an introduction from our Foreign
Office to the English Embassy at Brussels, whence I obtained another to the Burgomaster of Ypres, in order to
be allowed an inspection of the Records of the City. I
found several of the name of Priem who had holden this
office before our name was changed to that of de la Pryme,
and some of their names we discovered also on monuments
in the Cathedral, but I could find no living representative.
After I had left Ypres I met accidentally with one of its

---

[1] Mr Pitt declared to Mr Wilberforce that "Bishop Butler's work
raised in his mind more doubts than it had answered." *Wilberforce's
Life*, Vol. I. p. 94.

residents who told me that there was one old widow Lady surviving who bore the name of Madame Rix-Priem. On my return to England I wrote to her and sealed my letter with my arms. She sent me an answer couched in very civil terms,—though the ancestor who was the link between us had been ignored as a heretic.—Her seal bore the same arms as mine disposed in a lozenge.

I next visited Paris. It was during the period of the Republic, which was formed after the expulsion of Louis Philippe, and the present Emperor was then only its President. We saw several buildings which had been injured in the time of the Barricades,—and observed the words *Liberté*, *Egalité* and *Fraternité* still remaining over some of the Public Offices—the Boulevards were much injured by the loss of their trees, in the place of which young ones were planted.

Paris was more than usually empty at this time owing to the great Exhibition in England being open. I was shewn the *Institut* by Professor Blanquin, the Professor of Political Economy, to whom I had an introduction, being absent. I found among such Parisians as I conversed with a great freedom of speech in regard to Politics, and that they considered that Louis Napoleon was trying to conciliate the Clergy, which I afterwards thought might have been in order to obtain their support for the Empire which he contemplated even while affecting to refuse it.

It was with great interest that I visited Notre Dame, the Hotel de Cluny, and Père la Chaise. The ancient streets of Paris are now fast disappearing under the vast alterations made by the Emperor, in order to make way for others wide and magnificent indeed, but possessing no Historical associations.

I returned to England by way of the ancient Norman

Capital (Rouen). We saw there in antique perfection the Rue de la Grosse Horloge, in which the curious old clock remained, and the Place de la Pucelle, where the Maid of Orleans was burnt, and in the S. W. corner of which is the Hotel de Bourgthéroude, a sculptured mansion of one of the Norman Nobles, now converted into public offices. Some of the other old streets leading to the Quay had been displaced by a wide and splendid one called *Rue de la République*, which had been commenced by Louis Philippe, and which was then styled in honour of him *Rue Royale*. Since I was there I hear that it has been re-named *Rue Impériale*.

After a week's stay at Dieppe we returned to England, a few weeks before the Coup d'état by which, on the eve of a re-election, the President suppressed what freedom remained in France. I think of the future of that Country (now in 1864), that Louis Napoleon will gradually relax his iron rule, and give it more liberty; and that he will die upon his Throne.

[In 1850 the Commission was issued for inquiring into the State, Discipline, Studies, and Revenues of the University and Colleges of Cambridge. The Commissioners were the Bishop of Chester (Graham), Dean of Ely (Peacock), Sir J. F. Herschel, Sir John Romilly, and Adam Sedgwick. Mr Bateson (now Master of St John's College) and Mr Edward Bunbury were Secretaries. Their first care was to address questions to University Officers (my Father among them) intended to call forth their views. Their report was published in about two years, and filled a bulky blue book of 685 pages. Speaking of a part of their recommendations my Father said:]

I have often regretted that Lord John Russell had not been educated at either of the Universities. The disadvantage of this appeared, among many other things, in his proposing Commissioners of whom all were not intimately acquainted with the state and spirit of these Institutions.

[My Father, while regretting this "disadvantage," had a great admiration for what he termed "Lord John Russell's honest and straightforward, and continued self-education of himself as a Statesman." To the following extract in his own handwriting, "No error can be more fatal, than the belief that education terminates with School or College discipline. A wise, a truly great man, will continue to improve himself to the latest period of life[1]," he has added, "*e.g.* Lord John Russell." And he quotes elsewhere "the noble speech of Lord John Russell in June 1834."]

The Commissioners recommended the formation of ten new Professorships, three of which I venture to designate as fantastical. But they made no mention in any way of a Professorship of Political Economy. In respect to marriage the Commissioners adopted an exactly opposite course to the one which I suggested in my answer to their questions, deeming the celibacy of Fellows who did *not* hold College Offices undesirable.

In Trinity College there was little for the Commissioners to remedy or reform. The Fellowships and Scholarships were *there* completely open. Mr Tavel one day on coming into Hall told us that he had received a letter from a Military Officer enquiring whether his Son, who was born in India but within the British dominions, would be eligible to a Fellowship? "To which," Mr Tavel added, "I replied, 'I think I cannot give a better answer than to state I am myself a Swiss by *birth and family*, and that I am Fellow and Tutor of the College[2].'"

The Commissioners however recommended the alteration of the emoluments of our Scholarships. These have con-

---

[1] *Essays on Professional Education*, by R. L. Edgeworth, Esq., p. 337.
[2] Whosoever hath one English parent, although he be born in another country, shall be esteemed as if born in that County to which his English parent belonged. But if both parents were English, he shall be reckoned of that County to which his Father belonged. *Stat. Acad.* p. 268.

sisted of free Commons in the Hall at a table appropriated to Scholars of whatever standing, and a small sum of money. They suggested converting the whole into a mere pecuniary stipend. The College authorities refused assent to this change, showing therein a better knowledge of human nature; for I well recollect that we (as Scholars) felt far more gratification from the gratuitous hospitality of the dinner provided for us than we should have done from a payment of even greater value. It possessed another advantage too in being a slight encouragement to longer residence.

[The Commissioners, although they had published their Report, seem to have been sitting *en permanence*, for I find my Father writing to them some years later.]


PROFESSOR PRYME *to* THE HONOURABLE THE UNIVERSITY COMMISSIONERS.

CAMBRIDGE, 8 *Dec.* 1857.

SIRS,

Allow me, as Professor of Political Economy, to suggest for your consideration the expediency of adopting some plan to perpetuate a Professorship.

I began to give Lectures as a Master of Arts with the consent of the Vice-Chancellor, in 1816. The title of Professor was conferred upon me in 1828 by a vote of the Senate. But this is merely personal to me. There is no foundation, nor any emolument whatever, except a Dividend of Lecture and Certificate fees among certain Professors, which amounts to about £30 a year.

The Anatomical, Mineralogical, and I believe other Professorships, originated in the same way; on the first vacancy a Grace of the Senate voted them perpetual. And the Government made for each a vote of £100 annually from the Civil Estimates. None such (though I applied for it the first year) was granted to me.

My zeal for the Science induces me to continue my exertions in this department; but I much doubt if so trifling an emolument would ensure a successor.

I hear that it is contemplated at Trinity College to appropriate a Fellowship to such a Professorship; but unless the restriction of Celibacy were removed a privation for life would be inflicted, or a vacancy, by perhaps a fit Professor, be occasioned.

I am, Sirs,

Your obedient Servant,

GEORGE PRYME.

PROFESSOR PRYME *to* EDWARD BUNBURY, ESQ. SECRETARY TO THE CAMBRIDGE UNIVERSITY COMMISSION.

CAMBRIDGE, 30 *Jan.* 1858.

SIR,

I am honoured by your letter inviting communications from me as Professor of Political Economy. I am strongly impressed with the opinion that the Collegiate system is far preferable to that of Hostels, inasmuch as by the mixture of Students from different Counties and Schools, it tends to remove prejudices and give a knowledge useful in life, which mere Book-learning cannot bestow; while Hostels would probably become appropriated to particular tenets or districts, and thus strengthen instead of removing prejudices.

The latter plan (of domicile in houses of Professors) in the sister University is said to have worked well, but this is in contrast not to Colleges, but to the insulated state of out-door Students. I am strongly adverse to the opening of Fellowships to general competition by examination, for the reasons urged in Mr Latham's (Tutor of Trinity Hall) *Considerations on the Suggestions of the University Commissioners.*

I am equally adverse to the limited duration of Fellowships. I understand that it has worked ill in Wadham College, Oxford.

I beg leave to repeat what I stated in an early communication to the Commissioners—the want of attention to the English language and style; which I find in the sermons and publications of many men eminent for Classical and Theological knowledge. I then suggested the institution of a Professorship of English Literature.

With regard to the Professorship of Political Economy, I took the liberty of making a voluntary communication lately to the Commissioners.

I am, Sir,

Yours truly,

GEORGE PRYME.

[The communication of Dec. 1857, addressed to the Commissioners, seems to have been disregarded, for two years later my Father wrote again on the subject.]


PROFESSOR PRYME *to the* LORD BISHOP OF CHESTER.

CAMBRIDGE, 28 *March*, 1859.

MY LORD BISHOP,

Permit me to request your Lordship's attention as an University Commissioner to the state of matters as to a Professorship of Political Economy. I have twice sent a Representation through the present Secretary, who answered

that he would lay my letter before the Board, but I am
apprehensive that it may be overlooked unless one of the
Commissioners calls attention to it.

There exists no endowment whatever nor any Professorship of Political Economy.   The Senate by Grace in 1828
conferred on me the title of Professor.   The Professorships
of Chemistry, Botany and Mineralogy arose in the same way ;
and on the first vacancy the Senate passed a Grace for per-
petuating them.

I never had the £100 from the Government which those
others had, nor any emolument except my share of the
Certificate fees, which average about £30 a year, and I fear
that at my decease no one will be found to undertake the
duties of a Professorship in this Science of great and growing
importance[1] unless the Commissioners institute and provide
for the endowment of one.

I have the honour to be,

My Lord Bishop,

Your faithful Servant,

GEORGE PRYME.

[There were no visible results from these letters and appeals of
my Father to get his Professorship established on a firmer base, in
which case he would have immediately resigned it.   But perhaps his

---

[1] "Just notions of Political Economy are absolutely necessary to just
notions of History; and I should wish those young gentlemen who may
attend my Lectures to go first, were it possible, to my more learned
brother, the Professor of Political Economy, and get from him not merely
exact habits of thought, but a knowledge which I cannot give, and yet
what they ought to possess."   One present in the Senate-House told me
that this Sentence was followed by a ringing cheer from the Undergraduates in the gallery.   Extract from Professor Kingsley's *Inaugural
Lecture* delivered before the University of Cambridge.

ill-success prepared the way for a conclusion to his anxiety, which will be related in the next Chapter.]

1858. Lord Macaulay was elected (May 11th) High Steward of the Borough of Cambridge, and was entertained at a Breakfast at the Town Hall, when he made a splendid speech upon the occasion. He did not hold the office long, dying at the close of the following year. He was succeeded by the Duke of Bedford, a very shy retiring man, who did not like the publicity attending his inauguration into Office. He had known me in the House of Commons, and did me the honour to request as a favour that I would meet him at the house of the Mayor before proceeding to the Guildhall, in order to introduce him to the Aldermen, &c. I did so, and had the pleasure of sitting next him at the banquet which followed (April 11, 1860).

I was presented to Albert Edward, Prince of Wales, who was now a Student in our University, at a party this winter at Trinity Lodge. I ventured to tell him that I had been at his Great Grandfather's Court, and I was probably the only person in the College who could have said so. I thought him a most pleasing, unaffected young man, and very like the old King in countenance.

[If my Father was observant, the Prince was no less so. I have the kind permission of Sir Frederick Pollock (the late Chief Baron) to relate a remark made by the Prince to him, which evinces a tact and discernment quite remarkable in one so young as he then was; qualities that will be of inestimable value to himself and the Country hereafter.

"When I was at Cambridge, at Trinity Lodge, as Judge of Assize with Vaughan Williams, in March 1861, I had the honour, according to custom, to entertain the Noblemen of Trinity and the Heads of Houses. The Prince of Wales sat at my right hand, and made enquiries about Professor Pryme, whose countenance, he said,

had much impressed him, as indicating by its expression the high
qualities of mind, and the right use of them, which ought to belong
to a Professor; adding 'he has, to my mind, the true University-
Professor look[1].'"]

---

[1] I have met with a copy among my Father's papers of the qualifica-
tions required in a Professor at Melbourne. I have placed it in the
Appendix as an interesting evidence of the care with which a young
University selects its officers, and also because in many points it corre-
sponds with the same standard of excellence which uniformly guided my
Father in *all* his Votes.

# CHAPTER XXIV.

## 1860—1863.

1861. [I NOW enter upon the last Chapter of my Father's public life. He had failed to induce the University Commissioners to establish and endow the Chair of that Science of which he had himself, nearly 60 years previously, foreseen the importance, and of which most Ministers and Countries were now recognising the necessity in their Measures and Treaties of Commerce. Although it might perhaps seem at first sight unnecessary that, devoid as Political Economy is of the charm of Classic association and wholly utilitarian, an acquaintance with it should commence at the University, yet that is in truth the place where the model of the future Statesman is formed. It was already one of the accepted studies at Cambridge, and my Father's hope was to see its Professorship firmly established and endowed before he resigned it. His next attempt was on the Council of the University, and he therefore addressed the following letter to the Vice-Chancellor.]

Trinity College,
4 *Dec.* 1861.

Sir,

I beg leave to make a representation to the Council of the position in which the study of Political Economy is placed in this University.

A Syndicate being lately appointed for augmenting the Salaries of Professors inadequately endowed, I addressed a letter to the then Vice-Chancellor stating the case, and my apprehension that no successor would be found to undertake the office without a pecuniary augmentation. He answered that he would lay my letter before the Syndicate.

I was afterwards told by one of the Syndicate that an objection was taken of there being no Professorship of Political Economy; but only that the title of Professor had been conferred by Grace of the Senate upon me. This Grace was passed in 1828, after I had lectured twelve years, with permission of the Vice-Chancellor.

The Professorship of Mineralogy in my own time had its origin in the same way—by Dr E. D. Clarke first lecturing as M.A.; then having the title of Professor conferred upon him by Grace; and on his death by the institution of a Professorship. I have understood that the Professorships of Chemistry, Botany, and Anatomy had similar origin.

Since I began to lecture Professorships have been founded at Oxford, Dublin, Edinburgh and Glasgow; and have been added to those of Moral Philosophy in Aberdeen and St Andrew's.

Of the progress and importance of this study it is unnecessary in the middle of the nineteenth century to dilate, though it is comparatively recent at Cambridge. But it is more recent in the other Universities, which I mentioned.

In making these remarks I disclaim being actuated by any prospect of personal advantage. In contemplating my past career in life nothing affords me more satisfaction than the having been able to draw the attention of our University to the study of Political Economy—important in every country—and especially in ours, so connected with the commerce of the whole world. But I cannot expect to have strength to continue my Lectures much longer; and I am unwilling to imagine that the study of Political Economy, though not ignored, is not attempted to be established and perpetuated in the University of Cambridge.

I am, Sir, yours faithfully,

GEORGE PRYME.

The Syndicate recommended to the Senate the augmentation by one or two hundred a year of the Salaries of the aforesaid Professorships, but omitted any recognition of mine.

This was the more surprising as the Science being now recognised and included in the Moral Science Tripos, there was real work in the Examinations, and my Successor, if one were intended, could not have undertaken it on such conditions. But for this I would have resigned at once, but in the hope that some permanent basis might still be arranged I continued to lecture and to examine till advancing age and declining health rendered me unequal to the exertion.

1863. I communicated my wish to withdraw to the

Master of Trinity (Whewell), who had always taken a strong interest in promoting the cultivation of the Science.

PROFESSOR PRYME *to the* REV. THE MASTER
OF TRINITY.

SIDNEY STREET, CAMBRIDGE,
23 *Feb.* 1863.

MY DEAR MASTER,

As I have always considered you as the chief promoter of the study of the Moral Sciences in this University, I address this letter to you on the subject of a Professorship of Political Economy.

As it is 47 years since I began to lecture with the sanction of the University, and 35 since the title of Professor was conferred upon me by the Senate, I now feel myself less equal to the exertions required for the proper performance of that Office, and wish to retire from the duties of it. The absence of any endowment for a Professorship has made me hesitate as to offering this resignation, but as I have a confidence in the desire of the University not to let so important a study be neglected (and this would be the only University in the Kingdom where it would be so), I have no right to suppose that the Council and the Senate would not give effect to this feeling by making an adequate provision for the continuance of the Professorship's duties. May I beg of you therefore to communicate to the Council my wish to retire, and to consider myself as only holding Office until the appointment of my Successor?

Yours, most sincerely,

GEORGE PRYME.

[I have not found the answer which was sent to this letter—a kind one doubtless— but the best practical answer was in the Report (sent by Dr Whewell) of a Syndicate which was appointed soon after the Resignation was made known to consider it, and which is here reprinted from the original.]

CLARE COLLEGE LODGE.  *May* 1, 1863.

The Syndicate, appointed by Grace of the Senate, 20th March, 1863, to consider what steps should be taken by the University in consequence of the proposed resignation by Professor Pryme of the office of Professor of Political Economy, beg leave to recommend to the Senate :

1.   That on the resignation of Professor Pryme there shall be established in the University a Professorship to be called the Professorship of Political Economy.

2.   That it shall be the duty of the Professor to explain and teach the principles of Political Economy, and to apply himself to the advancement of that science.

3.   That the Professor shall be chosen and appointed from time to time by those persons whose names are on the Electoral Roll of the University.

4.   That the stipend of the Professor shall be two hundred pounds per annum, to be paid out of the University Chest, and that this stipend shall be increased to three hundred pounds per annum, so soon as the Lucasian Professor shall become entitled to receive the share of the income of Lady Sadler's benefaction allotted to the Lucasian Professorship under the provisions of the New Statute, confirmed by the Queen in Council, 7 March, 1860.

5.   That the above-named Stipend shall be payable out of the University Chest so long as the person who shall first be appointed under these regulations shall continue to hold the Professorship, and that it shall be open to the University to deal with the Stipend of the Professor as it may deem fit on the occurrence of a vacancy in the Professorship.

6.   That the Professorship shall be governed by the regulations of the Statute for Sir Thomas Adams' Professorship of Arabic and certain other professorships in common, and the Professor shall comply with all the provisions of the said Statute.

7.  That it shall be the ordinary duty of the Professor to reside within the precincts of the University for eighteen weeks in every year between the 1st of October and the end of the following Easter Term.

8.  That the fees to be paid by Students attending the Lectures of the Professor shall be the same as those settled in the case of the Professor of Botany by Grace of the Senate, 20 Nov. 1862.

> Edward Atkinson, *Vice Chancellor.*
> W. Whewell.
> W. H. Bateson.
> John Fuller.
> Joseph B. Mayor.
> J. Lempriere Hammond.
> Leslie Stephen.
> C. B. Clarke.

*The* Vice-Chancellor *invites the attendance of* Members *of the* Senate *in the* Arts' School *on* *Wednesday, May 13th, at Two o'Clock, for the discussion of the above* Report.

## Professor Pryme *to the* Rev. the Master of Trinity.

> Wistow, Huntingdon,
> 11 *May*, 1863.

My dear Master,

I have received your Report of the Syndicate respecting a Professorship of Political Economy, and feel gratified to find not merely that they recommend its establishment, but that Article 2 is in accordance with my practice and views instead of being, as at Oxford, on some particular branch which supposes a previous knowledge of the principles.

I am also satisfied as to the mode of Election.  The late Professor Tennant had meditated the foundation of a Professorship of Political Economy, and consulted me about the mode of Election, on which we agreed as to resident M.A.s. His intention was not carried out, as he was killed by an accident at Boulogne a few months after, and died intestate.

I am uncertain whether any further declaration of my discontinuance of Lectures and Examinations be expected from me. If it be so may I ask the favour of your informing me of it.

With thanks for your kindness in the matter,

Believe me,

Yours most sincerely,

GEORGE PRYME.

"LONDON,
"*May* 13, 1863.

"MY DEAR PROFESSOR,

"The result of the recommendation of the Council is yet uncertain. It will probably be offered in the Senate. Till the Grace is passed I shall think it not prudent for you to take any steps. You see probably that the matter is to be discussed in the Schools to-day.

"Yours very truly,

"WM. WHEWELL.

"*Professor Pryme.*"

[The debate was favourable, and on May 18 the Vice-Chancellor (Dr Atkinson) issued a notice that the Grace for the establishment of the Professorship would come before the Senate on Oct. 29. The reason for the delay was that the Long Vacation was shortly to begin. It would have been too soon to have brought forward so important a measure during the May Term, and therefore it could not be submitted to the Senate till the October Term had fairly begun, and all were in residence

Thus was achieved (virtually) one of the great aims of my Father's life, and which had been to him a hope too long deferred.

But it is only fair to the University Authorities to say, that until lately they had not the means to endow new Chairs, that even now their power is far behind their wishes, and that considering their means they have done a great deal. Those who knew my Father well understood for what purpose he had so long—so far beyond the usual time of man's health and strength—continued to discharge his Professorial duties. This cannot be better shown than by an extract from a note addressed to me at this time (May 23, 1863) by the present Master of Trinity. " We are all very sorry to think that Professor Pryme's periodical visits are likely to be further apart in future. He has however done the University a real service in insisting on its appointing a successor to his Chair. I for one shall always feel grateful to him for this act of firmness. *Now* I think the Grace will certainly pass, and the University will no longer be served gratis."

Four Candidates announced themselves for the vacant office,

> Mr J. B. Mayor, Tutor of St John's,
> Mr H. Fawcett, Trinity Hall,
> Mr Macleod, Trinity,
> Mr L. Courtney, St John's.

Even *before* the Professorship was established my Father was canvassed by influential people in favour of certain Candidates. To one of them he returned this answer.]

CAMBRIDGE,
4 *April*, 1863.

DEAR SIR,

I well remember your former communications on Political Economy subjects, and the satisfaction which I felt on perusing them. I feel some delicacy as to much interfering in the appointment of a Successor. A Syndicate is appointed to consider the permanent institution of a Professorship and report thereon before the end of next Easter Term.

The Election will probably be in the Electoral Roll. In giving a vote I have always adopted the rule of not making a promise till I knew who all the Candidates were, and then voting for him whom I thought best qualified.

I can only say that I place great confidence in your opinion, and will on every fair opportunity communicate it to others.

I am, dear Sir,

Faithfully yours,

GEORGE PRYME.

[In the following October a Grace passed the Senate establishing the Professorship of Political Economy, and endowing it with a stipend of £300 a year. It was carried by 98 to 40[1]. My Mother was in the Senate-House, and as soon as the Grace passed Dr Whewell went up to her, and in his earnest warm manner congratulated her. She told him she was extremely glad that her husband, who was now too old for work, had waited to such good purpose. " I was a proud woman that day," she said to me, " when I thought how disinterestedly your Father had acted."]

PROFESSOR PRYME *to the* REV. THE VICE-CHANCELLOR.

29 Oct. 1863.

DEAR MR VICE-CHANCELLOR,

In consequence of the Vote of the University Senate establishing a Professorship of Political Economy I beg leave to state, in pursuance of the notice which I previously gave, that I now intend to discontinue my Lectures and Examinations therein, which will of course be continued by the Professor to be elected according to the Report of the Syndicate now confirmed by the Senate.

I have the honour to be,

Dear Mr Vice-Chancellor,

Yours respectfully,

GEORGE PRYME.

[1] " Placeat vobis ut relatio Syndicorum vestrorum de Professore Œconomiæ Politicæ in Academia constituendo data 1<sup>mo</sup> Maii 1863, suffragiis vestris comprobetur."

THE VICE-CHANCELLOR *to* PROFESSOR PRYME.

"CLARE COLLEGE LODGE,
"*Oct.* 30, 1863.

"MY DEAR SIR,

"I beg to acknowledge the due receipt of your letter of this morning in which you announce your intention of discontinuing your Lectures and Examinations in consequence of the establishment of a Professorship of Political Economy by the Votes of the Senate yesterday. I think it will be necessary to refer to the Council the question whether any, and if so what, steps should be taken for making your intentions publicly known. And I will take care to place your letter in the hands of my Successor for that purpose, since there will be no further meeting of the Council during my year of Office.

"I feel in common, I believe, with every other member of the Senate that the University is under deep obligations to you for the manner in which you have for so many years gratuitously discharged all the duties of a Professor of Political Economy; and I have no doubt that it is to your services and exertions that the foundation of a permanent Professorship of that Science is due. I trust that you will still live in health and happiness to see the fruit of your exertions for many years to come.

"Believe me, my dear Sir,

"Yours very faithfully,

"E. ATKINSON, *V. C.*"

[My Father was always very desirous that his favourite Science should be kept distinct from Politics. He therefore, perceiving that there was a risk of their being confused in some minds on this occasion, addressed the following letter to the Editor of one of the local Journals.]

SIR,

The person who signs himself "A Conservative" in your last week's *Chronicle* seems to imagine from the name that Political Economy has some connexion with party politics. The word "Political" has been used merely to distinguish it from "Private Economy." It is true that Quesnay and his followers in the reign of Louis XIV. mixed their bygone system with approbation of *absolute* government; probably because they did not then venture to discuss subjects of national wealth without it. But Adam Smith, and I believe every other English writer, have not mixed any party politics with their investigations.

For myself, though a decided Whig, I have *scrupulously* done the same; and I have been told by at least two high Tories that they could not discover by my lectures what political sentiments I held.

Yours, &c.

GEORGE PRYME.

12 *Nov.* 1863.

["The Contest for the Professorial Chair in Political Economy took place Nov. 27th in the Senate-House, and created more interest than has attached to any Election of late. The real struggle lay between Mr Fawcett and Mr Mayor, but it is not too much to say that the friends of each of the Candidates strained every nerve to ensure the success of their favourite. The Senate-House was a scene of busy excitement throughout the day. At the close of the Poll the numbers were,

Fawcett.........90
Mayor ..........80
Courtney ......19
Macleod........13[1]."

My Father went over from Wistow in order to vote for Mr Fawcett, having, after much deliberation, thought him to be the fittest man.

He now finally quitted Cambridge, resigning the pleasant apartments in a private house, which by the kindness of a fellow-Townsman (Mr Ellis of Sidney Street) had always been specially reserved for his use. Before he left he sent a note of farewell to Professor Sedgwick, who was absent, asking him to visit him at Wistow. I insert the answer as a beautiful picture of a friendship which had lasted from youth.]

To Professor Pryme.

" Norwich,
" *Dec.* 14, 1863.

" My Dear Pryme,

" On Saturday I came hither on business. The Dean has called me into Residence to attend a Chapter summoned this day. Before we meet I will endeavour to answer the kind letter you left at my rooms before you went away from Cambridge. The only sheet of paper I can find is one they call *"foreign post,"* so thin that it will hardly hold the ink I can place upon it. But I hope you will be able to read my greetings. A thrice happy Christmas I send to you and Mrs Pryme—May God bless you both! and may He bless and preserve those who are most near and dear to you. I read your kind letter with an emotion of sorrow. For it sounded like a farewell letter ; and few are the old friends now left to me at Cambridge. You and I, my dear Pryme, have not long to live in this world. In course of Nature we must go before long, and the decline of life would indeed be cheerless were it not

---

[1] Abridged from the *Cambridge Chronicle, Nov.* 23, 1863.

lighted up by Christian hope. God grant that this hope
may brighten our declining days with Heaven's best light.
I believe that you have the Hope given us through Faith
in the power and love of our Redeemer. God grant that
this Faith and Hope may cheer us, and those we love, to
the last moments of our sojourn on Earth. The year of
1863 has been to me a year of very deep sorrow. But,
thanks be to God, that my health has been better than
during two or three preceding years. It will be a happiness
to me if during next Spring I can pay you a visit at Wistow.
You are one of my oldest friends, and I have generally
agreed with you in opinion: and even in points in which
we differed I have always honoured you as a man of principle. I was happy at the last Election of a Professor [1] to
vote at your suggestion.

          " Ever your true-hearted friend,

                  " ADAM SEDGWICK.

  " P. S. I am sure you will be glad to hear that the
Royal Society have this year awarded me the Copley
Medal. ' It is the highest honour they have in their power
to offer,' as the President told me in his Address."

       [1] Of Political Economy.

# CHAPTER XXV.

*Earliest Reminiscences of my Father—His Educational Theory—His patience in instructing—His energy—Accurate knowledge and memory—Republic of St Marino—Patriotism—Life at Cambridge—Anecdote of Sir John Campbell—Diversity of friendships —Tenderness to opponents—Anecdote of Baron Parke and Dr French—Resolution of the Cambs County Club—Visits to London — Lincoln's Inn Chapel — Lord Brougham's daughter — Dr Pusey's Sermon—Private Charities—Letters asking for advice— A legal Curiosity—Courtesy to inferiors—Their appreciation of it—Great power of illustration.*

THE Chronicle is now ended. Henceforth my Father had nothing more to do with public life. He retired to his farms and country occupations, but I trust I may be forgiven if, with a daughter's affection, I linger over the lineaments of his character. It was a very peculiar one, unlike, as a whole, any other that I have known. It was not at all a type of a class, but singularly independent, and not likely to be reproduced in its entirety in this or any other age. For his manners and his mind were fashioned in the formal mould of the last Century, yet he entered thoroughly into the progress and energy of this one. Deliberate in thought, and slow to generalise, he was, perhaps for that very reason, before his time, and had

not unfrequently to be overtaken by quicker and more en-
thusiastic spirits. He always kept sincerity and directness in
view, avoiding all kinds of exaggeration, and speaking of
"the delicious delight of reposing one's mind upon truth."

His habit was—like the Ancients—to meditate and converse in the open air. My earliest recollections of him are of
saying my Latin Lesson to him in his garden, and of his
sauntering in it with Professor Dobree. No sooner was he
returned home from one of his frequent professional journeys
than he was to be seen there, attended by a favourite Cat,
examining his flowers and fruit-trees, which last he always
pruned himself. His books, and his garden, with sometimes
a day's fishing at Grantchester, were his principal recreations.
However busy, he could still find time to hear his Children's
lessons, and his patience was unwearied.

My Father entertained a theory that up to a certain period (about 16 years of age) the capacity of girls to learn is
quite equal to that of boys. Of the mental difference between the two sexes he remarked that, "Though an Edinburgh Reviewer has instanced the want of any first-rate Poet
as a proof of the inferiority of women, yet the lesser opportunity of observing events and characters arising from their
more secluded education withholds the materials for poetry—
while attention to needlework and household affairs narrows
the mind." He put this theory into practice, and taught me
Latin and Italian, not in a slight and elementary manner, but
going deep down into the roots of these Languages, so that I
was, through his kindness and perseverance, able to read with
him the best Authors. Every place mentioned in them we
looked out both in Ancient and Modern Maps, and after a
lesson in Virgil or Tasso, he always read to me the translations of Dryden, Hunt, and sometimes quaint old Fairfax.
He would mark fine pieces of English Poetry to be got by

rote during his absences, and of Prose to be translated into
Latin, and immediately on his return would hear and correct
them. He also instructed me in Algebra and Euclid. He
taught my Brother Greek and Latin till he went to School,
and it was delightful to sit by and listen to his fine reading
of Homer. In the evenings he read aloud to us Gibbon's
*Decline and Fall of Rome*, some of Shakespeare's Plays, and
Scott's Novels.

How he found time for all he did surprises me[1]. Not only
had he to attend to his Profession, but when at home his
time was much taken up by claimants on it who had no real
business, but made the plea of consulting him an excuse for
moving his pity and obtaining money. He never seemed to
weary of listening to their affairs, or of relieving their wants.
One secret must have been that he rose early, and never
wasted a moment. If he were not writing he was reading,
and he was wont to have a book in his hand even while
driving himself in his open carriage with the other. And he
read "not to contradict and confute, not to believe and take
for granted, not to find talk and discourse, but to weigh and
consider." I have often seen him close a book and meditate
in silence. His incessant activity in business, and his absolute leisure for reading and teaching, remind me of one of
the men of the Elizabethan age, of whom it was said that
"he was so contemplative you could not believe him active,
and so active that you could not believe him contemplative."
Thus he accomplished a great deal in the course of his life,
but he did all in a quiet way as the occasion arose, not
seeking for or making it.

His power of fixing attention to *one* subject at a time,

---

[1] I find a note in his pocket-book for 1821. "Wrote 240 letters"
(this was in the days of heavy postage and long epistles); "travelled Post
1360 miles. By Coach 744. Total 2,104."

(though he was so versatile that nearly every thing engaged his thoughts from the drainage of the Fens to the Government of the Country) explains my Father's varied and accurate knowledge. He never relinquished a subject that he thought it worth while to take up till he had mastered and exhausted it, and this, aided by a remarkable memory, accounted for what Boswell calls "a precision in conversation." He never embellished a story, nor ever related it differently. Whilst dictating to me these "Recollections," he told me an anecdote, which I afterwards found that I had written down a year or two previously, and in precisely the same words. He forgot nothing worth recalling, and could quote and supply information on the instant to others who wanted it. He was staying in a Country house, and on the first evening mention was made of the Republic of St Marino in some book which was being read and discussed. "Who can tell us anything about it?" asked the noble host. No answer was made, and then my Father said, "If you will look in the second volume of Addison's Travels you will find an account of it." The other guests were superior people and strangers to him, and he felt during the rest of the visit the advantage this readiness had given him[1].

My Father took such a deep interest in the welfare and Government of the Country, and the times in which he lived

[1] The description is, like the Republic itself, a miniature. I met with it lately in an Annual Register of the last Century without a name, but who could fail to recognize in the opening sentences the hand of the great old master?

"I have been visiting the smallest of all Republics. I distinguished at some distance, and not without difficulty, at the top of a very high mountain, a town, the houses and larger buildings of what seemed to be rather a fairy vision than anything in reality. Venice appears, as one advances towards it, as if rising out of the sea; St Marino seems built among the clouds."

were so singular and transitional, that of course Politics and
the proceedings of Parliament were a chief topic in our house.
But I never once heard them spoken of in relation to self-
aggrandisement ; and I remember being rather surprised
when the invitation to represent Cambridge arrived.   Patriotism was really the mainspring of all my Father's political
exertions ; he "referred everything habitually to principles,"
and never allowed himself to be led on by partisans a step
further than his own judgment and conscientiousness allowed,
weighing every question involving a right or a wrong decision,
not by the opinions of others, but by a standard of his own.
I think it might be truly said of him, "his end was public
liberty ; his regulating principle was usefulness[1]."

Our life at Cambridge was a very pleasant one, for my
Father entertained many strangers of note who came to see
the place.   At all University Elections he kept open house,
and at the Assizes generally gave a dinner to the Bar.   I
remember one such being made for his friend Sir John Campbell, which brought out an illustration of Miss Martineau's
remark, that he delighted in telling his friends that he was
only "plain John Campbell."   He had gone down *Special* to
Huntingdon Assizes while Attorney-General (July, 1836),
and afterwards came on to Cambridge to dine with us.   He
arrived in the forenoon, and called directly on my Father.
Our house was recessed in a garden, and had two doors, one
for Visitors and one for Servants.   Sir J. C. came to the
latter, and was answered by a maidservant, who, taking him
for a farmer, informed him with little ceremony that he could
not see her Master, as he was in Court.   Sir John, wishing to
join him, requested that some one might go with him to
point out the way, to which the maid, as all the Servants

---

[1] From Sir James Mackintosh's description of Lord Somers.

were busily preparing for a great party, demurred. Sir John pressing the matter, she retired into the Offices to enquire, followed by him; here he found the Men Servants cleaning their plate, but one of them, after much pressing, agreed to go, saying, however, that he must first wash his hands. This was done in the presence of Sir John, who was afraid to lose sight of his guide, and then they set off. Not long after my Father returned with his guest, and of course he rang at the front door; the man Servant who answered it (the same who had attended Sir John to the Court) was surprised; but when he found, on his third appearance in the evening, that *this* was the very person for whom the party had been made, and whom he had treated so unceremoniously, his consternation was extreme. Sir John Campbell told my Mother the story, and enjoyed the joke.

It will have been seen that my Father's friendships took a wide range among men of very different political and theological views. His sympathies were also extended to those who were not his friends. And he often went out of his way to do a kindness to such. There could hardly, perhaps, be any one differing more from him in every way than Dr Turton, the late Bishop of Ely, yet I have before me a note from the latter couched in the warmest terms; he says, "I feel myself more obliged to you than I can express for the interest and trouble you have taken on my account. Nothing can be better than the manner in which you have stated the facts of the case. There is not too much of it, and in a small space you have brought forward all that is requisite. Pray accept my thanks for your kindness." This was, no doubt, in allusion to some little service such as my Father was always glad to render, as well to an opponent as to a friend.

Those were days, happily past away, when men of strong

political opinions were drawn up in opposing lines, and, in small societies, felt and spoke with bitterness of each other. Dr French, late Master of Jesus College, was one with whom my Father had no private acquaintance, and was always in public opposition, in the Senate House, and on the Hustings, yet only so that each, I am sure, could say of the other,

> "For though mine enemy thou hast ever been,
> High sparks of Honour in thee have I seen."

I remember Baron Parke calling one day, when, a Bishopric being vacant, the probable appointment to it was discussed. Parke mentioned that Dr French might not improbably be chosen, unless indeed his failing health should be a barrier. "Well," said my Father, whom we expected to be horrified, "if it would do him good, I should like to see him made a Bishop." "Ah!" rejoined his friend, "you think that the air of the See would benefit him." As a young man he had a strong hostility to certain Statesmen, Lord Castlereagh and others, whom he thought tyrannical; but after they were dead, he only mentioned them with kindness. To quote his own printed words, in speaking of some of them, " I therefore pass them by; for I am unwilling, without urgent necessity, to accuse so many individuals who can no longer defend them- selves before the earthly tribunal of public opinion." As he grew older, Seneca's line would well apply to him, "Lenior et melior fis accedente senectâ;" or, as Mr Browning has beauti- fully, and probably unconsciously, rendered it, "Yes, every- body that leaves life sees all softened and bettered."

My Father's old age came slowly on him,

> "An age that melts in unperceived decay;"

and he retained his faculties perfectly for 17 years more than man's allotted time. But if his life were calculated by his healthy days it was still longer, for, with the exception of one illness lasting a month, I never knew him take his breakfast in bed until a few days before his death. I almost think that there is a health of the body which accompanies that of the mind. His medical attendant told me that in all his practice he had never met with a pulse so regular.

It was in 1852 that my Father had his severe illness, and for some time after he was not equal to his usual exertions. Two years later he gave up farming himself, and sold his stock. He was now past seventy, and we wished him in other ways to curtail his occupations, but he could not be persuaded. A life of mere repose was distasteful to him notwithstanding his absorbing love of books, and he would take long journeys to transact various business connected with different Trusts and Societies to which he belonged. In 1854, he did resign the Hon. Treasurership of the Cambs County Club, after having proposed to do so some years previously, and withdrawn his proposal on an appeal from the members. This time it was accepted, but with a resolution, which gratified him much, as the greater part of this Club consisted of Conservatives.

"This meeting has received with sincere regret the resignation of George Pryme, Esq. their much respected Treasurer—37 years' acquaintance justifies this unanimous feeling. The President has the sanction of this meeting to express to him how sincerely they deplore the necessity which has led to such a conclusion as his resignation."

In going to live at Wistow my Father did not give up his visits to London, which he arranged to be in Term time, as he so much liked dining in Lincoln's Inn Hall and meeting his old friends. He continued this practice to the last year of his life. He used to attend the Chapel too, having a seat there as a Member of the Inn. He particularly liked the Services, and always, if he could, heard the

Warburtonian Lectures: I remember once going with him there on a Sunday afternoon to hear Mr F. D. Maurice preach. It was soon after the decease of Lord Brougham's daughter, and he pointed out to me where she was buried in the Cloister at her Father's earnest entreaty to the Benchers, and with a promise to be also himself interred there. I may not be quite correct in saying Cloister, some call it a Crypt. It is upon a level with the road, and over it is the Chapel upon low heavy pillars, and groined arches, with a sort of fan tracery, open to the light on every side except the West, where the entrance to the staircase and vestibule are. It was formerly used as a promenade or meeting-place, but is now shut in by iron railings between the pillars. There is on the Chapel staircase a mural slab in memory of Miss Brougham, containing some lines in Latin written by Lord Wellesley. Far away lies her celebrated Father under the blue sky of France. How different are their resting-places! Hers with a company of ancient Lawyers, and close to "the busy hum of men." His where the air is scented by the sweetest flowers, and musical with the soft murmur of a tideless sea.

While in Parliament my Father went regularly to St Margaret's Westminster or to Whitehall Chapel. At this latter place he happened to see two great Poets. He said to me, "I saw Walter Scott only once, when in Whitehall Chapel he sat together with Southey. After the Service a friend pointed them out to me as they walked away."

I may mention here a circumstance which shows the candour of my Father's mind, and his readiness to hear both sides. In the latter years of his life, when in Town, he generally passed his Sunday afternoons with me, and it was agreed on one very hot day that we should have an early dinner and go to Church in the evening. I told him that Dr Pusey was to preach at St Mary Magdalene in Munster Square, and proposed that we should go there. He evidently did not like this idea, being very much opposed to what was called "Tractarianism," so I pressed it no more. By and bye he said, that he thought he would go and not give way to a prejudice. He expressed to me afterwards the pleasure it had given him to hear "that admirable discourse," and said how glad he was that he had not persisted in his objection.

The number of people whom he assisted during his life was very great. Some by money, of which he was too profuse to those whose claims lay rather in their persistency in asking than in their merit. His ear was ever open to a tale of distress, and bank-notes were frequently enclosed in his answers to such appeals. Political Economy was forgotten in his charities, which were secret and unobserved, and of which we have found abundant proof since his death in grateful letters. But he gave also what was to him of more value than money, his time. He was always ready to help others by counsel or by exerting in their favour such influence as he possessed. This very day on which I write this page is brought a letter to my Mother from a Clergyman who speaks of having been "honoured by the friendship of your beloved and universally respected husband. You know, and perhaps you only, how much I was indebted to him for counsel and encouragement for the long period of five and forty years at least." Among the numerous letters which tell the same story we find those of a German Professor asking how to set about giving Lectures, a Civil Engineer wishing for a list of all the published descriptions of Scotland during the last 200 years, which he understands he has been lately (he was then 82) reading, a Doctor of Divinity about to become a

Magistrate, a youth going to College, a Lord Lieutenant consulting him in reference to County Meetings, and people of every sort and kind to whom his name was (as kindly said in the Cambridge Conservative Journal after his death) "a household word". One day, when he was past 84, he received a letter from a man who used to see him in Court when he went the Circuit, and who had not long before walked 40 miles to consult him, preferring his opinion he said before all others. As it is quite a legal curiosity I subjoin it.

*"June 25, 1866.*

"DEAR FRIEND,

"I hope this will find you well and yours as it leaves me at this present, bless God for it. I have another favour to ask you Another friend of mine is dead and left no Will and he have 270 pounds in the bank and his Father died in the French Prison and his Mother married again to another Man and is dead also and had Children but this Man that is now dead have his oldest brother's Son living and other Children living now will this second husband's Children have any claim with his Oldest Brother's Son would you have the kindness to give me your opinion weather the second Husband's Family have any Claim with the Oldest Brothers Son?

"And I wish you to send me word what your Charge is and I will send you it if spared for we rise in the Morning and now not what may befall us before Night.

"Yours respectfully,

———

"P.S. This man that is now dead had no Children."

My Father answered the letter but declined a fee. Not long after this person, who was quite an original and a worthy, good man besides, walked the distance again to see him, and was accompanied by "the oldest Brothers Son;" after which he sent a basket of fish so large that it feasted nearly all the Parish. This accessibility was a remarkable feature in my Father's character, for no man could enjoy his leisure more than he did; and he was not naturally of a yielding or passive temperament.

I have not yet mentioned, (though it must have been inferred,) my Father's great courtesy of manner to every one. More especially was it noticeable in his behaviour towards his inferiors. However humble or ignorant the persons, he put them at their ease directly by the gentleness of his demeanour and his studious consideration of their feelings and convenience. I have known him to be called from his books or writing many times in the day without a complaint, to listen, with "a courteous and invincible patience," to all the petty details that the humblest peasants brought before him as a Magistrate. They appreciated this, for some would say to his Servant, "I wish we could do something to keep Mr Pryme alive." "He is always ready with his pen and a helping hand." "He's such a gentleman, what shall we do without him?"

Although his own feelings on Politics and Religion were so strong that they might almost be said to amount to prejudices, yet he had great consideration for those of others. As a Magistrate he had often to administer an Oath, and a small Bible was constantly at hand for the purpose, but one day he came to my Mother and asked her for a beautiful little inlaid Crucifix she possessed, brought by Prof. Tennant from Italy. A poor Irishman, a Roman Catholic, was about to take the oath, and my Father respected his feelings so much as to wish to administer it in the way that he thought was most pleasing to him.

My Father had a great dislike to talking for the sake of talking. He would say, "I don't see the use of speaking unless we have something worth saying." Yet he was very kind in letting his family talk on the merest trifles while he was absorbed in reading. If asked whether it disturbed him he would answer, "Not at all, if you do not expect me to listen." He was always ready to be interrupted if it was to give information, and would take down Dictionaries and search for quotations even in the last few weeks of his life, rather than let a doubt remain in our discourse. The least question reminded him of something higher than the thing touched upon; as, for instance, to one enquiring the meaning of *Quidnunc*, he answered, "A man who asks, What now? Demosthenes said so finely, and so severely to the Greeks, , You ask what is new? can there be anything more new than that Philip of Macedon should ride rough-shod over Greece?'"

His power of quotation was unfailing. Some persons praising Alliteration, he remarked, "The best I know is in two lines in the *Rolliad*, written of Tomline, sometime Bp of Peterborough:

'Prim preacher, Prince of Priests, and Princes' Priest,
  Pembroke's pale pride, in Pitt's præcordia placed.'"

Once, when in penning these "Recollections," I proposed digressing to some subject not quite akin to the matter in hand, he said, "No, it is wandering out of the way, like Atalanta pursuing the apples." I needed no better proof of the richness and fulness of his learning than his absence from his earthly home gave me this summer. His Library remained, but the key to it was gone, and many of the illustrations and quotations I required in editing this book had to be sought for with patience and much trouble instead of coming immediately on my asking from the treasury of his great knowledge.

With all his love of solitude my Father was never more in his element than when in Society. He used to say of himself that he could never lead in conversation; but if that were so, and I am not sure that it was, no one could follow a lead better. A subject, no matter what, if within his own range, once started he was full of anecdote and information. Of this power I shall give some specimens in the next Chapter.

# CHAPTER XXVI.

## 1863—1868.

MY Father's country life gave him increased leisure,
and he partly employed it in re-reading the Classics
and the best Authors of the 17th and 18th Century. He
also read many modern books, but all in relation to each
other or with a definite purpose. When engaged on a book
of Travels he had always a map by his side, and he was
thus in his old age as conversant with Geographical discoveries as any younger man could be. As he grew older he
read books of Devotion more frequently. He had felt a great

desire to read *Cicero de Senectute* again, but on finishing he turned to Jeremy Taylor's *Holy living and dying*, saying,

"Saltem daretur in sacris literis tranquillè consenescere."

Time, too, was now beginning to give him many warnings, not in the failure of his own health or faculties, but in the withdrawal of his Contemporaries. One of the most distinguished of them died in 1861.

My Father went to Town as usual that year in the month of June to transact business. On these occasions, though he declined invitations, he used to call upon some of his old friends. An interview between him and Lord Campbell was arranged for one Sunday. My Father, however, not being very well on that day, wrote a note regretting his inability to go to him, and postponing the visit to another time. Within a fortnight the Chancellor, shortly after entertaining some guests, was "beckoned away" by the unseen Hand. We were afraid that, as they were born in the same year and month, it would have distressed him much. He felt certainly great regret at having missed that last possible interview, but was not otherwise affected. Thus a shield seems to be mercifully interposed to prevent the hearts of the aged from being wounded by the threatening dart.

In this Summer we had a Harvest Home at Wistow, the first of the kind in that part of the Country. My Father took a great interest in it; and, in order to set it well a-going, invited the older Farmers to dine with him after Church at an Upper table. He was now 80 years of age, but he presided and made the necessary speeches with a quiet ease and dignity which was natural to him.

The years that I have still to traverse I shall take in order, giving extracts from a Journal of my visits to Wistow.

which I began to keep in 1864 for the purpose of noting down in it some portions of my Father's conversations.

'Aug. 5, 1864. Yesterday was my Father's 83rd birthday. When I wished him many happy returns of the day he said, "It is little source of congratulation now, I must be thinking of another world;" and he rather objected to the Servants drinking his health, till my Mother said, "We may be glad that we have kept you so long." In the evening we gave an Amateur Concert in the School-room to the Villagers. My Father was present and enjoyed it extremely. Several of the Farmers were there, and one of them, knowing that it was his birthday, made a short speech, saying, that he hoped that they should keep him among them many more years; he answered, that he hoped so too, if it pleased God.

He is in the full possession of all his faculties, and his memory is as clear as ever. He never hesitates for a date, and is rarely at a loss for a name.

We have recommenced the Autobiography, and I am reading it over again to him from the beginning, in order that he may add to or correct it. We progress but slowly. On some days he feels bodily fatigue, on some the heat makes him incapable of more mental exertion than reading requires, and on others he is too much occupied with letter-writing or magisterial business.'

I have said that my Father continued his custom of dining in Lincoln's Inn Hall to the last year of his life. Two of these occasions are perhaps worth noting. In 1863 he had a pleasure which cannot fall to the lot of many. It is the usage at Lincoln's Inn that before being called to the Bar the Students—three times during their Studentship—should go up after dinner and be introduced by the Steward to the Senior Barrister at the head of the Bar table. Bows are interchanged, and the Student signs his name in a Register, and walks away between the two Bar tables, which stand parallel to each other across the Hall, so as to be seen by all the Barristers present[1]. It happened one day, that his Grandson, coming up to be presented when my Father, not knowing of it, was dining in Hall, it became his duty as the Senior to receive him. This he did very gravely, saying, with a quiet humour, " I think, Mr Bayne, that I have had the pleasure of seeing you before."

My Father described to me his seeing Lord Brougham for the last time. " He sat as a Bencher on the Dais. After the Grace was said, and when he moved to go, a low murmur of 'Brougham, Brougham,' went through the Hall, in acknowledgment of which he bowed three or four times as he passed through us, and was seen no more[2]."

My Father delighted to talk with his Grandson about the Norfolk Circuit, and to hear from him about his old friends still remaining on it. He would enquire especially about the Chief Baron (Pollock), and, when told that his summings up were still so admirable and so distinguished for good sense, he remarked, " It is not always that a Senior Wrangler attains such distinction in after life." He was interested also to hear of Lord Cockburn. He said, " I remember Chief Justices Kenyon, Ellenborough, Tenterden, Denman, Campbell, Cockburn. Denman was a distinguished man, a Johnian, and Classical Scholar. He took his degree

---

[1] This custom once proved a valuable safeguard, a Student having been recognized as a person who had formerly been convicted in a Court of Justice.

[2] Lord Brougham's last appearance in Lincoln's Inn Hall was on the 6th of June, 1864. A similar tribute was paid at the Middle Temple to Lord Eldon when 82 years old. He says in a letter, "As I walked down the great Hall in which we dined there was a general sort of acclamation of kindness from them all, which cheered an old gentleman."

in my Freshman's year, and therefore I saw nothing of him at Cambridge, but we became acquainted when I was in Parliament. Cockburn I knew when he was at College as an Undergraduate, introduced to me, long after I had left it, by his Father. Every one approved of his appointment to the Chief Justiceship. The *Times* made an excellent remark about him in describing a speech of his in the House of Commons, to the effect that, it was not so much the speech of a Lawyer exhibiting political knowledge as of a Politician shewing legal knowledge. He was quoted, in a company where I was, as an instance of a clever man occupying a high legal position without a University Education. I said in answer to that, ' He is a Fellow of his College at this moment.'

"This reminds me of a similar thing. Mr Heywood, late M.P. for Manchester, speaking at the British Association of distinguished men who owed nothing to a University Education, instanced Colonel Perronet Thompson, who wrote the *Catechism of the Corn Laws.* Mr Campion, of Queens' College, Cambridge, interrupted him, saying, ' He was a Fellow of my own College.' A greater mistake still was made about him when he was standing for Hull. The opposition Candidate was the London Agent of some Merchants in the Town, and in his speech on the Hustings he said, ' Gentlemen, what connection has this officer in the army with your Town? He has been in India, in Arabia, in South America, but that can give him no claim on you[1].'

---

[1] Colonel Thompson had served in all the four quarters of the Globe. Very early in his career he was taken prisoner in General Whitelock's unfortunate Expedition to Buenos Ayres. He was some years in India with the 17th Dragoons, during which time he was with one if not two Expeditions to the Arabian coast of the Persian Gulf, acting in alliance with the Imaum of Mascat against the Wahabees.

"Colonel Thompson said nothing till his turn came, and then observed, 'My opponent enquires what connection I have with this Borough? I will answer him that in such a house in High Street where my Father, who was a Banker in this Town, then lived, was I born, and that within a stone's throw of these Hustings is the Grammar School where I was educated till I went to Cambridge. Has the honourable gentleman any closer connection on his part with the Town?'"

While on the subject of Elections my Father went on to say, "Certain Elections were ordered by Act of Parliament to take place on a fixed day, so that if they fell on a Sunday it followed that they *must* be carried out, no mention being made of exception in the Act. I remember the Election of Vice-Chancellor, which is always on the 4th of November, being on a Sunday. The M.A.s assembled in the Senate House, but no other business was done, and they did not accompany him, as was usual on week-day Elections, back to his Lodge to partake of dessert. This custom of giving refreshments on those occasions is now disused. It is perhaps forgotten that the V.-C.'s weekly dinner used to be on Sunday. It was early, and he went afterwards, attended by his guests, in procession to Great St Mary's at three o'Clock. The dinner-hour was subsequently changed to four o'Clock[1]. Elections of Mayors and Sheriffs took place also under similar conditions to those I have spoken of. I remember being at the Charter-House Chapel at Hull one Sunday morning, and seeing the Clerk go out before the Sermon. I heard afterwards that he was a freeman of the Town, and went to vote for the Sheriff.

[1] These Sunday dinners were continued so late as 1833—4, during Dr King's Vice-Chancellorship. I believe it was Dr French who changed them to a week-day.

An Act has since been passed making it legal to alter the day to Monday if it fall on a Sunday[1]."

1865. I found my Father, when I visited him in July, sitting under his Walnut-trees, reading Bolingbroke's letters. I had brought him Lord Derby's *Homer*, which he directly commenced reading and comparing with the original. He was then 84. He was also reading this Summer Voltaire's work, *Précis du Siècle de Louis Quinze*. Speaking of it he said, "He gives a very just picture not only of the state of France at that time, but of Europe also."

I read to him an anecdote in the Newspaper of some Germans calling this Summer at the Vicarage at Wakefield, and asking to see the house and grounds, in the full belief that it was really the scene of Goldsmith's famous story. My Father was much amused, and said, "Dan Sykes told me that a Frenchman once said to him, 'I am happy to make your acquaintance, more especially as you come from the same port from which Robinson Crusoe sailed.' There was a family living at King's Lynn of that name (Crusoe), and they had one of their sons christened Robinson."

I drew my Father's attention to the announcement which I have put in a note below[2]. He said, "Well, it was no fault of his, the times were different from ours. To go as

---

[1] Although the day on which the death of George III. was announced was on a Sunday, according to the requisition of the Statute, 6 Anne, c. 7, both Houses of Parliament met.—Campbell's *Life of Lord Eldon*.

[2] "The death of the Rev. Robert Moore, Rector of Hunton, who had been principal Register of the Prerogative Court of Canterbury almost from his boyhood, and drew for about 60 years an income averaging £10,000 from his office." Bishop Spencer (of Jamaica) told me that he was once shown a cheque for £2,000 for a quarter's payment to Mr Moore. He was a son of Archbishop Moore, who had been tutor to his (the Bishop's) relative, a former Duke of Marlborough. It is right to add that Mr M. was "a most liberal and generous man, and made a good use of his wealth."

far back as to Sir Robert Walpole, he was corrupt, in so far
that it could be said of him traditionally that he believed
that 'every man had his price.' It has been asserted that
money was given in his time to secure votes in Parliament;
but there were many things besides money to offer. Pensions without limit, Sinecures, and even these reversions of
Places, which were often given to Children, and continued to
a later time. So that Cobbett, who had a deal of sarcasm
in him, writing in his *Weekly Register*, said, 'If you want to
see the Master of the Pells you will find him playing
marbles at Eton.' The fact being that some death had
happened earlier than was expected, and the reversion of a
place, given by Addington to a friend, had come to a Schoolboy. I remember a motion being made, when Spencer
Perceval was Prime Minister, to alter this. He spoke, and
brought all his influence to bear against it, and it was lost.
My impression is that these reversions could not be given
away to more than three persons. It was not altered until
Lord Grey's time[1]. As to bribes in money it was even said
that at the Ministerial dinners to which Members of the
House of Commons are invited, a Bank note was sometimes
found under the plate. I mentioned this once, when dining
at Bernal's, and said, I concluded it was gone by. Kaye,
who was of the party, and private Secretary to Lord H.
Petty, replied, 'Not altogether so completely as you think.'"

The Cattle Plague broke out this year all over the
country, commencing in the Dairies near London[2]. A Royal

---

[1] The office of Clerk of the Pells was abolished in 1834.

[2] From June 1865 to Feb. 1866 it appeared from the second
Report of the Cattle Plague Commissioners that there had been 120,740
cases of disease reported, and of these 17,971 had been in Cheshire
alone. 16,742 had been killed, 73,750 died, 16,986 had been under treatment, and 14,162 recovered.

Commission was appointed to enquire into it, and orders in Council were issued forbidding Cattle to be moved from one place to another without an order from a Magistrate. This gave very great trouble, especially to my Father, on account of the paucity of Magistrates in his part of the County, and of his always being at home; but he never excused himself, and went through all the tedium of it till the last year of his life, when it ceased. This, of course, brought him into contact with a variety of characters, some of whose peculiarities he did not fail to notice. He said, "I observe in my office of Magistrate that of the Foremen and better Labourers who come to make a declaration about their Master's Cattle only about one half can sign their names. At first I used to say, 'Can you sign?' but finding how many could not, to save their feelings I now ask if they will sign or make their mark? Mr Henry Okes, brother to the Provost of King's, who was a Merchant at Buenos Ayres, told me that the Merchants there did not sign their names, but had each of them a peculiar flourish of his own which did instead[1]. His name brings to my mind another thing that he told me. A quantity of skates and a large bale of hearthrugs were once shipped to him; with the former he could do nothing, but of the latter he made some use, by spreading one over his horse and riding on it through the Town, which set the fashion and brought him purchasers. I used this anecdote in my Lectures, to show how necessary it is in Political Economy to understand the wants of a

---

[1] In England individual marks were in use from the 14th to the middle of the 17th Centuries, probably much earlier, and when a yeoman affixed his mark to a deed, he drew a *signum*, well known to his neighbours, by which his land, his cattle and sheep, his agricultural implements, and even his ducks were identified."—*Nooks and Corners of English Life.*

people, and adapt the commodities offered to their tastes as well as their needs."

1866. I went down to Wistow for a short visit at Easter this year, and one of my first questions to my Father was, "What do you think of the new Reform Bill?" He answered, "I do not altogether approve of it; but I think that it should pass to allay the agitation throughout the Country. The old one went further than I wished. It went quite low enough in the Franchise, even though the people are better educated now, and would understand questions of Policy better. Spring Rice and I found *that* on the canvass for our second election. The Poor law Bill had passed previously, and there was a great prejudice against it among the lower orders. Perceiving this, S. R. and I determined to take the bull by the horns, and, at a large meeting at the Hoop Hotel, where we met our constituents, I said, 'I believe some of you are dissatisfied with certain provisions in the new Poor law Bill'—there was a murmur of assent—'I have heard that you believe that there is no relief for the aged Poor but in the Workhouse. I have the Bill in my pocket, and I will read the 17th Clause,' which provided that every poor person above sixty years might receive out-door relief. On the meeting breaking up, I said to a man, named Pryor, 'Are you satisfied?' and he answered, 'Perfectly.' Some days after we attended a meeting at New Town (a suburb), and again referred to the Poor law. This man Pryor was present, and called out, 'Read the 17th Clause.' But although these men were satisfied, the *lower* orders were still prejudiced; so much so that, as we passed by narrow streets and lanes, we were hooted. Spring Rice and I agreed that had the Franchise been lower than £10 we should have lost our Election."

My Father was extremely fond of flowers, and liked

me to gather them for him [1]. The morning on which I left I gave him some primroses. He smiled and said, "the rathe primrose." I asked if rathe were a word found in Shakespeare? He answered, "I only remember it in an old song,

> 'Life let us cherish
> While yet the taper glows,
> And the *rathe* primrose
> Pluck ere it close.'"

He then looked in Bailey's Dictionary for the word, but it was not there. A few days later he sent me the following little note—such was his accuracy.

WISTOW,
24 *April*, 1866.

MY DEAR ALICIA,

    I found the mislaid volume of Todd's Edition, enlarging Johnson's two volumes into three.

"Rath, adj. early, soon, coming before the usual time." Comparative "Rather." Superlative "Rathest."

Quotations:

> "The *rather* [2] lambs bene starved with cold."
> Spenser, *Shepherd's Calendar, Feb.*

> "Bring the *rathe* primrose that forsaken dies,
> The tufted crow-toe, and pale Jessamine."
> Milton's *Lycidas.*

Yours affectionately,

G. P.

It is singular that my Father had forgotten that the word was in Milton, for he must have been as well ac-

---

[1] My Father seldom spoke of his feelings, but when he did it was most touching. In a letter to me, dated Feb. 23, 1867, he says, "I have, and looked at yesterday; a flower which you gave me when you were thought to be on your death-bed. I have it with my Mother's last writing and a lock of her hair."

[2] Although *rather* is now used adverbially, it still retains its relation to the Saxon word *soon.*

quainted with *Lycidas* as with *Comus*, from which latter it
will be seen later on that he quoted a line so little remembered that I asked two or three fine Scholars in vain whence
it came.

My Father was very fond of studying the genealogy of
words. He remarked that "Editors of Shakespeare might
derive much assistance from consulting some one conversant
with the dialect of the Hills of N. W. Yorkshire and Westmoreland. Many of the phrases and words in use there
are merely Archaisms. My own knowledge is but imperfect, but in reading Malone's notes I have often found the
meaning of obsolete words or the different acceptations of
existing ones attempted to be proved by quotations from
old writers, which I can recollect to have heard used as
Shakespeare uses them. In Yorkshire they pronounce every
word with the same termination alike, and my Relative
quotes in his Diary an Epigram in which two lines rhyme
that end respectively in *grow* and *sow*, adding in a note
that in the S. Eastern Counties *grow* is pronounced like *sow ;*
whereas in Yorkshire it would be sounded like *now.* In
the Norfolk Peninsula, as I may call it, *prove* is pronounced
like *rove.*" This mention of the old country reminded him
to say, "The habit still lingers in the Yorkshire Dales of
calling people by their local designation. I can give an
instance of my own knowledge. 'Will by the fence.' I
had occasion before the Reform Bill was passed to examine
some of the Returns of Members to Parliament in the
reigns of the early Henrys and Edwards. These Returns
were always signed by a few Freeholders, and they had
put their Christian names only, with the name of the place
they lived in, thus, 'Richard by the Brook of Alconbury
Lane ;' 'William of Swaffham Lane.'"

' 1866, July 27. I find that my Father in his daily

reading begins with a Chapter in the Bible. He then goes to a folio work of Nicholas Bacon on the *Rise and Origin of the English Constitution.* "I like to read collaterally," he says, "and chose it, having just finished Bolingbroke's *Essays* on the same subject. He is an elegant and forcible writer but I think there is too much repetition of the same idea. It is said that he was an Infidel[1]. I am reading his letters to a Roman Catholic Peer, and I find nothing in them to confirm that notion. I should rather call him a Unitarian."[1]

My Father was of Socrates' opinion that it is well to repeat and consider beautiful things twice and even thrice; so he liked to read again and again works of Classic and Historic interest. He said to me one day in this visit, "I am going to read the Odyssey, which I have not done since I was a boy. (He was now past 85.) Pope's translation is a paraphrase; Cowper's is the literal one. Professor Thompson[2] advised me to read the latter with the original. Blair in his criticisms mentions that Pope often introduces words and phrases which are not in Homer, as

'When the Moon, refulgent lamp of night.'

The last four words are not in Homer at all. Pope with his fine style is yet appreciable by humbler minds. A man, who farmed his own land of 100 acres near Whittlesea, quoted from Homer once to me, and when I enquired how he became acquainted with it, he replied that he was a great admirer of the Translation and knew it well, 'although,' said he, ' my schooling never cost 3*d.* a week.'"

---

[1] Had he been one how could he have penned these words: "The shortest and the best prayer which we can address to Him, who knows our wants and our ignorance in asking, is this—'Thy will be done'?"

Bolingbroke's *Reflections upon Exile.*

[2] Now the Master of Trinity College, Cambridge.

Of course my Father, like all men who lived near those times, took a strong interest in the subject of Junius's letters. He used to discuss them with a great friend and neighbour of his who considered Sir Philip Francis as their author, and who had very strong arguments, almost amounting to proofs, on his side. My Father however said to me, " I am clearly of opinion, after careful examination and all things considered, that Sir Philip Francis did *not* write them. I once had a very interesting conversation with Lord Nugent about their authorship; it was at Aylesbury, during a contested election, where I, as a Freeholder of Bucks, had gone to vote. I had known Lord N. in the House of Commons, and he happened to talk to me of Junius in some interval in the Committee-room when none but ourselves were present. He told me that he, being related to the Grenvilles, had with some others of the family at Stowe been looking over the papers of George Grenville, and that they found a bundle of the letters of Junius with a note to G. G. tucked in as if they were connected. This note had in it an expression remarkably identical with one which appeared in a letter of Junius shortly after, and Lord Grenville and the other relatives considered it almost conclusive that they were by the same person, but Lord G. had requested that this might not be divulged in his life-time. Lord Nugent added, ' I may say so far that it was no one of those persons to whom it has been hitherto attributed.' An article in a recent Review considers from circumstantial evidence unconnected with the above that the second Lord Lyttelton was the Author, and I incline to that opinion."

1867. In March of this year Prof. Sedgwick paid a short visit to Wistow, promising a longer one next time. It was a great pleasure to my Father to see again this dear and old friend, towards whom he ever felt the strongest affection. His friends were thinning fast now. He received in April a letter from another old friend, Mr James Robinson of Chesterfield, Notts, who said, "I live a very monotonous life of pain and suffering. I often say to myself what Lord Byron so well says,

> 'What are the worst of woes that wait on age—
> What stamps the wrinkle deeper on the brow?
> To view each lov'd one blotted from Life's page—
> To be alone on Earth as I am now.'

Such is my fate, may it not be yours." Writing in answer my Father remarked, "You are now one of only three surviving Undergraduate friends, General Thompson of Queens', and John Wray of Trinity. Renouard of Sidney, one year senior to me, departed a few months ago[1]. This prolongation of life enables me to prepare better for my latter end." And truly it was so; as he approached nearer to it he felt a certainty of it unmixed with fear, and he began to set his house in order. It was in his garden, and his country life, in his books, and his time for quiet thought, that the preparation for departure commenced. One might have feared perhaps a little for one whose studies ranged so widely, and who was so accustomed to read all kinds of speculative Theology, yet the simple Faith remained with him to the end. He would say to me, "I delight in the Day of rest, and look forward to it through the week, and confine my reading on it to religious books." When unable to bear the

---

[1] The Rev. G. Cecil Renouard, B.D. died at the advanced age of 86, and had been for 49 years Rector of Swanscombe in Kent. He was reputed one of the best Oriental Scholars of his age, and took an active part in the work of translating the Holy Scriptures into the Turkish language for the Bible Society. *Guardian*, Feb. 27, 1867.

*long* morning Service at Church he read the Litany at home, a part of our Liturgy that he deeply valued. Quite 20 years ago he regretted that instead of building so many new Churches an arrangement was not made for multiplying the Clergy in each Parish, and opening the Churches many times in the day and for shorter Services ; this plan is now beginning partially to be adopted.

I went as usual to Wistow this Summer, and found little or no change in my Father. On his 86th birthday he was in good health and spirits, had one or two friends to dinner, and related anecdotes containing accurate quotations. His health was not quite unbroken, but he could take his usual exercise, and ride on a favourite old pony about some of his fields near home. He had ceased to attend the Bench at Ramsey, but still acted as a Magistrate at home. His faculties were as acute as ever, and his interest in all things as great, from the political and social questions of the day to the pruning of his vines and fig-trees. His love of books was undiminished. Writing to a relative in this year he said, " I am now in the 15th Vol. of Burke's works, and in the 2nd of Dryden's 12 volumes."

In his drives he noticed not only the state of the crops and the culture, but also trees, birds, (which he recognised by their plumage and their songs), and especially the beautiful forms and colours of the clouds at sunset. Alluding to these last he said, " On my return from Cambridge a few days ago I saw a beautiful bank of grey clouds, which looked like mountains, and reminded me of the first ride that I took at Sedbergh. I was then going towards a village where Burn lived, who wrote the book which has lasted, with very few emendations, through all the changes of the English Law. He was a Clergyman and Magistrate in Westmoreland, and compiled the volume for the guidance of himself as well as others[1]."

*Apropos* to a hawk he remarked, "I have seen persons hawking. It was very useful before Gunpowder was employed to bring down the game. It is astonishing after the invention of gunpowder how slowly guns came into general use. Within my memory there was a great limitation on sporting. None might take out a license for shooting (Gamekeepers were privileged, but limited to certain Manors) who had not £100 a year in landed property of his own, or were not the Heir to a Knight of the Shire, a designation by which any were called who possessed £500 per annum. It now only lingers in the County Member. Town members were called 'Burgesses of y⁰ Borough,' and Oliver Cromwell was unable to be elected for Cambridge until he had been first made a freeman."

He always looked with a pleased eye at the allotments for the poor, and, speaking of the enclosure of Wistow, which had taken place in his time, he said, "When I went to College the villages all around Cambridge were unenclosed, Coton, Trumpington, Chesterton, Cherryhinton, and Barnwell, which last was a small village in the midst of fields. From the backs of the Colleges in the direction of Coton was one vast plain. Towards Ely it was quite open, and when about half-way to it I have roused wild ducks as I rode along. In my Uncle's time there was, he told me, good snipe-shooting at Cherryhinton. I have seen Bustards, birds which the natives called '*Wild Turkey*,' and which are now nearly if not quite extinct in the Eastern

---

[1] "Burn, Richard, author of *The Justice of the Peace;* born at Winton, lived and died Vicar of Orton in Westmoreland."

Counties, flying over the Gogmagog Hills[1]. Between How House and Fenstanton, a distance from Cambridge of 9 or 10 miles, the fields were quite open, and rye, which the soil suited, was the corn chiefly grown on them. It was mostly sent Northwards, as it is preferred there to wheat for bread. There was always a loaf of it on the breakfast-table at Milton, as well as some of the other kind."

1868. In the Spring of this year a Petition was got up at Cambridge in favour of the Bill for the abolition of all religious Tests in the two Universities. It was sent to my Father, but he declined to sign it, and doubtless gave his reasons. Shortly afterwards he did sign a Counter Petition brought to him by the Rector of his Parish.

It was not that his Political feelings had stagnated, for he was still interested in the General Election of that year; but he felt that a stand must be made somewhere, and he could not consent to alter the religious character, nor entirely change the tone of those Institutions which it had been his pride to belong to and to uphold as far as in him lay. There is a fable of the wise old Æsop that it might be well in these days to recollect, in which it is related that those who admitted others to share their home soon found themselves barred out[2]. It is quite consistent with liberality towards others to maintain one's own inheritance; and I think that this was in my Father's mind when he would not sign that petition.

It is pleasant to turn from times of instability and unrest to the constancy of a friendship. My Father received in that Spring a Book and the following letter:

[1] Dr Johnson thanked his friend Mr Bennet Langton for a pheasant and a bustard.

[2] Many years ago a chief present mover in the Nonconformist ranks said that they wanted no emoluments or offices; nothing but a degree.

"MY DEAR PRYME,

"I have come to this place, where my Niece has fixed her residence, that I may breathe the pure air of the hills and have the pleasure of her society.

"My health is not what I could wish, but I am better than I was; and I have a view from my window of such beauty (especially during this glorious Spring weather) that it seems enough to put life into a skeleton. So I hope soon to be well. Just before I left Cambridge I revised the last *proof-sheet* of a Pamphlet I have printed, which relates to the Valley of Dent; and to-day I have sent you a copy of it by the Book Post, for you are a Brother Yorkshireman, with the blood of sweet Wensleydale flowing in your veins. And you know the Northern Dales, their humours, and their dialects. At any rate, pray accept it as a little token of my goodwill, and a proof that you live among those whom I rejoice to treasure in my memory. For you are my oldest and most honoured friend. With the little book I send my kindest Christian greetings to you and Mrs Pryme. You can take no interest in the Memorial; but I hope that in the Appendix (commencing with No. IV. p. 36) you may find some points of local history that may amuse a leisure hour.

"The last time I heard from your daughter, Mrs Bayne, she and my Goddaughter were at Nice. When you or Mrs Pryme write to them pray give my love to them. May God bless and preserve you and Mrs Pryme and all whom you love! Ever, my dear Pryme,

"Your true-hearted old friend,

"ADAM SEDGWICK.

"*Professor Pryme.*"

The letters of old men to each other are inexpressibly touching. My Father wrote several to his remaining friends this year which seemed like Farewells. One of them was to Dr Clark (late Professor of Anatomy) at Cambridge, who made, feeble as he then was, a great effort to answer it himself. The few sentences were so minutely and closely written that it required a magnifying glass to decipher them, but when enlarged they were beautiful in the expression of a tender friendship.

Whoever does not know Prof. Sedgwick and would have some faint idea of the charm of his conversation, his goodness of heart, his quaint and rich phraseology, may gain it by reading the Memorial mentioned above. It was printed at the University Press, but I fear the copies are very scarce. I have his kind permission to publish what I please of his correspondence with my Father, and I could not but take advantage of it to give the two letters which appear in this book.

My Father went to Town as usual in June. He had a great pleasure in seeing again two of his oldest friends who went to call upon him. As he and Sir Frederick Pollock sat together on a sofa in the Hall of the Reform Club they attracted attention from their venerable appearance, and my Brother was asked who they were. "Two old College friends," he answered. Next day General Thompson visited my Father and sat with him in the same place; the same question was asked, and the reply given was still more singular, "Two old Schoolfellows."

August 4. We went down for my Father's 87th birthday. He seemed quite well, and gave us Champagne to drink his health in. He grieved with his usual compassion over the destruction of a wasp's nest, and hoped it was done without cruelty. In these latter years he had a great dislike to have

small birds or anything killed, and would carry stray ear-
wigs and caterpillars into the open air, saying, "Poor
harmless little things." When reminded that such creatures
could not be allowed to multiply, he remarked, "True, or
we should be destroyed by them,

> 'And the wing'd air be dark't with ·plumes[1].'"

This was his last Summer. He felt the heat very much, and
though he rallied as Autumn came on he was evidently less
capable of bodily exertion. His mental powers were undiminished, and he read and wrote many hours in the day,
being called so early as half-past six A.M. He never found
the day too long. In his books, his garden, his family, and
his own reflections, he found happy employment for the
whole of it. At night he read prayers at half-past nine,
and then retired to rest.

One day my Father and I were driving out alone, and
on those occasions the talk was always a little graver, and
he opened more. He spoke to me with great affection of
my Mother and of her looking so young still; and related
to me a touching speech of her Father, which I had never
heard before, and who had died previously to her marriage.
It is singular that people will often speak in this way
before some change takes place. I knew a gentleman who
for half a lifetime had never spoken of his dear and lost
wife, and a month before his death he talked of nothing
else. When we got to Bury we overtook what is the most
affecting of all sights—except it be a Soldier's—a village
funeral. The procession was unusually long, for there were
numerous sons and daughters who followed their mother,
a Farmer's widow, to her grave. We had to wait while they
all defiled into the fine old Church. I was afraid that my

---

[1] Milton's *Comus.*

Father might see in it the shadow, as it were, of his own
burial, but he preserved his equanimity. I asked the meaning of the old phrase, "He lays by the Wall." "It was," he
answered, "derived no doubt from the time of the Plague,
when they laid the deceased and infected persons outside
the wall of the Town. It is an expression I have heard
used, among others, by old Bowtell, of the University
Library." We spoke of people being buried in woollen,
about which there had recently been a discussion in the
Newspaper, and I asked him if he remembered it. He said
" The Act was in force in my early days, and a penalty of
£5 was attached to its neglect, but people evaded it, having
a dislike to it, like ' poor Narcissa,' and were often wrapped
in linen with a woollen outer cloak. They were bad Political
Economists in those days, and did not understand that
whoever spent 30s. in woollen had not that sum to spend
on linen or other produce¹. There were many similar and
absurd enactments, which have been repealed within my
time. I remember when there was a penalty on covered
buttons²."

The Village fruit and flower Show was held as usual
on our Lawn one fine day in September. My Father came
and sat out among his friends for a time, and was as animated as ever in a conversation with one of them with
whom he loved to talk of old and new times. A few days
later our Harvest-Home Festival took place. It was on
a sweet autumnal afternoon, and as I was going to witness
the games, &c. I stopped to speak to my Father as he sat

¹ "The Act was repealed in the middle of the last Century, about
the time when Dyer published his *Fleece*. This led to its being wittily
said of the poet (whose poem was dull and ponderous), that when he
died, 'he, at all events, would be still buried in woollen'."

² Buttons covered with cloth were prohibited by law in 1721, and poor
old men wore their coats fastened by hooks and eyes.

reading beneath the shade of his old Mulberry-tree. The Church-bells were ringing a merry peal, and but for them, all field labour having ceased, there would have been entire stillness. I lingered to talk with him, for I feared when we had all left him that he would feel that he was no longer able to be one of us, or to enjoy what we enjoyed. But he did not view it in that light. He said he liked to hear the Bells chiming, and to think that the people were enjoying themselves in their way as he was in his. He had come to the time when

> " Life's strong lights and shadows seem
> Soft as the visions of a dream[1]."

October 5. My visit was now drawing to a close and I took my last drive with my Father. He noticed with his usual observing eye the various objects of interest; the Homesteads so unusually crowded with stacks after the abundant Harvest, the fresh ploughing, in preparation for the next, the fine autumnal tints. We went to the little Town of Ramsey, and as we stopped in it here and there, it was pleasing to see the people bowing or coming up to the carriage to hope my.Father was well. It was as if they had some presentiment that they should never see their old Magistrate again, and he was gratified with their attention. But there was so much simplicity in his character that he would say when farmers and labourers who were strangers to him in the more distant villages through which we drove, took off their hats to him, "I do not know these people, it is very kind of them."

October 7. I left Wistow. My visit had been unexpectedly prolonged for ten days, and in that time my Father had dictated to me the Chapter which contains the account of

---

[1] J. Mitford's *Poems*, 1811.

Huntingdonshire. This was the last of his "Recollections;" what comes after that in this book had been done previously, for, as I have said in the preface, we did not strictly continue in the order of time. On the day previous to my departure he not only exerted himself to complete what we had in hand, but he read with a young Relative the 2nd Epistle of Horace (Lib. 1), and he had drawn out for his future reading a list of Books, or *Legenda* as he called it, which might have lasted him for years.

Before leaving he expressed to me how glad he had been of my lengthened stay, and how much he looked forward to my return in the Spring. "Then," said he, "we will read over and complete the Autobiography." I was glad to see him hopeful, for he had told me some little time before that he did not think he should survive the winter. I left him,

"Waiting his Summons to the sky,
    Content to live, but not afraid to die."

# CHAPTER XXVII

## 1868.

O World, I must forsake thee
And far away betake me,
   To seek my native shore.
    \*      \*      \*

I wish not now for gladness,
   Earth's joys to me are o'er.

*Henry of Loufenburgh.*

ON Nov. 29th I received a Telegram at Torquay, saying
that my Father was "seriously unwell." I set off
directly, and by travelling all night had the satisfaction of
arriving in time to hear his last words. As I stood by his
bedside I perceived that he would never rise from it again.
He was just awakened from a tranquil sleep into which he
had fallen after receiving the Holy Communion with his
wife, having been able to repeat the Responses clearly and
with great devotion. He knew me, and made an effort to
utter a few sentences. He expressed his pleasure at seeing
me, said that he had but two or three days to live, and
that he had just partaken of the Sacrament of the Lord's
Supper. He never spoke again beyond a single word at
intervals. He recognised my Brother and my Son, who
arrived soon after I did, and he was able to put out his hand
and to pronounce their names, but he could not converse.

The history of the short illness was that he had been unwell for two or three days and seemed to be getting better, when his appetite suddenly failed. He then bid the world adieu at once, desiring that no more letters might be shown to him, and that he might see his Rector daily. He took his medicine from our hands, but showed no anxiety about recovering, in fact, after what he said to me, it was evident that he was only waiting for his summons. He was quite conscious even to the end, but his weakness was great, and he was sometimes disturbed by convulsive pain which he bore very quietly. As we knew not how much he could bear us to say it seemed almost impossible to break the solemn silence of the sick room by reading to him or speaking. He evidently liked us to be there, and that was a comfort.

It was on the morning of Monday that I arrived, and each day he grew weaker; his medical Attendant said the pulse was perfectly regular, and all the organs perfect, but that nature was exhausted. On Wednesday night towards ten o'clock he was a little restless, and then slept quietly; presently he awoke, opened his eyes, put out his hand as if for farewell, and again slept. For a short time the breathing was soft and regular, and then it almost imperceptibly ceased. "Calm death to end a healthful life" was come.

There is a time-honoured custom at Wistow of tolling for the dead. The next morning at 8 o'clock the mournful sound gave the message with the Church's own voice to the Villagers. They had been most sympathising during my Father's illness, and had been expecting to hear that solemn voice each day. One cannot imagine a more beautiful way than this of announcing to them that their chief neighbour and friend was gone.

So completely had my Father prepared for his death that he had described to his Rector the precise place in the Churchyard where he would be buried, and had desired that one of his tenants should make his Coffin. It was of polished oak, and was made with such care and pride that it looked more like a beautiful Casket, having eight massive burnished brass handles, and a plate of brass inlaid upon the lid with the words finely chased upon it,

Professor George Pryme, aged 87.

The written sympathy of relations and friends came to us very shortly, and the public journals contained eulogistic notices of my Father's life, which were most gratifying, and almost surprising to us; for, after twenty years withdrawal from the world's eye, we had supposed him, in these ever-hurrying days, almost forgotten. But it was not so, and nothing could be more cheering to us under such a loss than to find how well he was remembered and appreciated.

It was remarkable that in nearly every letter we received, the words "honour" and "courtesy" were used. It seemed almost as if this last was a rare thing, so prominently was it alluded to. A friend writing from Trinity College, said that everyone in that Society from the Seniors downwards, spoke of my Father with a great regard; and that even the Junior Fellows, with whom he could have had latterly but little intercourse, made mention of the courtesy, or of that which has been well described as "the polished deference" which he exhibited towards those who conversed with him. By putting together only a few sentences of some of the letters which we received from his friends, the Astronomer Royal, the Deans of Lincoln and Salisbury, Bishop Thirlwall, Professor Sedgwick, &c. a com-

plete portrait of my Father is given as he appeared to
their eyes, and which may perhaps show that the one I
have attempted to depict has not been too highly coloured.

" I felt deeply the sad event, and sympathise in your grief
for the loss of your excellent Father. I learned at Cambridge to respect Professor Pryme's public position, and to
esteem his high and honourable character in academical and
political matters—I received from him, on all occasions of
our meeting, the same unvarying courtesy and kindness.
Notwithstanding so great a loss, you are fortunate in being
able to reflect with satisfaction on his long, honourable, and
most consistent career, and I am convinced that in your sorrow for its termination, you will not forget how much subject
it affords for pride and gratitude—Your dear Father had for
many years shown me unvarying regard, and I felt sincerely
attached to him. He formed one of the few remaining links
between past and present times, and there was a peculiar
charm in the genial spirit with which he carried us into days
gone by. His loss will be felt by many, for he was a most
tender-hearted and benevolent man—Your excellent Father
was one of my earliest friends, and I shall always cherish his
memory with feelings of regard and respect. He was a most
able and consistent man; kind, just, and honourable, full of
truth and consideration. Though he was as decided in his
politics as a man could be, yet his mind was a fair and judicial mind, not given to exaggeration or vehemence, and
capable of looking calmly on both sides of a question. There
was an evenness of temper about him and a dignified self-
control, which I never saw disturbed under even great pro-
vocation—For one whom we loved to go to his rest in peace,
without pain, and in full self-possession, after a long and
active and useful career, is certainly the crown of all earthly
blessings, the greatest any one can wish for himself or his

friends, and one placed beyond the reach of change—God will be your comforter in this sorrow. My eyes are dimmed with tears as I write this. How kind your loving God, your Redeeming Saviour has been to you in giving such a calm, cheerful old age to your late Father! and at length allowing him to drop gently into his grave with a soul unclouded, with his thoughts turned towards his Redeemer, and in the loving presence of those whom he best loved. These thoughts will comfort and support you now, and with God's blessing, will be a fountain of Christian joy to you all so long as you live."

At the time of his death my Father was the Senior of all the Societies to which he belonged. From the two chief of these we received official letters of sympathy. From the Master and Seniors of Trinity College an assurance of the deep sorrow they felt at the loss of so old, and so warmly attached, a Member of the College, to whom they would gladly pay their last respect by having the Dead March in Saul played before the Anthem on the Sunday following his death.

The Benchers of Lincoln's Inn sent "the offer of their condolence, and their deep sense of the loss sustained by the departure of a venerable member of the Society, whose sound professional knowledge, general acquirements, and social qualities, conferred upon it so much honour." The Treasurer (Mr Montagu Chambers, Q. C.), who conveyed this message kindly added, "had the day of the funeral been known to me, I should have paid to his memory the melancholy tribute of directing the Chapel Bell to be tolled, an exceptional course which I am satisfied all the Members of our Bench would have willingly sanctioned."

I will add one more trait of regret, and that came from a poor man, a kind of pedlar, who was accustomed, in his

yearly rounds, to see my Father walking in his garden, when
he would gratify him by purchasing some trifle. He appeared
at the gate not long after his decease, and enquired if anything were wanting. "Nothing, thank you," said the Servant, "our poor Master is dead." "Dead!" repeated the
man, and his eyes filled with tears, as he exclaimed, "God
rest his soul," and walked away without another word.

On the 9th of December, a day quite remarkable for its
sunny warmth and clearness, my Father was to be buried.
His coffin was not closed till that morning, that we might
be able to look at him each day, as he lay quite unchanged,
with a look of profound peace upon his features, his hair,
still brown, disposed upon his temples. He was carried to
his grave by eight of the Sons of his own Cottagers, followed
by his Son and Grandson and myself as mourners, his farm-
tenants, and his servants. The little procession was met at
the entrance to the Churchyard by the Rector of the Parish,
the Rev. Thomas Woodruff, and by the Rector of Woodwalton, the Rev. Henry Stowers. The Coffin was placed in
the centre of the pretty Church, in whose renovation and
adornment he always took a great interest. It was filled
by the villagers, and by others who had come from a distance
to testify their respect, and the greater part were in mourning.
After the beautiful chapter from Corinthians had been read,
a hymn was sung by the choir.

> Brief life is here our portion,
>     Brief sorrow, short-lived care;
> The life that knows no ending,
>     The tearless life, is *there.*
>
> O happy retribution!
>     Short toil, eternal rest:
> For mortals and for sinners
>     A mansion with the blest.

The morning shall awaken,
  The shadows shall decay,
And each true-hearted servant
  Shall shine as doth the day:

Jesu, in mercy bring us
  To that dear land of rest;
Who art, with God the Father,
  And Spirit, ever blest.

The procession then moved into the Churchyard, the Rector saying the concluding portion of the Service. Mindful of his love of flowers, I placed a wreath of the last lingering roses and of holly on the Coffin of my beloved Father as it was being gently lowered, amid a respectful silence, to its final resting place; there to await

The Resurrection of the body,
And the life everlasting.

# APPENDIX.

## I.

## VERSES BY MRS BYRON.

I FOUND among my Father's papers a copy of verses in his handwriting; "Mrs Byron" was written below them. As he had passed his youth in Nottinghamshire I thought it possible that these verses might really have been composed by Byron's Mother, and a copy of them passed from one neighbour to another. I showed them to those who were better judges than myself; but they had never heard of Mrs Byron possessing a poetic turn, and much doubted her having written these verses. A few weeks ago however I saw the following notice in the *Athenæum*.

"There is, or ought to be, somewhere a book which is almost as well worth inquiring after as the Charlemagne Bible. The mother of Lord Byron collected all the criticisms on her son's *Hours of Idleness*. She had the whole bound and interleaved. On the blank leaves so inserted she wrote her own comments on the poet, the poem, and the reviewers. These are said to have been written with wit and ability. Does anyone know of the whereabouts of this volume?"

Not having observed any answer to this Query I have resolved to print the verses I have spoken of as perhaps bearing upon it, and also in order to raise another question: Did Lord Byron inherit from his mother his poetic power, or are these verses a very early effusion of his own?

26

1.

"Alas, the bright Chivalric day is past,
　No more its graceful influence to cast
　　On scenes that gladly once confest its power;
No more bold Barons head their lordly trains,
Urge the swift chase, or list to Minstrels' strains,
　　Or yield to peerless dames in painted bower.

2.

"Yet not unvalued are the artless lays,
　That celebrate the deeds of other days:
　　Imagination loves to catch the theme,
And fondly lingers in fair fiction's fields
To cull each flower her gaudy harvest yields;
　　The perfume gone, the tints more beauteous seem.

3.

"So when I've marked the close of Summer's day,
　And paus'd to watch the Sun's departing ray
　　Gild some sweet spot adorned by nature's hand
*The glow luxuriant, and the dubious light*
*Have left a charm upon approaching night*
　　*The day's meridian hour could not command.*

4.

"So o'er thy soul, to taste and genius true,
　The memory of the past 'its radiance threw,'
　　And shewed the wish sublime, the thought refin'd:
As moonlight glitters on the distant streams,
As joys present themselves in pleasant dreams,
　　As soft, as sweet the visions of thy mind."

I feel a conviction that the above are either by Lord Byron
or his Mother, and a family likeness will at once be observed if

the lines which I have italicised be compared with three others in the first of the " Hebrew Melodies " wherein the same thought occurs :

> "And all that's best of dark and bright
>
> \* \* \* \* \* \* \*
>
> Thus mellow'd to that tender light
> Which Heaven to gaudy day denies."

It seems to me also that the thought of the remainder of the " Melody" may be traced in the 4th verse of my copy; and it will hardly fail to be observed that the word *gaudy* is used both in the last line I have quoted and in the 2nd stanza of the copy. It is not impossible that Mrs Byron may have asked her gifted Son to respond for her to the " Lines sent to a Lady." If so, he may at a later period have repeated, with that subtle power which he possessed of making old things new, the best idea in other words. Or—if it were his Mother's composition—he may have borrowed from it unconsciously[1].

[1] My Father once said to me, " Literary coincidence is often a more proper phrase than plagiarism," and I was told by Mr Crabbe Robinson that Goethe remarked to him that there was no such thing, that all must borrow of those who have gone before them, and that he himself had only learnt of three persons—Shakespeare, Spinoza, and Linnæus.

Since writing the above the following information has reached me from the Cambridge University Library.

Partenopex de Blois

a

Romance
in four Cantos
freely translated
from
The French of M. le Grand
With notes
by
William Stewart Rose.
London :
Longman & Co.
1807.
(printed by Ballantyne & Co. Edinburgh.)

It is illustrated by Engravings by Richard Smirke. There is no dedication. From the preface it appears that an extract from the poem was first published in the *Bibliothèque des Romans* under the title of *Partenuple de Blois*, but that M. le Grand made his translation from a Manuscript of the 13th Century. It is probable therefore that the verses I have appended above were written some years before the " Hebrew Melodies " were composed, when Lord Byron was about 19 years of age.

## II.

The following is a list of Fen Plants grouped under the Heads of "Probably extinct," "Lingerers" likely to disappear, "Once Common, but now Rare," but not likely to disappear altogether.

### *Probably extinct.*

Senecio paludosus.  
Cineraria palustris.  
Sonchus palustris.  

Malaxis paludosa.  
Sturmia Lœselii.  

### *Lingerers.*

Lathyrus palustris.  
Comarum palustre.  
Cicuta virosa.  
Helosciadium inundatum.  
Œnanthe Lachenalii.  
Selinum palustre[1].  
Valeriana dioica.  
Carduus pratensis.  
Villarsia nymphæoides.  
Menyanthes trifoliata.  
Pedicularis palustris.  
Veronica scutellata.  
Teucrium scordium.  
Pinguicula vulgaris.  

Anagallis tenella.  
Myrica gale.  
Orchis latifolia.  
,,    incarnata.  
Epipactis palustris.  
Luzula multiflora.  
Sparganium minus.  
Schœnus nigricans.  
Cladium mariscus[2].  
Eleocharis acicularis.  
Eriophorum angustifolium.  
Lastrea Thelypteris.  
Osmunda regalis.  

### *Once Common, now Rare.*

Ranunculus lingua.  
Nymphæa alba.  
Nuphar lutea.  
Nasturtium palustre.  
Bidens cernua.  
Achillea ptarmica.  
Carduus palustris.  
Utricularia vulgaris.  
Alisma Ranunculoides.  

Butomus umbellatus.  
Triglochin palustre.  
Scirpus fluitans.  
Carex pseudo-cyperus.  
,,    ampullacea.  
,,    vesicaria.  
Calamagrostis lanceolata.  
,,        Epigejos.  

W. M.

[1] It is on this Plant that the Swallow-tailed Butterfly (Papilio Machaon) feeds.

[2] This was once largely used for lighting fires at Cambridge, and is now to some extent.

## III.

### For a Young Lady's Album.

Amor volea schernir la Primavera
Sulla breve durata e passeggiera
Dei vaghi fiori suoi;
Ma la bella Stazione a lei rispose;
"Forse i piaceri tuoi
Vita più longa avran delle miei rose!"

"Thy flowers," one day cried Love to Spring,
"Scarcely survive their blossoming:
Fleet one short month, frown one dark sky,
They in their very cradle die!"
Lightly the taunt sweet Spring retorted,
As in her bower, all bloom, she sported,
"The joys forsooth thy reign discloses
Will flourish longer than my roses!"

### Idem Latine redditum.

"Flores, quos medio e sinu profundis—"
Ad ver sic Amor est (ferunt) locutus—
"Vix fulgore oculos ferire, nares
Vix contingere suavi odore possunt:
Quæ nasci hora videt, videt perire."
Huic Ver contra, ut in hortuli rosetis
Ludebat, nimis acriter jocanti
Respondit; "Tua scilicet corolla,
Quam nectis juvenum choris gerendam,
Nostris vitam aget heu rosis negatam!"

FRS. WRANGHAM.

Chester,
*Sept.* 1836.

## IV.

QUALIFICATIONS REQUIRED FOR A PROFESSOR IN THE UNIVERSITY
OF MELBOURNE.

"It is considered expedient that the persons whom you may deem eligible for the Office be men *not* in holy orders; of *approval worth* and *moral standing;* and of such *stability of character as to command respect.* Literary attainments, however remarkable, unaccompanied by amenity of disposition and power to enforce by admitted or accessorial superiority, should not alone recommend the Candidates. A devotedness on the part of those selected to the cause of literature, and the interests of the University, is deemed to be of great moment; inasmuch as those interests must be held paramount to any pointing to prospective individual advancement by taking pupils, imparting instruction by public Lectures or otherwise, which are all strictly prohibited by the Statutes.

"A total abstraction from political or sectarian interference must be rigidly enjoined, and, these general suggestions being submitted, it will be considered desirable that the Professors should be men *under the middle age; of approved diligence in literary pursuits; Graduates* of one of the Universities of Oxford, Cambridge, London, Dublin, Edinburgh, or Glasgow; and designated by *some particular excellence in their Collegiate career;* accustomed, if possible, to the inculcation of knowledge (with clearness and readiness) in the department to which they propose to apply themselves; and more especially *of such habits and manners as to stamp upon their future pupils the character of the loyal, well-bred English Gentleman.*"

CAMBRIDGE: PRINTED BY C. J. CLAY, M.A. AT THE UNIVERSITY PRESS.